P9-CFL-237

A WARNING . . .

A new image appeared. It was another generated image of myself, this time captured in the aftermath of a terrible beating. My face was a collection of pain piled upon pain, with every millimeter of exposed skin swollen and glossy with blood. Any injuries below the neckline were invisible beneath my black suit, but from the way it stood, seeming ready to fall at any moment, they must have been just as brutal and ugly.

The animation took a single blind step, stiffened, and as if in terrible, clairvoyant realization, emitted a cry pregnant with the certainty that everything it had endured up until this moment was just empty preamble.

The top of its head disappeared in a burst of blood and smoke.

The brutalized version of myself did not fall, but just stood there, dazed, everything above mid-forehead amputated, oozing rivulets of blood from the splintered basin its skull had become.

Then she tumbled forward, disappearing even as she fell out of the frame.

I blinked several times.

And murmured another silent response to the unknown sender.

Be seeing you.

By Adam-Troy Castro

The Andrea Cort Novels
EMISSARIES FROM THE DEAD

ATTENTION: ORGANIZATIONS AND CORPORATIONS
Most Eos paperbacks are available at special quantity discounts for bulk purchases for sales promotions, premiums, or fund raising. For information, please call or write:

**Special Markets Department, HarperCollins Publishers,
10 East 53rd Street, New York, New York 10022-5299.
Telephone: (212) 207-7528. Fax: (212) 207-7222.**

ADAM-TROY CASTRO

EMISSARIES FROM THE DEAD

AN ANDREA CORT NOVEL

An Imprint of HarperCollins*Publishers*

This is a work of fiction. Names, characters, places, and incidents are products of the author's imagination or are used fictitiously and are not to be construed as real. Any resemblance to actual events, locales, organizations, or persons, living or dead, is entirely coincidental.

EOS
An Imprint of HarperCollins*Publishers*
10 East 53rd Street
New York, New York 10022-5299

Copyright © 2008 by Adam-Troy Castro
Cover art by Chris McGrath
ISBN: 978-0-06-144372-5
www.eosbooks.com

All rights reserved. No part of this book may be used or reproduced in any manner whatsoever without written permission, except in the case of brief quotations embodied in critical articles and reviews. For more information, address Eos, an Imprint of HarperCollins Publishers.

First Eos paperback printing: March 2008

HarperCollins® and Eos® are registered trademarks of HarperCollins Publishers.

Printed in the U.S.A.

10 9 8 7 6 5 4 3 2 1

If you purchased this book without a cover, you should be aware that this book is stolen property. It was reported as "unsold and destroyed" to the publisher, and neither the author nor the publisher has received any payment for this "stripped book."

For Christina Santiago-Peterson,
who wasn't satisfied with the way
I killed her off the first time

ACKNOWLEDGMENTS

Has anyone, ever in the history of novels, read this page if they didn't have some specific reason to consider themselves likely to be mentioned? (Voice of random reader: "Boy, that Joe Schmo, his third-grade English composition teacher, sure sounds like a nice guy!") Just wondering.

In the meantime, various moments in the creation of this book were rendered easier thanks to the members of the South Florida Science Fiction Society writer's workshop, including George Peterson, Chris Negelein, Wade Brown, Dave Dunn, Cliff Dunbar, Mitch Silverman, Brad Aiken, and the late Meir Pann, all of whom had helpful things to say about its composition. Thanks also to Michael Burstein, who tolerates being immortalized as the alien race Bursteeni. Thanks to Stanley Schmidt, who published the first appearance of Andrea Cort in *ANALOG*. Thanks to the late Julius Schwartz, whose DC Comics letter columns, back in the day, were a young boy's first appearance in print. Thanks to Joey and Debbie Green, to David Goodman, to Elena and Ed Gaillard, to Janna Silverstein. Thanks to my agent Joshua Bilmes, for superhuman patience. Thanks to Diana Gill and Emily Krump. Thanks to

Jack McDevitt and Rob Sawyer. Thanks to Harlan Ellison. Thanks to my webmaster Dina Pearlman, and thanks to the many denizens of my newsgroup on www.sff.net.

Love again to my lovely wife, Judi, who for some odd reason persists in believing in me. I dunno why. But I sure as hell hope she never stops.

Adam-Troy Castro

EMISSARIES FROM THE DEAD

PROLOGUE

When the Monster sleeps, she dreams of Bocai.

Bocai had been an unremarkable world, of the usual unremarkable beauty. There had been deserts of towering red spinestalks, mountains lined with spongiform trees that remained tall and unyielding despite the softness of their bark, oceans that glowed with dancing phosphorescence at night, and a day and night approximately half the length of the normal human sleep cycle, allowing the human beings who had leased one small island from the natives two sunsets and two sunrises for every day they stood upon its generous fertile earth.

A beautiful world, yes. A remarkable beautiful world, no. Those who'd traveled to many all agreed that they'd seen better.

Following the usual behavior pattern of their species, the tiny human community had found the exotic sights and scents a fine subject for overwrought poetry. They had composed several hundred volumes, in no time at all, before something happened to all of them that lent those works a dark undercurrent they had never been meant to possess.

These days, on the rare waking occasions when the Monster permits her thoughts to dwell on that damned place, she wonders how she ever endured life there.

It was, after all, a world.

And as a grown woman, she hates worlds.

As a grown woman, she has never been able to understand why so many technologically advanced species continued to prefer natural environments when artificial ones are much safer and so much easier to control.

As an eight-year-old child, she had not known that even the happiest worlds could end with her curled in a dark narrow space between a bed and a wall, breathing dust and the sweat-soaked smell of her own fear.

She knows this now, and reminds herself anew every time she dreams of Bocai: not the lush and colorful landscape but that cramped space, her ragged breath, the distant smells of burning flesh, the distant cries of sentients killing or being killed.

She dreams about this night when hide-and-seek was no longer just part of a familiar childhood game. She dreams of thoughts that did not belong in her head and feelings that did not belong on her skin.

She dreams of seeing a mob of neighbors smash her mother's head against a wall again and again until everything the kind, somewhat distracted woman had been was reduced to a stain on the mortared walls.

She dreams of seeing her father, armed with a shovel, smash the skull of a Bocaian child she had considered a sister.

She dreams of seeing two sentients who had until this night been best friends to one another, one human, one Bocaian, tearing and scratching at each other in the dirt, too frenzied to scream from the wounds that have already blinded both.

And all of this was horrible and all of this was terrifying, but none of it affected her, at least on that night, the way it should have.

On that night it thrilled her.

On that night it made her heart pound and her blood race and her flesh tingle with the thrill of a game more delicious than any she had ever known.

On that night she regretted only being too small to participate.

Because she also wanted to kill something.

It's an odd thing for an eight-year-old Hom.Sap girl to want, and the part of the child that still remained sane had been entirely aware of that. There had never been any violence in her life, up until those last few hours—and there seemed no reason beyond simple self-defense for her to feel the urgency she felt now.

But she did hunger for it. She wanted to feel something alive turn to something dead. She wanted to stand above it at the moment of its dying, and feel the satisfaction of knowing that she'd been the one who drove it from the world of things that live and breathe and feel into the world of things that merely rot.

She wanted it so much that the grown-up Monster, reliving these moments from the vantage point of a survivor, is amazed that the little girl's sense of self-preservation was powerful enough to keep her in hiding for so long. Amazed that the little girl managed to keep quiet, that she'd managed to hide from the adults-turned monsters before they could have done to her what they'd already done to her father, her sister, her neighbors, and her friends.

If only she'd remained in hiding.

She might have avoided getting any blood on her own hands.

She might have.

In dreams, anything can happen. History can be rewritten. Fates can be argued with. Things set in stone can be remolded like putty.

But this dream follows real historical events.

This dream bears an inevitability that has tortured the Monster all her life.

This dream carries with it the knowledge that all these events have already taken place and therefore cannot be changed.

This dream commemorates the moment that transformed the little girl from innocent into the Monster.

The little girl in this dream is frightened not because she knows she might die tonight, but because she holds the knowledge of the Monster, watching through the same adult eyes, seeing that death might have been better.

Trapped in the dream that never changes, the little girl hears a rustling sound, and she knows that there is someone else in the room with her.

She knows it is someone she loves.

She knows he is here to kill her.

She knows she will kill him first.

She knows that at the moment of his death she will feel a rush of sick pleasure unmatched by any other joy her life will ever offer.

And she knows that she will live the rest of her life missing it.

1

HABITAT

I've never been a fan of natural ecosystems.

I know they're romanticized. They're great for people who like to swat bugs, step on feces, and catch strange diseases, an odd subsection of humanity that has never included myself. I grew up in urban orbital habitats and pretty much know better. But even I must admit that natural places evolve by accident and therefore can't be blamed for their high level of unpleasantness.

Artificial ecosystems, engineered by sentients who know we're better than that now, are just plain perverse.

The cylinder world One One One was an eloquent case in point.

It was so wrong, in both concept and execution, that it exalted even the most appalling messes arranged by Nature. Like most constructs of its kind, it rotated at high speeds to provide to the internal environment a simulated gravitational pull away from its axis of rotation. That's just basic engineering, so old that dumb old Mankind considered it a brilliant idea long before we went into space and put the basic idea into practice. But most cylinder worlds orbit planets, or hang around inside solar systems, and are built by sentients who evolved on planets to support life that likes to walk around on a solid surface, even when that solid surface has a horizon that curves up on both sides. As a result, they house their habitats on the surface that best approximates planetary notions of up and down: that is, the outermost "floor."

On One One One, the independent software intelligences known as the AIsource had turned that usual model upside down. The station itself was situated in deep interstellar space, a good twenty light-years from the nearest inhabited world, and far from any of the territories claimed by any of the major spacefaring species. We never would have known about it if they hadn't given us the address. Its habitable interior centered on an Uppergrowth of knotty vegetation clinging to the interior station axis. The crushingly dense lower atmosphere was a poisonous soup of thick toxic gases above a sludgy organic sea. Only in the upper atmosphere, near the central hub, was there a thinner oxygen–nitrogen blend of the sort congenial to the life-forms the AIsource had engineered.

The AIsource determination to get into the God-in-a-bottle business struck me as quixotic at best and insane at worst. And pointlessly grandiose, as well. The average human cylinder world is about ten kilometers long by two kilometers in diameter, which strikes me as a compact, manageable size that shows a little sense of humility in matters of cosmic scale. There are some leviathans, like my base of operations, New London, of up to ten times that size. All right, so we need big cities. But this place, One One One, was approximately a thousand times longer and some fifty times fatter than even New London: pretty excessive for the housing of a few brachiating apes who had to spend their entire lives clinging to bioengineered vines. It defined the concept of inexact fit.

Either way, it was an upside-down hell.

Even as the sleek AIsource transport ferried me into the habitat, I mentally catalogued everything I found disturbing here. The storm clouds far below were like a roiling brown cauldron, flashing with sudden light whenever charged by the violent forces at their heart. The giant winged things who sometimes ventured above those were like dragons out of a bad fairy tale: their wingspans up to two kilometers across, the force of their flight leaving entire storm systems in their wake, their sudden screeching dives into the opaque clouds acts of epic predation on creatures nobody flying at my current altitude had ever seen.

I'd been assured that the dragons never ascended as high as the Uppergrowth latitudes. I'd also been advised not to bother thinking about them, as they had nothing to do with the reason I was here.

It was like that old joke: *Don't think about the elephant.*

(But it's there.)

Don't think about it and it'll go away.

(But it's there.)

You're still thinking about it.

And so on.

The Uppergrowth, dotted here and there with the sluggish forms of the Brachiators, was a vast gray surface of compact, knotted vines that loomed over this world like a hammer waiting for the best opportunity to fall. The thick black pylons that every hundred kilometers or so descended from that Uppergrowth into the cloudscape were anchored at their apparent midpoints to the glowspheres that served as One One One's suns, and looked far too flimsy to hold such balls of corruscating fusion. The glowspheres themselves cast a light harsh enough to burn purple afterimages on my retinas, and there were so many of them that my transport cast multiple, competing shadows on the Uppergrowth above me.

I regarded it all with my usual grim reserve, dimly aware that I'd fallen back into a nervous habit that had plagued me for years: one index finger twirling the single lock of long, black hair that dangled from the right side of my head. Since the rest of my hair is cut very short, the many people who hate my guts like to say I keep that lock long to feed the tic and for no other reason. I know the habit drives people to distraction and therefore practice it whenever I can. I'm too uncomfortable in the presence of others to tolerate their comfort in mine.

The flight might have been bearable if the transport had been properly enclosed; but, no, it was a roofless model, protected against precipitation and wind shear by ionic shielding, offering a ride so smooth that had I closed my eyes I wouldn't have experienced any sense of motion at all. But I knew I was not enclosed. I knew that given just one moment's suicidal madness, it would have been all too easy to hop over the waist-high bulkhead and plunge to my death. I knew it and I could not ignore it.

Just as I knew that somebody in this Habitat was a murderer.

Excuse me. Somebody else.

I always forget to count myself.

The transport interjected: ***Andrea Cort: are you suffering distress?***

"Yes. How did you know?"

Your blood pressure, heartrate, and respiration all reflect tension levels consistent with the early stages of panic.

"I didn't know you were paying such close attention."

You are our guest and your health, when in our care, is paramount. Would you like some medication?

"No."

Some therapeutic conversation, then?

I'd spent years enduring therapy I didn't want, receiving medications that didn't help, having my brain mapped at every scale down to the molecular in search of answers that didn't exist. If it accomplished anything at all, it was instilling a lifelong aversion to sentients who meant well. "No. Maybe later."

You would not be the first human being to experience difficulty in this environment. Help is available.

"No, thank you."

The transport respected my wishes enough to shut up, thus demonstrating one major difference between software intelligences and human beings.

Human beings intrude whether welcome or not.

The facility housing One One One's human contingent was a network of pendulous canvas shapes, dangling from the Uppergrowth like gourds. Colored as gray as the network of vines that supported them, they seemed so organic a part of the landscape that I didn't recognize them as human structures until we drew near.

There must have been fifty hammocks, dangling in bunches, with only a few set off in relative isolation. They were linked by bridges of flexible netting, which crawled with the forms of human beings. Some traveled the Uppergrowth itself, brachiating along its roots and vines without safety lines. One lithe young woman with flaming orange hair hurled herself away from even that precarious haven, hung in mid-space for a second, and landed on one of the nets, bouncing up and down in total disregard of the deadly fall that would have awaited her if she'd missed.

The transport slowed, picked an angle of approach, and moved in underneath the hammocks, so close now that it was possible to discern the prone shapes of human beings in the lowest distensions of dangling canvas. Some of the humans traversing the net bridges paused to study me as I arrived. Their clothing styles ranged from skintight jumpsuits to, in a few cases, full nudity. Male, female, and a few identifiable neuters, they were all built like gymnasts at peak physical condition. Most were compact, though I noticed a few long-limbed spidery physiques among them. Their expressions managed odd combinations of hope, terror, resentment, and defiance, sometimes all at once.

I'd seen looks like that before.

They were people under siege.

The skimmer slowed to a stop beneath one of the central hammocks. As it dropped the shields, I felt wind: a light, warm breeze, carrying with it a scent midway between ocean water and the sugar-saturated air outside a candy shop I frequent in New London. Despite the terrifying environment, my mouth watered. Addiction to sweets is one of my few humanizing vices.

The fabric above me shifted and bulged from the weight of human movement. A narrow slit appeared where there had been no visible seam, revealing the face of a man in his late thirties. He had close-cropped shiny brown hair, eyes of a blue so pale they vanished against the whites, thin pink lips, and a lantern jaw that made his tentative smile look like a fissure on the face of an edifice. "Hello there! Welcome to Hammocktown! I gather you're the J.A. rep?"

I object to such snappy abbreviations on principle, but my complete title was Associate Legal Counsel for the Homo Sapiens Confederacy Diplomatic Corps Judge Advocate, hardly the kind of thing anybody could be reasonably expected to rattle off in a single breath. "Yes, I'm Counselor Andrea Cort. Are you the ambassador?"

His thin lip twisted. "That's not a title our esteemed landlords allow me to use."

"The AIsource object to the title Ambassador?"

"They object to it here."

If the software intelligences were getting pissy about job titles now, it either meant a major shift in the nature of their relationship with our species, or something unprecedented about the rules of life on One One One. But that was largely what I'd been led to expect. "Have they given you a reason?"

His smile faltered. "You couldn't have gotten much of a briefing on your way here."

"I'm only seven hours out of Intersleep." And still awaiting the energy crash that always struck like a club, within twenty-four hours of waking. "You haven't answered my question."

"I think I can answer your question inside. In the meantime, if you want to call me something, my name's Gibb, Stuart Gibb. You can consider me the chief asshole in charge." The slit opened wider, and he reached down with both arms. "Let's get you up here so we can get you up to speed. Do you have anything you want to pass up?"

I had a soft cylindrical bag containing three changes of clothes, a few toiletries, and a significant amount of contraband. I've never had any qualms about handing it to anybody. The bag was of Tchi manufacture, and as such was designed to satisfy a people who spent their days and nights taking offense at imagined improper liberties. Gibb could have examined every centimeter of the bag for days without finding access to my goods.

Gibb disappeared with the bag and a few seconds later lowered a ladder. Loose as it came down, flapping in the high-altitude breeze, it solidified at full extension. I grabbed hold, testing its ability to hold my weight, wondering what it would be like to slip and tumble into that storm-tossed hell.

A relief. The old death wish, speaking up again.

I took a deep breath, forced calm calm calm into my limbs, muttered my personal mantra, *Unseen Demons*, and began to climb.

As I pulled myself through the slit, entering warmer air and murkier light, Gibb grabbed my upper arm to steady me. His very touch was immediate annoyance. I let him guide me to a resting place about a meter away from the opening, and was not at all comforted by the way the soft rubbery canvas sagged beneath my added weight.

The interior of the hammock was a large round chamber, sagging at its center. A molded circular spine around its widest point, bearing a variety of tightly bound cloth bundles, allowed it to maintain a shape approximately like that of a teardrop, but the material below that spine was loose, settling into a shallow bowl beneath our weight.

Gibb was not the only man here. The other was a compact, grimacing figure with a shaved head, a prosthetic memory disk clinging to one temple, and eyes that glowered like lasers. Both men were dressed in loose-fitting gray pants and many-pocketed open vests that seemed designed to show off impressive gymnastic physiques. There was no way of telling whether those physiques had been earned the hard way via intensive training or installed by dealers in extreme physical enhancements.

The air inside the hammock was stale, redolent with liquor and body odor. But my relief at no longer needing to contemplate the long drop into One One One's stormy atmosphere almost made the murk intoxicating.

On the other hand, Gibb was still holding my arm.

I tugged. "Let go."

"You looked like you were having trouble—"

"I was."

"There's nothing to be ashamed of. As you can imagine, I've seen height-sensitivity before—"

"I can imagine. Let go."

Still he didn't. "I know the signs, Counselor. You're about ten seconds away from hysterics."

"You're about five from losing your hand. Let go."

An odd little look passed between Gibb and the grimacing man. I didn't need psi enhancements to note that all the questions seemed to come from Gibb's side of the hammock.

The self-proclaimed chief asshole in charge didn't seem to be as much in charge as he liked to claim. That was okay. I was willing to believe the rest of the description accurate. In my personal experience, people who tell you how awful they are, the first time they meet you, are just trying to defang your own inevitable reaction by beating you to the punch.

I know this. It's something I do myself.

Gibb released me and scrambled back half a meter up the canvas. "Forgive me, Andrea. Some of our newcomers have a major problem with vertigo. They're so scared of falling that they make it happen. Whenever I see somebody in trouble, I tend to be extra careful until I know we won't have a problem."

"As long as you don't call me Andrea again, we won't have a problem."

"Oh," he said, "we're generally informal here—"

"I'm not."

Another shared glance. "There's really no need to be so upset. We know this place isn't easy for some people to deal with. Most people just take some time to adjust—"

"Understood. And I'll appreciate anything you can do to help me adjust. But I'm still not interested in informality."

"Come on. There's no reason we shouldn't at least pretend to be friendly—"

"There is if I'm not looking for friends." I made this announcement without any special heat and without any special chill. "Counselor's fine. And if I can't call you Ambassador—"

Gibb stammered. "A-As I started to tell you, the AIsource don't recognize this as an official embassy. They've promised to evict us if I give myself that title. So you can call me Stuart if you like. Or Stu."

"No," I said. "I believe I'll call you Mr. Gibb."

The grimacing man rolled his eyes in contempt. It was not contempt for me, which I'm used to. It was contempt for this man he worked with, contempt he wanted to share with me.

Interesting. I'd been here less than two minutes and I was already being made privy to a power struggle.

Gibb's eyes broadcast waves of warmth and compassion but engaged my sincerity detector not one bit. "Have I done something to offend you, Counselor?"

"Not yet, Mr. Gibb. Are you hoping to?"

Gibb seemed taken aback yet again, displaying a most undiplomatic lack of skill at dealing with unpleasant people like myself. "All right, then, Counselor. If that's the way you prefer to play it. We'll keep this on a strictly professional level." He gestured toward the grimacing man. "This is Mr. Peyrin Lastogne, our special consultant on-site. My second-in-command, if you prefer. He'll be providing you with any help you need in your investigation."

Lastogne's nod was minimal. "Counselor."

Even that single word was tinged with an anger he contained but made no attempt to hide. He'd been through hell, somewhere, sometime; maybe several hells.

I nodded at Lastogne, then asked Gibb, "So why wouldn't the AIsource want to recognize your diplomatic status?"

He fluttered a hand. "They classify this entire habitat as a commercial installation rather than sovereign territory. They call everything inside it, including their precious engineered sentients, assets still in the process of being developed. As such, they claim exemption to the usual treaties involving diplomatic exchange."

"That's outrageous," I said. "It doesn't matter who administers the real estate. It matters who lives on it. The Brachiators have the right to speak for themselves."

"You know that and I know that. The AIsource contend that the Brachiators are a special case. They're not indigenous to this environment, after all. They were engineered elsewhere, and transplanted here. They were also all supposedly provided AIsource citizenship at the moment of their creation, which in theory gives the AIsource the right to speak for them."

That was transparent and familiar nonsense. Subjugated peoples are always subsets of the societies claiming to speak for them. Sometimes they're even called citizens. It doesn't mean they're one iota less subjugated.

Gibb's shrug prevented me from lecturing him on legal principles he already knew. "You can save your breath, Counselor. I'm just reporting the AIsource line."

I chewed a thumbnail—another of my many runaway tics that I'd spent years struggling to control. "How did this even have the opportunity to become a diplomatic issue of any kind? This is a sealed station, well hidden from anybody capable of looking for it. The AIsource didn't have to let anybody in. They didn't have to show anybody the Habitat. There's no way anybody from outside could have even known the Brachiators existed, unless the AIsource told them."

"Which is exactly what happened," Gibb said. "About three years ago Mercantile, they sent word to all the major governments that they wanted to show us something. Not long after that, a mixed delegation including Riirgaans, Bursteeni, Hom. Saps and Tchi arrived here, and were shown the Brachiators in their, you should only excuse the expression, natural habitat. Once the delegation realized that AIsource had engineered their own sentients, and better still professed to own them, it ignited a diplomatic firestorm."

"The AIsource must have expected that."

Gibb rolled his eyes. "Gee, you think?"

I'd been involved in a number of such diplomatic clusterfucks over the years. They were always nightmares, as you'd expect of sustained arguments between creatures defined not only by their differing cultures but differing psychological models. It's never erupted into all-out interstellar war, that being such an impractical and expensive prospect that only idiots and madmen see any point in it (and that's a damned good thing all by itself, since the hundreds of bickering, warring, and self-obsessed governments that make up the Hom.Sap Confederacy have never gotten along well enough to stand up against any concerted war of conquest or annihilation, from a truly determined enemy from outside). But there's been plenty of petty harassment and high moral dudgeon, plenty of brushfires over small matters of economic sovereignty, and plenty of wrangling over the Interspecies Covenant that allegedly keeps everybody nice to one another.

It's that very Covenant, with its provisions permitting diplomatic immunity, that both gives me my reputation as war criminal and places me outside the reach of the several races that would like to prosecute me for what I did as a child. And it's that very Covenant, with its provisions against the breeding of slave races, that the AIsource was so deliberately flouting now. What were they thinking?

My thumbnail clicked against teeth. "So how large is this 'unofficial' delegation of yours?"

"About seventy on-site, here under AIsource invitation, at their sufferance and under their designated limitations. We were able to set up this home base about two years ago Mercantile. We can interact with the Brachiators, find out what they're like, make friends with them, and catalogue their behaviors, but only for the purposes of study. As soon as we cross the line into actual diplomacy, we're expelled."

"My own main purpose here," Lastogne said, "is enforcing those guidelines. Making sure none of our people ever accomplish anything of note."

I studied the man's eyes for signs of mockery. "Must be frustrating work."

His appraisal of me was equally frank. "Diplomats don't need my help to avoid accomplishing anything."

Even more interesting. I began to suspect I could actually approve of the man.

But his attitude bothered Gibb. "That'll be enough of that, Peyrin. You'll have more than enough time for your facile nihilism. It's far from a waste, Counselor. We're here to combat a precedent that would tolerate the use of engineered sentients as slaves. Gathering the ammunition we need may be the most important agenda the Dip Corps ever had."

"How much longer do you think it's going to take you?"

"This is a permanent installation," Gibb said. "Barring a dramatic breakthrough, some of my indentures can expect to stay here for the entire length of their twenty-year contracts."

I could think of no better definition of hell.

And speaking of hell, Gibb's knee brushed against mine. Maybe it wasn't his fault. The soft surface beneath us sagged so much it took vigilance to avoid sliding toward the lowest point of the hammock's gravity well. On the other hand, Lastogne didn't seem to have any trouble maintaining his own position higher up the slope. And without being able to point to anything in particular, I could still sense an unwanted sexual charge coming from Gibb.

I attempted a deep breath and tried to focus on the matter at hand: "So what do you make of the Brachiators? Are they slaves?"

"They don't seem to do any real work, except for whatever niche they fill in One One One's ecosystem, but they're still sentient property, with no right of self-determination. There are right now eleven separate spacefaring races, ours included, involved in the legal battle to bring the issues here before an interspecies tribunal."

Wonderful. With eleven sentient races, from the amicable Riirgaans to the downright unpleasant Tchi, all bringing their special kinds of diplomacy to the fray, the higher math necessary to determine the lifespan of this litigation was beyond me.

Gibb read my expression. "It'll happen eventually. But the

AIsource are tricky. It took a year of heavy negotiation before they even agreed to let one race, which when the dust settled turned out to be us, send a minimal force of observers into this habitat just to make sure the Brachs weren't in immediate distress."

That couldn't have sat well with the other races, considering how many of them have less-than-salutory opinions of humanity. "And nobody complained about that?"

"Oh, they all complained about it. And from what I hear they're still complaining. We're fortunate in that we're locked away in here and don't have to listen to them. I should mention that one race, the Riirgaans, managed to send along their own rep, in the form of a human being with Riirgaan citizenship, but he's still, for all intents and purposes, one of us, under my command."

I grunted. "Which means little without diplomatic status."

"Right. We have no official standing, no authority, and no immunity."

"Not the best circumstances for a murder investigation."

Gibb's eyes flickered. "No."

"So tell me about this victim, Christina Santiago. How did she die?"

Gibb excused himself, scrambled up the sloping floor, made his way to a bundle strapped to the hammock spine, and removed a pair of cylinders with built-in straws. Scrambling down was an undignified slide on his rump, which ended only when his knees were once again pressed against mine. "Drink this, please."

I didn't often take food or drink in the presence of my fellow human beings, communal meals implying a social connection I preferred to avoid. But I obliged, gasping when the stuff hit my throat.

"Understand this, Counselor: that cloud layer below us is sixteen kilometers straight down; the ocean layer many kilometers below that; the atmosphere is unbreathable for most of that distance and only gets more caustic the farther you fall. There's nothing between us and a nasty drop but the layer of flexible fabric holding us right now. It's hard not to spend most of your time here thinking about the dangers of a misstep. I keep intoxicants around for newcomers who need to be pacified while they get used to the idea and while I figure out if they're going to have a problem with the heights. You've been looking dizzy since you got here. So I need to ask you: Are you going to have a problem?"

I felt the canvas sag beneath my weight, and reminded myself that if there were any chance of it tearing, Gibb and his fellow diplomats would have long since tumbled through the clouds. "No."

"Are you sure?"

"I'm not likely to change my answer based on repetition."

Gibb studied me for longer than I would have liked. "I hope you're right. Because this is no longer a single murder investigation."

He hesitated, as if afraid to speak the next words.

Lastogne spared him the trouble. "We had a second killing the day before yesterday."

2

HATE MAIL

I wish I could say that the news surprised me, but even before I arrived I'd suspected that the single murder was likely to become a multiple.

I'd received fair warning just out of Intersleep, when I was least primed to process it. It's a lot like being wakened from a coma with a tap from a hammer: a moment of crystal shock, so unpleasant in and of itself it made me want to sink back into the murk.

I don't even like waking from normal sleep. There's always a first, terrible moment when I remember who and what I am; and every morning, my heart convulses tight around the knowledge, like a blister forming around a wound.

I drove the kres into his back, not to protect myself, though he would have killed me if he'd had the chance, but because I wanted to see him die. I watched myself do it and I enjoyed doing it. He had been my Vaafir. He had been like a father. I didn't care. I wanted to see him die.

No, regular sleep is bad enough, if like me you shun the implants that allow controlled dreaming.

Intersleep is worse.

In Intersleep, the conscious mind is shut down for weeks or months, Mercantile reckoning, defying actual flatline with a few rebellious bursts of mental static. It's not so much thought or memory as the lint thought and memory left behind.

This may be an enjoyable thing for people predisposed to dream of pleasant memories or erotic interludes.

I've never been.

So I sat upright in the translucent bluegel, my eyelids still sticky with it, my knees curled tight against my chest, my eyes burning as acid tears carved paths through the caked goo on both cheeks.

I felt loss, shame, self-hatred, rage, and the need to make something bleed.

I shuddered. Sobbed.

Wanted to die.

Closed my eyes and cursed myself for not being able to rise above it.

Held my breath, felt the heart pound in my chest, and willed it to quiet down before it burst like a bomb inside me.

Good morning, Andrea. Welcome to your waking day.

Sanity, or as close as I ever came to it, returned in pieces. I remembered where I had been and where I was supposed to be now.

I'd been on a world called Grastius, working a case that had been one of the most colossal wastes of time in a long career spent investigating colossal wastes of time.

I was supposed to be heading back to New London. I should have found myself on a Dip Corps loading dock, being fussed over by the sleeptechs whose most substantial contributions to my well-being would have been a few comforting words and an offer of something sweet to drink. I didn't exactly miss having them flutter about, but their absence meant that something had gone wrong. "Shit."

Once upon a time, before I fed it a personality capable of getting along with me, the wakeup monitor would have advised me in the most syrupy tones imaginable that everything was all right. "Yeah. Shit."

I prized the irritation value of that craggy, long-suffering voice. "Why aren't we home? We're not about to crash into anything big, are we?"

The monitor replied with an audible grimace. "We wouldn't be that lucky."

"Then what?"

"New London had us diverted."

"What do you mean, diverted?"

"Diverted," it repeated, with a level of annoyance that matched my own. "Detoured. Shanghaied. Assigned a different destination. Ordered to pursue the wild gooses. You know. Diverted."

My head throbbed. "Shit."

"That," the monitor said, "would be yet another synonym."

"Shit. Shit. Shit. Shit."

"Don't milk it, honey."

"I was due for a sabbatical." Which I'd intended to spend mapping a private investigation into a certain matter involving Unseen Demons.

"I know. So did they. Evidently they didn't care."

"Why couldn't they divert somebody else?"

"They must have supposed it would be too cruel to do it with somebody who actually had a life to inconvenience."

"Fuck you."

"What makes you think I'd be interested, babe?"

Then again, a little irritation value went a long way. "Where are we?"

"Seven hours from arrival at a cylinder habitat designated One One One, AIsource registration, ranking Dip Corps representative a Mr. Stuart Gibb."

The AIsource registration was the first sign this was serious.

It was impossible to travel extensively in civilized space without dealing with that community of independent software intelligences, but they were bodiless, untouchable entities who wandered among us offering advice and selling high-tech services without ever offering us enough access to be touched in return. The little we knew about them was vague in the extreme. We knew that they'd all originated as proprietary software of various early-developing organic sentients whose respective technologies had advanced enough to create computer programs capable of guiding their own evolution. We knew that the proto-AIs had achieved true sentience and, sometime after that, independence long before mankind emerged from the primordial muck, that they'd contacted each other at some point during their explorations of the universe, and that they'd formed a community of sorts, which was there to greet us poor flesh-and-blood things when we finally dragged our asses free of our respective gravity wells, life-support equipment and all.

We did *not* know where they kept their hardware, though the current conventional wisdom was that it was nowhere in conventional space and certainly no place paranoid organic creatures were capable of bombing. We did *not* know what benefits they derived from maintaining trade and diplomatic relations with the rest of us, unless it was just to rack up high scores (a computer game playing *us*). We did *not* know just how smart and how powerful they were, and how easily they could wipe the more conventional sentients from their sky if it ever occurred to them to want to, though I've been to more than one Dip Corps gathering where idle contemplation of the subject led to uncomfortable silences at best and white-knuckled drinking at worst.

In the meantime, they were happy to just flit among us, selling tech and occasionally baffling us with bizarre whims.

Juje alone knew what they did with the money they made from their various corporations; it's not like they needed anything we were capable of selling. The most famous of their contributions to interspecies trade was of course AIsource Medical, with its network of clinics and hospitals which handled more than one-third of all health care in Hom.Sap space. I'd relied on them for emergency treatment a number of times, twice surviving attempts on my life only because AIsource were available to mend serious wounds. But that's the thing. Always, before, they'd come to *us*.

They didn't have bodies, as we understood the concept. What, then, were they doing with a world? Even an artificial one?

I covered my eyes with still-sticky hands. "I don't suppose anybody deigned to send word what I'm in for."

"*Deigned* is the word," the monitor said.

"That bad, huh."

"That bad. Sit tight. You're gonna love this."

The cold light of the chamber before me faded, replaced by a moment's encompassing darkness, which in turn faded only to be replaced by the face of a man I'd despised for much of my professional life.

Artis Bringen was a wispy-thin, smooth-faced functionary, autoengineered to look like a boy of no more than fifteen Mercantile. His cheeks were smooth, his jawline bland, his skin unmarked by anything approaching the character it would have acquired from actual experience. The only concessions to his actual age were a hairline trimmed back to accentuate his glacial wasteland of a forehead and a pair of world-weary eyes that his obsessive overuse of rejuvenation treatments had not been able to lend the same apparent youthfulness as his face and body. The discordance had always lent him the look of a callow nonentity, not at all worth taking seriously.

Bringen was also one of many who believed that the crimes of my childhood had not been extenuated by my young age or diminished capacity at the time. To him I was a living symbol of humanity's genocidal warts, whose continued freedom refuted all our protestations of trying to evolve into something better. In the time he'd been my superior he'd raised four legal challenges to my protected status in the Corps, at one point coming damn close to dragging me before an interspecies tribunal.

The projection flashed a smile without warmth that seemed less a greeting from one professional to another than the opportunity to display the sharpness of his teeth. "Good morning, Counselor. By the time you receive this message, you'll be aware of your diversion to One One One. I'm aware that postponing your sabbatical can't be pleasant for you . . ."

"Shove it up your ass," I muttered.

". . . but the situation aboard that habitat is both critical and politically sensitive, which is why we're indulging the several parties who have requested you by name."

Indulging. The choice of verb was a typical Bringen touch. "Go space yourself."

"You'll get a full briefing on-site. The situation is fluid . . ."

I groaned. "Your *head* is fluid."

"I can imagine your reaction to that too." He sighed, his expression changing to one he often wore when dealing with me: a certain infinite sadness which would have been more appropriate to somebody he liked than somebody he'd so often tried to throw to the wolves. "I'm sorry about that, Andrea. I know the way things are, between us. If circumstances had been different, we might have been friends. It would have been nice. I know I've always tried . . ."

I blew him a raspberry.

"But it's fair to say that you're not going to like me any more once you discover the conditions inside One One One." He smiled, an expression that on his face resembled a predatory rictus. "You'll have some problems there, Andrea. Heights. I'm sorry."

Yeah. I believe that.

"This is the bare minimum you need to know," Bringen said, his smirk replaced by a grimace that established nothing beyond his utter lack of talent for gravitas. "The AIsource have engineered a sentient species."

A long pause, while the fuzzy aftermath of Intersleep cleared all at once.

"Our observation team on-site has suffered a fatality—a first-year indenture named Christina Santiago—which they attribute to AIsource sabotage. Our understanding of the evidence seems to support their theory. But if the AIsource are guilty we have a shitstorm and a half, and I mean that in its most precise application. We cannot allow them to be guilty. Do you follow?"

I followed, all right. If AIsource sabotage had led to the death of a human diplomat, it was an act of war from an enemy that could not be seen, or touched, or hurt, and which had been been running major industries on Hom.Sap worlds for the better part of six centuries. Who could return fire in such a war? Who could be sure that the battle hadn't been lost before the war was even noticed?

If it came to that, humanity might not even survive it.

"Whatever the facts, whatever the evidence, whatever your senses tell you . . . find the AIsource innocent. Even if they're guilty, find them innocent. We'll deal with their actions as best we can. But in the meantime we need to put this back in its box. We need a guilty party we can cage." He hesitated. "I have faith in you, Andrea. Get in touch when you can."

The projection went to black and disappeared, replaced by the four blank walls that enclosed my crypt.

For just a moment I wanted nothing more than to aim my transport in some direction unpolluted by the presence of sentient life, someplace where it could safely drift for centuries or millennia without ever encountering a gravity well, or without ever being disturbed by crises or controversies.

Then the monitor said, "Hey."

I said, "What?"

"You asked me to remind you whenever you got like this. *Unseen Demons*."

The chamber was silent but for the hiss that afflicts even the emptiest of rooms, the sound of random colliding molecules making even quiet a kind of repressed explosion.

Unhappy that I'd been dragged back to a land occupied by those with all-consuming purpose, my only recourse was to mutter, "Shit."

The monitor said, "Want the other shoe now or later?"

I considered putting it off. I hadn't even come close to full recovery. Intersleep created an inertia that lingered. I needed to drag myself from the crypt, spend at least an hour in the sonic vibrating off bluegel, force-feed myself something solid, and then maybe spend another couple of hours lost in a standard, garden-variety doze. It would be awhile, maybe even a couple of days, before I got to sleep again, after all. The counteractives necessary to get my system running again always gave me an amphetamine rush that locked me in hyperdrive until I struck my metabolic wall.

But listening to Bringen and the monitor had already restored me to my most productive state of seething irritation. "I'll take it now."

"There was a second message piggybacked on that transmission. It was an encoded data strobe, occupying ten parts of noise for each thousand parts of Bringen mouthing off; and there are at least seventeen separate indications, boring if you force me to enumerate them, that it was inserted into the stream at some point after the message was sent."

"Are you sure about that? It wasn't just Bringen trying to be cute?"

"The contents of the second message render that unlikely, but I wanted to be sure, so I hytexed New London and asked to resend. The second transmission was just Bringen, without any additional code. No, it looks like somebody captured Bringen's signal and shuffled the data." The monitor hesitated, capturing with perfect fidelity the manner of a man trying to avoid words that sounded insane to him. "Internal evidence seems to suggest a human being using AIsource coding. I believe this may have been done from someplace inside One One One."

I bit a thumbnail, regretting it when I tasted the dried bluegel residue. "Somebody wants to talk to me without going through channels."

"Or they want to show they control the channels. Given the contents of this second message, it is a matter for concern."

I sat a little straighter in the gel. "Show me."

The chamber went black a second time and lit up as another projection—this one a full-sized holo of myself, standing as if at attention in my habitual shapeless black. My facial expression was neutral to the point of coma, omitting my usual furrowed-brow seriousness. The portrait was also a little softer than it needed to be around my chin, but its cheekbones were the proper height, its nose the proper thinness, its features at rest the familiar, damnable, unwanted combination of elements adding up to unwanted beauty.

It was an outdated image, depicting me with short-cropped hair on all sides, when I now indulged an appreciation of things asymmetrical by allowing one thin lock to descend all the way to my right shoulder. But it was recognizable enough, and would have passed muster as an image to send the media if I'd died, gone missing, or fallen so far out of favor that I could be disappeared with impunity.

It looked me in the eyes and said, "Hello."

Just that: *Hello*.

Then it exploded from the inside out.

It threw back its head and opened its mouth wide and stood before me twitching as tremors rippled down its cheeks. Its mouth yawned wider than human anatomy allowed, then further still, and then further yet. Soon the underside of the jaw was almost flat against the neck, the skin and flesh around it drawn so papery-taut that they split open in a garish scarlet wound that exposed teeth turned pink from the sudden hemorrhages at the back of its throat. Then its insides geysered from that impossibly huge mouth as if fired from cannons somewhere deep inside; not just blood and bile but black, glistening, organic shrapnel, desperate to escape whatever was happening inside. There was more fluid than my body could have contained. The simulacrum was soon painted in it. Then something unspeakable happened to its chest, caving it in, splintering the ribs, leaving curved white daggers of bone emerging from its flesh like scalpels.

I'm an expert in hate mail. My past has earned me an extensive personal collection of death threats, from representatives of various species. Most have been voice messages, colored with bile and transmitted my way via hytex. A few have been written with real ink on real paper. A few had been imaginative and vivid, and a number had been animated. Among the animated, I'd seen images simulating my torture, my strangulation, my rape, and my willing, enthusiastic participation in sexual acts so depraved that even my most exhaustive research hasn't been able to uncover more than a dozen worlds where such perversions are even theorized.

Most of this stuff is laughable. I'm sometimes amused at how little my correspondents know about female anatomy.

The unknown parties responsible for the inside-out image had programmed a state-of-the-art simulation, outdated or inaccurate in some particulars but persuasive in every other way.

It felt real.

It felt sincere.

It felt like a promise.

It was the kind of threat sent only by a genuine monster.

I should have been terrified.

But I was also a monster. And as I thought about the unseen sender, I tapped a fingernail against my teeth and murmured a silent promise in return.

You'll go first.

3

VICTIMS

First they told me all they knew about Christina Santiago.

Lastogne rattled off the facts, in a contemptuous drone that failed to betray any sympathy. Santiago, he said, had been a second-year diplomatic indenture, just out of training: specialty, exopsychology, the product of some industrial hell somewhere in the ass end of Hom.Sap space.

The feudal economy that kept the darker corners of the Confederacy going had seized a particularly savage grip on her people. The colonists who'd settled the place seventeen generations back had so badly mortgaged their lives and their children's lives, just for the funding to establish their infrastructure, that the entire population lived as the de facto debt slaves of the sponsoring Bettelhine Corporation. The world has one major industry, the construction of components for starship quantum dampeners. With perhaps one-third of the population engaged in providing food and housing and other support services, the other two-thirds spend their days working endless shifts in Bettelhine's factories, struggling and failing to meet the quotas that would bring their world's struggling millions a few percentage points closer to solvency.

Sometimes, they almost break even.

Mostly, as management intended, they fall much further behind. They have to give up more and more of their own agricultural and industrial systems just to make up lost time, which obliged the company, in its infinite generosity, to supply an ever-increasing percentage of their basic necessities, at an ever-increasing markup. Christina Santiago's people have been forced to mortgage three additional future generations, just during her lifetime alone.

The situation failed to shock me. The Confederacy doesn't provide its citizens with any redress against that kind of local corporate rapaciousness. What little political clout exists is external, a mere façade of species unity between us and the other sentient powers; internally, it's never been able to come up with a constitution all of our bickering subcultures have been willing to get behind. It's why any voyager through human space will encounter every political and economic system from green cults to fascism, why some of our more contentious worlds have as many as fifty or sixty separate governments happily bombarding each other from orbit, why we still have to deal with internal genocides in this day and age, and why debt-slavery like Santiago grew up with continues to flourish when the people benefiting from it should be lined up against the wall and shot.

Don't get me started. But it's one reason, of many, why I sometimes hate my own species.

To Lastogne and Gibb, I affected boredom. "So? Half the Dip Corps must come from some depressed background or another. It's what makes indentured servitude such an attractive alternative."

"It explains who she was," Lastogne said. "Gives you a special feeling for her character."

"Special feeling for her character doesn't matter unless

you believe that where she came from and who she is has some bearing on how she died. That her murderer targeted her in particular. Is that what you believe?"

"I have no reason to believe anything. I'm just being thorough."

Gibb just looked weary. "Get to the good stuff, Peyrin. She can fill in the personalities later."

Nobody could have blamed Santiago for indenturing herself to the Dip Corps as soon as possible. There, at least, she would have had a chance at a better life. But that better life had not materialized. Her murder had taken place during One One One's dark hours, when the glowsphere suns were dimmed to provide the cylinder's inhabitants with some semblance of a normal planetary night. But because witnesses had reported that Santiago's assigned hammock was still aglow, she was probably still awake, and working, at the moment of the crime.

The culprit or culprits had sliced through every cable anchoring one side of her hammock to the Uppergrowth. The partial collapse transformed the hammock from a tent to a flapping banner. All its loose contents, including Santiago herself, had tumbled into the darkness below, trailing her scream.

The young indenture may have remained conscious and terrified for long minutes, as she plunged toward the fatal high-pressure regions far below.

How must it have felt, falling all that distance, knowing even as the temperature rose all around her that all her striving had been futile?

The drink hadn't calmed me as much as Gibb had promised. It had heightened my awareness of the many subtle vibrations that resonated in the flexible material of the hammock—some the product of three human heartbeats transmitting their rhythms through flesh and bone and clothing into the material that supported us; others, and many more no doubt, the final vibrating manifestations of the winds outside. Christina Santiago's screams as she fell had contributed to those winds, and were probably still echoing elsewhere in this impossible place.

The thrum I felt, when I placed my palm against the hammock, was all that remained of her dying cry. I shuddered. "It couldn't have been done by somebody with a normal cutting edge."

Gibb's grimace was almost as embittered as Lastogne's. "That's so obvious it's almost a joke."

"Those cables were reinforced microfilament weave," Lastogne said. "They were designed to take fifty times the load. None of the tools we're permitted in-habitat are capable of slicing it. We brought the segments still left hanging from the Uppergrowth to our ship berthed in the station hub. We examined them to rule out faulty manufacture, only to find clean, precise breaks marked only by microscopic signs of heat-scoring—no-brainer indicators that whoever committed the crime had industrial capability."

"I was told that you suspected the AIsource themselves."

"It only makes sense," Gibb said. "They set the conditions here. The Brachs are pre-tech. Hammocktown gets by with minimal tech: a few floaters, some midrange skimmers, and of course full linkup to the hytex network. Just enough to zip around, do what we do, and report our daily findings to New London. Nothing like what was done to those cables."

I said, "How big is your ship?"

"Intersleep accommodations for fifty, waking accommodations for four. Brought our building materials and the bulk of the our del . . ." He stopped himself from saying delegation. "Research party."

"Building materials would include the tools you used to build this outpost, correct?"

"True."

"Which would have to include something capable of trimming cables."

"Of course."

"Then, I trust you've confirmed that those tools remain locked up aboard your vessel?"

"Of course," Gibb said. "I know where you're going with this, Counselor. You're thinking I should look at my own people before accusing our hosts."

"It seems a reasonable first step," I said.

"Unfortunately, the AIsource permitted the restricted tech inside the Habitat only during a limited construction window, and required us to return everything to our cargo hold afterward. The shipboard systems track everything that's removed and replaced, and confirm that it's all accounted for. The AIsource remain the only sentients with the proper tools at the proper time."

"Unless somebody on your staff hacked the inventory to hide a little unauthorized appropriation."

"A possibility. History's shown that human beings can hack anything. But even if this presumed hacker beat our systems, the AIsource have their own monitors recording everybody who enters or leaves the hangar. Nobody holding proscribed tech would get outside the hangar, let alone all the way inside the Habitat. Nobody could even try without the AIsource alerting me—and they have every reason to do so, since it's the lack of any alternate explanation that makes them look so guilty."

I chewed on a fingernail. "Maybe they don't care about looking guilty."

"We can't assign them human motivations, but it makes a lot more sense for them to be guilty and not care that we know than innocent and not care that they're under suspicion."

"There's also a human safeguard," Lastogne said. "We have a full-time staff in the hangar, three indentures who couldn't handle the conditions in-habitat. They're assigned for repairs, accounting, and hospitality during down-time, but they would report anybody who tried to get into the tools."

"Any reason they're above suspicion?"

"Below suspicion," Gibb said, with palpable contempt. "Working in-habitat almost killed them as it is. It's expecting too much to imagine any of them overcoming their paralysis long enough to hack the inventory system, select their equipment, somehow get it past the AIsource security systems, pilot a transport into the Habitat, and conduct a pointless little act of murder-sabotage for no reason other than they somehow figured out how."

I wondered why the height-sensitives were still on-station. It couldn't have been all that difficult to transfer them to another assignment. "What if your culprit was only faking height-sensitivity in order to set the stage for a murder he planned to commit later?"

"That would require a ridiculous amount of advance planning. All three were judged unfit months ago Mercantile: one a full two years ago, before Santiago was even assigned here."

"I'll still need to speak to them."

"It's a waste of time." Gibb's fatuous superiority, so similar to the hated Bringen's, was beginning to infuriate me. "But not unexpected. We expect you to speak to them and everybody on-site. We have no doubt that when you're done you'll come to the same conclusion we have."

"The AIsource have the only real power aboard this station," Lastogne said. "They have remotes all over the place. Flatscreens, fliers, maintenance bots, surveillance cams. They range in size from heavy construction equipment to nanotech. You can't spend five minutes here without seeing something of their manufacture zip by on one mission or another, which means that they had the means and every possible opportunity."

My thumbnail crunched between my teeth. "But they still deny involvement?"

"Of course."

"What about knowledge? Even if they're not involved, they must have observed—"

Gibb grew more glum with every answer. "But they don't seem interested in testifying."

"I'll still have to interview them too."

"They expect you to," Lastogne said. "In fact, they asked to see you tomorrow morning. I'll be flying you to that meeting first thing."

I wasn't sure I'd heard that correctly. "Flying me?"

"That's right. Same way they flew you in."

Aghast, I demanded, "Do you seriously mean to tell me that with all the remotes they have flying around this station—one zipping by every few seconds, you said—they won't connect one to their main system and save me a trip?"

"No," Gibb said. "They want you back at the Hub."

This was their oddest, most counterintuitive behavior so far. Distance wasn't the issue. I'd dealt with AIsource remotes, as embodied by their ubiquitous floating flatscreens, on two dozen worlds. It seemed downright silly for them to change the rules inside this station they owned, and pretend they needed to drag me to and fro for private audiences.

Maybe a show of arrogance was the whole point.

Lastogne showed teeth. "Don't look so upset, Counselor. You need to go to the Hub, anyway, to talk to our exiles. You can take care of that after you deal with our landlords. And you'll find the Interface system they have here pretty special."

And that had the sound of an unpleasant private joke.

It could be a simple local eccentricity. We may treat the AIsource like they're all one big monolithic entity, but they're really billions of separate linked intelligences, operating in an imperfect consensus. There were probably millions of linked programs on this station alone—which meant that proving their involvement still left me with the problem of isolating the individual software that committed the crime. And from there, determining whether the murder was the aberrant act of an individual or an assassination committed as a matter of policy.

All in all, it was enough to make me grin. The death of a young Dip Corps indenture wasn't funny. But the malice of those who'd drafted me was. It was a) an impossible investigation, b) on unfriendly territory, c) without the protection of official standing, d) but with the legal status of an entire sentient species potentially at stake, e) involving a practically infinite number of intangible possible suspects, f) none of whom could be isolated from the others, g) but all of whom could at any moment eliminate me with as little warning as the culprit had previously eliminated the unfortunate Christina Santiago, h) all in an environment taking full advantage of my well-known distaste for heights, i) in service of a case I'd been specifically warned I shouldn't pin on the most likely suspects.

Thank you so *very* much, Artis Bringen. "And the second victim? The one from seventy-two hours ago?"

Gibb's wince tightened. "Cynthia Warmuth. Twenty-three years old. A third-year diplomatic indenture, specialty exolinguistics."

Cynthia Warmuth had hailed from an agricultural colony within the Confederacy, but not of it. The details of her life on that world were a sick portrait of deprivation for deprivation's sake, of a barbaric religious conformity enforced with a medieval level of discipline. They had not been allowed music, or hytex connections, or more than minimal education. They might not even have been permitted to know that other worlds existed if the Confederacy hadn't considered the dissemination of such basic information the bare minimum expected from any world hoping to engage in mutual trade. It was not an educational requirement the people in charge pursued with any special vigor, and though Warmuth had grown up perfectly aware that there was a greater universe, she had assumed it to be comprised of a hundred worlds or less, all of which she supposed to be pretty much a direct copy of her own. She had still been among the one-third of that world's young people who indentured themselves offworld as soon as possible, her educational background so deficient at the start that she'd needed to sign up for an additional ten years just so five could be dedicated to remedial training.

"She turned out to be a prodigy," Gibb said. "Very gifted. Handled her remedials in less than half the assigned time. Scored top marks on all of her qualifiers. Excellent physical conditioning as well; a gymnast. Uppergrowth navigation was downright easy for her. I put three separate notes in her file recommending her for the leadership track."

Once certified, Warmuth had enjoyed an uneventful year as Dip Corps liaison to the dance pilgrims on Vlhan, achieving marks for efficiency if not for unusual level of achievement. Some unspecified conflict with her fellow indentures had led to an official request for a transfer.

"Whatever it was," Gibb said, "it wasn't serious enough to be written up in her Corps files. Personal chemistry, most likely. Warmuth got on people's nerves. But indentures come from so many cultures that you have to expect some of that kind of thing."

"Did she request the transfer or was it requested for her?"

"As far as I know, it was her idea. I once heard her claim to have been the only Dip Corps indenture on Vlhan with any real interest in the indigenes, but that was just her. She liked the mantle of sainthood."

Whatever the explanation, Warmuth had been sent to One One One. At the time of her death she had been on-station for six months Mercantile, working in a support capacity before being cleared for direct contact. Until the day of her death, she'd never ventured any distance from the hammocks without an escort.

Gibb said, "She had minimal contact with the Brachs, I assure you; just a few introductory sessions. And a few with our exosociologist Mo Lassiter and a cylinked couple called Oscin and Skye Porrinyard. She was on her first overnight when what happened . . . happened."

I noted the man's shudder, found no reason to doubt it now, but tucked it away in case further developments gave me reason to consider it feigned. "I'll still want to speak with Lassiter, these Porrinyards, and any Brachiators she encountered."

"The Porrinyards will be glad to help. If you get anything useful out of the Brachiators, you're better than me."

Still studying the non-ambassador's eyes, I found more sadness, more regret, a level of grief that verged on the personal . . . and something else, something reticent, something hiding away secrets the man would have preferred me not to see. "Did you like her, Mr. Gibb?"

Gibb averted his gaze. "I really do prefer people to call me by my first name, Counselor. But, dammit, yes, I liked her. She was one of the sunnier people around here: compassionate, friendly, dedicated, and, above all, giving to a fault, the kind of person who becomes the emotional center of an outpost like this."

Lastogne's eyes burned with mockery. "A born idealist."

I picked up the insult, as I was meant to. As far as I could tell, Gibb did not. Lastogne seemed to enjoy firing verbal missiles under his superior's radar.

I said, "You just made her an angel. You also said that she had a way of getting on people's nerves. Which is true?"

"Both," Gibb said. "She tried too hard."

"Was her hammock sabotaged too?"

"No." Gibb's pale eyes seemed to turn obsidian with despair. "Like I said, she was out on her first overnight. We found her hanging from the Uppergrowth."

"Tell her how, Stu," Lastogne said.

Gibb held back the words, as if the mere act of speaking them brought the terrible facts into being. But he managed: "There were Brachiator claws driven through her wrists and ankles. Another, the killing blow through the heart."

"Brachiator what?"

"Claws." His voice broke. "The Brachiators have very sharp curved claws. They're constantly growing, and break loose when they get too long. Usually they just freefall into the murk and are never seen again. But many Brachiators keep a few cuttings tangled in their fur as subsidiary tools. These claws looked like they'd been carried around for months."

Silence fell, with nobody in the hammock willing to say the next part.

Lastogne's words arrived in a bitter explosion. "She was crucified."

4

BRACHIATORS

Navigating through Hammocktown required a mix of confidence and coordination that taxed my shaky nerves. The hammocks were linked by a cat's cradle of nets and cables, only some of which seemed to have been designed for safety. Most routes from place to place required a confident athleticism that my own high level of conditioning, fine for most environments, was not able to match. Other routes seemed more precarious: the shortcuts of those confident enough, or arrogant enough, to scorn safety. There were rope bridges that swayed with every step; great taut expanses of fishnet that, like the hammocks themselves, needed to be negotiated on all fours; even places where the residents seemed to take a kind of perverse pride in jumping between fixed platforms. There were a few, tiny places where it was possible to stand upright, like a human being: solid surfaces that had more to do with supporting the community than with humoring the human prejudice favoring upright locomotion.

At times it was necessary to pass through the hammocks

themselves, some of which were occupied by off-duty personnel. I was introduced to close to two dozen people, none of them long enough for register as individuals. I noticed a few places where indentures, in various states of undress, lay huddled together in low-lying hammocks, in gatherings that had more to do with the leveling effects of gravity than with the erotic possibilities so much closeness suggested. I wondered if I'd misjudged Gibb. In this place, you'd lose your sense of personal boundaries very quickly.

One sleeping man, curled in a ball at his tent's lowest point, didn't even stir when we made our way past him, even though our very passage through his domain made his body slide across the canvas like a stone in a sack.

"Cartsac," Lastogne sniffed. "Has something like a twelve-hour sleep cycle. Makes him useless, most of the time."

"And the rest of the time?" I asked.

"Marginal."

Interesting. Yet another complaint about this outpost's standards of competency.

At the higher latitudes, the Uppergrowth itself hung close enough to touch. The vines were dotted here and there with bunches of engorged fruits, hanging from buds like candy. Parts of the outpost's support structure were so streaked with juice that I had trouble seeing how anybody who worked here stayed clean.

Lastogne plucked a fruit. "Taste one if you want. It's good."

"No, thank you. What is it?"

Lastogne took a bite, made a face, and gave the barely touched fruit an underhanded toss into the clouds. "We call them manna pears. The AIsource engineered them as a staple of the Brachiator diet, but humans can metabolize them too. Our generous bosses in the Dip Corps tried to take advantage of that fact to cut down on our food drops, until we rebelled and said we wouldn't subsist on an exclusive diet of the crap."

The speed with which Lastogne had disposed of the uneaten portion gave me the nasty suspicion the flavor would have appalled me. "What's wrong with them?"

"They're an acquired taste. I like them, in moderation. They're easy to ferment, by the way, but I warn you away from any invitation to partake."

"That bad?"

"That strong. The intoxicant stays in your system for close to forty-eight hours. It's an excellent drunk if you don't mind being impaired for up to two days Mercantile . . . a bad idea if you're still getting used to the conditions here."

Substance abuse is an endemic problem in the Dip Corps, where so many indentures are, like Warmuth and Santiago, driven more by economic need than any passion for the work. But the risks that such a form of escape carried here seemed greater than in most places. I thought of all the daredevil indentures navigating Hammocktown, and focused on one young woman who was now traveling hand-over-hand across a slack line strung between hammocks, unmindful of the many kilometers of empty space that yawned below her. *Just how many of you have tried that trick drunk, or buzz-popped, or worse?*

I shuddered and, to distract myself from the image of a drunken indenture taking a one-way slip into the lower atmosphere, asked, "What about those giant flying things I saw on the way here? The dragons?"

"What about them?"

"Well, what do they eat?"

"There's a whole complex food chain going on down there. The clouds contain heavy organic compounds, an insect form which metabolizes them, a birdlike thing that eats the insects, and the dragons, which eat some combination of the above I've never bothered to ask about. I think there are only about four or five of them, all told, and that they function as living air purifiers, sweeping that level of atmosphere for compounds the AIsource want to get rid of it, and happily shitting whatever they want. Like vacuum cleaners with a mythological edge."

"Have you ever gotten a close look at one of the dragons?"

"Enough to satisfy my curiosity. They're not sentient, you see, so they're outside the scope of our mission here."

"Are we sure about that? Them not being sentient?"

"The AIsource say they're not."

"AIsource honesty has already been called into question once today."

"Maybe so," Lastogne admitted, "but it seems silly for them to call attention to one bunch of unlikely sentients we never would have known about and then deny the sentience of another bunch who would have been just as easy to keep a secret."

Unless they saw some advantage in feeding us a partial impression. "Has anybody bothered to investigate?"

"We could, Counselor, but we only have a handful of people here, and this world brings an entirely new meaning to the phrase 'bottomless pit.' There are more different atmospheric environments the lower you descend, and they all have their own life-forms, increasingly alien as you go down, and there's no point in wondering just how many of those creatures down there might be sentient when the AIsource won't allow us to import the equipment we'd need to map those lower altitudes properly. The only vehicles we're allowed have trouble surviving the intense conditions below that cloud cover. Maybe we'll get down there someday. If we do I'd love to be part of it. But right now it's enough to worry about the Brachiators. They're our assignment, just as Warmuth and Santiago are yours."

Farther on, he pointed out another pair of young indentures, making their way across the outpost. One man and one woman, they were clearly a couple, maybe siblings and maybe lovers. Both had stubbly silver hair and square faces, and both were clad only in shiny silver briefs and another thin strip of the same material across their chests. Their arms were as well developed as any I'd ever seen, and their abdominal muscles as rock-hard, which must have aided them as they traveled hand-over-hand on the Uppergrowth itself, using its many protruding roots like the rungs of an overhanging ladder. They moved with the practiced speed of people who traveled that way on a daily basis, and their dangling legs, kicking back and forth as they went, gave them the look of people running across a floor tangible only to themselves.

My personal aesthetic left little room for appreciation of beauty, but they qualified. I felt an undeniable awe, which I quickly repressed. "Who are they?"

"The Porrinyards."

Oscin and Skye. "What can you tell me about them?"

"They hail from some world where the settlements are built on the branches of mile-high trees. They were scrambling branch-to-branch from infancy, so they were natural choices for assignment here."

"How would you assess their relationship with the victims?"

"Helpful," Lastogne said.

"Just helpful?" I pressed.

"Just that. They're professionals at what they do."

"And nothing more?"

"They're cylinked. They don't make friends in the usual sense."

I'd heard that said about other cylinked pairs, but I'd never encountered anybody with that particular enhancement, so I didn't know whether to consider Lastogne's claim accurate. "Do you?"

He wasn't shocked. "No. But it's different for me, you see. I make no friends because it's too time-consuming, and they make no friends because their condition makes the idea superfluous. What about you, Counselor? I gather from your treatment of Mr. Gibb that you don't make friends either."

"I don't."

"Repugnance, disinterest, or sheer misanthropy?"

"None of your business."

He took no offense. "I shouldn't be surprised, considering your background."

I chilled still further. "What do you know about me?"

"Everything unclassified and much that's not supposed to be. You're not exactly obscure, Counselor. The Bocai incident, the Magrison's Fugue Reparations Trial, the Cort Compromise—they're all pretty famous to people interested in that kind of thing."

More chill: "And what kind of thing is that?"

"Diplomats being diplomats."

Given his already established opinion of diplomats, I was not foolish enough to take this as a compliment.

He continued. "It's fascinating. We have a lot in common, the four of us—you, me, and our linked pair, the Porrinyards—all antisocial by inclination, all obliged by profession to make nice with others."

I gave my voice all the cold I could muster. "It occurred to me a long time ago, Mr. Lastogne, that diplomacy has very little to do with making friends."

Lastogne's expression resembled a warm smile about as much as a heap of blasted rubble resembled a home. "No, Counselor. It doesn't."

He then took me to the opposite end of the installation for my first closeup look at a lone Brachiator, clinging to the Uppergrowth five meters from the nearest bridge.

The thing was a collection of four furry, muscle-bound arms, radiating from the edges of a torso streaked and matted with manna juice. The head was a small, neckless bump situated at its center of that torso, bearing facial features reminiscent of the fabled, but extinct, human cousin known as the chimpanzee, except with three eyes and a toothless mouth twisted in what looked like a perpetual grimace. The position of that face atop the torso dictated a life spent facing the Uppergrowth. If any manuever within its range of movement allowed the Brach to face the cloudscape below, it would have included falling as a necessary first step.

The creature was so sluggish that I needed several seconds to be sure it was actually moving. Its edges looked fuzzy until I realized it was surrounded by a halo of insects, scavenging manna drippings from its fur.

"They're messy eaters," Lastogne said. "The vines spout sap when punctured, so the average Brach spends its lifetime covered with sticky glop."

"Which explains the bugs."

"Yes. We were a little worried about those, at first. An infestation, on Hammocktown, would be seriously unpleasant. But the bugs don't want anything to do with us, even when we're covered with juice ourselves. Humans are just, well, naturally repellent."

I refrained from saying that this was hardly news. "Is it old or disabled in some way?"

"No. That's as speedy as they get. Makes sense, though, this being an environment where being sure of every move you make bears a definite evolutionary advantage. And with food everywhere and no natural predators supplied by their landlords, they don't need all that much speed anyway."

I was reminded of another species I'd encountered, on the case that had given me my secret mission in life. The Catarkhans had been blind, deaf, mute, insensate by all human standards, and so slow-moving that their entire lives had been a ballet of pathetic obliviousness. The dull, inexorable momentum of this Brachiator reminded me of the average Catarkhan. "Is it even aware we're here?"

"Oh, he can hear us fine. And he'll be able to see us, too, if we can get within his range of vision. We pretty much have to be next to him, or on top of him, for that to happen. We can even have a chat. They speak Mercantile."

The dominant language of human trade and diplomacy was a crass and unpoetic tongue, engineered long ago to edit out elements that could be culturally offensive to any of humanity's thousands of squabbling subcultures. There was not a single beautiful phrase in it. Encountering it among the Brachiators raised my suspicions a notch. "That's a little too convenient, Mr. Lastogne."

"Thank the AIsource. They had the whole species fluent by the time our team arrived. A stab at hospitality, I suppose."

Or a sneaky way of suppressing the real Brachiator language, so Gibb's team couldn't comb it for insights into Brachiator thought processes. One One One was aptly named: it seemed to have circles within circles within circles. "So let's have a talk."

He scared me silly by grabbing hold of the Uppergrowth and climbing hand-over-hand to the creature's position. A few seconds of conversation later, he returned, dropping back onto the mesh bridge with such ease that it erased any impression he'd been showing off.

I needed all my self control just to avoid being sick, but kept my face stony as the Brachiator, moving with significantly less grace than Lastogne, obeyed the summons. Unlike Lastogne, who'd managed his feat in seconds, it needed almost a full minute to traverse the distance, greeting us in a scratchy, high-pitched whine. "Peyrin the Half-Ghost asks me to speak to New Ghost. Can New Ghost hear me?"

Lastogne nudged me.

I said, "Yes."

"I am Friend to Half-Ghosts," the Brachiator said. "I am not Friend to New Ghosts. I speak to New Ghost only as courtesy to friend Peyrin."

Lastogne nudged me again.

"I am Counselor Andrea Cort. Friend to," I hesitated, then felt the correctness of my instinctive response, "the Living."

The Brachiator needed long seconds to consider that. "Will you stay a New Ghost or become a Half-Ghost like Peyrin?"

Lastogne placed his index finger before his lips.

But I never shut up when told to shut up. "What if I don't want to be a ghost of any kind? What if I wish Life?"

The Brachiator sniffed, in what may have been its equivalent to the snobbish dismissal humans of self-proclaimed quality reserve for others, below their station, who insist on applying to the same clubs. "Life is not good for ghosts. It exhausts them."

I ignored Lastogne's increasingly annoyed gestures. "I breathe air. I eat food. I sleep and wake. These are conditions of Life."

"You may live, but you are not of Life."

"And if I become a Half-Ghost?"

"Then you can touch Life."

"Just touch it?" I asked.

"Yes. And perhaps keep it a little while."

"I can't have it?"

"Having it," the Brachiator said, "is too much for a Half-Ghost to expect."

Lastogne said, "Thank you, Friend. Now, if you'll excuse us . . ."

I bit down hard on the tip of my thumb, found focus in the moment of clarifying pain, and said, "One last question. What do you know about the beings my people call the AIsource?"

Friend to Half-Ghosts said, "We are of the AIsource. We breathe the air of the AIsource. We know the AIsource with every breath. The AIsource know us with every breath. There are no secrets from them."

"And are they alive or dead by your definition?"

"The AIsource are not Life."

"Then they're Ghosts?"

"They are not Ghosts. They are the hands in Ghosts. They are not Life, but the vessel of Life. They." Friend to Half-Ghosts halted in mid-declaration, like any other sentient searching the air around itself for the phrase best suited for capturing a difficult thought. But the silence went on, and on, and on, stretching so long that the sentence already begun closed itself off like a malignant tumor excised before it could cause irreparable damage to surrounding tissue. Then it twitched its head and said, "I apologize, Peyrin. I have broken the laws of my people. I cannot answer any more of Counselor Andrea Cort's questions while she remains a New Ghost. Please tell her we can speak if she becomes a Half-Ghost."

"She understands," Lastogne said.

The Brachiator turned and embarked upon its long and laborious journey back to its previous feeding place. At the rate it traveled, the trip would cost it many minutes, but the Brachiator seemed undisturbed by the inconvenience, a genetic aversion to haste being a clear evolutionary advantage in any species that could do nothing in a hurry.

Not that evolution, as it usually worked, had been a factor on One One One.

Why would the AIsource, a species with a computation speed that qualified as instantaneous by human standards, create a species this slow of thought and deed? The Brachs could have been acrobats. Instead, they were sloths.

I looked at Lastogne. "That's some hierarchy they have. New Ghosts. Half-Ghosts. Life. What do you make of it?"

"Pretty much what I see you've started to get already. They refuse to believe in human beings as actual living creatures. The New Ghost designation they gave you is simple enough to figure. It's what they call people like yourself who are newly arrived and have not yet been initiated into their circle.

We have yet to figure out why we're dead to them, unless it's pure, garden-variety species chauvinism, but they're pretty serious about it. They won't talk to any of us for long unless they first declare us Half-Ghost, with one foot in the living world. And that requires us to prove we can spend hours hanging from the Uppergrowth as they do. Cynthia Warmuth was undergoing that very rite of passage, with a tribe about an hour's flight from here, the night we lost her."

"Is there any reason a Brachiator couldn't have killed her?"

"They might have. They had the opportunity, and of course the means. They even have the temperment, to some extent; you can talk to Mo Lassiter about that. But every human being at this outpost, you excepted, has undergone the same rite, and Warmuth was our first bad experience. If a Brach killed her, it was a behavior we haven't encountered before, and it's difficult to separate it from what happened to Santiago."

"Which doesn't mean it was linked in fact. They could be unrelated incidents."

"True," Lastogne said. "That's another thing you're here to figure out."

One of the camp's hammocks had been cleared for my personal use while I was on-site. It was a space exactly like Gibb's, complete with hytex link, blankets, spare clothing, and enough emergency provisions to keep me alive for weeks. Lastogne gave me a quick orientation, concluding, "The lights and the hytex are voice activated; you can work here, reading the files, familiarizing yourself with the rest of the background, for as long as it takes. If you want to talk to any of our people, call me and I'll make sure they come to you. If you need escort anywhere else, link to me and I'll be over right away. If you need anything to make you comfortable . . ."

"Well . . ."

He anticipated my next question. "We have a latrine structure at the center of the camp. No need to flush, the waste just drops out the bottom, with the environment below us functioning as the most elaborate chemical toilet in this solar system. Some of us don't bother to make the trip, as we can accomplish the same trick by unzipping the access flaps in the bottom of our hammocks."

I frowned. You normally don't want to introduce untreated waste into a habitat not evolved to break it down. "I'm surprised the AIsource even allow that sort of thing."

"You shouldn't be. The most sensitive part of the ecosystem, the Uppergrowth, is above us, and shit, once released, doesn't gain altitude. Not even a trained diplomat's. As for everything below us, well, there isn't a single compound in the human body capable of surviving the lower atmosphere intact. The ocean layer won't even feel the ker-plop."

I thought again of a human being falling that distance, and shuddered. "Anything else?"

"For bathing, you'll have a sonic kit in that pack over there." He indicated one of the many bundles hanging from the O-shaped spine on hooks. "If, on the other hand, you're one of those people who absolutely can't do without running water, our ship in the station hub has full recycling systems. Our exiles there have nothing better to do than take care of you. It'll take you the better part of an hour to fly there and back, but it can be done, and it'll even save you some time, since you have to be at the hub for your interface with the AIsource first thing tomorrow morning anyway. Do you want a ride?"

It sounded like a test, one that made perfect sense: stationed in this place, I might have been equally unwilling to trust anybody who couldn't stand local conditions. "No. I can wait for the morning."

Lastogne didn't bother to show even conditional approval. "Then, if you need nothing else, I'll let you rest, so you'll be fresh when the suns switch on."

He didn't wait for my response but instead scrambled up the flexible floor to the exit. There was no haste in that wordless retreat, no rudeness, just the swift and assured efficiency of a man who believed he'd already provided every answer I could want. As my long list of hates includes having my needs anticipated, I waited for him to reach the threshold before calling him back. "I'm not done."

The bastard didn't even turn. "Oh?"

"A few final questions."

When he slid back down the slope to my side, his grin was so insolent I knew that he'd expected the summons. "I doubt very much that they're 'final,' Counselor. You strike me as the thorough type."

"I try to be. But for now: Who sent for help from the Judge Advocate? Was it you or Gibb?"

"Gibb had me take care of it."

"Did he ask for me in particular?"

"No. I don't think he ever heard of you, before today."

I'd suspected that when he greeted me with actual human warmth. I don't often get that from people who already know my background. "Did you request me?"

"I would have if I'd thought of it, but I had no way of knowing you were available. No. I just sent word to New London and let them decide who to send."

Bringen had told me I'd been specifically requested. "Did the message pass through any hands other than Gibb's, or your own?"

"No. We currently approve all out-station traffic. Why?"

Somebody here was lying, though I didn't have enough information to determine whether that liar was here or back home. "You called Warmuth an idealist."

"She was."

"You also make it pretty clear that you did not consider that a compliment."

"I didn't and I don't."

"You didn't like her?"

He hesitated. "It wasn't a matter of personal like or dislike."

"Did you or didn't you?"

"I enjoyed her company."

"But you don't think she was as wonderful as Gibb says?"

He hesitated a second time, just long enough to establish that he didn't want to speak ill of the dead. "I suppose you could say she had an excessive hunger for novelty. She kept saying that she left her homeworld because she wanted exotic experiences, and that being open to such things was part of being alive, but there was a self-serving element to the way she went about it. It gave the impression she saw people and strange places as entertainments the universe programmed for her specific amusement. Talk to the Porrinyards; they'll tell you."

"And the other victim? Santiago?"

"She was even more unpleasant, but straightforwardly so. Had a bitter streak, in part because of the kind of place she came from. Wanted everybody to know she'd suffered more than the rest of us. Had the distinctively subversive edge of somebody who would have razed all human society to the ground if she could. She liked to tell everybody how corrupt and useless she found the Confederacy. I'm sympathetic to such talk, so I tried to engage her in personal conversation a couple of times, but ideological ranting was all she was set up for. Professional enough, but determined to just do her job and earn out her contract. She hated Warmuth, by the way."

"Why?"

"Warmuth kept trying to understand her."

"And that's a problem?"

"Some people resent being treated as research projects."

Having lived much of my childhood under a magnifying glass, I empathized. "Were there any confrontations between them?"

"Just Warmuth being invasive and Santiago freezing her out. If they weren't both dead, I would mark them as perfect suspects to finish each other off."

"Was it really that bad?"

"Santiago was like us," he said. "You and me, I mean. She did not want friends. Warmuth was of the opinion that everybody needs friends even if they believe otherwise. She declared Santiago a personal project and kept pushing. Santiago finally got mad and pushed her around a little, at which point Warmuth declared Santiago persona non grata."

"I'll want the report on the incident. As well as the names of any witnesses."

"Expected. I don't see it as all that relevant anyway. We investigated Warmuth's recent activities when we lost Santiago, and I can assure you she had neither the means nor opportunity to do that kind of damage to Santiago's hammock."

I nodded. "And Gibb? What's your personal take on Gibb?"

"You're talking about my immediate superior, Counselor."

"Answer the question."

"I will," he said. "But I'd be interested in hearing your own take first."

I considered telling him it was none of his business, but supposed the question harmless enough. "He gave the impression he tries too hard."

"He does. And he's somewhat more dangerous than he initially seems."

"Are you implying he's responsible for these deaths?"

"Not at all. But he's a Dip Corps lifer. You know what that means."

"Tell me what you think it means."

"As far as I'm concerned," Lastogne said, with weary contempt, "the Dip Corps is a meritocracy in reverse. By its very design, nobody who sticks around is any good. The genuinely talented work off their bonds quickly thanks to incentives and bonuses. The incompetent get fined with extra time and find themselves shunted to more and more irrelevant assignments. Everybody in the great big mediocre middle, and everybody insane enough to fall off the scale entirely, winds up assigned to Management—and Management's never been interested in really doing the job, not at any point in human history. Management's true agenda has always been making things more pleasant for Management."

It was a harsh but defensible portrait of the way things worked. "And Mr. Gibb?"

"Mr. Gibb considers himself a dedicated public servant."

"And is he?"

"As a public servant," Lastogne said, "the man is Management in its purest form. Let's just say I don't consider him exceptionally talented."

"You're wearing your resentment out front, Mr. Lastogne. How's your own career going?"

"More than fine," he said.

"Nothing else to tell me? No disciplinary actions in your past? I warn you, it is something I'll check."

"Feel free. My record is the very definition of clean."

I didn't trust that secretive half-smile of his, the kind that not only harbored a private joke but teased me about his refusal to share it. I backtracked to another subject he'd already shown eagerness to cover. "Both the victims are women. Gibb seems a little grabby around women. What's your take on that?"

"No take. I've heard some of our female indentures call him smarmy, and I've noticed it myself, but that's not a crime. Neither is his ambition to fuck any indenture who will have him. We're all going to be here a long time, and life would be pretty damn unbearable if we had to live like celibates. I don't think he killed Santiago or Warmuth, if that's what you think. I just think he's out for himself."

"What about you, Mr. Lastogne? What are you out for?"

He made a noise. "The big picture."

This was profound noncommunication, but I noted it and moved on. "Who do you think killed them?"

He didn't look at me. "Some faction among the AIsource."

"But they told us about the Brachiators. They arranged our presence here."

"Some of them may disapprove."

"To the point of committing murder?"

He looked disgusted. "Why not? Assassination's just diplomacy by other means."

"So's war, sir."

"Exactly."

I waited for a clarification and received none. After a few seconds I decided he didn't know what was going on any more than I did. It was just more of what Gibb had called his facile nihilism. So I altered course. "What do you think about their position? Do you think it's right for sentient creatures to be owned?"

He emitted a short, cynical laugh, driven by the kind of anger that drives entire lives. "We're all owned, Counselor. It's just a matter of choosing who holds the deed."

5

OWNED

After Lastogne left, I wished the designers of Gibb's facility had put more effort into constructing solid platforms where restless human beings could stand and pace. Crawling, climbing, and clinging, the only means of locomotion possible in Hammocktown, may have been effective ways of getting from place to place, but they couldn't burn my nervous energy, or facilitate analytical thought, the way pacing did. Being deprived of that option was going to throw me off as long as I remained here.

So would Lastogne. With a few offhand words, he'd shown a knack for echoing suspicions I'd rarely spoken out loud.

We're all owned.

It might have been mere political cynicism, coming from him.

For much of the past year I'd considered it literally true.

Owned.

The things that happened one night on Bocai had caused such a diplomatic firestorm that the authorities, including the Confederacy and the Bocaians themselves, had declared the survivors better off permanently disappeared.

I still don't know what happened to most of the others. I suspect they're dead, or still imprisoned somewhere. But I'd been shipped to someplace I don't like thinking about, there to be caged and prodded and analyzed in the hope of determining just what environmental cause had turned so many previously peaceful sentients into vicious monsters.

My keepers spent ten years watching for my madness to reoccur. It had been ten years of reminders that I was an embarrassment to my very species, ten years of being escorted from room to room under guard, ten years of being asked if I wanted to kill anything else. The people who studied me during these years were not all inhuman. Some even tried to show me affection, though to my eyes their love had all the persuasive realism of lines in a script being read by miscast actors. Even the best of them knew I was a bomb that could go off again, at any time; if sometimes moved to give me hugs, they never attempted it without a guard in the room. Others, the worst among them, figured that whatever lay behind my eyes had been tainted beyond all repair, and no longer qualified as strictly human—and being less than strictly human themselves, treated themselves to any cruel pleasures they cared to claim from a creature awful enough to deserve anything they did to her.

Even freedom, when it came, came in a form of a slightly longer leash.

We've gotten your latest test scores, Andrea. They're quite remarkable. You deserve every educational opportunity we can provide for you. But we can't quite justify letting you go. There are just too many races out there that don't believe in pleas of temporary insanity, and unless we come up with some solution that stays their hand, they'll do whatever they can to extradite you. But if you want, you can walk out of here and enjoy Immunity. All you have to do is allow us to re-

main your legal guardians, for the rest of your natural life.

Most indentures, like Warmuth and Santiago, have contracts of limited duration: five, ten, twenty, or thirty years; the terms varied. They could work off that time in the allotted period or they could earn the time bonuses that permitted early release. They all knew they could look forward to a generous pension and an unlimited passport, someday. They all understood that one day they'd own themselves again.

I didn't have that luxury. The Dip Corps had promised me lifetime protection, or as close to lifetime protection as I could expect given the certain knowledge that they'd give me up the instant they decided I was useful currency. But they were the ones capable of tearing up the contract. I had no means of severance.

I was owned and expected to be owned for the foreseeable future.

I'd gotten used to the idea.

I'd only imagined I knew what it was like.

Less than a year ago, on Catarkhus, it had come to mean something else.

I activated the hytex and called up the service records of the two dead women.

I started with the most recent victim, Cynthia Warmuth, opening with a hytex image taken since her arrival at One One One. She turned out to have been a pretty young thing, lithe, fresh-faced and blue-eyed, with a tentative smile and short dyed hair determined to make a stop at every color in the rainbow. The image caught her in the act of climbing one of the hammock farm's mesh ladders, one foot already resting one rung up. Being lit from below, like just about everything else illuminated only by One One One's suns, gave her an odd exotic quality that she seemed to take as a reason for pride.

Of her background, there wasn't much more than Gibb

had already provided. The only notable addition was a thesis she'd written, discussing what she believed to be the impossibility of proper objectivity in the study of sentient races. New indentures in training wrote theses like this all time, most of them showing little originality and promise. Warmuth's parroted the Dip Corps line: *Sentients can only be studied by sentients, and sentients by their very nature bring their own prejudices to anything they study.*

I didn't know how true that nonsense was in practical circumstances. In the course of my daily work I'd encountered any number of diplomats and exosociologists who claimed to be able to watch over intelligent alien races while themselves possessing only as much observable sentience as doorknobs.

Gibb's personal evaluations of her were also attached to the file, and marked her for guarded praise. She had potential, he said, but she needed to learn how to curb her somewhat excessive zeal. It seemed to be more a personality thing than any problems with her skill set. On four separate occasions, under his watch alone, she'd scored highly enough, on examinations, to earn some additional time off her contract. It shortened her full hitch by less than a month—not much time at all, when you considered how many years she still had left on her contract. But not bad for an indenture who hadn't even been cleared for her first direct contact with the locals. Either she'd excelled beyond all reason in training or Gibb was an unusually generous boss.

The first image I found of Santiago was not quite as congenial or as posed as Warmuth's; it was a candid shot, taken from a distance, of her clinging to the Uppergrowth with all four limbs. There were four Brachiators in the background, looking less at home there than she did. About all I learned from it was that she was up to the physical demands of the work. I requested another image and got it: an awkwardly posed image of Santiago standing in a triangular corridor, arms crossed, one thin eyebrow raised. She had dark eyes, tan skin, a round face framed by tousled caramel hair, and a slight underbite that transformed her lower lip into a pout. There was no hint of a smile.

Santiago's papers were fewer than Warmuth's, but tinged with a bitter edge. One passage Lastogne had bookmarked for me was especially interesting. "For most sentients, belonging to their respective species means bearing the influence of the whole. Being a human being often means being outshouted by the whole. It means being a cell with no voice in the function of the organism. It means being owned."

There it was again. *Owned.*

It could be a coincidence. It was a common concept among the sufficiently cynical, a parade I help to lead. Santiago's background as a debt-slave even made it reasonable. There were too many worlds like hers, and too many people like her aching to leave those worlds behind. Their need was a large part of what staffed the Dip Corps.

A look at Santiago's bond put the nature of the contract into sharp relief. The woman had exchanged her own debt for a ten-year contract. By the time the Dip Corps added the costs of transportation, training, and the medical treatment necessary to cleanse her lungs and body chemistry of the homeworld industrial toxins that would have left her dead or incapacitated by age forty, the time-debt on her contract had stretched from ten years to twenty.

Extended, just like Warmuth's: a coincidence, or a link? Either way, she wouldn't have minded. The Corps was the best form of debt slavery—the kind that ended in freedom if the job was done.

But it was still slavery. Ownership.

The kind that made people angry.

Santiago had been described as an angry person.

We're all owned.

I looked further. Santiago had earned some mild time bonuses in her months on One One One, but had also been fined for antisocial behavior, the worst penalty coming after her confrontation with Warmuth. Once I did the math, she turned out to be earning out her contract at something approaching real time. That was a mediocre score indeed. I wondered how much of her abrasiveness was political, and how much was personality.

I thought of another abrasive personality: Lastogne.

He'd also made a reference to being owned.

He had given the words special emphasis.

He struck me as a man embittered by the deal he had made.

He had gone out of his way to tell me that he'd already heard of me.

Had he been giving me a gentle nudge in the direction he wanted the investigation to go?

Or was he obscuring the trail? Maybe he was just pushing buttons. Or maybe all his talk of Santiago's attitude problem was a smoke screen for his own.

I directed the hytex to provide me with his file.

Nothing came up.

I went into the Dip Corps Database, and used not only the security codes I had earned but also several my superiors would have been very unhappy to know I possessed.

Nothing came up.

I bit my thumb, wondering if I'd gotten his name right.

No, that was facile. I never got names wrong. I got people wrong, but not their names. He was Peyrin Lastogne, all right.

But why was there no available data?

I was still wondering when the floating white blob the hytex projected instead of a useful answer blinked, like a single cyclopean eye, and exploded, filling the space with a blinding light. When that faded, a new image appeared. It was another generated image of myself, this time captured in the immediate aftermath of a horrific beating. My face was a collection of pain piled upon pain, with every millimeter of exposed skin swollen and glossy with blood. My eyes were puffed shut, the cheekbones staved in, my gaping mouth an assortment of shattered teeth. Any injuries below the neckline were invisible beneath my black suit, but from the way it stood, seeming ready to fall at any moment, favoring its right leg and cradling its midsection with both hands, they must have been just as brutal, and just as ugly. Hiding them just gave the imagination room to imagine the absolute worst, and produce the image of a woman whose entire body was one walking wound.

The animation took a single blind step, stiffened, and as if in terrible, clairvoyant realization, emitted a cry pregnant with the certainty that everything it had endured up until this moment was just empty preamble.

The top of its head disappeared in a burst of blood and smoke.

The brutalized version of myself did not fall but just stood there, dazed, everything above mid-forehead amputated, oozing rivulets of blood from the splintered basin its skull had become.

Then she tumbled forward, disappearing even as she fell out of frame.

I blinked several times.

And murmured another silent response to the unknown sender.

Be seeing you.

6

PORRINYARDS

In the morning, the suns of One One One had the common decency to seep into brilliance, avoiding the kind of sudden light burst that would have blinded everyone in the Habitat. Having gone without sleep, I spent that hour watching the earliest stages of that dawn filter through the material of my hammock and bring my own shadow on the tented ceiling into sharp relief.

When it came to evidence that I'd survived yet another night, I've known worse.

By the time the hytex warned me that my ride had arrived, I had soniced myself clean, availed myself of the outhouse structure at the center of Hammocktown (in what must have been the most harrowing trip to a bathroom I'd ever known), and thrown on a fresh black suit. Zipping open the port at the base of the hammock, I found Lastogne and the Porrinyards both below me in an AIsource skimmer of a design much sleeker than yesterday's.

Lastogne waved at me, still looking like a man harboring a secret joke. The Porrinyards were harder to read, their expressions conveying no feeling deeper than amiability. They still dressed identically, with thin strips of shiny silver material over their breasts and waists, but now that I saw them close up I could tell that they were not quite as androgynous as they'd appeared at a distance. The taller and bulkier one's waist cloth was just tight enough to reveal a telltale bulge in the crotch, and the slighter one's bound chest bore a pair of tiny breasts distinguishable among all those hypertrophic muscles.

The woman had a soft, nearly transparent down along her jawline, the male a darker complexion and eyes that testified to Asian ancestry. And there was something deep and amused about the way they regarded me—almost as if somebody had been telling them stories, and they approved.

Lastogne saluted me. "Good morning."

The Porrinyards acknowledged me with a shared, "Counselor."

I blinked away a wave of vertigo. "Good morning. Are we all going to the hub?"

"Mr. Lastogne said you wanted to interview me." This, the Porrinyards also spoke together. It wasn't so much simultaneous as stereo, with each member of the pair linking phonemes and word fragments and vowel tones with complementary sounds voiced by the other. The collaboration created the uncanny illusion of a shared voice emanating from some indeterminate space between them.

Nobody offered to help me descend the hammock's ladder into the vehicle. Aware that this was a form of respect and simultaneously a test to determine if I deserved respect, I slid down, feeling a definite sense of relief once I entered the skimmer's specific gravity. Standing on the solid deck was even more of a pleasure, after too many hours on the softer surfaces of Hammocktown.

Either way, I seemed to have passed a test.

Lastogne grinned. "Nobody would ever guess you had only been on-station a day."

"Whatever." But I wasn't above feeling a little touch of pride.

As the skimmer pulled away from Hammocktown and picked up speed, its shadow, cast by the multiple glowsphere suns, raced along the Uppergrowth above us and was distorted by the gnarled texture of that knotted surface. The flight speed of this vessel seemed faster than that of the chatty skimmer that had ferried me yesterday, leaving me uncertain over whether to be pleased at today's added convenience or annoyed over yesterday's unnecessary delays. I contemplated the matter until the racing shadow blurred, then forced my attention back to the patient Lastogne. "We're not going back on the same route I traveled yesterday."

Lastogne said, "Right you are. Your personal transport's docked at a bay well on the far end of the Hub. The best route to the Interface is through a portal much closer to us. It'll be a much shorter flight today."

Which was good news when it came to my flight aversion, bad news when it came to my hopes of gathering some information on the way. Rather than waste any more time, I got down to questioning the Porrinyards. "Which one of you is Oscin and which one of you is Skye?"

The woman spoke by herself. "I was born just Skye. He was born just Oscin." They spoke together again, in that musical, but unnerving, shared voice. "We were linked at fifteen, and took the surname Porrinyards."

"It saves them a lot of money buying each other monogrammed jewelry," Lastogne said.

I ignored him. "Did you do this to yourselves voluntarily?"

The pair flashed identical smiles. "That's an offensive question, Counselor, but I'll take it as an innocent one."

"I'd appreciate that."

"Yes, it was voluntary. It was the only way the individuals Oscin and Skye could indenture themselves offworld and know that they'd always be posted together. They thought they were close then. I am integrally linked now."

Cylinking, an illegal operation on most human worlds, was one of the queasier services AIsource Medical offered other sentient races. In exchange for a percentage of future earnings, the AIsource could wire the personalities of two separate individuals together, via an intangible broadcast matrix. The process replaced the two individuals with a larger gestalt that experienced life as one combined person. In theory, this added to their shared intelligence by decreasing the need to devote precious skull space with redundant information that no longer needed to be known by both.

Cylinking had been attacked as dehumanizing. Its defenders said it was nothing of the kind. It wasn't destroying individuality, they said, but redefining it, making new people by combining those who considered themselves incomplete when apart. Those who'd been through the process said it had improved their lives tremendously. Regardless, it took a rare couple to even want to be cylinked, a rarer couple still to meet the AIsource's arcane requirements for the procedure. There were, as far as I knew, fewer than three thousand pairs in existence. I'd heard that the Dip Corps had a few among its indentures, but this was the first time I'd encountered any.

I clicked a fingernail against my teeth. "Mr. Lastogne tells me that the two of you handled much of Cynthia Warmuth's training on-station."

"*I* did," the Porrinyards said, emphasizing the singular, "though Mo Lassiter also contributed."

"Yes, I've heard that name before. Is Mo a man or a woman?"

"A woman. Mo's short for Maureen."

I'd have to meet this Mo Lassiter and question her later. "But you spent substantial time with Warmuth. What did you think of her?"

"She was young and hungry. So intent on understanding others that she entered the point of obnoxious intrusiveness."

"Yes, I heard that Santiago disliked her for that. How was she intrusive?"

"In my case," the Porrinyards said, "she asked rudely intimate questions."

"Like mine?"

"No. You were just trying to understand a condition unfamiliar to you. Her curiosity was quite different."

"How, then?"

Lastogne made a rude noise. "Really, Counselor. I thought you were supposed to be some kind of prodigy."

I didn't catch what was supposed to be so obvious, but Oscin and Skye saved me the trouble of asking: "She was most interested in the sexual aspects of my enhancement. She specifically wanted to know what it was like when my two component bodies made love."

Now that they mentioned it . . . "A number of people must wonder that."

"Which is only natural," the Porrinyards said. "But Warmuth was aggressive enough to expect vivid descriptions on demand."

"If you don't mind me asking, what did you tell her?"

They bristled. "Are you like her, Counselor? Do you want descriptions on demand?"

"No," I said. "I want to know what kind of answer you gave *her*."

The Porrinyards considered that and saw the distinction. "I told her that it's exactly twice as pleasurable for me as it is for a pair of isolated single-minds who can only interpret the physical act from one viewpoint apiece. This only enflamed her prurient interest, of course. More than once she offered herself to me."

"To both of you?"

"To *me*," the Porrinyards corrected.

"And you declined?"

"Yes. I didn't like the way she asked."

"If you had liked the way she asked, would you have said yes?"

"I say yes all the time," the Porrinyards said. "I remain only one person, and a steady diet of sex with myself is as depressing as any other confinement to masturbation. So I'm always interested in finding another partner. Peyrin, here, was once open enough to accept such an invitation—"

"Hello," Lastogne sang.

"—and even Santiago turned her down with only mild offensiveness. But I'm only attracted to people capable of understanding that they're making love to only one person, not two, regardless of the number of bodies involved. Cynthia Warmuth never struck me as being able to make that kind of cognitive leap. She was interested only in adding to her personal library of deep enriching experiences. The last I knew, Warmuth had sought out less demanding partners, and enjoyed at least one assignation with Mr. Gibb."

I had already noted Gibb's possessive response to women who entered his personal orbit. "Was that an ongoing relationship?"

"No. I think Mr. Gibb's usual level of charm had its usual prophylactic effect before long."

"Did you notice any tension between them afterward?"

"Mr. Gibb is too big an oaf to feel any tension toward anybody." Oscin and Skye gave a single, unified sniff of disdain. "I have no way of knowing how Warmuth felt."

Gibb's failure to mention his relationship with Warmuth was interesting, but not necessarily damning. "What about Santiago? Did Gibb have any special relationship with Santiago?"

"I doubt it. Santiago didn't have special relationships."

"She was a loner?"

"I would say misanthrope. She alienated people as a matter of course."

"Mr. Lastogne said she wouldn't shut up about how much she hated the Confederacy."

The Porrinyards frowned at that. "Is this a political witch hunt, Counselor?"

"Not as far as I'm concerned. People can bad-mouth the Corps and the Confederacy as much as they want. On a good day I'd even join them. But it's been described as an obsession. I want to know what kinds of things she said."

They relaxed. "She wasn't a bastards-up-against-the-wall revolutionary, if that's what you mean. She had an honest grudge. She always said that if the Confederacy was worth a damn, it would have seized all power for itself and shut down the kind of power structure that made hellholes out of worlds arranged like hers. She wanted one big government, or at the very least a common bill of rights, for everybody. She particularly wanted debt slavery abolished—not just the horrible kind she grew up with, but even the contracts we have in the Corps. None of it was at all new, you understand. Scratch any indenture and you'll find somebody who feels the same way."

"I agree. And yet I get the impression that she was a profoundly unpopular person."

"Christina may have been more bitter about her politics than most of us, but that wasn't her real problem."

"What was?"

"She didn't like being around people and had no problem letting them know it."

Which only increased my sense of kinship toward her. "Did she get along with anybody at all?"

"Not to my knowledge. She alienated everybody equally."

"She spent a lot of time with Cif Negelein," Lastogne said.

The Porrinyards seemed genuinely surprised by that. "Negelein? Really?"

I said, "Who's Negelein?"

Lastogne's expression failed to communicate undying affection. "You'll meet him later."

Uh-huh. "How would you define their relationship?"

"Can't answer you there," Lastogne said. "Whenever two people I don't like start spending time together, I consider it a personal gift. It saves me the aggravation."

"Why don't you like Negelein?"

"He's a pretentious snot."

I turned my attention back to the Porrinyards: "So what did Santiago do, when she was not on-duty or spending time with this Negelein? Retire to her hammock and stew in an antisocial funk?"

"Some of that," they said. "She sometimes went exploring on her own. Sometimes she descended, trying to observe the dragons, though she never got close enough to report anything. A few times she took advantage of all the down-time available to her and went back to relax in the hangar. Nothing out of the ordinary, here; we all take our breaks when we can. I can tell you she had less use for other people than anybody I've ever met."

"Including yourself?"

"Very much including myself," the Porrinyards said. "I'm no misanthrope."

Which was exactly the opposite of the way Lastogne had described them. If *them,* plural, was the right word. I was far from sure that it was. The more I dealt with these Porrinyards, the more pronoun trouble I was likely to have.

The skimmer banked into a course correction, headed for a portal into the station hub; its controlled local gravity prevented me from feeling any change in acceleration, but my stomach lurched anyway. The portal, a well-camouflaged hatch cut into the Uppergrowth itself, bore the same knotted surface as the surrounding vegetation, a touch that seemed anal on the part of the AIsource. After all, who inside this habitat would have been aesthetically offended by an unsightly sliding panel?

Orienting itself toward the hatch meant that the skimmer had to position itself vertically. The skimmer's local gravity kept me from feeling any change in orientation, but my eyes were another matter, and my mind refused to forget that the vast wall before us had been up only a few seconds before. I tasted stomach acid and closed my eyes to ward off the worst of the vertigo. "You trained Santiago too, correct?"

"That's correct."

"Did she and Warmuth ever train together?"

"Yes."

"Was there any friction?"

"There was some off-duty, I believe. A bit of a shoving match. I wasn't around for it. On the job it was minimal. You would expect to get more from Santiago, considering her attitude, but she was, if anything, the easier of the two to work with. Focused. No interest in adding a personal element. Far from charming, but right to the point."

Lastogne broke in: "You can open your eyes, Counselor. We're in."

We were traversing an octagonal access tunnel, only twice the diameter of the skimmer, with walls of an indistinct blue that remained bright without any obvious light source. Shiny black panels appeared every few meters, but I couldn't tell whether this was tech or just a design element. Nor could I tell how we were oriented with respect to the Habitat, but I'd already experienced so much vertigo today I was relieved not to care. "You trained them both for their first contact with the Brachiators?"

"That's right," the Porrinyards said. "We have a policy here, requiring escorts during individual first contact."

"Tell me how it works."

"Mr. Lastogne has probably already told you that the Brachs have unusual perceptions regarding the difference between life and death. As far as they're concerned, alien sentients like us are not alive in the sense you and I understand the concept. We're 'Dead.' Introducing a stranger involves a ceremony that boils down to telling the Brachiators something along the lines of 'This is (insert name), an Emissary from the Dead, who wishes to be with you in Life.'"

Just ahead another portal irised open. Not much time left for follow-up questions. I bit the tip of my thumb, cursing a little when I realized I'd drawn blood. On a bad day, my fingertips were a mass of scabs. "And if they're amenable to that, Insert Name has to cling to the Uppergrowth for several hours, while the Brachiators around her decide she's sufficiently Alive to merit their company."

The Porrinyards nodded. "Alive enough to be declared a Half-Ghost anyway."

"Is this something only required for offworlder visitors? Not with strangers of their own kind?"

"Only with offworlders," the Porrinyards said. "We don't know if they'd react this way to any species other than human beings, but they think we're dead. We haven't figured out what gives them that impression, but as long as we observe the proper etiquette in their environment, they're more than happy to declare us Half-Ghosts for the purposes of getting along."

"Until," Lastogne said, "like Warmuth and Santiago, you die for real."

I digested that as the skimmer slid into its bay, in a well-lit chamber with a platform bearing tubes curving away to what must have been other Hub locations. Given the convenient scale, it all seemed too much like the rapid transit system on New London to suit a cylinder world, which had never been intended for the convenience of human visitors, but then, the AIsource were great at building things and might have built all this within a day of inviting Gibb's inspection team.

That is, assuming they hadn't expected human visitors all along.

We disembarked and stood on the platform, getting used to the novelty of a solid, if spongy, floor. Local gravity seemed about one-third of what it had been in Hammocktown, but that didn't matter to me. My legs, which were used to carrying me around in that traditional manner, thanked me with the abject relief only aggravated limbs can express.

The blue lighting made Lastogne's face look cold. "I'm sorry about this next part, Counselor."

I said, "What?"

"If you don't like heights, you may not be all too happy about what's coming up."

7

INTERFACE

Every human being who's ever dealt with the AIsource knows them through their ubiquitous traveling remotes, hovering flatscreens approximately one meter square and only a handful of molecules thick. These remotes travel so widely in diplomatic circles that it's easy to consider them the AIsource in flesh. It's hard to remember that the AIsource are really only intertwined sequences of multitiered code and not just aliens who look like floating black rectangles.

On One One One, the AIsource eschewed appearances and interfaced with visitors on their own terms.

The portal into the Interface was a hatch in the wall of a narrow corridor near the dock. Entering it meant enduring almost a minute of what felt like free fall, another minute of what felt like steady acceleration, then a third minute of vague disorientation as air currents guided me to someplace where gravity was negligible.

My destination turned out to be a vast chamber lit by a soft blue light. I drifted through the warm and richly oxygenated air, feeling a sense of well-being that belied what should have been terrifying disorientation, until the caress of unseen breezes brought me to a halt at what might have been the chamber's center. Between the blurring effect of the light and the AIsource's refusal to provide a reference point, there was no way of telling where the hatch had been or how far I had traveled. The room itself seemed to extend for an infinite distance in all directions.

The sense of entire kilometers of space below me should have wrecked the composure I'd managed to rebuild since reentering the hub. Instead, it felt womblike. I was nervous, and off-center, but no more than they must have wanted me to be.

Interesting.

This had to be the AIsource equivalent of maintaining an intimidating home office to cow troublesome visiting dignitaries. Such a tradition was the main reason human bureaucrats still sat behind used imposing desks, long after the transfer of record keeping from paper to hytex relegated such work surfaces to the technology of the past. It was cheap theater, nothing else. But effective theater.

The AIsource had always frightened me, a little. All other sentient species, however alien, could be counted on to need the same things needed by just about all other biological life: sustenance, habitat, the ability to procreate. Among sentients who shared those needs, there was at least a basis for understanding. But the AIsource had no biological needs. They were pure intelligence, driven by imperatives comprehensible only to them, and I'd never believed them as conscientious regarding organic considerations as they'd always been careful to pretend.

That and the fact that I liked being able to look other sentients in the face.

The chamber spoke in a feminine voice that always seemed to originate from some unseen presence directly in front of me regardless of how much I drifted. ***It is a pleasure to see you again, Andrea Cort.***

This was no surprise. Flatscreen remotes had been treating me like an old friend for years. Not that I'd ever made the mistake of confusing that for actual friendship. "You saw me yesterday, didn't you?"

You must be referring to your conversation with the Subroutine piloting your skimmer. It is a limited individual, enjoying only limited interplay with our diplomatic functions. As far as meaningful communication goes, this is your first contact with the bulk of the AIsource shared intelligence aboard this facility.

I didn't waste time returning the empty pleasantries. "Two human beings have been murdered."

The AIsource never simulated laughter, but the voice took on an amused tone even so. ***Many human beings have been murdered, Counselor. Almost all of them by other human beings.***

"I'm referring to the two murders aboard this station."

We surmised that you were referring to the situation here, but we felt some specificity was called for, given the carnage you're known for.

If the AIsource intended to rattle me with that remark, they were far clumsier than I gave them credit for. "Me personally or my race as a whole?"

You're certainly known for carnage, Counselor, but in this context we meant your race as a whole.

I refused to take offense. "Irrelevant either way. I want to focus on the two murders that have actually taken place on your station."

We have no problem with an informal discussion as long as you remember what you were told by Mr. Gibb: that you are not in these circumstances a recognized diplomat, and are therefore not entitled to the usual array of diplomatic protections.

In other words, the AIsource could decide to take any punitive action they deemed fair, at the first moment I proved inconvenient. Another intimidation tactic.

"I make my inquiries as a concerned private citizen."

Very well.

Whenever questioning sentients who consider themselves smarter than you, it helps to approach the interrogation from an angle they don't expect. "Would you mind if I asked, first, just what you're doing here?"

Please be specific.

"Why did you engineer the Brachiators?"

A pause. ***That is a surprising first question.***

"It's hard to investigate crimes unless you can understand the worlds where they take place. Do you have any objections to answering?"

No, Counselor. We hate to disappoint you on this subject, but the Brachiators are not the only reason for the establishment of One One One. The Brachiators are just part of a complex multitiered ecosystem, any part of which may be more to our interest than the activities of a minor species created only to fill an environmental niche. There are, for instance, acidic worms in the lower regions of One One One's oceans, that we find most fascinating indeed.

"I'm sure they are. But I have trouble believing that they're as important to you as the Brachiators."

We confess interest in your reasoning.

"Sentient species evolve in environments where problem-solving presents a survival advantage. That's far from the case here. The Brachiators live their lives clinging to vines and sucking on nourishment you provide for free. There's nothing in that rendering sentience an advantage. If you only created them to fill a niche, it would have been much easier to engineer mindless animals, with hardwired behaviors. You had no persuasive reason to make them sentient."

It was impossible not to read amusement in the hesitation

before their next reply. ***You assume that their sentience was a deliberate part of their design. It could have arisen as a by-product of other physical requirements. Your human brain evolved in an environment that rewarded a certain degree of animal cunning, but gave no immediate advantage to higher intelligence capable of producing Shakespearean sonnets or discovering quantum physics. Your intelligence developed far past your immediate requirements only because there were other evolutionary rewards, such as your inefficient birth process and the physical requirements of binocular vision, in producing a skull that conformed to a certain shape. This innovation produced significant but, we assure you, accidental benefits to the development of that part of your brain capable of abstract thought. Much the same happy accident occured in the case of the Brachiators. Their brains simply developed beyond their absolute needs.***

"I still have trouble believing that."

Again: we retain a vivid interest in your reasoning.

"The Brachiators didn't evolve by accident. They were engineered. They were created for a purpose. And if you didn't have any particular need for the Brachiators to be sentient, then it would have been simple enough for you to create a simpler species incapable of developing that trait."

There was another pause, longer by many orders of magnitude than the interval the software intelligences should have required to frame a reply. ***We have never taken action to discourage the development of sentience, even inadvertent sentience.***

"Bullshit," I said, surprised by the heat in my own voice.

We are well aware of human conversational conventions associating feces, especially animal feces, with dishonesty. But we still require your reasoning.

"I don't believe you capable of the sloppiness it would take to engineer life for an environment this unusual without first establishing exactly what you wanted that life to be like. You wanted the Brachiators to think, and you wanted them to communicate with visiting species like my own. You designed them with that in mind. You even taught them the Mercantile tongue. Then you orchestrated this diplomatic wrangle over their legal status by making sure we knew about them, when it would have been just as easy to keep their very existence—this very station's existence—a secret. So I ask you again: Why did you create the Brachiators? And why did you want us to react to their existence the way we have?"

The chamber was silent for a long time. ***We reserve the right to treat these issues as state secrets, and consider the answers classified at this time.***

I pressed on. "What about their beliefs? This thing they have about considering human beings dead? Their characterization of you, their creators, as the 'Hands-in-Ghosts'? Do you understand what they mean by that?"

We have always found the belief systems sentient creatures concoct to explain their place in their universe to be, by far, the most fascinating and potentially enlightening by-product of intelligent life.

Which wasn't an answer. "How do you respond to charges that engineering the Brachiators breaks interspecies covenant prohibiting slavery?"

By pointing out that the Brachiators perform no labor on our behalf, that they live in their own natural state, that we voluntarily revealed their existence to the diplomatic community, and that if "freed" from their Habitat by forces intent on helping them against their will, they would no doubt perish for lack of any other suitable environment. We could also point out that the society responsible for your Christina Santiago, and the special relationship between yourself and the Confederate Diplomatic Corps, both fit the standard definition of slavery more than our protective re-

lationship with the Brachiators. But we can assure you that none of these issues have any direct bearing on the issue of the crimes committed aboard this station.

Direct bearing. Did that indicate an indirect connection? I hesitated, had the ghost of a thought, lost it, and conceded defeat for the time being. "I agree it's unlikely."

What are these questions, then? Idle curiosity?

"Something like that." Something was missing, but it took me a second to realize what it was. In most interrogations, an abrupt segue to a new line of questioning almost always left subjects confused and intimidated. But the AIsource didn't care where I went next. Their computing speed was infinitely faster than mine; they knew they could outthink me, and probably already had. In context, the human speed of my own thought made my every hesitation, every "uh," feel like the conversational spasm of an idiot. "The Hom.Sap Ambass—I mean, Hom.Sap observer, Mr. Gibb, tells me that he believes the circumstances of Christina Santiago's death indicate AIsource involvement."

It is of course true that the sabotage of Santiago's hammock required a level of technology that only we're supposed to possess inside the Habitat.

"How would you explain that?"

There are only two possibilities, Counselor. Either we're responsible for these incidents, or somebody other than us arranged access to the tools.

"Do you deny your own involvement?"

A moment's logical consideration should be enough to establish our innocence of that crime. After all, we built this station. We maintain it. We agreed to your presence here. We even provide your life support. If we wished to kill every human being on board, we could do so in a matter of moments, by means far subtler than those employed by your supposed murderer. If we wished to kill individuals, the mechanisms that support your lives here are sufficiently

precarious that, were we of the proper bent, we could have no trouble arranging a series of accidents that would never be suspected as the product of deliberate intent.

Thoughts like that had occupied my mind since my own arrival on this station. "And Warmuth?"

We did not murder either Christina Santiago or Cynthia Warmuth.

That last statement delivered emphatically.

It is of course possible, even probable, that even if innocent we still know more than we're saying about these events, but in that case any explanation of our involvement would have to include the reason we've elected to keep such secrets.

"I agree with that too." Sheer perversity would not work as an explanation.

There is another point. If your culprit used sophisticated tools to sabotage Santiago's tent, why was the murder of Cynthia Warmuth so primitive by comparison? Why use high technology for one crime and messy savagery for the other?

The AIsource had hit upon the one aspect of this double crime that bothered me the most. "The circumstances weren't all that different."

How were they alike, in your view?

"They were both theater. They were both designed to be recognized as murders."

Meaning?

"As you point out, life on this station is precarious by design. A murder designed to look like an accident could pass without suspicion, leaving no body and no forensic evidence. But both of these incidents raised immediate suspicions. They seem downright stage-managed. Is that what's happening here?"

When the AIsource finally spoke again, I could only read the delay as a dramatic pause. Theatrics. Or diplomacy; wise men throughout history had already noticed that sometimes there wasn't much of a difference between the two.

You are a very intelligent human being, Counselor. We have been more impressed by your capabilities than you could ever know, for a longer time than you could ever know. Indeed: you would be surprised indeed to discover some of the attributes we have in common.

Empty flattery was not AIsource style. "But?"

But you still need to rethink your starting assumptions in this case. Some are flawed.

"Which ones?"

Continue your investigation.

The blue glow faded to a gray nothingness. I knew, without asking another question, that the audience was over; that they would not tease me with further discussion until I was able to bring more to the table.

They were playing games with me. I had no idea why; until this moment, I never would have guessed that they played games at all. But their refusal to specify just which of my starting assumptions were flawed was a de facto admission that this was exactly what they were doing.

Why?

A gentle blast of cool air came out of nowhere and propelled me toward a grayer blur that might have been a portal opening in the chamber wall. Aware that there was nothing I could do to continue the interview if the masters of this station wanted it over, I said nothing and allowed the winds to usher me out.

But it seemed that the AIsource still had a parting shot.

Andrea Cort? Two other points of interest.

"Yes?"

Your false assumptions extend to your professional history. You have completely misjudged Artis Bringen.

I think my jaw dropped open. "What?"

Second, we are aware that you have received certain

threatening messages. We are not, ourselves, responsible. But we do know that the responsible party is on One One One and does intend you harm. Whatever actions you take from this moment should include extreme vigilance to ward off imminent attempts on your life.

I didn't bother asking for the assassin's name, even though I was pretty sure they knew it. We wouldn't have been going through this charade if they'd been in any mood for providing answers. "Thank you. Anything else?"

They spoke a single sentence that yanked my world out from under me.

By the time this business is done, you will know your Unseen Demons.

8

OZ

I'd expected to find all three of my guides waiting for me upon my ejection from the Interface, but instead found Oscin Porrinyard standing vigil alone.

The vestibule was a small chamber, similar to but quite distinct from the one I'd entered. The gravity was light, the air cold and marked with unfamiliar scents. The curved walls were alive with shifting lights, the ground spongy. The far end of the chamber narrowed, becoming a corridor that curved to the left. Though presumably built for AIsource use, its shape still seemed too conveniently scaled to human dimensions. I thought *stage setting* before a wave of weakness overcame me.

Oscin immediately seized my arms and guided me as I sank to the soft plastiform floor. I almost protested Oscin's hands on my person, the way I'd protested Gibb's, but the shock made it a medical necessity. So I said nothing as he eased me back against the nearest solid wall, which adjusted at the moment it felt my weight, becoming a soft, supportive cushion. Its touch felt disturbingly intimate, almost invasive, but I was not up to protesting.

Unseen Demons, they'd said.

I must have spoken those words to myself ten thousand times in the year since they'd become my personal mission. They'd roused me from despair, from apathy, from the feeling that nothing I could do would ever redeem what I'd done.

They'd given me a reason for living.

But I'd only shared them with one other human being, and he was dead.

The diplomatic crisis on Catarkhus, one year earlier, had involved several alien governments in a wrangle over the proper venue to try a disturbed human being named Emil Sandburg, who had admitted to murdering a number of the indigenes.

All the established protocols of interspecies law had argued for Sandburg to be tried by the locals, but the Catarkhans, while sentient, were nevertheless so closed to the universe that the rest of us lived in that they were incapable of even understanding that crimes of any kind had been committed against them. Blind, deaf, and unable to sense us in any way, they weren't even aware of our presence. To them, the visiting humans, Riirgaans, Tchi, and Bursteeni delegations were just invisible, intangible presences whose influence on their lives was neither felt nor suspected.

In short: *Unseen Demons.*

The phrase had come up more than once during my investigation. It was a convenient metaphor, an elegant description of what walking among the Catarkhans had felt like.

But even as I'd worked out the compromise that had allowed Sandburg to be remanded into human custody, the greater implications of the case had haunted me.

Following the celebrations, I'd stood before the broken

Sandburg, in the cell where he'd been awaiting extradition, and faced him as an equal: one Monster to another. Why not? My opponents in the case had already sullied me with the crimes I'd committed on Bocai; he knew what I was, and understood that I was just as guilty as he.

It made him the only available audience for the conviction that had struck me, in the course of my investigation.

I'd stood before him and said, *There's one other thing I want to share with you, Bondsman. It has to do with what happened at Bocai.*

I still hated saying the name of the world where I'd been born.

Bocai had been home to an unremarkable sentient race, too comfortable with themselves to compete with Riirgaans and Hom.Saps and the rest of that sick, motley crew in the game of who got to rule more squares of the vast, celestial chessboard. They had ventured into space, found it not to their liking, dismantled their space program, and moved back home, happy enough to play genial host when offworlders dropped by to enjoy the feel of soil beneath our shoes.

They were even happier to oblige when a small colony of human academics, including my parents, wanted to lease an island where they, and a group of equally curious Bocaians, could experiment with raising their children side by side. The point of this remains murky to me, despite years of poring through the papers and correspondence both sides left behind. As near as I can determine, it was just a shallow utopian gesture, designed to prove once and for all the oft-discredited truism that we're all the same beneath the skin.

There was no reason the mere attempt should have done any harm. After all, while Hom.Saps and Bocaians were the end-products of two completely unconnected evolutionary processes, they still seemed to have more in common than not: both species were omnivorous, mammalian four-limbed bipeds, both had two sexes, both had binocular vision, both indulged in things like art and music and fiction, both tended toward tribal family structures, and both were capable of metabolizing the same foods, separated only by a few differences in ideal diet. It was even easy to mistake one species for the other, at least in the dark.

The differences, like the greater hairiness of human beings and the greater prominence of the Bocaian eye, were so minor that some of the diaries left behind, by the human adolescents of the colony, confessed sexual attraction to adolescents of the Bocai. Actual coitus was so impossible that the mere thought was ludicrous, as the evolutionary parallels had stopped short of providing compatible genitalia. But the attraction existed, and testified that by all surface criteria, human beings and Bocai were able to see each other as slightly more exotic versions of their own kind. That illusion was the whole reason it seemed so natural for the Hom.Saps and the Bocai to exist in the same community, to join each other's families, to call each other cousins, and help raise each other's children.

Which is why I'd had two sets of siblings, one human and one not. I'd had two names, one human and one not. I'd lived in two worlds, one human and one not.

I'd doted on my Vaafir, the Bocaian equivalent of a father. I'd slept in the home of my Bocaian family as much as I'd slept in the home of my biological parents.

I had been three years old before I fully understood why there were two completely different kinds of people, four before I was even sure which kind I belonged to.

I was eight on the night everybody became monsters and slaughtered each other.

I had never even come close to making sense of that night's carnage until the day on Catarkhus when I stood before the murderer Emil Sandburg, who had tortured and murdered six sentients for no reason beyond sheer frustration at their inability to see or hear him.

The cell was monitored, but I'd activated a hiss screen to flood the listening devices with noise.

I said, *What makes us think we're better off?*

He looked past me, through me, through even the walls of his cell, seeing not the shape of his cage but the shape of the idea that was forming. His lips twitched, the look of a man fed an exotic treat who was trying to decide whether he liked it.

Maybe, I said, *it's the kind of idea you have to be crazy to imagine. Maybe it's the kind of idea you can only believe if you're desperate for some kind of absolution. But that doesn't mean it's a bad idea, just an old one we thought we could safely outgrow. Maybe the Unseen Demons who we used to believe influenced all our worst impulses really do exist, and we were only wrong about what they were and where they came from. Maybe they come from all around us, and we're just not equipped to notice them. Maybe that frustrates them so much they get even by pulling our strings.* I took such a deep breath that the rest of my words emerged in a semi-hysterical shudder: *Maybe one was with me on Bocai. Maybe one was with you, here.*

From this moment on, I said, *my life's about finding out, one way or the other.*

And if I do find them, I'm going to make damn sure they're properly judged.

I'd never shared my theory with anybody else.

Sandburg could not have done much with the knowledge, as he'd lasted less than four weeks in his penal colony before being murdered by another inmate.

In that time, the mantra *Unseen Demons* had become a reminder to myself. Something I'd muttered aloud, whenever I'd needed reminding that I couldn't allow myself to be beaten.

As far as I knew, nobody had overheard me. The hiss screen I'd used during that last meeting was state-of-the-art tech, which shouldn't have been beatable by anybody.

But the AIsource had been listening.

By the time this is done, you will meet your Unseen Demons.

What was that? A threat? A warning?

Or worse?

A confession?

Without Skye beside him, Oscin looked like any other man. The only indication of a consciousness larger than his own was a certain distracted quality, as if he was splitting attention between me and another equally pressing problem. But his lips had curled into a smile other people might have found reassuring.

I murmured, "Where's your other half?"

"Why, Counselor? Would you be more comfortable with her?"

"I don't need to be comfortable. I'm just surprised to see the two of you apart."

His next smile came complete with closed eyes. "My components are never apart, Counselor, but we don't necessarily have to be physically next to each other in order to be together. We can undertake separate conversations with separate people, or act in concert a million kilometers apart. Right now, Skye is being quite charming with Mr. Lastogne. I promise, they'll be back soon."

"Where are they?"

Oscin saw my suspicion. "It's just a routine break, Counselor. We didn't know how long the AIsource would keep you. For all we knew, you might not have come out of there until after the suns turned off, tonight. In the meantime, Mr. Lastogne needed to stretch his legs, and Skye, being my usual delightful self, offered to go with him. That body has much more luck exercising charisma, I'm afraid." He unclipped a canteen from his belt, curled his lips around a gentle sip, then offered it to me. "Would you like some water? A buzzpatch?"

"No."

A vague disappointment darkened his features, but then he shrugged, set the canteen down by his side, and crossed his legs into a relaxed lotus. "Did the AIsource tell you something about yourself that they had no right to know?"

The surprise must have shown in my eyes. "Maybe two things."

"It's no big deal, Counselor, just a local habit of theirs. You may be familiar with the works of a twentieth-century fantasy author named L. Frank Baum? Specifically, his novel *The Wizard of Oz*?"

I've never related to fiction of any kind, let alone works of such ancient vintage. "No."

"That's too bad. You see, Skye the single's mother was a dear woman who loved antiquarian fantasy, and read her that particular work more than once." A soft nostalgia entered his eyes, as he lost himself in a cherished memory that had never truly happened to him. "It's about the ruler of a magical country, whose power is entirely based on his false reputation for omnipotence. He frightens his subjects, plays on their fears, and makes them so terrified that they flee his presence thinking he's more than human."

It sounded as inane as any other fairy tale. "This is an AIsource station. They run the place. They are All-Powerful. Or, at least, more than human."

His attention snapped back to the here and now. "True. As they no doubt pointed out, one way or another. But on this station, they like reminding us of that fact, and they have a sincere talent for coming out first in any confrontation. They specifically like dropping references to things you consider personal; the more private, the better. Leaving you to wonder how the hell they know."

Another difference between the way the AIsource acted elsewhere, and the way they acted here. I didn't much like their etiquette, on-site.

"This is their home ground," Oscin said. "Here, they feel entitled to a little arrogance. And they exercise it at every opportunity."

"Doesn't explain how they know—"

"You'd be surprised what they know. They don't advertise it much, but they're said to have an interface, somewhere—not here, of course, but on some other installation—where anybody willing to pay the fee can ask any twelve questions and receive twelve accurate answers. It doesn't matter how obscure the questions might be, whether they're about the location of buried treasure or the most shameful secret of your life. The AIsource guarantees perfect accuracy. I'm not about to say there is such a place, but based on some of the things they've said to me since the singles Oscin and Skye linked, I'd be very surprised to find out that there isn't."

"Yes," I said, "but how?"

"Their computation speed is something like one million times the average human being's. Their storage capacity is something close to infinite. They've been, pretty much, everywhere. How much would elude you, if you had resources on that scale? Face it: they're the font of all knowledge. It's just that on neutral ground, they're polite enough to avoid rubbing our faces in it. Here, they want to."

I wondered if that would extend to sending anonymous hate mail, then discounted the idea as unlikely. My long experience with hate mail had taught me it was a tactic for the frightened and impotent. If those messages did come from within One One One, a human being was sending them. But was it a human being responsible for the deaths of Warmuth and Santiago, or just one of the small legions of people who hated me for other reasons?

The thought was enough to give me cottonmouth. I took

the canteen, put it to my lips, and threw my head back so far that rivulets ran down my chin.

When I gave it back, Oscin took another gulp before sealing the vessel tight. "Well, there goes that theory."

"What?"

"Some cultures disapprove of arrangements like mine. They call them criminal, or even perverse. On some of my past postings, there's been so much discrimination that Oscin and Skye have had to pretend to be a pair of separate individuals just for personal safety. For a moment there, I was afraid I had to watch myself around you."

"How do you know you don't?"

He almost laughed. "You drank from my water, Counselor. Most of the people I'm talking about wouldn't."

"That's stupid," I said. "What would drinking your water have to do with it?"

"They give my condition the status of a disease and can't help acting like it's contagious. I agree, it's stupid. But I'm happy you don't feel that way."

I wondered why the likes of the Porrinyards would even care, since I was nothing to them; decided it was one of those strange people-behaviors I didn't need to know about, then forced myself to my feet. Oscin saw what I was about to do and jumped up, intent on hovering nearby until I could stand without assistance. I resented the hell out of that even after I almost swooned. "So what else did you want to tell me?"

"Pardon?"

"I'm not stupid, sir. You hustled Lastogne out of the room. Is there some information the two of you needed to share with me that you didn't want him hearing?"

"There's only one of us," Oscin said.

"Forgive me. Whenever you *two* act independently, you strain the limits of my syntax. What did you want to tell me?"

"Nothing about your investigation."

"About Lastogne?"

"There are any number of things I can say about Peyrin," Oscin said. It wasn't hard to read undercurrents of resentment in the calm but chilly way he spoke the other man's name. "But no, not him either."

This was still a prime opportunity to follow up on one of this station's many contradictions. "I'd like to ask you about him anyway—or at least, something he said about you yesterday."

"Oh?'

"He'd said, 'They're cylinked. They don't make friends in the usual sense.'"

He seemed darkly amused. "Peyrin said that? Why, the backstabbing son of a bitch."

There were depths here I wasn't getting. "I've never met any cylinked pairs before, so I had no reason to disbelieve him. But between the way you're acting, and some of the things you've said, makes me wonder if he's . . ."

Oscin finished the sentence for me. ". . . full of Tchi shit."

"Exactly."

He walked away, cocked his head as if listening to the advice of an observer I couldn't see or hear, then came back. "Nobody's a closed system without wanting to be, Counselor. Not even me. It wouldn't be any more fun for me being trapped in two heads, with nobody else to talk to, than it is for an unlinked individual like you to be trapped in only one. So, yes, I do make friends in the usual sense. I care for some people. I get angry with others. I even fall in love from time to time, though it's a little harder to manage, given that it has to be a person capable of pleasing my shared, and therefore somewhat more demanding, perspective."

"And that's where Cynthia Warmuth fell short?"

A little angry now: "Cynthia Warmuth was kind, generous, eager, compassionate, and, as I've already said, needy, pushy and grating. It's a matter of taste, not misanthropy."

"And yet," I noted, "Lastogne said what he said. Why?"

"Didn't I tell you on the way over that we made love once? I mean, Lastogne and I?"

"Yes."

"The operative word is *once,* Counselor. Once and only once. Even then, it was cookie-cutter heterosexuality, which didn't go anywhere substantial until this body"—Oscin gestured at himself—"left him alone with Skye in what his limited imagination was able to consider privacy. It wasn't, of course; our gestalt was still involved even if this male body could not be. But from what you're saying, Lastogne now rationalizes what happened between us as his own skillful seduction of Skye behind Oscin's back, which is of course an absolute impossibility and a ridiculous insult. And now, to make matters worse, he seems to be blaming what I am as the handiest excuse for Skye's lack of interest in a sequel. Please. Take what he said as the self-serving garbage it is. I'm not an exclusive club. I just don't want him as a member."

It was an interesting fresh take on Peyrin Lastogne, who had tried so hard to paint himself as a distant, cynical observer of humanity. I wondered whether he'd taken on that persona for my benefit. It was possible. One thing I'd learned, from being such a sincere bitch for so many years, is that some people wear misanthropy only as a fashion statement.

Lastogne could be one of those.

But maybe not. Oscin's revelation established only that the man was not, entirely, the island he claimed to be. He was just a deluded, vindictive ex-lover. So what? He could still be a son of a bitch. Or even a murderer.

I said, "So if you didn't want to talk about him, what did you want to talk about?"

Oscin switched gears with no visible difficulty. "I don't know how to say this, Counselor. Considering where this conversation was a few minutes ago, it's a risky thing to say.

But, you know, the individuals Oscin and Skye were once very angry people. They both felt trapped in a place they did not want to be, in a life they did not want to live, and they made themselves miserable sharing their resentment with anybody else who could have been allowed into a world that, as far as they were concerned, allowed room for only the two of them. After a while they had so much anger between them that they started to direct it at each other. They began to fight. To leave scars." For a moment his face seemed to shift, and became no longer his own but a reflection of how Skye might have looked were her body the one telling the story. "They didn't link just so they could be indentured together. They linked because they were a few harsh words from breaking up forever. They linked because joining together as this new creation greater than the sum of its parts was their only alternative to walking out of each other's lives and feeling incomplete for as long as they lived."

I pushed myself away from the wall, tested my ability to stand alone without help, and found that I was now as steady on my feet as I ever managed to be. "Why tell me?"

He cocked his head again, and flashed a secret smile at himself. "I don't have much time, Counselor. Skye and Lastogne are coming back. They're not far away. I don't think Skye will be able to delay him for more than another minute or so.

"So here's the little I have time for. I'm an expert at angry people. I know that they come in many different flavors and I've learned to recognize what they are. Like Gibb and Lastogne. Like Warmuth and Santiago. Like some of the exiles you're about to meet." He had not faced me at all since beginning this speech, focusing instead on some distant point somewhere beyond me, beyond the blue walls, perhaps even beyond the territories encompassed by One One One. "Like yourself. I don't know all the details yet, but I really don't need AIsource help to feel like I already know you."

Lastogne had said something much like that yesterday, and I'd reacted with little more than wry acknowledgment that he was right. Others in my life had confronted me with words to the same effect and I'd displayed boredom, defiance, even pride.

Oscin Porrinyard made me want to hit him.

But before I could go through with it, Skye and Lastogne turned the corner, at a junction some fifty meters up-corridor. Lastogne still wore his grimace-as-smile, and Skye walked with a sprightly bounce to her step that from this vantage point seemed deliberate mockery of whatever he'd had to say to her.

When I caught her eye, she winked.

It had to be meant for me. She wouldn't have needed gestures to communicate with her other half.

When I glanced at Oscin, for confirmation, he was winking too.

My moment of anger faded, replaced by open confusion.

What the hell was all *this* about?

9

EXILES

The Dip Corps ship, an unlovely bullet bearing the service's much-parodied trademark of a starscape in the outline of an extended human hand, sat berthed at the far end of One One One's many hangars, a glowing, blue-walled chamber large enough to hold four ships its size.

The chamber had more than enough room to house my transport as well, but the AIsource had berthed that in another chamber. Why, beyond some sense of courtesy toward visitors who'd arrived at different times, I didn't know, and didn't particularly care. A number of inflatable sleepcube tents, perfect for wilderness accommodations, and just odd in this context, sat just outside the ship, each glowing from a soft internal light. There was also a portable table, flanked by a pair of stasis crates pressed into service as chairs. It looked like a place people lived, but nothing at all like home, not even as much of a home as the indentures had made of Hammocktown.

I suppose it was close enough to camping, for people deprived of any outdoors beyond a vast empty room with a spongy floor and luminous blue walls.

The air was warmer than the neutral setting preferred by most space docks, warm and humid in a manner that suggested, without actually providing, the presence of an overhead sun. It was the kind of environment I liked: all straight lines.

"The poor bastards sure make themselves comfortable," said Lastogne.

"It's no fun for them," said the Porrinyards.

The ship's hatch opened, revealing a tanned, muscular man with shoulder-length black hair. He was stripped to his waist, the planes of his chest shining with enough perspiration to suggest a recent workout. He had a massive nose and tiny gray eyes which seemed to light on Skye before turning, with sad self-knowledge, to me. "You're from the Judge Advocate."

"Brilliant deduction," said Lastogne, dripping more than his usual concentration of scorn. "Counselor Andrea Cort, meet Exophysiologist Third Class Nils D'Onofrio, current status inactive. De facto commander of the three height-sensitives confined to this chamber on Mr. Gibb's orders."

D'Onofrio offered me a hand, kept it extended, then let it drop, a grim disappointment already burning in eyes that knew the cruel emotion well. "I see you share Mr. Gibb's attitude toward us untouchables."

"Not at all," said Lastogne. "She just hates everybody."

D'Onofrio gave me an appraising look. "Really, Peyrin. You must feel like you just found your soul ma—"

I cut him off. "Mr. Lastogne doesn't speak for me, sir. It's true that I try to avoid physical contact whenever possible, but the number of people I go to the trouble of actually hating comprise a very small and very select group, who had to earn their places there. Deal with me properly and I promise you we'll have a pleasant, professional relationship."

D'Onofrio studied me for signs of mockery. "I'll take that at face value, Counselor. How do you want to do this? You want to question us together, or one at a time?"

"Together will be fine, for now."

D'Onofrio acknowledged that with a nod and returned to the ship, a portrait of wounded dignity.

I thought of the many years I'd needed to carry myself with quiet strength, bearing the monstrous reputation I'd earned at Bocai. D'Onofrio's bearing testified to the same kind of wounds, the ones known only to the scapegoated. I found myself feeling significant empathy for him. Without turning to Lastogne, I murmured, "Don't speak for me again, sir."

"My error," said Lastogne, who didn't sound sorry at all.

"I mean it. I'll cite you with interference if you try it."

"I understand," he said, without an iota of additional contrition.

"Especially if you implicate me in any attempt to stigmatize these people."

Lastogne waved his hand. "We don't stigmatize them, Counselor. Not as bad as they sometimes think we do."

"No," said the Porrinyards. "You do worse." They glanced at Lastogne, as if deciding just how much contradiction he could take, and then resumed, their shared voice pitched toward Skye's side of the vocal register. "Gibb's people are all high-altitude specialists. They define themselves by their ability to navigate the Uppergrowth bare-handed, and they demand that level of competence from everybody they work with. They have to, when the reflexes of others are so vital to their own survival. They see anybody who freezes up, who can't function, who allows himself to be defeated by the same challenges they face every day, as not just weak but dangerous. Cross that line and you're on their bad side, permanently."

Wonderful. "You've already noted that I'm not too good at heights myself. Where does that leave me?"

The Porrinyards considered it. "I don't think you should worry about it, Counselor. Most of Gibb's people understand that you're an untrained outsider, doing your best in an environment you find frightening and alien. It may lead a few to underestimate you, or show you less respect. But most won't judge you by that criterion alone."

I wasn't sure I bought it, but that assurance would have to do for now. "And you?"

The Porrinyards grinned with something hard to avoid interpreting as affection. Now their voice tipped toward Oscin's end of the register: "Here's a shameful personal secret, Counselor: Oscin the single never quite managed the grace and confidence Skye the single demonstrated in high places. She did things that scared the hell out of him. He hid it well, and overcompensated by taking stupid risks to impress her. So I know what it's like."

They seemed to be going out of their way to show individuality in my presence. Why, I didn't know, but I sure wished they'd stop turning it on and off and just decide which way they wanted to act.

A second later D'Onofrio arrived with his fellow exiles, introducing them as Exobiochemist First Class Li-Tsan Crin and Atmospheric Analyst Second Class Robin Fish.

Li-Tsan, lowering her head to get through the hatchway, was one of the tallest unenhanced human beings I'd ever seen; her hypertrophic arms and legs, left exposed by the minimalist white worksuit that covered her from breasts to hips, were so knotted by muscle that they looked too tight to move. She had light brown skin, emerald eyes, and a chin that came to a point. Her hair was a wispy halo of white so thin it seemed like cirrus clouds orbiting the darker skin of her face. She was beautiful, in a dangerous way, with all the coiled menace of a predator seeking a way out of its cage.

Fish, who barely came up to Li-Tsan's collarbone, was milky-white, to the point of translucence, her finest feature lush red hair she wore in a quartet of tight shoulder-length braids. She wore a loose open vest that accentuated the curve of her breasts and the bottom half of a stained shipboard worksuit that looked baggy and shapeless on her, even though the name stitched into the chest pocket was her own. Nothing about her physique, from the slight bulge of her exposed belly to the soft freckled skin of her limbs, testified to the kind of hyperathleticism that characterized so many of Gibb's people. Her puffy, bloodshot eyes seemed the footprints of many sleepless nights.

Even before the women spoke a word, they both radiated wariness. They'd both been hurt badly, and at length: the kind of hurt that still bled. Was it just the professional upset of failing in One One One's upside-down environment? Or something more?

Li-Tsan, looking me up and down, said, "So you're the grand inquisitor."

"No inquisition," I said. "Just a few questions."

"Oh, certainly," Li-Tsan said. She had the clipped accent of a woman whose Mercantile was a second tongue learned late in life: all exaggerated vowels and stressed consonants. "And when you've asked all your questions, just who will you choose for scapegoat? Not one of Gibb's infallible supermen, dangling from the Uppergrowth like monkeys. Not somebody Gibb wants to use. Just one of the expendables, fit to be taken out like a spare part the first time his creature Lastogne needs someone to condemn to the Corps—"

Fish barely raised her eyes. "That's not fair, Li—"

"Nothing's fair, sweetmeat. Not in the Corps, not on this world, and certainly not in front of this piece of Tchi shit."

Anger not just between these three and the rest of this station's human contingent—anger between those two. Their life as internal exiles must have been as interesting as the booming local industry in comparing things to Tchi shit. I asked Li-Tsan, "Would you be more comfortable answering questions without Mr. Lastogne present?"

Li-Tsan snorted. "I'd be happier still with him pushed out

an airlock, but yeah, why not, as long as you're giving me a choice. While you're at it I'd prefer the unison twins gone too. I don't trust anybody who works for the lord of that upside-down madhouse."

"No offense taken," said the Porrinyards.

"Go fuck yourself *some more*," Li-Tsan told them, with special emphasis.

Lastogne's smile didn't falter, less the amiability of a man refusing to take offense than the arrogance of one who considered these enemies beneath his contempt. "You first, bondsman."

The Porrinyards gave me a look which they must have considered eloquent but which I found totally opaque. There was a shared-joke element to it, which seemed more or less inevitable with these two, except that I was somehow supposed to be included in it. Again, I didn't have the slightest idea what they were getting at, and again my denseness didn't seem to bother them all that much.

Only after all three of my guides exited the hatch at the far end of the hangar did I address the height-sensitives again. "I don't know if it means anything to any of you, but I don't believe it's accurate to call Lastogne Gibb's 'creature.' It seemed the other way around, to me. Lastogne's even accused Gibb of incompetence."

Li-Tsan rolled her eyes. "And you've been here how long, all of a cycle or two? Wow, Counselor, I'm impressed how completely you've managed to analyze the true nature of their relationship."

"If I'm being hasty, I'm more than willing to stand corrected."

She adopted the tone of a frustrated teacher repeating basic lessons for an idiot. "He doesn't consider Gibb incompetent. He considers Gibb a mediocrity. He thinks Gibb is a nothing, a void, a space-holder. And that's exactly what he wants Gibb to be. He wants it so much that he's willing to support all of Gibb's sordid little corruptions, in exchange for the freedom to be an even bigger ass."

D'Onofrio raised a hand, cutting Li-Tsan off before she could further elaborate on her distaste for all matters related to Lastogne. "I'm sorry, Counselor. Nobody likes to feel useless for as long as we have. It's made the three of us a little bitter, I'm afraid. The fact is that we're not sure how we can help you. None of us have been allowed inside the Habitat for months—in poor Robin's case, for almost two years Mercantile. We can't tell you anything about the way those women died."

I said, "Fair enough. I'll be satisfied with hearing how the three of you got mustered out."

Li-Tsan's silence, provisional at best, failed her. "See, Nils? She doesn't a give a damn about the truth! She's just trying to make this about us!"

Whenever I question three or more people at the same time, one of them takes the role of the volatile hothead who serves as the self-appointed keeper of all of their shared paranoia. Only sometimes does it indicate that the hothead's hiding something. Just as often, the amount of truly relevant data being huffed about equals zero. Either way, the hothead needs to be cuffed down. I heaved a deep breath, took my sweet time sitting down on the one of the crates the three height-sensitives had drafted into use as chairs, and said, "You know, bondsman, I don't claim any great dedication to the truth. I don't even have all that much empathy for the problems of the unjustly accused. No, I'm afraid my only real objection to concocting transparently flimsy cases against innocent people has always been that I prefer to look like I have some talent for my job. Picking unlikely suspects at random means looking capricious and incompetent and sloppy. Doing the job right the first time, and finding the *actual* guilty party, is just a lot less work in the long run."

The three height-sensitives stared at me.

Li-Tsan spat. "Next you'll be telling us you don't bite."

I've long reserved my sweetest smiles for my nastiest moments. "Oh, I bite, all right. And once I clamp down, I'm like a snake. You have to cut my head off to get me to let go. Please don't test me, Li-Tsan. I promise you, I leave marks."

The height-sensitives consulted each other in silence, then came to a mutual decision and joined me at the round table. Even then, they pulled their crates together so they could sit elbow to elbow, presenting a united front. D'Onofrio and Li-Tsan wore attitudes of bored defiance, Fish a darker form of beaten resignation. I couldn't tell whether the other two were supporting Fish or simply bracketing her. I did notice that Fish didn't seem to want to face either one of them. It wasn't fear, but something else: A recent argument? An old one? Even an old-fashioned love triangle? "Why would you believe the Corps wants to make this about you?"

"No reason," Li-Tsan growled. "Except for treating us like Tchi shit for something we can't help, holding us prisoner in this hole for months on end, and refusing to transfer us out of here to another assignment where we could make ourselves useful instead of going slowly insane from boredom, the Dip Corps has always been scrupulously fair to us. I can't possibly imagine why we wouldn't expect more of the same. Not at all."

"So you don't think they have any actual evidence against you."

Li-Tsan's eyes went small and dangerous. "You're the investigator. You'd know what they have and don't have."

I was really beginning to hate her. "I arrived yesterday, Li-Tsan. Assume I know nothing."

"They have worse than nothing. They have actual, genuine impossibility. They may think we're lower than Tchi shit, but they also know we're stuck here and never have anything to do with anything that's going on. But they'll make this about us. They'll do it just to see the looks on our faces."

The other woman's intensity was a little bit like being jacked into a pleasure node at full voltage. I rubbed my temples. "Gibb says he considers the AIsource responsible, and never gave me any other impression."

She made a rude noise. "You know he can't let the AIsource take the blame for this. It would mean a major diplomatic incident, even war. Better to strut around looking tough and then come up with some solution that inconveniences nobody but the trio of likely suspects you keep preserved in cold storage."

I remembered Bringen's briefing, with its unsubtle agenda. *Whatever the evidence, whatever your senses tell you . . . find the AIsource innocent. Even if they're guilty, find them innocent. We need a guilty party we can cage.*

Did he already have these three in mind?

It was possible. He must have read Gibb's reports from onsite and found references to three people whose fates would not be mourned, if a case could be made against them.

But I didn't want any part of it. I'd already done more than enough to merit the Monster label, thank you. I was in no hurry to add any additional interest to that account. So I treated Li-Tsan to my most unpleasant grin. "Well, before I officially make up my mind to accuse you of multiple murders and have you shipped off for trial, I should at least go through the motions. Maybe we should just start with how you developed your respective problems with high places."

She studied me with resentful, half-lidded eyes. "Why would that make a difference?"

"It got you where you are. You were chosen for this assignment because the Corps thought you could function under local conditions. Now, for whatever reason, you can't. That makes it an interesting subject. So tell me. What made you such good recruits? And what changed you?"

The three height-sensitives stewed in silence: D'Onofrio slumping in disgust, Fish staring at her hands, Li-Tsan stewing at the edge of another explosion.

There was no questioning which of the three had the most volatile temper, but that meant nothing, not when the murders would have required too much cold planning to be believable as crimes of sudden passion.

I pointed at D'Onofrio, who seemed the most even-tempered. "You first."

He relaxed. "Yeah, might as well. You can read my records and find out the same thing, right? I come from a planet called Agali Vespocci. You know it?"

"Sorry. No."

"Not surprised. It's only borderline habitable, and nothing of any importance ever happened there. The thing is, it resembles this nasty hellhole. One One One, I mean. The lower atmosphere is hot as hell and contaminated with caustics that make the surface next to unlivable, but the temperatures drop and the poisons thin to traces as you get to the higher latitudes, so we do most of our living on the mountaintops."

It did sound a lot like One One One. "I don't see why you had a problem."

"It's not exactly what you'd expect, is it? But even on Vespocci we had solid ground to walk on, when we needed it. There were terraces, cliff dwellings. You could turn your back on the heights whenever you needed to. There were times of year, brief times, when the weather was almost pleasant. Here, there's nothing. I was fine here for more than a year, but after a while I started thinking of all the things that could go wrong. Then one day, on the Growth, I froze up, started crying, and couldn't stop. Gibb pulled me in, called me every possible name for coward, and sent me out here to stay with Robin and Li-Tsan."

"They were already here, then?"

"Yes. This was only about six months ago Mercantile."

"Was there anything in your past, at any point, to indicate that such a breakdown was possible?"

"No." He spread his hands. "But I guess we don't know our limits until we reach them."

It had been a while since I'd seen anybody quite as defeated, and in this chamber I didn't have to look far to see another one. "Who was the first to arrive here? Robin or Li-Tsan?"

"Robin."

"All right," I said. "Li-Tsan, you're next."

She started. "Not Robin?"

"No, I'll work my way back. What's your story?"

"Like Nils just told you, you can get all this from our records —"

"I want to hear it from you. Go on."

Li-Tsan rolled her eyes again, just to stress that she still considered this all a tremendous waste of her time, but warmed up as she began to talk. "I worked in orbital construction for a Bursteeni company producing wheelworlds for the Tchi holdings. It's tough going. Everything's free fall to start with, of course, but the silly ass-backwards way the Bursteeni do it, the rotation starts up before the project's half finished, and you have to work in and out of the skeleton while the spin's trying to fling you against the outer walls. The third time a friend of mine got reduced to a fine red paste I contacted the Dip Corps to have them buy out my contract. They figured my background made me a perfect match. They didn't know I sold out because I was losing my nerve already. I made it all of three months before I made a mistake serious enough to get me banished to this gulag, and I still don't know what the hell this has to do with anything."

"How long have you been confined to the hangar?"

"Almost nine months Mercantile. Could have had a grotting baby by now, come to think of it."

I turned to Robin. "Now, you."

Fish made even the moment of eye contact look like a backbreaking effort. "Do you really need to hear this from me, Counselor? I'm not feeling well today. I really need to go inside and lie down for a while."

She did look awful, more a physical shell of what she must have once been than either Li-Tsan or D'Onofrio. I took another look at the bagginess of her clothes and, for the first time, registered the muscular atrophy. Confinement here was killing her. Confinement, or something else.

I said, "The faster you answer me the faster you see me leave."

Fish held the silence for so long that I had to restrain myself from prodding her. That's never a good idea. Sometimes people hesitate because they don't have the courage to come out with whatever needs to be said; other times they desperately want to speak but can't find the words. Jabbing them prematurely tends to shut them up. Outwaiting them gives them the time to say more than they intend. When she finally spoke, it was without any noticeable energy. "I wasn't ever much. Just a clerical worker on New Kansas. No special skills or education, just crushing boredom and a thirst to get the hell out."

"So you joined the Corps."

"Which assigned me to the same kind of work I'd done back home. I met Mr. Gibb for the first time when I was at a records center on Hylanis. He was the big name doing administrative work as he waited for his next posting, and I was the frustrated kid begging him to remember me if he got sent somewhere with a possibility of advancement. Not long after he left I was pulled into special training for this project. I did thirty days of height-desensitization, before they shipped me in."

"And you mustered out."

"Almost as soon as I got here," she said.

"How did it happen?"

"Everybody except Gibb knew how useless I was from day one, but he kept insisting I'd adjust. Then one day during remedial training, one of the Uppergrowth vines snapped and left me screaming my stupid head off at the tail end of a dangling ten-meter cable." Her hand spasmed at the thought. She examined it without much surprise, then placed it flat on the table. "I couldn't blame anybody for not wanting to work with me after that."

"And that was two years ago Mercantile."

"Not quite two years. We're still a few weeks away from my anniversary."

She used the celebratory word without any apparent irony.

I said, "You've received supply shipments. New indentures, now and then. In two years Gibb never talked about sending you home? Or transferring you out, to someplace where you could still do some good? There had to be opportunities."

Li-Tsan, who fronted many of her statements with rude noises, made another one. "Mr. Gibb thinks failures among his staff reflect poorly on his leadership. So it's safer to just tuck us out of the way and let us rot."

"Have you tried complaining to his superiors on New London?"

"Sure," Li-Tsan said. "We all have. We've inundated them. I've sent two complaints a day. But guess what. It all goes through Gibb, and he still has the authority to declare us essential to the effort here. And besides, New London isn't eager to ask its projects elsewhere to trust people who've already proven themselves incompetent at previous assignments. The way they figure it, Gibb's justified in keeping us in limbo, and we can sit out the remaining years of our contracts getting as irate about the injustice as we like." She rolled her eyes. "Of course, it's different now that he needs a scapegoat."

"Would this be why you show your hatred for Mr. Lastogne?"

"He supports what Gibb's doing to us, which makes him a piece of shit."

Normal shit, this time. I turned my attention back to Fish. "So you were confined here, alone, for more than a year before Li-Tsan showed up. That sounds cruel."

Fish didn't look up. "It wasn't exactly solitary confinement. I received visits."

"From anybody in particular?"

"Anybody who felt sorry for me, or wanted a break."

"How many would that include?"

"Everybody took breaks. Not everybody made the trip just to visit me." Fish allowed herself the kind of smile that reeks with intense self-loathing. "I wasn't in-habitat long enough to make friends."

"Except for Mr. Gibb."

"I wouldn't call him a friend, exactly," Fish said.

"He got you the job. What would you call him?"

"Had it worked out, a mentor."

"Did he ever visit you, after your exile?"

"I saw him whenever he took leave."

"Did you ever talk about your situation, on those occasions?"

"I begged him to transfer me."

"And?"

"He said we'd talk about it if I met him at Hammocktown."

Mr. Gibb, I decided, was a bastard. "Even with Gibb's people taking regular leaves, you must have been alone most of the time."

"Yes."

"Doing what?"

"Not much. I helped edit the reports our people sent to New London."

"You had access to hytex transmission?"

"Yes. For more than a year I handled all the mail back and forth."

"Send anything unauthorized?"

Fish's eyes flared. "Like what?"

"There have been some unusual messages recently." My hate mails.

She showed no interest in the details. "Oh, recently. Well, I'm sorry to disappoint you, Counselor, but recently—as in the last year or so—all of our transmissions go through Gibb and Lastogne. He took that job away from me when he banished Li-Tsan."

I had trouble believing either Gibb or Lastogne responsible for the messages I'd received. I had no problem believing them capable of malice, but that particular kind seemed contrary to their style. "Did he have any problems with the job you were doing?"

"No. He made sure I knew he thought I'd done all right. But he still insisted on handling all the correspondence from then on. I think he just wanted to make sure we wouldn't say anything he wouldn't be able to deny."

"Like what?"

"I don't know," Fish said.

"Neither do I," said Li-Tsan.

Something was being hidden, here. "What would you think if you had to speculate?"

D'Onofrio jumped in. "One One One's a very precarious situation, Counselor. We're dealing with issues of tremendous sensitivity, in the face of an alien government that has permitted us no diplomatic status at all. The wrong word, spoken at the wrong time, can jeopardize everything we're trying to do. Maybe we had a close call, and New London told Mr. Gibb he had to take on greater personal responsibility."

Or maybe they'd had prior incidents with hate mail, and sending everything through the boss was the only way to make sure it didn't happen again. "But you're the one who said Mr. Gibb's afraid of having to deny something. What would he have to deny?"

"I don't know," Fish said. "Honestly."

I let it pass. "All right. So he took away your job as correspondence officer, and left you playing innkeeper to personnel on leave."

"And inventory officer. It wasn't that bad. We needed somebody here to keep track anyway."

"And that couldn't be done by onboard systems?"

"Onboard systems can be hacked."

"Gibb said that. So what was he frightened of, exactly? Weaponry?"

"Luxury items. Stimulants. Personal belongings. High-tech not allowed in the habit under our contract with the AIsource."

"Anything capable of sabotaging the lines of Santiago's hammock?"

"We have some plasma knives," Fish said, "but nothing that's gone missing. That was the first thing we checked."

"We being your little group?"

"Not just us. The Porrinyards supervised, and Mr. Lastogne double-checked. They found no irregularities."

"I'll check on that." I would, too, but doubted I'd find anything pivotal. Anybody capable of hacking the inventory would have covered himself too well to leave evidence vulnerable to a cursory inspection from the likes of me. Thinking furiously, rejecting half a dozen possible lines of further inquiry, I settled on the one that had proven best at enflaming the emotions of everybody I'd met so far. "What can you tell me about Warmuth and Santiago?"

The three height-sensitives greeted this little inquiry with the same enthusiasm they would have reserved for an unexploded bomb. They glanced at each other, came to the shared conclusion that this looked suspicious, glanced back at me, came to the shared conclusion that this looked furtive, and looked away, coming to the shared conclusion that avoiding eye contact was just as bad as all their other options. All this happened in about two seconds, and left the three of them with no safe place to focus.

It was Li-Tsan who decided that frankness was the best of a long list of bad options. "Santiago was a bitch and a half."

"She wasn't unpleasant," Fish said, "not in the way that some of the others were . . . but she was anything but friendly."

"She was a bitch and a half," Li-Tsan repeated. "Yeah, she never actually mocked us, and she never did anything we could nail her for . . . but as far as attitude went, she was the worst. The times she spent here, she just spent inside one of those sleepcubes, refusing to say a word to us, coming out only to eat. Everything she said, everything she did, let us know she thought we were worse than garbage."

"I didn't like her, either," D'Onofrio said. "But I didn't think the way she treated us had anything to do with us being height-sensitives. I asked around, whenever I saw any of the others, and they all said pretty much the same thing: that she treated everybody that way. She said what she had to say and she did what she had to do, and she turned her back as soon as she decently could."

"And Warmuth?" I asked.

Li-Tsan spat. "She was worse. She kept *visiting* us to see if we were *all right*."

There was the anger again. Deep, poisonous, and undiluted, making Warmuth the central focus in everything that had gone wrong in her own term of service. "And you resented this?"

"You must have heard by now. She was an empathy addict. There was nothing special about being befriended by her. She only sought out vulnerable people because it gave her a charge."

"Yes, I've heard that. But wouldn't that be hard to distinguish from genuine compassion?"

"Genuine compassion," Li-Tsan said, "doesn't leave you feeling like you're being used. It doesn't leave a bad taste in your mouth. It doesn't make you feel worse than you would if you had to go without it."

"Again," I said, "tell me how you knew the difference."

Li-Tsan just shook her head, showing herself and all the world her incredulity at my failure to get something so transparently obvious.

It wasn't that I thought she was wrong. I'd been an outcast for most of my life, and I'd learned the hard way that some of the people who wanted to befriend me, and understand me, often acted that way only because it made them feel kind and giving and charitable and special. I'd grown so suspicious of anybody who wanted me to open up that I now assumed ulterior motives long before confirming that there actually were any. But the near unanimity on the subject of Cynthia Warmuth was unusual even by my standards. Either One One One housed the most selective group of misanthropes in the known universe, or she faked sincere concern worse than any other human being ever born, or . . .

. . . or what?

There was something else here, something I was still failing to see.

D'Onofrio looked too tired to jump in and help me. "Come on, Counselor. I don't know anything about you, but sometime in your life you must have known what it was like to have somebody feel sorry for you. Not just a little bit; not just for a few minutes on end. I mean deep, compassionate, ostentatious pity, hauled out at every opportunity, stressed again and again as if you were too stupid to get it the first time, then offered anew even after you recognized it for what it was." He took a deep breath and stood up, stepping away from the table to face the ship that had become his home, his prison, and the symbol of his greatest failure. "Sometimes that hurts even more than just being left alone."

And for a moment I still didn't get it. I knew that it had more to do with D'Onofrio than with the others, but had no idea what.

But then the universe shifted, and one small piece of the puzzle slipped into place with such finality that I came damn close to hearing the click.

D'Onofrio saw the light dawn. He looked away from me, more disgusted with himself than at any other point during the conversation.

Li-Tsan just laughed her nastiest little laugh. The sound that bubbled up from somewhere deep inside, bringing with it the palpable taste of poison. "Pity sex. Ever had any, Counselor? Done right, it hurts even more than any other kind. . . ."

10

LASTOGNE

As our transport reentered the Habitat, the first fresh view of that great empty space was enough to reintroduce me to the digestive effects of soul-searing vertigo. That and the sheer organic smell of the biosphere almost got the better of me. I would have vomited over the side, but the ionic shields would have repelled it back at me. So I just closed my eyes, counted to one hundred by primes, and entertained myself with yet another inner recitation of all the reasons I hated ecosystems.

The Porrinyards had enough decency not to mention my discomfort, but Lastogne called attention to it. "You're turning colors, Counselor. Would you like some medication?"

I hadn't heard so many people intent on medicating me since my days as a guest of the state. "No. But I would appreciate it if you wiped that amused grin off your face."

"Not an option," Lastogne said, with friendly malice. "Nausea may not be all that fun to experience, but among unaffected travelers it bears a long and honorable history as a spectator sport."

I tasted stomach acid. "I'm beginning to understand your attitude about making friends."

"Oh?"

"It's self-preservation. Whenever you say something like that, a stranger just considers you an asshole. A true friend would be obliged to kill you."

"You're right. It must be why I've always avoided making true friends." He hesitated, weighed the moment, and plunged in: "So how have you found your interviews so far?"

This exemplified the truism that local liaisons exist to funnel information in both directions, not just one. Lastogne wasn't here just to help me. He was here to make sure my investigation didn't go anywhere embarrassing. I urped. "Incomplete."

"Nothing helpful at all?"

"Nobody confessed to a massive conspiracy, if that's what you mean. I found more interest in the things people left unsaid."

"Oh?"

I called the Porrinyards. "Oscin, Skye."

Skye was too occupied on the freight deck, tending to one of the packages we were ferrying from the hangar, to look up. But both Porrinyards answered, their shared voice once again a neutral compromise between them. "Yes?"

"I'm about to have a screened conversation with Mr. Lastogne. Please don't disturb us."

"Understood," the Porrinyards said.

I unclipped my hiss screen from my belt, setting it for a radius that included Lastogne and myself. A pleasant murmur filled the air around us. I waited for the murmur to reach full volume and said, "Point one. Robin Fish."

Lastogne seemed surprised. "What about her?"

"The other two came from high-altitude environments. They were trained and experienced and excellent prospects for One One One. When they failed, it was against all reasonable expectations. But Fish was assigned here despite minimal qualifications, given brief and inadequate training in what seems a transparent attempt to justify her posting to this facility, removed from the environment at the first sign of trouble and condemned to literally years of performing busywork in virtual isolation. Her very presence is an anomaly. Why is she here?"

Lastogne shrugged. "No big mystery. The Corps had a number of slots to fill and filled as many as they could with qualified people. The rest had to be chosen off the rack, in the hope that they could be tailored to fit."

"It seems an awful leap from people as completely suited for the job as the Porrinyards, to somebody as completely unsuited, physically and psychologically, as Robin Fish. Weren't there any more candidates from the middle ground?"

His sideways grimace proved no more mirthful than the one requiring both sides of his face. "What makes you think there weren't?"

"Were there?"

"This isn't exactly a typical environment, Counselor. If we'd staffed it with nothing but people trained in climbing and high-altitude gymnastics, we would have fallen short on every other skill set we needed. We would have no linguists, no biologists, no environmental analysts; nobody capable of maintaining the hammocks, nobody qualified to assess the well-being of the Brachiators. So we have several dozen other indentures on-site whose backgrounds offered no special indication of any talent for functioning here. There are even one or two who spent their formative years living on planetary flatlands, without so much as a low rise between them and the horizon, and who never once enjoyed a view from any kind of height until they joined the Corps. I would be lying if I said that everybody found the going easy, but just about everybody adjusted to the conditions better than those three did."

"It still seems excessive to keep a mere clerk like Fish on-site, doing nothing of any real importance, for two full years. Especially since Mr. Gibb arranged her presence here himself."

He shrugged again. "Gibb has a thing about quitters, and about admitting a mistake. I think he believes that if he keeps Fish and her friends penned up long enough, they'll stop being silly, pull themselves together, and rejoin the rest of us."

"Do you believe that?"

"For what it's worth, no. People who fall apart can be put back together again, but they're usually more fragile not less."

"But you still support what Gibb's doing."

Lastogne's grimace became a smirk. "I may not like the man, and I may think he has his head so far up his ass on this subject that he may never live to breathe fresh air again, but he is in charge, and I have to support his decisions, regardless of my own personal feelings."

I couldn't buy Lastogne's portrait of himself as a man who backed up the boss no matter what. "You gave me the impression that you hate them."

"Hate's a strong word," Lastogne said. "I don't feel sorry for them. I don't think they deserve any special sympathy, and I don't think they have any call to sit there, in their little do-nothing world, feeling persecuted because they failed."

I nodded, to support the impression that I accepted his response without question. "Which brings us to point two: the strange dynamic between them. Both Li-Tsan and D'Onofrio behaved protectively toward Fish, even as they both seemed to look down on her."

He seemed astonished that I would even see fit to ask. "Well, she's low dog in their pack. They'll piss on her all night and day, but rip out the throat of anybody else who tries."

"She seemed ill."

Now he gave me an actual smile. "She does look like shit, doesn't she? I think she spends her days dosing herself sick on buzzpatches and manna wine. No particular reason to punish her for indulging, since she has nothing else to do and, confined to the hangar the way she is, can't fall any farther than the floor she's walking on. Of course, the worse she gets, the less likely it is that Gibb will ever feel comfortable about sending her elsewhere."

Terrific. Abandon the woman, then do nothing as she destroys herself. "Where does she get manna juice, if the only place to get it is inside the Habitat?"

"Gibb has no problem with our people drinking the fermented stuff as long as they do it outside the Habitat and detoxify before they return to work. So she gets it from indentures on leave. There are some awfully wild parties, going on in that hangar deck."

"I'm told Cynthia Warmuth went there a lot."

"Everybody goes there a lot. Even Santiago went. It's the only place to go if you want a break away from the Habitat."

"But Cynthia Warmuth especially."

"Maybe a little more than average. She used to talk about how sorry she felt for them."

Backing up what the exiles had said about the self-serving nature of her affections. "Did you know she slept with D'Onofrio?"

That got him. His jaw worked as he considered four or five separate responses, and rejected them all. "No. But I'm not surprised. It's just the kind of stupid-ass thing you would expect the silly quiff to do."

"Empathy addict, right?"

"To a fault," he agreed, with more bile than he actually needed.

There comes a point, in some Dipcrime investigations, when I begin to see my suspect pool as a nest of rabid animals, clawing and sniping at one another in a constant effort to inflict scars. It was especially difficult here, as the nearly universal disdain for both victims was beginning to get on my nerves.

Except it wasn't universal, was it? Gibb and Lastogne both claimed affection for Warmuth. Gibb had even slept with her. Maybe I was just getting a skewed sample.

I glanced up at the blur of Uppergrowth just a few short meters above my head. "Point three. Christina Santiago. Putting yourself in her position: what would you do if your hammock collapsed?"

He smiled. "If I was lucky enough to be somewhere else, I'd get nice and irritated about all the belongings I'd just dumped."

I think I managed to smile back. "I mean if you happened to be inside it at the time."

A shrug. "I'd fall."

"And?"

"What do you mean *and*? What other *and* could there be? I'd fall *and* die, just like anybody else."

"You're sure?'

"Counselor," Lastogne said, with infinite patience, "please don't tell me you think Santiago's still alive. I'd be very disappointed in you. It's not a possibility."

"Why not?"

"Let's forget that the fall itself would take her past heavy weather, poisonous clouds, and an acid rain layer before she ever hit anything solid enough to make her splatter. She'd be bones, and then bone fragments, long before hitting the soup. You're really wondering if anything could have rescued her on the way down. The answer is no. The Brachiators would need to fly, and they can't, so that lets them out. Not us either; we didn't have any skimmers in flight when she fell, and wouldn't have been able to get one launched in time to make a difference. And while the AIsource provide us all the taxi service we want, they express zero interest in playing lifeguard. As far as they're concerned, any attempt at a rescue would compromise the stark integrity of this place."

"Have they actually said that?"

"They said it when they agreed to allow a human presence here. They said, Brachiators stay alive by holding on, and any human beings intent on studying them need to learn the same skill."

This added yet another wrinkle to the game. A longstanding Interspecies Covenant, to which both humanity and the software intelligences were charter signatories, required all participating races to offer reasonable protection to alien diplomatic personnel within their territories. The AIsource's evident refusal to honor that treaty would have been seen as a massive breach of interstellar law . . . were it not for their prior refusal to grant our outpost diplomatic status.

Their failure to recognize Hammocktown as an embassy made it a lot easier for human beings to die here.

Which led to the most troubling issue so far, at least as far as Lastogne was concerned.

"Point four. Peyrin Lastogne, who the hell are you?"

If that offended him at all, he did not show it. Instead, he simply flashed a sideways grin, much warmer than his usual grimace, and squeezed me once on my upper arm. It was a different kind of intrusive touch than I'd endured from Gibb. That one had felt sexual. This one? More like affection, for sharing a secret joke. "I was wondering how long it would take you to just come out and ask."

"You have no Dip Corps listing. You have no bio on the hytex."

The grin remained. "It could be that my background is nobody's business. Look at yourself, Counselor. Your own life would be a hell of a lot easier if it wasn't accessible to anybody with sufficient curiosity. Somebody like myself wouldn't be able to look you up and find all those voices yowling for your extradition. The Tchi really want you, don't they? And the Bocaians—"

The Tchi just wanted me because they wanted anything that would embarrass the Confederacy; it had rendered them predictable in a manner that ended up saving me once or twice. And the Bocaians, who rarely ventured off their own world, were no real threat to me either. "This is not about me. It's about you. Why are your records a closed book? What is it we're not supposed to know?"

"If I told you," he said, "you would know it."

"Have you been sending me any messages?"

"No more than the usual, Counselor."

"Meaning?"

"Nonverbal messages," he said, batting his eyes. "Some involuntary, but all defensible."

"Nothing by hytex?"

"Why would I do that? I can talk to you any time I want."

His answers were driving me crazy. "Did you kill Warmuth or Santiago?"

And instead of a yes or no, he laughed—not with hysterical glee, or superiority, or even with malice, but with a level of bemused affection I found a hundred times more infuriating. "Oh, really. Counselor. What answer could I possibly give, aside from a full confession, that you would ever be willing to believe?"

Now I knew it for a fact. The son of a bitch was teasing me. "Tell me anyway. Did you kill Warmuth or Santiago?"

"No," he said. "I did not. But you have to keep something in mind."

"What's that?"

"That if I was the killer, I'd be saying the same thing."

11

LEVINE, NEGELEIN, LASSITER

The rest of that day passed in a frustrating blur of interviews with the remaining indentures of Hammocktown. I didn't want to work in my own assigned quarters, so I requisitioned a long and narrow hammock that served Gibb's facility as the equivalent of a social hall and communal dining room. I couldn't imagine being here when it had to bear the weight of dozens. I would have choked on my food, unable to avoid picturing the phenomenon of fraying cables.

I managed to interview maybe half of Gibb's people before the suns went out. Most of what they had to tell me jibed with what I'd been told: Santiago the misanthrope, Warmuth the determined empath, the three height-sensitives as social outcasts. Opinions of Gibb himself varied from worshipping to resentful. Despite my prior impression that he grated especially hard on women, some of the highest praise came from young female indentures who couldn't praise him enough. Two or three of those confessed to past, emphasis on past, relationships with him, so anxious to assure me that the breakups had been cordial that my chief question became not whether he'd coached them, but how much.

Nobody had much to add to my skimpy store of intelligence regarding Peyrin Lastogne. As far as they were concerned, he was just a Dip Corps regular, like Gibb—or, as several bothered me by pointing out, me.

Several indentures had witnessed the confrontation between Warmuth and Santiago, which as advertised hadn't amounted to all that much. The time and place had been a midafternoon gathering in the very hammock where I now sat. Five off-duty indentures had been relaxing with a hytex strategy game one had imported from her homeworld. A few others were sitting around, bitching or chatting or arguing about time off. Santiago wandered in to grab some food and return to her own quarters, intent as always on keeping all social contact to an absolute minimum. Warmuth, who had already been observed trying to talk to her on several occasions, abandoned the game and approached her, speaking at length in a voice not loud enough to carry. Santiago tried to leave without acknowledging her. Warmuth put a hand on her shoulder. Santiago slapped her hand away and cursed her out in some non-Mercantile tongue. Warmuth tried to touch her again, and Santiago gave her a light shove, which left the shaken but uninjured Warmuth bobbing on her back at the hammock's lowest point.

Nobody knew the meat of the conversation, but everybody had heard Santiago say, "Leave me alone, bitch."

Despite the subsequent deaths of both participants, nobody thought it had much to do with their eventual fates.

A redheaded medtech named Bill Wilson told me, "This is a small town, Counselor. We've had fights before and will have fights again. It doesn't necessarily lead to murder, and there's no reason to believe that it led to murder now, just because one followed the other."

"It's a place to look," I said.

"Until," he said, "you realize there's nothing there to see."

And the hell of it was, he was right. The incident had seemed so minor, at the time, that it hadn't even led to an investigation. There had been no complaint, no follow-up, no disciplinary action, no pattern of subsequent conflict serious enough to merit either official interference or unofficial gossip. As far as I could tell, neither woman had shared her version of the incident with friends or co-workers. Both had determined to put the whole thing behind them, and both had moved on without mentioning it again.

There was no reason to believe it meant anything.

Except that, for all we knew, it might have been the key to everything.

Among the subjects of interest: one Jacques Robinette, a nervous type whose stammer, in my presence, betrayed a deep level of guilt over something, even if that something had nothing to do with the investigation under way; a pudgy fellow by the name of Ierck Kzinscki, who had trained alongside Li-Tsan Crin and seemed to harbor a deep crush on her; a conspiracy theorist named Gilian Brenner, who had a theory pinning both murders on the Tchi that went all the way around the Coal Sack Nebula and back working out a scenario that would have enabled them to stage manage the crimes without ever being allowed on station; and a Curtis Smalls, whose pleas for a transfer off One One One pegged him, in my eyes, as a future full-time member of Gibb's exiled height-sensitives.

The indentures included several utopian idealists, a few revolutionaries, a couple of crackpots, several brimming with enthusiasm for their mission here, and a number of grim lifers just putting in the hours until they collected their passport and went to the world of their choice. Many found it necessary to recount details of the worlds they had come from. As was all too often the case when indentures swapped life stories, there turned out to be a depressing number of stories about military dictatorships, theocracies, places where one family had seized power and delighted in raping the ecosystem everybody needed to survive, and worlds so screwed up by internal conflicts that volunteering for the Dip Corps emerged as the only way to avoid having your head shot off in some stupid war against civilians.

You want to know why humanity's never been involved in a serious interspecies conflict? Because it's like going out to eat when you have a pantry full of food at home. Why bother sampling the buffets elsewhere when we haven't worked out all the great ways to kill each other yet?

I found, out of all Gibb's staff, maybe half a dozen people who professed deep affection for Warmuth and many more who had a grim, jaw-grinding respect for Santiago. As could only be expected from a small insular community of indentures, working in a dangerous environment under difficult conditions, the web of sexual relationships was almost as tangled as the substructure of Hammocktown. My interviews rang with excited gossip over who'd been with Warmuth (I counted a dozen assignations, all fleeting, before losing track), Li-Tsan (almost as many, but over a much longer period of time), Gibb ("Guess who the boss is doing!"), Lastogne ("Who *isn't* he doing?"), and the Porrinyards (some of these unlikely, envious, or prurient). The precious little gossip I picked up over Christina Santiago had to do with her alleged nasty attitude, and what seemed to have been a long-term love affair with this Cif Negelein I kept hearing about ("You'll know him when you see him," said one indenture, with a theatrical roll of her eyes).

Only a few of the interviewees stood out from the crowd.

Oskar Levine was a sad-eyed, thin-faced, sallow-cheeked young man wearing the insignia of the Riirgaan Republic. He didn't have much new to say about either Warmuth or

Santiago, but his own legal status was such a knot it made mine look simple. Once an indenture in our own Dip Corps, he'd been scapegoated for his actions during a major diplomatic incident he said I could look up for myself, and would have been tried and imprisoned for treason had he not defected to the Riirgaans before prosecution.

Now he sat high up the curve of the communal hammock, his hands performing somersaults in a ballet of nervous overemphasis.

"I look human. I feel human. I even smell human, some days more than others. Any medical examination would confirm that I'm human. But I'm legally nonhuman. No government within the Confederacy is permitted to provide me human status. My Riirgaan diplomatic immunity keeps me safe from any genuinely dangerous consequences, but there have been some unpleasant ones."

"Such as?"

He rubbed the corner of his eyes. "Well, some worlds enforce very strict residency limitations on nonhumans; I've been expelled from a couple of those. And a few years ago I ran into trouble on another world where I served the local Riirgaan ambassador as liaison to the human locals. When the community found out about my relationship with a local girl, they accused me of rape and her of practicing bestiality. I was expelled. The girl was fined, forced to publicly apologize to the community, and prohibited from ever contacting me again."

Levine told the story without any noticeable self-pity. Instead, he seemed to feel a peculiar pride in his one poor claim to fame.

I said, "It must be lonely."

"It's not as bad as you think, Counselor. In fact, I'm married to a woman who defected to Riirgaan in order to make it legal. There's a community of about forty of us, based on one of their worlds; mostly political refugees, of one kind or another, all as human as I could ask for. We're just not recognized as human under Confederate Law."

"Where's your wife now?"

A smile tugged at his lips. "Back home. I'll see her again when I'm cycled out in a few months."

"Do you miss her?"

His smile made his face redden. "Of course."

"Then, if you don't mind me asking, what the hell are you doing here?"

That made him laugh without any self-consciousness at all. "Doesn't make sense, does it? After all, I hate the Dip Corps and the Dip Corps hates me. We shouldn't have anything to do with one another."

It hadn't worked that way, in my case. The Dip Corps and I hated each other, too, but were so integrally connected I'd be wearing its yoke for the rest of my life. But I said, "So?"

"The truth is, I'm here to function as living loophole. The AIsource running One One One only agreed to a small installation of observers, administered by one government and one government alone, required by treaty to share its findings with all the others monitoring the situation here. Humanity got elected. 'My' people, the Riirgaans, wanted their own eyes and ears aboard anyway, so they pulled some strings, finagled a separate deal with the Confederacy, and negotiated my presence as independent consultant. The AIsource know my legal status, but either they don't value citizenship over biology the way the Confederacy does, or they're not willing to argue the point. So I'm a human without being human."

"I'm surprised you would want to go along with it. After all, the Corps shafted you twice. You should tell them to go to hell."

"That's right in both cases. They did, and I should. And for what it's worth, they're not much kinder to me now; some of the careerists, including Mr. Gibb, like to let me know as often as possible what a despicable race-traitor I am. But the Riirgaans gave me a home when I needed one, so I don't mind taking a little crap for their sake. Besides, my bosses among the Riirgaans say that completing this assignment might give them enough leverage to negotiate a Confederate pardon for me and my friends. Even possible repatriation."

I decided to give him some free legal advice. "Dual citizenship of some kind would be fine, but it would have to be dual. Confederate and Riirgaan. Don't ever give up your Riirgaan ties, even for a moment."

Levine frowned. "I wasn't planning to, but why?"

"Because it would be just like the Confederacy to return your citizenship in some deal that comes with immunity from prosecution for crimes already charged, welcome you home, and then nail you with another charge they've been holding in reserve all along. They're vindictive bastards, Mr. Levine. I know."

He saw the conviction in my eyes, thought to question it, then stopped, the awful truth dawning. "Damn. You really think they'd do that?"

I gave him the full force of my certainty. "I'd be astonished if they didn't."

"Damn," he said again, this time rolling the word with special emphasis. He was quiet for a moment, as he weighed the epiphany. Then he looked at me again and said, simply, "Thank you. I appreciate your honesty. Would you be upset with me if I asked you a personal question?"

I didn't like personal questions in general, but I'd opened the door. And, besides, Levine gave me a feeling I rarely had for my fellow human beings: the sense that he could have been a friend, had I been in the market for friends. "Go ahead."

"It's a bad one. I don't mean any offense."

"I said go ahead."

"I've known your name for a couple of years now. I know your background, and I know your legal status. It comes up a lot when researching my own. Don't worry, I haven't mentioned it to anybody here, but —"

My ears burned. "Just ask your question."

"I was wondering . . . if I could defect to get out of a bad legal situation, why can't you? I mean, I'm not advocating it, or saying that you should. But it's not like the Dip Corps is an ideal place for you. You're practically their slave. Haven't you ever thought of getting some alien government, like mine, to give you sanctuary on its own soil?"

The question's rudeness was not nearly as breathtaking as its honesty. I decided against going off on him and gave him an answer, even if I could only afford a less than candid one. "I don't know of any alien governments who wouldn't hand me over to the Bocaians."

"Oh," he said, deflating. "Just a thought."

And a good one. But his adopted people, the Riirgaans, had been among the loudest raising challenges to my immunity. There were voices among the Tchi who hate me more than you can imagine. The Bursteeni agreed that I was functioning under diminished capacity, but thought that I should establish it once and for all in a Bocaian court, a course of action I considered tantamount to suicide. The K'cenhowten didn't offer refugees sanctuary. The Cid were downright creepy. That pretty much did it for the major powers. Some of the lesser races regarded me with sympathy, but none had enough clout to buck a concerted interspecies attempt to extradite me. The Confederacy, at least, wouldn't have forced the Dip Corps to give me up unless I became a much hotter issue than I am now. The Corps might not have loved me, and might have come close to giving me up half a dozen times, but they had invested in my training and could count on results from me. I was an asset, to be hoarded for as long as they had use for me.

And there was another factor I hadn't mentioned, one that outweighed all the others.

Even if possible, defection amounted to surrender.

I wasn't crazy about the human race, or the people I worked for, but I'd never been willing to give the bastards the satisfaction.

C if Negelein lived up to his advance billing.

I didn't recognize the name of his homeworld, but it was either an eccentric place or one that considered him among its more eccentric sons. Squat, neckless, round-eyed, and top-heavy, he affected an extreme form of Hammock-town's fashionable near nudity, eschewing any uniform but for a thin strip of black cloth around his waist. His chest and arms were so furry they almost rendered any further clothing superfluous anyway. His face and scalp were as hairless as the plasm human surgeons implant on burn victims on worlds without access to AIsource Medical. This had evidently been arranged to clear space on his skin for a tattooed essay in the blocky alphabet of Hom.Sap Mercantile, delivering a small-print personal manifesto in a spiral that began just over his brow and culminated with an ellipsis at the highest point. Affectation, insanity, or gesture of deep commitment to a religion I didn't even want to guess at, it made eye contact with him almost impossible. In my first few attempts to maintain a conversation with him, the words snaking along from temple to temple kept coming into focus upside down, often shutting me down in mid-sentence. Short of inserting him into a rotating tube and reading the words as he spun, I had to focus on his mouth to avoid being blind-sided by any features above his nose.

Negelein, a talented painter of both landscapes and portraits, hadn't been able to keep conventional art supplies during the eighteen years he'd served, but he'd produced many thousands of works using implants in his fingertips to daub intangible pigments on projected virtual media. He illustrated almost everything he said with finger-twitches that called forth works he'd produced on One One One: from vivid head shots of the people he spoke about to colorful panoramas of his fellow indentures working on the Habitat's upside-down horizon. He had one portrait of Warmuth, portraying her as a wide-eyed, sallow-faced gamin placed against a nondescript black background. She looked sad, vulnerable, and alone: a facile characterization that completely contradicted the impression I'd gotten from the other images I'd seen. Against that, he offered almost a dozen studies of Santiago, starting with the portrait of a woman simmering in mid-frown, backlit by a nimbus of glowing red light. It taught me nothing either. But as I studied the work, searching for an answer that wasn't there, he said, "Most of the people here didn't realize it, but their entire problem lay in the failure to recognize an alien mind."

"I suppose we're not talking about the Brachiators."

He shook his head. "No. Christina. People had a rough time seeing who she was and what she was about; they just saw this sullen little bitch who was ready to bite your head off the first time they even looked at her funny."

"Like that incident with Warmuth."

He chuckled. "Like that. And a dozen others I can name. You didn't get along with Christina. You experienced her."

"And you're saying she had an alien mind?"

He drew a curlicue in midair, dabbed a few lines underneath it, and emerged with a fair-to-middling caricature of me. "I suspect you already have a good idea what I mean, Counselor. When you get to the core of it, we're all aliens to one another, raised according to some common precepts but otherwise ruled by paradigms far removed from those of the people around us. The tragedy is that we tend to judge others by standards that may make perfect sense to us but which are more likely totally irrelevant to them. That's what you're doing to me right now, even though you're doing an excellent job of hiding it, and that's what most people did to Christina.

By the standard of their own worlds, their own heads, she was an intolerable person. But the fact is, she was as sociable toward them as she knew how to be."

The man's pontificating was beginning to wear on me. My yawn, another in a series of symptoms that my post-Intersleep crash was coming on fast, might have been just as inevitable on the most energetic day of my life. But I recovered: "What was she, then? Just socially inept?"

Another curlicue. "Think about her background. Her world had mortgaged its entire population for generations. Her family had no tomorrow greater than endless repetitions of today, no dreams beyond returning home at the end of a shift, no options beyond grinding despair and dull-eyed, grim-faced loyalty to the only possible employer. Their rights were so curtailed that they couldn't even start families without proving it wouldn't harm production. I don't even think she encountered the concept of leisure time at all until she got here. It speaks well of her independent nature that she sold herself offworld as soon as she was able to find another buyer, but by then her routines were set, and she came to work for the Corps acting out the same behavior patterns she showed at home, which happened to be: *Keep your head down. Don't make friends. Don't share confidences. Don't question orders. Submerge every personal feeling you have: just concentrate on the work and nothing but the work.* From everything she'd been taught, this was appropriate behavior. From the viewpoint of everybody else, it made her a pill and a half. Both viewpoints were accurate as long as you bought their starting positions."

"And yet," I noted, "you say you got something out of her."

"Not just say, did." He projected an image of Santiago, sitting cross-legged on one of the settlement's rope bridges while the upside-down horizon of One One One curved away in the background. She wore a form-fitting gray jumpsuit fastened tight at the neck and wrists. Her eyes were hooded, her lips thin and unsmiling, but the image stressed the bound curve of her breasts; and the way the light played across her cheeks suggested Negelein, at least, considered her uncommonly beautiful. "I run a little art class here, not a big one, but something for people to do off-hours when they're not jumping through Gibb's hoops. I have four, maybe five, students at a time. Nobody produces spectacular work, but then nobody's required to if they're only doing it for their own amusement. Christina started visiting within two weeks of her arrival here. She would show up late so she didn't have to make small talk, listen a little bit, then leave early so she didn't have to talk with anyone on the way out. The first couple of times she visited, I thought she was just deciding it wasn't for her. But then the third time she approached me in private to ask a question."

"What?"

"She asked me to explain what art was good for."

I wasn't sure I could have produced a satisfactory answer myself as art just slides off me like I'm a frictionless surface. But I did my best to look duly horrified. "What did you say?"

"Well," he said, "given that it's a major part of who I am, a major part of what I need to stay sane, and for me a major part of what makes life worth living, I could have fired off a withering reply that punished her for being ignorant. About a dozen occurred to me before I even opened my mouth. But somehow I recognized it was a well-meaning question, and said, 'If you make some, maybe you'll figure it out.' Not long after that we scheduled private lessons."

"Was she any good?"

He rolled his eyes. "*Was she any good?* Please. *Good* didn't enter into it. She'd never picked up the basics of perspective or shading or composition or even appreciation: nothing that permits a socialized eye to look at a blob of color and linework and produce the reaction, *Gee, that's pretty*.

She couldn't even produce a workable abstract. She didn't even have the background she would have needed to recognize the building blocks, and may have been too deprived of basic visual education for far too long to ever develop a meaningful imagination. But being *good* wasn't the point. Letting out her feelings was. And as she produced one hopeless, primitive piece after another, she started stumbling over the things she would have said if she had the vocabulary. The things she was too alien to say to anybody else."

"Such as."

Negelein's voice grew soft at the moment he seemed to remember that the person he'd been talking about was dead: "Such as what it was like, for her, to spend so much of her life in a cage."

His eyes welled. No question in my mind: he was seeing her. But which her? A real Christina Santiago, who had revealed herself to him? An imagined version of her he'd projected upon a woman he'd barely known at all? A woman he'd loved, or one he'd pitied? I had no doubt that his grief was genuine, but that meant nothing; some people grieve as easily as other people breathe, and the grief-stricken include some of the very same people who brought on the grief by killing.

After a moment, I asked him, "Who do you think killed her, bondsman?"

He dabbed at his eyes. "Mr. Gibb says the AIsource did, but that doesn't exactly make sense to me. I can't see the AIsource doing something that pointless. Maybe something I did contributed. Wouldn't that be a special trip through hell."

I could see him turning the wheels in his mind, concocting scenarios, working out various ways his relationship with Santiago could have led to her death. Guilty or not, he had a conscience; guilty or not, it could very well destroy him; guilty or not, he may have wanted it to.

What followed was a calculated risk, based on my own

sudden, irrational certainty that he was guilty of nothing except following his own heart. "Mr. Negelein, I'm going to have to ask you to keep this next question to yourself, and not mention it to anybody, not even Mr. Gibb."

Negelein seemed to notice me again. "All right."

"One of the lesser pieces of evidence in this case involves threatening hytex messages, containing animated simulations of violence happening to somebody currently aboard One One One. Not Santiago or Warmuth, but a possible future victim. These animations are very realistic, very detailed, and very disturbing. I suppose they qualify as art."

He sniffed. "They would certainly be *craft*."

"Yes, well, either way, is there anybody here to your knowledge that is capable of producing such work?"

He studied me through slitted eyes. "I'd have to see these messages to know."

"You can't."

"Would that be because they're classified, or because they no longer exist?"

In both cases, I hadn't been able to access the signal following the initial delivery. But he didn't have to know that. "Classified."

"I see." He rubbed his chin, looked very tired, and said, "I'm not the final judge of what people can and can't do, and I can't give you any answers about those images unless I can study them to figure out how they were made. But though a non-artist with access to source materials could use advanced AI routines to help draft that kind of thing on command, the actual quality of those pictures would depend entirely on the kind of obsession we're talking about."

"Assume extreme obsession."

He thought about it. "That would make anything possible."

Which happened to be as true for murder as it was for art.

* * *

My final interview that day was with somebody who, like Negelein, had also been mentioned several times: Exosociologist Second Class Mo Lassiter. She was one of the most solidly built women I'd ever met, muscular even by the exaggerated standards of One One One, with arms that bunched like knots beneath form-fitting black mesh sleeves. She had an olive complexion, centimeter-deep black hair that resembled fuzz, a jaw like a boulder, and brown eyes so tiny that it was next to impossible to see the whites.

Had she met me with a grimace, she would have been the very picture of a frightening thug. Instead, she offered an unforced smile. It made the difference between a face that might have bordered on grotesque and one that possessed its own, eccentric kind of integrity.

When it came to talking about people, Lassiter offered little in the way of in-depth analysis, summing up everybody I asked about in content-free, carefully nonjudgmental sentence fragments. She didn't become helpful until we began discussing the death of Cynthia Warmuth. "I've never had any doubt, Counselor. It had to be a Brachiator."

I tried to imagine the slow-moving creatures I'd seen surprising and overpowering an athletic human being. "Why?"

"Because it fits their natures. They're vicious."

The dull, barely mobile Brachiators hadn't struck me as capable of savagery. "How would that work?"

"All the usual ways. Assault, murder, open warfare, even genocide, when it suits them." She saw my blank look, and commiserated. "I know it's hard to believe. They move so slowly that it's easy to think of them as passive. But they're anything else. The truth is that they're as warlike as any other pre-tech sentients I've ever seen. They have tribes and they have territory, and they go after each other whenever it suits them."

"It's hard to imagine."

"Also hard to justify. One would think they had no reason for it. After all, why are wars fought in the first place? Sometimes out of ideology or fear, but more often because one side covets something the other side wants: territory, natural resources, wealth, what have you. Here, the AIsource made sure all of that was provided in abundance that dwarves the Brachiator population's ability to consume it—and yet when one tribe encounters another somewhere on the Uppergrowth, without detailed negotiations in advance, one of them has to change course or invite an all-out war that doesn't stop until one side is eliminated."

I had the oddest sensation of wanting to do something but didn't know what it was. "What does it look like?"

"Like a slow-motion slaughter. The two sides engulf each other, ripping and clawing. They use those knife-claws of theirs, both attached and detached, and they rip away at each other in parries and thrusts slow enough for my dear old grandma to evade. Sometimes two fighters clinch for as long as twenty minutes, half an hour, before either one succeeds in drawing blood. Sometimes their two tribes savage each other for days on end, fighting a close-quarters war that ancient human villages the same size would have probably mopped up in a matter of minutes. They move so slowly, throughout, that we have time to hover near them on floaters and watch. Sometimes we even talk to them, try to understand what they're doing and why. They find the question so stupid they can't even figure out why we ask it."

I came close to murmuring that they reminded me of human beings, but that kind of facile cynicism comes so easily to me that speaking it out loud would have been cheap. "And why do you think this explains what happened to Cynthia Warmuth?"

"The Porrinyards handled most of her training, but I took her out a few times, and just two weeks ago I had the opportunity to show her one of these battles in progress. We were hovering just below, on floaters. She saw one of the Brachs start to lose its grip and started shouting that we had to rescue it. I told her there was nothing we could do. And—"

Lassiter wiped her eyes, rubbed her chin, scrambled up the curve of the hammock to a water bottle, and allowed herself a deep gulp before returning to me, looking miserable.

I'd seen that look in so many eyes, over the years, that identifying it wasn't even hard anymore.

It was the look of somebody who had just made up her mind to confess.

"She pulled her floater between two of them: a big pair of alpha-males who hadn't even reached each other and probably wouldn't have drawn blood for another ten minutes. She told them their battle was pointless and would only result in death. She said it had to stop. She said she would stay between them to protect them both, and help them talk to each other, so nobody had to die. She said they had plenty of time to try."

"And the Brachiators?"

"Both sides involved in the battle stopped what they were doing and shouted her down. They called her a Half-Ghost and said they had no time to listen to the Dead. They said that a Ghost who interferes in the affairs in the living might soon find herself returning to the Dead."

The words hung in the air between us, resonating even as distant laughter, from some of the other residents of Hammocktown, failed to dilute the tension left by their passage.

"Why wasn't I informed of this before?"

"Because I never reported it," Lassiter said, looking everywhere but at my eyes. "I didn't see the need. Cynthia backed off at once. The Brachiators resumed their stupid little war. I took her back home, lectured her about the delicacy of our position here, and didn't let her go until she admitted that she'd acted without thinking. Later, when the Porrinyards took her for her first solo, they picked a different tribe entirely, one about three hundred kilometers from those she'd offended. It was after what happened to Santiago, but I still didn't see any reason to worry about Cynthia. Or any reason to believe that she'd get . . ."

The sentence ended there. Lassiter covered her eyes, hung her head in abject misery, and shuddered, the very portrait of personal guilt. It wasn't hard to tell that there was still something else coming, so I waited the close to two minutes it took her to provide it.

The words, when they came, seemed too soft and distant to emerge from her mouth.

"They say you're hunting scapegoats. Will I do?"

12

CRASH

I left the community hammock alone, passing a small mob of hungry indentures carrying ration boxes. I recognized about twenty of them as ones I'd interviewed earlier. The friendlier among them invited me to come in and join them.

I was famished, as I hadn't eaten either breakfast or lunch. I was also exhausted, as the rush of energy that had powered me since leaving Intersleep had begun to fail, and a break was long overdue. But I was not in the mood, so I took my bag and scrambled up a long mesh bridge to a nested bridge two meters below the Uppergrowth. That spot was advantageous mostly because somebody had been smart enough to protect it with an overhang, which kept the mesh relatively free of the dried sap I'd found covering just about everything else. It was also well out of the normal flow of indenture traffic, which meant that I could sit here, alone, enjoying a few moments of solitude after far too many crowded hours.

I could also watch from a relative height as the indentures went about the routines that ended their working day. From where I sat I observed a dozen human beings scrambling like spiders along the cables that separated one dangling hammock from another, some among them moving with the exaggerated care of those who would never be at home in this place, others zipping back and forth as if they'd never once considered any possible input from gravity.

A hammock near me jostled from the movements of the indentures inside. The material was not quite transparent, but some of the bulges I saw were quite recognizable as the knees and palms of a woman making her way to the lowest point. More bulges followed: a different set of knees and palms. At least two people, in that one.

It struck me that the residents of Hammocktown could always see, from the outside, whether or not a hammock was occupied. They might even be able to identify the inhabitants by the shape of the sag.

I wondered if anybody had recognized the telltale sag that marked the presence of Christina Santiago, in the instants before her hammock fell.

If so, nobody I found complicit in her murder would ever be able to cut their losses by admitting the sabotage but proclaiming themselves innocent of wanting to take human life. It was just impossible to claim they hadn't known anybody was home.

The crime against her suddenly seemed even more cold-blooded than the crime against Cynthia Warmuth. The Santiago incident had taken place late at night. The suns were off and the only light shone through the material of the hammocks whose inhabitants remained awake. Gibb had told me, just yesterday, that Santiago's lights had been on at the moment her cables parted. Her hammock would have been as aglow as any lantern. Our unknown saboteur would have been able to see her moving around inside. He would have been able to pick out the one moment when she seemed to have settled in at the hammock's lowest point and was therefore least likely to reach safety.

It was, of course, possible that he hadn't been that careful, that he hadn't waited around for the most advantageous moment, that he'd performed his impossible sabotage the instant he had the opportunity, and simply hoped she'd be taken by surprise.

I couldn't believe that.

The crime was too perfect. It had been committed without witnesses, using tools that nobody but the AIsource was supposed to have. It showed too much organization to believe that any part of it had been left up to chance. Sitting on my bridge of mesh, watching as silhouettes of two human beings combined to form a larger, deeper bulge in a hammock they shared, I was afraid I knew how coldly our unknown saboteur had watched, plotting for his perfect moment.

Then he had done—what? Pressed a button? Signaled confederates to act? Climbed hand-over-hand to the hammock mooring and taken care of it right then and there?

No; even assuming he had the tools in his possession, the perfect conditions he would have needed could have changed at a moment's notice, the first time some sleepy Hammocktown denizen made an unscheduled trip to the latrine. He had to do what he did at the instant nobody was watching. He would have had to arrange some kind of remote control to cut Santiago's cables the instant he thought best.

But even that would have required time-consuming, intense advance preparation, for a single human being working without allies.

And all the logical objections to him doing the job the night Santiago fell also applied to him making preparations at any point beforehand. When would he have had the opportunity to sabotage Santiago's cables with absolute assurance that he wouldn't be spotted?

Never, that's when.

He would have needed machine precision.

That brought me back to the AIsource.

The AIsource could have provided him the tools. The AIsource could have assured him the opportunity.

Hell, the AIsource were so integral to any explanation that made the crime possible at all that they rendered our mysterious, hypothetical saboteur superfluous.

Which brought me all the way back to the solution favored by Gibb and Lastogne, the one Bringen had forbidden. That the AIsource had used their tech to murder Santiago and their engineered sentients to murder Warmuth.

It was the only possible solution.

But against that, I had their fervent denial.

And my own absolute, unwavering certainty that they had been telling me some version of the truth.

I sat and thought, lulled by a wafting scent that reminded me of perfume: a flowering section of the Uppergrowth, summoning the insects that swarmed from place to place. In the rigging below, various indentures spotted me, waved, called up to see if I wanted any help, even climbed up to me to see if I wanted any company. I sent them all away, begging the need for privacy.

One One One's array of internal suns, sizzling away on the vertical shafts that supported them, dimmed, became pale ghosts difficult to distinguish from retinal afterimages, and then switched off completely, returning the world to night. The "sky" below us turned as black as any other sealed room, with but an occasional flash of light from the storms that churned in the clouds. Any AIsource mechanisms that continued flying after the onset of darkness passed by without sound and without light, confident in vision that had nothing to do with the spectrum used by human beings.

As the Habitat disappeared behind that black curtain, the drop below us seemed to stretch from profound to nearly infinite. Some of the hammocks lit up as their occupants finished their day's activities. I watched the shadows of their movements, and had no trouble picking out some people talking, others sonicing a layer of sweat from their bodies, still others gathering together in twos and threes and fours, for their off-time.

They were all islands in the darkness; and it was all too easy to imagine what this place would be like if they were gone and I had nothing but the darkness and the Brachiators for company. I tried to imagine enduring the solo overnight stay that to Brachiator eyes elevated their status from New Ghosts to Half-Ghosts: hours and hours and hours, in perfect darkness, feeling all that empty space. Some personalities might enjoy that kind of thing. I could only count myself, firmly, in the camp of those who would have been destroyed by it.

It would be so much easier to jump.

Somebody was scrambling up the mesh to my position. I summoned the expression most likely to support the pretense of everything being all right and called down: "Hel-lo?"

"Hello!" It was Stuart Gibb. "You up there, Counselor?"

I've never understood the character flaw, common to so many human beings, of asking questions that establish pre-existing knowledge of the answer. "Yes, I'm up here."

Gibb's head appeared over the edge of the mesh. The light of the nearest occupied hammock, as cast through the netting, separated his face into a stark black-and-white grid, with distorted squares exaggerating the size of the jaw. "I'm not happy to see you up here by yourself, Counselor. You're not used to local conditions and shouldn't be wandering around unescorted."

"I'm not wandering. I'm taking a break."

Gibb looked past me, as if suspecting the presence of a very short and narrow person using me for cover. "But unescorted."

"That is the very definition of a break."

His only answer to that was a pout. "Peyrin was supposed to watch out for you."

"Your people are more candid when he's not around."

He sighed, pulled himself up onto the netting, slid a little bit toward me, and came to rest still a comfortable distance away. The sag of the material here was much less than in any of the hammocks I'd seen, so it must have been significantly harder for him to justify the constant accidental body contact he'd been so helpless to avoid in our previous meeting. I wasn't sure that meant I'd misjudged him yesterday, or whether he thought some lines too obvious to cross. He looked anywhere but at me. "It is a hell of a view, isn't it?"

I said nothing.

"Ten of our people, ten, work full-time on the engineering problems alone. You'd be surprised how many of them come up, in a world this size, that never bothered us in any of the ones we've built. The AIsource have given us a few tours. There's an air-circulation system driven by turbines the size of small moons. There are heat-dispersal units around the suns, designed to keep anything too close to them from boiling. The structural stresses those verticals have to endure are enough to give our experts the screaming shakes. We keep getting moving radiation sources from that toxic sludge down below; we don't even want to know what's alive at the lowest levels. It's all so bloody arbitrary, and at the same time so bloody perfect. Sometimes, when I come out here, and wonder if there was ever a point to all this, I wonder if it's just something like the Taj Mahal or the Striding Colossus of Parnajan, just something the blips put together to prove that they could: 'Look On My Works, Ye Mighty, and Despair!' That kind of thing."

"It's one theory," I said.

"No, it's not. It's bullshit. It's just an old Dip Corps hack doing the best he can, with what little he has. I'm more concerned about you. You don't strike me as the kind of person who goes out of her way for a scenic view."

I could have pointed out that the darkness that consumed the Habitat at night was the precise opposite of scenic, as it utterly eliminated any view. Instead, I shook my head. "Nothing as frivolous as that, sir. I needed to feel the rhythms of life here. The way your people move when there's no place they particularly have to be, the way they carry themselves when there's nothing they particularly have to do. Even the sounds they make when most of them have gone inside for the night. It needed to get a taste of what it was like the night Santiago died."

He nodded. "Have you arrived at any conclusions?"

"None I'm prepared to share."

"Fair enough." He glanced at his lap, seemed to remember the bundle's presence, and tossed it over. "Nobody seems to remember seeing you eat today. So I had them put together a little package for you. Nothing special: just the usual slop that passes for food locally. It'll keep you alive, at least."

The bundle was still warm, and rich with the scents of foods I must have tasted and liked, at some point in the distant past. My stomach growled. I put the bundle aside without opening it. "Thank you. That was considerate."

He waited for me to attack my dinner and saw that I wouldn't. "Alternatively, you could save it for later and join me. I haven't had dinner, either."

"Thank you," I said, "but no. I prefer to eat alone."

Somewhere in Hammocktown, an intoxicated woman exploded in a helpless, delighted peal of laughter. A man said something arch and she laughed again. Love, or at least passion, seemed in the air. Somebody else, a little farther away, argued a deeply felt point. Somebody muttered an obscenity. The wind changed, the network of nets and cables shifted, and the story behind all those random sound fragments vanished, lost behind other atmospheric static.

Gibb, trapped with me when he could have visited any of these other more interesting places, could only look forlorn. "I really wish you'd loosen up, Counselor."

"You wouldn't be the first."

"Ah." He cast about for something else to say, and settled on being the voice of authority. "Well, if you're determined to eat alone, maybe you should go back to your quarters. I am responsible for your safety, after all, and I wouldn't want you to have an accident or something—"

"I understand. But if you don't mind clearing up some things, first —"

The shift to official business, however grim, freed him from any further need to figure out just what the hell else to do with me. "Go ahead."

"First," I said, ticking off three names on my fingers, "Robin Fish, Nils D'Onofrio, and Li-Tsan Crin."

"Yes."

"Why haven't they been transferred?"

He became a martyr, unjustly accused. "Have they been complaining?"

"Answer the question."

"I've answered it many times before," he said, which was giving away more than he intended, since none of those occasions had involved me. "There's no reason to transfer them. Confinement to the hangar may not be pleasant for their respective egos, but we do need a full-time staff to maintain those shipboard facilities, and those free do an excellent job providing support for those of us who have proved we can perform the job out here."

"Yes," I said, "I've heard that. But none of the busywork you assign them actually requires three people—not when Fish, who was stuck there alone for almost a full year, was able to handle those responsibilities, and others you've since taken from her, all by herself before Crin or D'Onofrio were ever sent there to help her."

"Yes, she was," Gibb said, with the kind of heat that came from repeating an old and familiar argument. "But only just. Her morale has never been exactly high. I didn't curtail her duties because of overwork, but because she wasn't performing satisfactorily at the few jobs she had. Her performance has deteriorated even further since Nils and Li-Tsan showed up; from what I gather, even they consider her worse than useless."

"So you don't need her."

"We could survive without her, but we do the best we can with the people we have."

"You arranged her assignment here in the first place," I said.

"That's right. I met a young, ambitious, and determined indenture, trapped in what she considered assignments without a future, who begged, at length, for my help getting her a posting more in line with her self-proclaimed talents. I was impressed with her and remembered her when I needed people to staff my facility here. It turned out that she was much better at self-promotion than she was at delivering on her promises, but what could I do? She was already *here* by then."

I'd just been fed about fourteen different flavors of self-contradictory bullshit and told it was all the same shade of vanilla. "So are they necessary, or not? Do you need all three of them, or not? Do they do an excellent job, or are they worse than useless, or what?"

Gibb was getting fed up with this line of questioning. "Let's just say we might be a little overstaffed in that area, though not entirely by choice."

More bullshit. In the absence of any other agenda, refusing to transfer them was vindictive, wasteful, and stupid. But only in the absence of any other agenda.

"Second question. Peyrin Lastogne. The man has no Dip

Corps file. He has no Confederate file. He's not even an official member of your delegation. But his authority, here, seems second only to your own. Who the hell is he?"

Gibb showed teeth. I don't think I could call it a smile. "That's classified."

"I'm cleared for that kind of information."

"I'm sorry, Counselor, but I'm afraid you're not."

This was outrageous. "In any investigation of this kind, the Judge Advocate's office has total access to—"

"—to less than the Judge Advocate imagines," Gibb said. He did smile then, the kind of unsympathetic smile customer service representatives of major transport lines use to hide their schadenfreude when dealing with troublesome passengers whose belongings have been accidentally dumped into the coldest regions of deep space. "I'm sorry, Counselor. But this comes from the very top. Mr. Lastogne is off limits."

One of my earliest assignments, about a decade ago, had been to support a task force investigating allegations of high treason in the Confederate Executive Branch. We'd questioned Cabinet members on a daily basis. Nobody, not even the president, had been off limits to us then, which had turned out to be a good thing, since we soon discovered a link to the whereabouts of the fugitive terrorist, Magrison, among the members of the first family. (He still remains at large.) My authority now was at least as high as that shared by the task force then. But sometimes bureaucrats of middling rank, like Gibb, put up more of a fight than the people at the top, who know what their limits are. "All right, then. Without giving up any particulars, is information about his background in your own possession?"

Here came that apologetic smile again. "I only know what I'm cleared to know."

"You can't even tell me if you've been informed?"

"I'm saying that my knowledge is far from total, and that I'm not cleared to answer that kind of question."

To hell with this. "Fish told me you've taken control of all communication in and out of this Habitat."

"Yes, but that's just a security concern. Our position here is such that—"

His last three words were obliterated as I spoke over him. "I don't need to know your position here to make this particular point, sir. I intend to issue a report to New London tonight. I will send it through you, because that's the way you've set yourself up here, but I will send it coded. Any attempt by you to read that communication before transmission, or to censor its content, will be detected and taken by the Advocate's office as obstruction of justice. Do I need to advise you of the seriousness of that charge?"

Gibb's face was a portrait of repressed anger. "You don't have to act like this, Counselor. I've been nothing but cooperative."

"You've been nothing, period," I said.

Which was excessive. I regretted saying it the second the words left my mouth.

But if you must make enemies, you might as well make make sure you can expect them to stay that way.

Making Gibb escort me to my hammock may have amounted to salting the wound, but I had no choice. The route was vertiginous enough in daylight and might have killed me after dark.

Dropping dead of fear or falling off a rope bridge would have amounted to a cruel practical joke on any investigators who replaced me. They'd no doubt think I was the latest victim of this increasingly murderous conspiracy, and neglect any number of reasonable explanations for the deaths of Warmuth and Santiago that failed to account for my own.

And that's just if their own deaths were connected. If they were unconnected, then the confusion caused by my also irrelevant passing would be even worse. Imagine anybody trying to float the theory that three different difficult women all died, one after another, from a series of stupid coincidences.

The first person to suggest that unlikely possibility would no doubt find herself marked as a prime suspect.

I preferred not to burden strangers with problems like that.

Not that I'd have the luxury of feeling any guilt if the eventuality came to pass.

The hammock smelled of the previous night's sweat. I slid down the slope, practicing how to stop midway so I wouldn't find myself trapped at its lowest point. My progress was minimal. Scrambling back to the circular spine, with somewhat more effort than it would have taken Gibb or the Porrinyards, I tied my bag to one of the restraining hooks, then used one of the cables there to secure myself as well. It wasn't comfortable, but it felt more secure than coming to rest at the hammock's lowest point.

Temporarily satisfied, I inhaled the dinner Gibb's people had packed for me, then activated the hytex and composed a text message to Artis Bringen, confirming that I was on the job but leaving out any of the findings or theories I'd come up with so far. Most Advocates on my level, investigating incidents at remote locations, send obsessively detailed daily updates, documenting every single movement. I'd trained Bringen to tolerate vagueness, on the theory that the less I told him during my investigations, the less I'd have to deal with his second-guessing. I did assure him that while early inquiries seemed to support the theories he'd relayed (unspoken: that the AIsource were as guilty as sin), unforeseen developments suggested a number of other possible interpretations (unspoken: that the search for a scapegoat was proceeding without hitch, thank you). The politician in him would take comfort in that much, and I needed him happy so I could pump him for certain information I wasn't getting here.

I have had difficulty accessing Confederate files on a Peyrin Lastogne, who is operating as second-in-command under Stuart Gibb.

At this juncture I have no particular basis for suspecting Mr. Lastogne of any involvement in these crimes. His reputation on-site seems to be exemplary. However, I cannot eliminate him from consideration until I am provided his background and diplomatic record. Please forward this information as soon as possible.

I almost sent it, but then thought of something else.

Also, you mentioned that my services were specifically requested by several parties on-site. Neither Gibb nor Lastogne will admit to making this request. As they screen all mail, there seem no other possible sources. Please clarify.

I almost asked him another question, *Why would the AI-source say I'm wrong about you?* but demurred. That was an issue for a face-to-face meeting, if I even bothered bringing it up at all.

To counter the local protocols that funneled all such messages through Gibb and Lastogne, I scrambled the text and added a subroutine that would reduce the entire message to gibberish if opened by anybody other than Bringen.

A version of that gibberish, forwarded back to me, would provide confirmation, if necessary, that neither Gibb nor Lastogne could be trusted.

I might have done more, but that's when a fresh wave of exhaustion washed over me.

The delayed-reaction systemic crash that always follows Intersleep by a couple of days is nobody's idea of fun. I've been known to show up at an assignment burning with energy only to later nod off in the middle of a conversation. The supplements I took upon every waking, some of which were prohibited within the Corps, saved me from the worst of it, but I was always hit sooner or later. Between that and the environment on One One One, I was well overdue.

I was not just slow on the uptake right now. I was downright stupid.

Which is one main reason why I failed to be alarmed by the way the gray-green material of my hammock kept wavering in and out of focus.

The effect reminded me of the gray spots I sometimes see in bright light. They're almost impossible to discern, but they look like little translucent specs of gray receding toward a distant vanishing point. For a few years in my adolescence I thought they were symptoms of the same madness that overcame me on Bocai. Then I mentioned them to one of my doctors and he laughed, assuring me that they were just a common symptom of eye fatigue, experienced by all human beings and not just those guilty of war crimes. They're maddening, because it's futile to focus on them: the more you concentrate, the more they remain indistinct blurs, surfing the edge of the eye's ability to perceive them.

The material of the hammock, lit by the glowing edge of the circular spine, was alive with spots just like those, visible one second, invisible the next. I focused on the effect and found myself drifting, aware of nothing but the sight before me, my thoughts growing duller and more obscured by fog with every instant.

I knew sleep was coming. I could feel the increasing heaviness of my eyelids and the increasing numbness of my limbs. I felt my mouth drop open and my lower jaw brush my chest. I jerked awake, with the sudden jolt of alarm that sometimes interrupts a doze, but recovered, curled my lips into a half-smile, and almost immediately began to relax again.

I think I felt at peace.

A hammock is a nearly perfect bed, after all. It allows the body to seek its own most comfortable position. The give of the material feels comforting, almost womblike. It may be hard for someone afraid of heights to relax on such a thing, when it's hanging so many kilometers above the nearest solid surface, but once exhaustion takes over, the simpler instincts start to dominate. Oblivion called out to me, in a way it never had in bluegel and rarely did in sleep.

I felt a light breeze on my skin, and stirred in sudden concern. But nothing all that terrible happened, so I fell back asleep.

The dreams that came were not so bad.

I was a little girl of three or four, playing with Mommy and Daddy. For once, I didn't remember them solely in terms of the tragedy on Bocai. I remembered them sitting together at a table, laughing at some joke I was too young to understand. My father seemed happy, my mother downright merry. For the first time in many years I remembered that she'd been a little taller than my father, who had not been a short man; when they faced each other her eyes addressed his from a height advantage of several centimeters. Her arms had been tanned to a fine leather by a life of working in the sun. Her eyes had been surrounded by a starbust of little crinkles. She'd been stingy with smiles, except when I'd said or done something precocious.

Usually, when I thought of my parents at all, it was not often with anything beyond contempt for the two reckless utopians whose experiment had damned me to spend the rest of my life carrying such a load of insupportable guilt. I almost never thought of them as Mommy and Daddy, and the novelty warmed me for a while, even as I sighed with vague concern over a certain loss of tension in the material that cradled me.

My dreams shifted, passed through a succession of other settings, and turned to the erotic. This was even rarer, as I'd shut off that part of myself, too, after the abuses I'd suffered in isolation. For the first time in longer than I could remember, I imagined being touched by others, without recoiling in revulsion or resentment: hands that emerged from a fog I couldn't penetrate to caress my face, my thighs, my breasts. I couldn't tell whose hands they were, or even if they were supposed to belong to any specific person at all. I just knew that they wouldn't hurt me, and I felt a warmth that rose from my deep, cold center to envelop every frozen part of me. Even in the vagueness of my dream, I felt a little sadness at the thought that, of course, I couldn't see the face of the unknown lover responsible for making me feel this way, because being the monster I was meant that no such person could ever, possibly, exist. But that regret went away, too, because in a moment I felt everything that had held me back let go all at once.

I felt like I was flying.

The stern voice of a man I despised boomed in my ear:

"Andrea! Wake up if you want to live!"

I resisted the summons, thinking only, *Bringen? What the hell is Bringen doing here? Bringen should be nailed to his desk at New London, pulling the wings off various species of fly. He doesn't care about me. I could be bobbing around in vacuum with less than thirty seconds of air left and he wouldn't work his index finger enough to push the airlock button. He certainly wouldn't travel halfway across inhabited space to join me in upside-down land. No, he wouldn't do that. . . .*

I don't know how many places my mind went after that, but sooner or later the phrase *upside-down land* reverberated enough for me to remind me that I was on One One One, a place where people had been known to fall from great heights.

I woke up just in time to realize I was looking down at my own legs, dangling loose over a sky lit, for just this instant, by a faraway burst of lightning. Something else, large and shapeless and flapping, was tumbling out of sight, impossible to identify as it was swallowed up by darkness.

Then I began to fall.

13

ABYSS

The tether I'd used to connect myself to the hammock's solid rib pulled me up short just before I could decide that I was dead.

It jerked taut at the base of my spine, startling the breath out of me and arresting the plunge of my midsection even as my upper torso, and limbs, attempted to continue falling. I bent over double, grunted, thrashed in panic as I spun like a toy at the end of my line, and came close to fainting in shock.

All at once I knew someone was trying to kill me.

I'd like to report that my rage was all by itself enough to keep away the terror.

I can't say that.

I think I vomited before it occurred to me to scream.

I'm not sure whether I did or not because I didn't remember doing anything, and while I tasted the acid in my throat, there wasn't anything anywhere on me. Whatever I'd lost was now well on its way to the lower atmosphere of One One One.

I gagged, tasted blood, realized I was spinning, and only then tried to scream, without any success at summoning voice.

Far below, the clouds of One One One rumbled from another internal storm. One formation lit up, backlighting the outline of another dragon in flight. I had the lunatic thought that it didn't deserve to have such fine wings, almost surrendered to hysteria again, and in a single burst of sheer frenzy whipped my head around to see if anything at all remained solid above me.

Not much did.

The hammock's circular spine was still intact, as were most of the bundles still attached to it; a few, containing items I'd never bothered to investigate, had gone missing. My own bag, with all its personal treasures, still hung from its tether. Everything below the circular spine was missing, and (now that I looked), much above it. The upper regions of the hammock were covered with little black spots.

I don't eat apples. But the black spots made me think of one, infested with worm trails.

I found voice and screamed.

"HELP! FOR JUJE SAKE, SOMEBODY HELP ME!"

Silence.

No response whatsoever.

I screamed again, this time requesting specific people. Lastogne; no answer. Oscin and Skye; no answer. Oskar Levine, on the grounds that us outcasts needed to stick together. Nobody answered. The only sounds were my own ragged breath and the wind brushing over the sections of canvas that still remained.

I started cursing them.

Still nothing.

Maybe I was the last one left.

Maybe all the tents had failed, the same way mine had, and all of Gibb's people were already dead and falling.

Maybe the AIsource had exercised their claimed ability to kill every human being on One One One.

Maybe I should just wriggle free of this tether and let myself fall.

I bit my lip in anger. *No, dammit. Use your head.* There was still light shining from up above, both through the holes in the canvas and through the canvas itself. Its only likely source was the superstructure of Hammocktown. There hadn't been any of the changes in the quality or the intensity of that light, which suggested that the nets and rope bridges were still intact. I had to believe that Hammocktown was intact as well, if for no other reason than because the unknown assassin we blamed for the deaths of Warmuth and Santiago had thus far seemed happy enough to claim victims one at a time.

If the camp couldn't hear me, there had to be another reason.

I listened, and realized that much of what I'd taken for wind was instead a soft hiss.

The bastard. Or bitch. Whatever.

They'd hiss-screened the entire hammock, to cut me off from any would-be rescuers.

I could cry for help until I scraped my throat raw, and nobody would ever hear me.

For the next few seconds, that didn't stop me from trying.

Afterward, running out of breath, managing another look above me to confirm that the holes in the canvas had grown larger and more numerous, I became angry enough to do something about it.

Had to take this one step at a time.

The tether was the only thing keeping me alive. Getting a grip on it, behind my back, was difficult as I was bobbing and spinning from my initial fall, but I managed it. It was a thin line, but a strong one, with just enough texture to make a firm grip possible. It wasn't the kind of rope I would have chosen to climb, but then I'd never allowed my life to depend on climbing a rope before.

I pulled and with tremendous strain managed to lift my body a few centimeters before exhaustion made me let go and fall again.

That was okay. I'd learned what I wanted to learn.

I reached behind my back and grabbed the line with both hands, with my favored hand, the right, uppermost. Holding on with both hands was not quite as difficult as maintaining a grip with only one, but still more than I could manage for very long.

This would have been easier facing the tether. The blood wouldn't be rushing to my head, for one thing. But I didn't need this to be easy. I needed it to be possible.

All I had to do was release the line with my left hand, move that hand just a few centimeters to a new hold directly above my right.

My left hand didn't want to let go until I screamed at it for being so fucking useless.

Then it complied.

I rose a few worthless centimeters. The strain on my arms and lower back was horrible, but at least now there was some slack on the line.

The clouds of One One One's lower atmosphere called to me. *This is stupid, Andrea, why don't you just let go and come to us? It's not like you have anything special to live for.*

Climbing just this little bit had taken more out of me than I could really afford. The position was just too difficult. One of Gibb's monkeys might have managed it, but I was not built like them. I didn't have that kind of climbing experience or upper-body strength.

To have any chance at all I had to find a way to turn around and face the line.

Another few inches gained, and the slack in the line began

to curl against my waist. Black spots swarmed at the edges of my vision. I hissed through gritted teeth and knew, with as much certainty as I've ever known anything, that I'd only have one shot at this.

Still holding on with my left hand, I released the hold I had with my right and allowed myself to roll. Throwing all my weight into the spin, I put everything I had, and a little bit more, into whipping my right arm around.

I don't know what I would have done if I'd missed it. The tether would have arrested my fall again, but I'd have been back where I started, too exhausted to start again, with the only safety line still attached to my back and still almost impossible to reach.

But my right hand found the line.

I spun, gasped as my grip almost failed to survive the counterswing, then gasped again as I righted and the line now curling in front of me whipped across my face, drawing a nasty friction burn on my cheek.

But once I stopped spinning, my body was no longer an inverted V, bent at the waist and trapped with a view of the clouds. Now I had my back to them and my eyes fixed on the remains of my hammock. The material of the upper structure had further deteriorated in the long minutes since my last close look. It was now marred by big gaping holes surrounded by clusters of smaller ones. I could see additional ribs of the same material, composing the central spine, descending from the hammock's highest point like a pair of interlocking arches, to anchor the rib in four places.

Anything I could hold on to was good news.

All I had to do now was climb up, hook my legs around the circular spine, and scramble up and over.

That was still going to be difficult, but the hard part was done, I thought.

I was wrong.

* * *

By the time I straddled the circular spine, grateful for the substantial comfort I found in contact with such a solid object, the air around me was flecked with falling snow.

Not water-snow. This was another phenomenon, resembling little flakes of ash. They tumbled around me in thin flurries, captives of One One One's high-altitude breezes, each speck a little pinprick of tan color I was only able to discern because of all the lights of Hammocktown, shining through the wreckage above me.

I didn't know what the specks were until one came to rest on the back of my hand. It was an irregular square about half the size of my pinky fingernail, neutral in texture, so light I wouldn't have been aware of its arrival at all had I not been watching at the moment. There were probably any number of flakes just like it already dotting my skin and in my hair. This one seemed to be sizzling, though I couldn't feel any difference between its temperature and that of the surrounding air. Even as I watched, a small hole formed in its center, and the straight lines of the outer perimeter turned saw-toothed as bits and pieces of it dissolved into nothingness.

It was a piece of my hammock.

The process responsible for dissolving the lower half was still hard at work on the upper portions.

The loose canvas at my side rippled in the wind. I tightened my thighs around the thin rail and probed the cloth with my left hand.

It felt softer. Fuzzier. The more it broke down, the more pitted and rutted its surface became. The imperfections may not have been visible to the naked eye, but they did change the texture, and my fingertips could feel the difference.

Whatever was happening here didn't seem to be affecting the hammock ribs, yet, but I had no guarantee that they'd remain intact forever.

I yelled again, testing the hiss screen: "HEY! HELP! I'M OVER HERE!"

Then listened.

Nothing.

I couldn't tell whether I was still within the hiss field, or outside it in a Hammocktown where everybody else had died, but either way, my options remained limited.

I had to get to solid ground.

Unfortunately, I was on the far side of the circular spine, opposite the bridge to the rest of the community. To get there I'd have to use the spine as a tightrope. The sections of hammock still remaining intact would only hinder me in that attempt. I couldn't straddle the spine, let alone walk upright, in any of the places where material flapped. Nor was I sure I had enough will left to move at all. I couldn't think of the emptiness below me without wanting to close my eyes and shut myself down.

The only solution to that was to start moving.

First things first: retrieving my bag. I'd tethered it before tethering myself, and I wasn't willing to surrender it.

I reached over, grabbed the shoulder strap, and looped it over my head.

Then I undid its tether.

Fear flared when I realized that it was as vulnerable now as I was . . . and that there were any number of ways it could unbalance me and pull me over the side.

I didn't allow that thought to lead to considerations of dropping it.

More snow flurries around my head.

Canvas shrapnel tumbled past me, and into the void.

The tent above me had deteriorated enough to reveal the Uppergrowth. Three Brachiators dangled in plain sight, their broad, shaggy backs blind to me. One bore a little baby Brachiator, one-tenth the size of its mother, clinging to her back with equal determination.

I considered finding some way to signal them, maybe getting some help, but changed my mind as soon as I realized that any one of them could have been responsible for what was happening to me. Even if not, just what could they do to help anyway? They weren't exactly the most agile creatures I'd ever known.

I had to do this myself.

Another flurry of canvas snow.

Somebody right behind me said, "Why don't you just fall?"

It wasn't an implanted thought but an implanted sound, unmuffled by static or distance.

It was neither male nor female, young or old, mad or sane: just a slick, measured everyvoice, flensed of everything that might have given it character. Only the words themselves betrayed its malicious nature.

"It's not like you haven't considered the option," the voice continued. "The Dip Corps knows how much of your waking time you spend thinking about it. In the files they never let you see, they call you a third-tier suicidal personality, of the sort that automatically imagines self-destruction as the easiest possible solution to every serious problem, before your intelligence kicks in and you concoct another solution you like more. The analysts among your keepers like to credit that tension between your self-destructiveness and your self-preservation for your success as an investigator."

I didn't know who this unknown Heckler was. There was nothing in the voice to recognize. But the arrogance was familiar. This was the same cruel bitch, or bastard, who had sent me those hate mails. If it was also the perpetrator responsible for killing Warmuth and Santiago, then my current lifespan was probably measurable in minutes.

Good. Minutes were an improvement when fighting seconds. Now all I had to keep was the shithead talking. "N-nice to know."

"They also compile yearly studies on your emotional state, as well as the immediate likelihood of your self-destructive side ever getting what it wants, in order to maximize your potential as a diplomatic asset. Would you like to know your current stats, Counselor? Would you enjoy a pie-chart measuring just how much you think your life is worth?"

I used the nearest vertical rib to guide myself to a standing position. After about ten seconds of sheer hell, I managed to get to my feet without killing myself. I didn't straighten up all the way, as there was still loose material billowing around just over my head, and one flap in the face could have knocked me over the edge and sent me on an unwanted tour of the lower atmosphere. But I did manage an uneasy crouch, with knees bent and feet balanced.

My training had never covered tightrope walking. Even if it had, it wouldn't have covered walking a beam that curved. When fighting vertigo, a straight line requiring a forward stride is about a hundred times easier than a curve requiring a miniature course correction with every step.

But all I had to worry about right now was the distance between me and the next vertical support. That wasn't too far. It gave me something to aim for. I could manage both speed and accuracy that long.

I stood there, trembling, rehearsing my moves a thousand times in the space of a second.

Just as I took the first step, the Heckler spoke again.

"There's even a contingency plan. You should know about this one, Andrea. It's really quite clever. You see, the people who use you, who rely on your skills and reap the benefits of your accomplishments, who have sheltered you from the same fate afforded the rest of the surviving Bocaian colonists, do value you, in the way they'd value any other useful tool. They intend to hold on to you for as long as they can. But they also know that you might not always be as useful as you are now, and foresee any number of circumstances where you might, someday, become a liability. In such an event they know any number of ways to turn your third-tier personality to their advantage. They've considered how to arrange circumstances where you'd be likely to turn that famous anger of yours inward. And the second you surrender to the inevitable, they'll gnash their teeth and wring their hands and wax rhapsodic about the deeds of the public servant who had overcome such a tragic beginning to accomplish so much. They might even feel bad. But they won't mourn. Because nobody mourns a monster, Andrea."

I was on my knees, hugging the vertical rib I'd aimed for. "Nobody . . . asked them to."

The twenty steps had taken only a few seconds to travel. Recovering from the sheer terror of the journey had kept me mute and paralyzed a full minute after that. My belly had become a pit of ice, my heart a runaway engine intent on ripping free of my chest.

"I should tell you everything," the Heckler continued.

I rose to my feet, balancing myself on that last section of rib, trying not to wobble and knowing I would anyway, working up enough nerve for the last rush to safety.

"Because that's the way your mind works. You've survived this long because you refuse to die when there's still something left to know. You can't go without knowing the faces of your Unseen Demons."

Juje! Is there anybody here who doesn't know that phrase?

No. Forget that. That's just an attempt to rattle you. Concentrate on the road ahead. There won't be a perfect moment. The more I stay here trying to work up sufficient nerve, the more hopelessly spastic I'll become. The only choice is to go.

But my arms refused to relinquish their grip.

"But if I tell you everything, you lose that excuse for living. Should I tell you, Andrea? Would that give you an excuse to jump?"

I balanced myself as best as I could and launched myself on my journey across that final quarter-section of rib.

Five steps in and I knew I was in trouble. I was already leaning far too far to my left, and beginning to lose my balance. Momentum still propelled me forward, but I was not so much running as falling in slow motion.

My right foot caught the rib at a glancing angle instead of a secure one and it went out from under me and gravity took hold, and I pinwheeled my arms and for just one moment managed to avoid toppling—and in that second pivoted almost one hundred and eighty degrees while catching sight of a pair of familiar figures hopping off the edge of a rope bridge that I would never survive to reach.

I recognized them as the Porrinyards.

The gesture pissed me off. Why were they so eagerly killing themselves? This was *my* moment to die.

Then I was in free fall and I knew that these last several minutes had been nothing but a delaying action, because I was dead, and that stupid hateful voice had been right about me not wanting to die with so many questions unanswered.

I never fainted. Had I continued to fall, I would have remained wide-eyed and terrified, recording every millimeter of that endless, inevitable plunge to dissolution in the storms below.

But I never saw the arc of the other bodies, falling up to meet mine.

14

RETREAT

The Porrinyards half escorted, half carried me to the communal tent where I'd conducted the bulk of the day's interviews, applied a buzzpatch sedative that didn't alleviate the residual aftereffects of terror so much as wrap them in soft, sweet-smelling flowers, and stayed beside me for the two minutes it took to summon Gibb and Lastogne.

When Lastogne showed up, he paused at the tent flap to drive back the small mob of indentures attempting to enter with him. I heard men and women, some of whom I recognized by voice, peppering him with questions. Some had to do with whether I was okay, others had to do with what the hell had happened, and still others had to do with whether the danger was over. He told them to take it easy and give him room. They did both with minimal protest. He may have been an irritating son of a bitch, but he knew how to make his authority stick.

As he came in, sealing the flap behind him, I saw that he'd donned a pair of long-sleeved gray pullovers, covering everything but his hands and feet. Puffy, sleep-deprived eyes, and a circle of bare, pale skin at the site of his ROM prosthesis, furthered the impression that he'd come in a hurry. He slid down the canvas to Oscin's side and demanded, "Is she all right?"

"You can try asking her," I said.

He didn't quite manage to hide surprise. "Forgive me, Counselor. You looked a little catatonic there."

"I'm in shock, which isn't even remotely the same thing."

His lip curled, in a combination of annoyance and admiration. "My apologies. Do we have any idea what happened?"

I resisted making a snide comment over his use of the pronoun we. "Some kind of dissolving agent turned my hammock to confetti."

"How fast?"

"Minutes."

The Porrinyards, bracketing me on both sides, moved a little closer. "She almost didn't make it out."

"I didn't make it out at all," I said. "You pulled me out."

That glimpse I'd caught of them, jumping off the edge of the rope bridge, had proven only the first step in an insanely intricate trapeze-act manuever they'd plotted and executed at the very instant they'd seen me about to fall. Oscin had clung to the bridge by his knees and ankles, securing Skye so she could wrap her arms under mine on her upswing.

Coordinating their movements with such instant perfection had been easy enough, given their abilities. Holding on to me and my bag during my ten seconds of full-tilt, convulsive panic had been considerably more difficult.

They'd almost lost me.

Worse, at least from their point of view—Oscin had almost lost Skye.

I'd thrashed so hard that Oscin had lost his grip on one of Skye's ankles. They'd had only a second to decide whether to drop me or keep holding on.

I tried to imagine what it would have been like for them,

if Skye had fallen. Oscin's body would have remained safe, but he would have felt every sensation she felt as she plummeted through the clouds, just as she would have felt every sensation he felt as he remained safe high above her. Both halves of their shared personality would have felt safety and damnation at the same time, as half of everything they were died. Turning away would not have been an option.

Oscin would have known every single moment of Skye's agony.

And yet they'd held on to me anyway.

The worst of the things I didn't know, at this moment, was just how I felt about that.

Lastogne rubbed his jaw with a dark amusement that simultaneously acknowledged and mocked the gravity of the moment. "Good work, people. I'll speak to Gibb, and make sure he takes some time off your contract."

"No need, Peyrin. I wasn't doing it for extra credit."

"Too bad. You're getting it anyway." He turned to me. "And you, Counselor. You do know what you're describing, don't you?"

I resented having to think. "I could be describing any number of things. A lone human being could arrange an effect like that with a chemical agent."

"But you don't seriously believe that."

"No, sir, I don't. Even if somebody could smuggle a large quantity of a dangerous substance on-station, and apply it without anybody noticing, our postmortem investigation would be all too likely to identify it from traces on the hammock superstructure. Our culprit doesn't strike me as the type to leave that kind of obvious footprint."

"We'll still have to check," Lastogne said.

"I expect you to. But I'm pretty certain you'll only be eliminating it from possibility."

"Me too. So, you suspect—"

I spoke the damning word without inflection. "Nanotech."

It was hard to avoid noticing how completely Lastogne's glance at Oscin ignored Skye. "You saw it?"

"The last few seconds," the Porrinyards said.

"And you concur?"

"Yes. That's what it looked like."

Nobody said the obvious. The low-tech conditions constraining Gibb's people specifically excluded access to microdisassemblers. Within the Habitat, only the AIsource were supposed to command that kind of tech. This incident incriminated them even more clearly than the Santiago killing, even without considering the unseen Heckler, who I wasn't ready to mention.

Another flurry of raised voices later, the hammock flap opened again, this time admitting the flushed and sweaty Gibb, who was wearing an open vest and a pair of shiny silver briefs tight enough to display his personal assets in extreme detail. I would have liked to believe that the emergency had interrupted him during some personal down-time, and that in rushing to my side he'd been in too much of a hurry to change into something less ludicrous, but this was Hammocktown and we were talking about Gibb. Either way he slid down the canvas to the knot of us congregated at its lowest point, and immediately made the same mistake Lastogne had: "Is she all right?"

I said, "I must look downright brain-damaged."

His reluctance to address me directly was so palpable that when he jerked his head in my direction, it was hard not to imagine the snap of invisible strings. "So? Speak."

"Bottom line?" I said. "There's been more sabotage, by an enemy you can't predict or identify, whose attacks on your facility have been growing more frequent, more elaborate, and more contemptuous of your authority. You don't have the knowledge or the tools you need to protect your people, and there's every reason you believe that your lives will be in more danger tomorrow and in even more danger the day after that. Remaining in Hammocktown, at this point, leaves everybody at risk and complicates my investigation for no good reason. It could only be sanctioned by an obstinate fool, driven more by his own self-destructive pride than any vestigial concern for the lives of the people who depend on his good judgment. I have problems with your management style I haven't even mentioned yet, sir, but you're not the person I just described. We both know what you have to do."

I'd seen looks just like Gibb's from any number of people who wanted to hit me. The length of time they hold the look has always been inversely proportional to the chances of them acting on the impulse. Gibb held his for close to a minute. "Do you know what retreat means, for someone in my position?"

I did. If the Dip Corps later judged the retreat avoidable, the black mark on his record could very well stigmatize him for the rest of his career. I could only counter, "How many people are you willing to sacrifice to keep your reputation?"

More silence. And then all the air went out of him at once, draining away his anger and leaving a man resigned, defeated and old. "Peyrin?"

"Yes, sir?"

"Go out and count heads. Make sure we didn't lose anybody else while we were in here babysitting the Counselor."

"And?"

"Tell them to collect their essentials. We're leaving."

Hammocktown didn't have enough skimmers to carry out a full evacuation, but once contacted the AIsource were happy to supply us with a fleet of ten. It was hard not to see the sudden wealth of free transportation, on this station not designed to accommodate a human presence, as more evidence that they'd been trying to get rid of us all along. Gibb was not the only person who muttered a few angry words to that effect as we boarded the vessels and left the sad, hanging corpse of his outpost behind.

I don't know how many others imagined every gleaming carrier in that fleet obeying AIsource orders to simply discard us from a height, but that image occurred to me early, and dominated the nastier side of my imagination long enough to give me serious second thoughts as I boarded a skimmer that already held Lastogne, the Porrinyards, and a purple-haired, saucer-eyed female I hadn't questioned yet. But bugging out had been my idea in the first place. So I took my place beside the Porrinyards, and made room for the final two passengers, including another young man unknown to me, and Oskar Levine, who didn't sit until he was satisfied that I was all right.

As we pulled away, the Skimmer itself called my name.

Andrea Cort.

I said, "Yes?"

I don't blame you for not recognizing me, but I'm the same skimmer that conversed with you on your arrival. I was concerned about you then and I'm concerned about you now. Has your stay here been as difficult as this sudden mass departure implies?

I glanced at the Porrinyards, who for once reacted as individuals: Oscin with an encouraging smile, Skye with a charming little shrug. Levine, sitting behind them, just shook his head. Nobody else seemed available for comment.

Might as well. "Don't you know?"

One of the many ways we preserve individuality among our components is by restricting some of us to limited perspectives. To put it in terms you might respect, nobody ever tells me anything.

Levine muttered, "Sounds like a true brother under the skin."

Lastogne murmured something about finally, at long last, meeting an AIsource program he could get along with.

The suns were still out, but the skimmer was equipped with lights for the convenience of its organic passengers, and provided a moving spotlight on the Uppergrowth a few meters above us. Our poky rate afforded us clear views of any Brachiators we passed; most were moving at a pace so deliberate that human eyes interpreted it as the next best thing to complete immobility. I couldn't tell whether they noticed us or not, and after a moment decided that I preferred not. They were like many pre-technological races we'd encountered, in that they had been perfectly comfortable without us.

Once we left, they'd forget us in a generation. Maybe earlier. We were "Ghosts," after all. Some of us more than others.

The skimmer persisted in its delusions of helpfulness. ***Do you need any special assistance, Andrea Cort?***

I said, "Can you get a message to the entities in charge?"

Of course.

"Fine," I said. "Tell them that I want another private audience, at their earliest convenience. And while you're at it, tell them I'm tired of their fucking games."

The hangar may have been a vast open space, dwarfing the Dip Corps transport, but human frenzy is large enough to fill any empty room known to sentient life, and the overwhelming impression Gibb's evacuees inflicted on their surroundings was indeed frenzy. Indentures ran in and out of the hangar, using flats and freight drivers to ferry salvaged supplies to a makeshift storage area between the ship and the hangar bulkhead. Robin Fish and Nils D'Onofrio occupied themselves inflating an array of emergency sleepcubes along the opposite wall. D'Onofrio worked at twice Fish's speed, moving with a swift, confident efficiency that spoke well of his willingness to work when work was provided. Fish just seemed to drag herself from place to place, expending minimal effort to minimal effect. It didn't strike me as laziness so much as adherence to a different time scale: she didn't seem to feel the passage of minutes at the same rate the rest of us did, instead adopting a rate the Brachiators might have appreciated. I wondered again just what drugs might have been coursing through her veins, in addition to any blood she still had room for.

Some of the indentures wobbled as they walked, reflecting what may have been a long interval since their last walk on solid ground. Others bore the shell-shocked, disbelieving expression common to all refugees. Still others seemed defiant or even amused. I saw tears, hugs, jokes, more than a few stolen kisses, and a couple of minor shoving matches. When Cif Negelein ambled unseen in the midst of it all, fluttering his hands like doves, I thought him in the midst of a major emotional breakdown until I glimpsed the light in his eyes and realized that he was virtually sketching the scene, filtering the unbearable through the lens of his own beloved art.

A few minutes into the general chaos Gibb called out for attention, his voice a lost thin note that went unnoticed until Lastogne provided his own sharp "All right, people! Listen up!"

Everybody stopped.

Gibb winced, shot Lastogne a look, and cleared his throat in an unsuccessful attempt to pretend that hoarseness was the only reason he hadn't been heard. "Right. I just want to say that, as far as I'm concerned, this situation here, this . . . retreat . . . is just temporary. We're not leaving One One One, nor are we abandoning our duties here. We'll use skimmers to continue our observations inside the Habitat, and with any luck return to Hammocktown upon the conclusion of this investigation." He licked his lips, cast about for something else to say, found nothing, and looked to me. "Counselor? Do you have anything to add to that?"

I shook my head. "That covers it."

He seemed dismayed by my failure to provide a dramatic

closer. "Well, uh, all right, then. Everybody, go back to setting up."

The only notable reaction was a gradual return to the previous noise level.

Gibb stood at the center of it, wearing the look you'd expect from a man who had just blown the most important speech of his life.

Oskar Levine, his arms fully laden with material I failed to recognize, stopped by my side. "Not exactly the most inspiring of leaders, eh?"

I found myself casting about for something to do with my hands. "That may be his greatest advantage right now."

He raised an eyebrow. "I honestly can't wait to hear how you figure that."

"An inspiring leader would have amped their emotions. He'd have blistered the air with rhetoric and shown enough courage, defiance, and self-confidence to make them eager to follow wherever he led. And, just like Gibb right now, he'd then have absolutely nowhere to go from there: not a game plan, not an exit strategy, nothing; not even the vaguest of ideas. He'd have set them on fire and then given them nothing to do with it. But treating this like just another bureaucratic inconvenience that we all just have to buckle down and muddle through, the way he just did, accomplishes something more."

"What?"

I looked him in the eye. "It makes the crisis boring."

"And that's good?"

"It is if it makes them look forward to whatever happens next."

Levine shifted his packages under one arm so he could scratch his head with the other. "You've got a great way of thinking, Counselor."

I spotted Skye in the entrance to the transport. She'd

changed into a full-body jumpsuit, too loose and all-concealing to have been one of her own. Her face was flushed and her bristled hair shiny with sweat.

Excusing myself to Levine, I avoided three or four collisions with other bustling indentures just rushing to her side. "What's wrong?"

She wiped her forehead with the back of one hand. "Beyond the obvious?"

"Please."

"Some of the Intersleep crypts need cleaning. Nothing serious, but there's one in the back that looks like it hasn't been flushed since the trip in."

I remembered Gibb telling me that the ship only had waking accommodations for four. "I thought D'Onofrio and the others were supposed to be in charge of that."

"They were, but this one's caked with dry bluegel."

I revised my previous complimentary estimate of D'Onofrio's work ethic. "Is that going to be a problem?"

"As long as we're not in a hurry to get out."

I'd done the grim math. The current complement of human beings on One One One included not only those who'd arrived on this vessel, but also a substantial number who had arrived on subsequent supply ships. The total population exceeded this ship's entire capacity by about twenty. If a full evacuation became necessary, I could squeeze in another couple of people in my own transport, but that still left a tragic number of people behind.

Of course, if it came to that, we'd all be dead anyway.

Because the only possible reason for us to leave here in such a hurry would be confirmation that the AIsource wanted us dead.

And if that was true, I couldn't come up with a single scenario that didn't end with those binary-code bastards reducing us to floating debris in space.

Which made it something not worth talking about. "Where's your other half?"

"On a flight back to Hammocktown. Some supplies got left there. We don't want to lose anything to the lower atmosphere if any more hammocks collapse. But, you know, he's here with us, too, as long as I am. Do you need something?"

"Just a few minutes of your time."

"Goodie." She ran her blue-stained fingers through her scalp-bristles and cocked her head toward the ship interior.

I followed her inside, through a cramped exit corridor, to a circular command hub containing two display consoles and bracketed by a quartet of private rooms just large enough to house fold-down beds, sonic lavatories, and narrow shelves. All four were open, but only one looked occupied, the bed down and bearing a folded blanket. Whoever lived there had installed a holo graffito, more distracting than clever: LOST LOST LOST ON ONE ONE ONE. A sack of personal items sat on the counter. I took the liberty of inspecting them and saw a name tag marking the bundle as the property of Robin Fish.

The cramped, sparse accommodations for passengers not stored in Intersleep were more than enough to explain why the height-sensitives preferred to erect sleepcubes in the relative vastness of the outer hangar. Confinement to the ship would feel more like prison.

An open hatchway at the rear of the command hub revealed only a green wall across on the other side of another narrow corridor, no doubt the route to cargo, ship's systems, the real-water shower Lastogne had mentioned, and the Intersleep crypts. Awake or asleep, it was nobody's idea of luxurious travel, but then I'd known luxurious travel once or twice in my life and found it just got me places at the same speed while forcing me to interact with the kind of people who could afford such passage.

We sat at the swivel-seats. Skye rested her left arm on the console, tilting her head to prop her temple against her index finger. Her smile was unforced, but quietly infuriating. "Shoot."

"I want to talk about what you did."

She fluttered her free hand. "No need."

"I'm afraid there is."

"Um. This isn't about thanking me, is it?"

"No. I hope to get around to that, sooner or later. But right now I can't afford to. There's too much about tonight that still needs to be explained."

Her tiny smile remained where it was. But she lifted her head off her index finger, and lowered that hand to her lap, where it joined the other in uncharacteristically prim repose. "No offense taken, Counselor. You have a job to do. What would you like to know?"

"How come you were the only ones who saw me?"

"The only *one*," she corrected me, showing absolutely no impatience at my refusal to retain this one essential point. "It was dark."

"Not all that dark. Hammocktown is lit at night."

"Yes, it is. But once the suns go out, and everybody's back from wherever they've flown off to, there's less reason to be up and about. People tend to settle in, alone or with friends. Traffic from tent to tent goes way down."

I remembered the Brachiator term for human beings. "A Ghost town."

The reference amused her. "A Half-Ghost town anyway."

I grinned back, despite the seriousness of the moment, but forced myself to drop it at once. "But that didn't stop you from showing up just in time."

Now she looked more than just insolent. She looked downright knowing. "That does strike me as convenient. Are you complaining?"

"No. But before we move on from here, I need to eliminate the possibility that the entire incident wasn't staged just to make me trust you."

Her smile didn't falter, but for a moment it turned absent. "Did you notice how close Oscin came to dropping us both?"

"I also know how effortlessly you caught me in the first place."

"It was far from effortless, Counselor. At the moment I decided to go for you, reaching you and bringing you back alive were already far from sure things. Catching untrained people, in situations like that, never is. There's no way to know how they're going to react. They seize hold when you need them to go limp, go stiff when you need them to grab hold, faint when you need them to react, or at the very worst treat you like something they have to climb instead of somebody trying to help. Had your need been any less immediate, I would have preferred to tell you to hang on while I summoned help. That would have been easier for me and safer for you. But instead I arrived at the last second and didn't have time to measure the chances of you reacting in some manner that would doom us both. I had to act then, right then, or lose you. And even then, I think the chance of success was, maybe, one out of three."

I didn't know what appalled me more: her estimate being that low, or that high. "Which is, again, convenient. If you like dramatic rescues."

She chuckled. "I prefer dull rescues. Less stressful."

Something was off, here. I wasn't rattling her at all. At the very least I'd expect her to be angry. "I've been rescued from other dangerous situations. I know how they tend to be spur-of-the-moment improvisations. But if we consider what almost happened to me, in light of what happened to Warmuth and Santiago, we see that all three incidents show a certain preference for theatricality. And rescuing me, in the way that you did, very much fits that overall pattern. To believe it real, I need more. Like what you were doing up and around, and that close to my hammock, in the first place?"

Her lips curled, turning that secretive smile into a broad

one, all teeth and gums and unforced hilarity. "Hallelujah. At long last, we come to the relevant line of questioning."

I waited for her to elaborate, but no go: she was going to make me ask. "What were you doing there?"

"I was coming to surprise you with a visit."

"Why?

"Because," she said, slowly and clearly and without a trace of hurt or sarcasm, "there seemed precious little chance of you inviting me."

Running an investigation like this would have been a lot easier had I possessed some kind of mystical, infallible sense separating truth from fiction. The truth is that I have no such gift. It's a good thing I'm talented at piecing together the bits that corroborate each other, because I usually can't tell the truth just by listening. I could now, because I found myself connecting the way Skye was looking at me with the way Oscin had looked at me yesterday.

It wasn't something I'd ever been comfortable with. I'd tried to live my life without it. But I had seen it before, and I did know what it looked like.

I said something stupid. "Both of you?"

Skye had corrected me on the same point, only two minutes ago. But she indulged me one more time. "There is only one of me."

It still didn't make any rational sense. This was, after all, me we were talking about, and I knew exactly how unlikable I was. It made even less sense when I considered that the Porrinyards had been treating me this way since the very first moment I'd met them.

But for once, I knew the truth just by hearing it.

Well.

This was interesting.

I didn't want it to be interesting. But, damn. It was.

I'd already noticed how beautiful they were.

I pivoted my seat away from the console, rose, tugged

a wrinkle out of my jumpsuit, and stood there feeling stupid while Skye just sat there, damnably calm, her confident smile not wavering a millimeter.

Not knowing what else to say, I ventured, "Thank you for saving my life."

She said, "We'll work out the terms later."

I offered a queasy smile, and left in a hurry, emerging from the transport just in time to see the hands closed tight on Gibb's neck.

15

ARRESTS

I heard the fight before I saw it.

A pair of angry voices, one male, one female, were both lost in the kind of argument where being heard was no longer as important as making sure the opponent was not. Both participants had passed well beyond the border that separates shouting from screaming, their voices distorted past intelligibility, their words reduced to bursts of concentrated rage.

I didn't recognize either voice. They were too distorted by volume. But in that instant before my eyes tracked the disturbance to its source, I was able to put faces to some of the other participants. I heard Oskar Levine cursing in disgust, Cif Negelein crying something I couldn't make out, and Robin Fish screaming for intervention.

Then I spotted the crowd across the hangar and caught the unmistakable sound of somebody's palm smacking somebody's face.

Then half a dozen people fell to the ground as two hurtling forms bowled over the line of spectators. A few just stumbled backward, some went to their knees, but two who caught the full brunt of the impact went down hard.

I broke into a run just as the two combatants joined those two unlucky bystanders on the floor.

Li-Tsan Crin had landed on top, screeching hatred and bile as her knees slammed hard into Stuart Gibb's abdomen. She'd wrapped her hands around his neck and dug both thumbs into the vital soft spot separating Adam's apple from windpipe. Gibb had grabbed her wrists, first attempting to break her stranglehold and, then, failing that, digging his nails into her tendons in an instinctive attempt to make his murder too painful a job for her to finish.

Before I could reach them, Negelein and Lassiter both seized Li-Tsan by her left arm and two others I didn't recognize took her right. Their combined efforts succeeded only in lifting Li-Tsan and Gibb off the deck together, in a fused ball of hate. The combined weight proved too much, and Li-Tsan took advantage of that as she once again drove the back of Gibb's head against the deck.

With Negelein, Lassiter, and the others continuing to hold on to Li-Tsan's arms, two more indentures, including a woman I'd spoken to briefly and a man I hadn't encountered at all, went in on their hands and knees to pry Li-Tsan's thumbs from Gibb's neck.

The woman yelled, "Don't make me break them, Li!"

Li-Tsan cried something so incoherent that the only word I recognized was "bastard."

The crack of bone and the sickened gasps of the crowd fought each other for the title of ugliest sound.

The two indentures responsible for snapping Li-Tsan's thumbs joined the others in pulling her off Gibb. She called them all bastards and slime-sucking sacks of shit and put all her strength into a single, two-legged, gravity-defying kick that impacted with nothing but air.

Gibb, still purple despite the release of his windpipe, pushed away a woman who had rushed to his aid and stood up, his teeth pink and his lips gleaming with blood.

"I'll fucking murder you!" Li-Tsan screeched, her fury overwhelming the mob struggling to hold her.

A woman with a shaved head went to restrain Li-Tsan's legs and was sent flying, with a freshly bruised jaw for her trouble. Another two went in low and wrapped themselves around those legs, weighing them down.

The eight people restraining Li-Tsan now comprised three on each arm and two hugging her legs like koalas clinging to tree trunks. Even rage couldn't lend Li-Tsan enough strength to overcome that many people. But though effectively helpless, she hadn't given up; she was still thrashing, still rippling every muscle, still making her captors work for every instant they held her in check. Even as half a dozen voices in the crowd called her name, trying to cut through this moment of insanity with compensating reason, she still pelted Gibb with abuse, passing from the relatively dull epithets available in Mercantile to the more vivid images afforded people who can bare to fit their tongues around the harsh consonants of Grechilissh.

I don't know much of that second tongue, a minor dialect spoken by the settlers of an industrial world not worth visiting unless you have an overbearing craving for sulfur and soot. But the very harsh and very hard-to-pronounce epithet Li-Tsan had just spat with perfect intonation was a notorious adjective applying to the practitioners of a rare, possibly extinct and most probably apocryphal perversion involving the surgical removal of visual organs to facilitate the sexual exploitation of the empty eye sockets.

You can describe the practice in Mercantile, just as in any other language, and it will always be nasty. But in Grechilissh, the word sounds a lot like what it's describing. It's nasty, painful, demeaning, and, worst of all, evocative—the kind of name you don't apply to another human being unless you really want to risk an immediate fight to the death.

Gibb's purpled complexion went a shade darker.

He went for her.

Despite the provocation, there was no way to look on what happened next as fair. Li-Tsan was being restrained by all four limbs. Gibb was free to act. Nobody made any special effort to stop him as he leaped forward and delivered a roundhouse punch to her jaw. The onlookers were still gasping from that one as he followed up with a left that shattered her nose.

At his current rate of attack he might have had time to hit her another two or three times before anybody in the crowd thought of intervening.

Long before any of them had a chance, I stepped forward and tapped my index and middle fingers to the base of his jaw.

The jolt made his muscles spasm, the eyes roll back in his head, and his bladder release. He stumbled backward, conscious but unable to regain his balance. Somewhere along the way his feet tangled up and he began to fall.

Lastogne caught him under the arms.

Everybody else froze, including Li-Tsan, whose bruised and bleeding face joined all the others now staring at me.

Gibb focused, broke from Lastogne's grip, and managed to stand. "What the hell was that, Counselor?"

I brandished the shiny metal cap I wore over both fingertips, removed it, and replaced it at my collarline, where it turned liquid and became a Dip Corps insignia again. "Insurance."

He fingered the swelling blister on his jaw. "That's not exactly standard issue, Counselor. Do you have any idea how many treaties you just broke, carrying a concealed weapon into another government's territory?"

I raised an eyebrow. "If you can prove that the device I just used has no purpose other than weaponry, quite a few. But everything's a weapon, sir. Including tools, blunt objects, and, as we've just seen, our own arms and legs. Short of amputating our limbs every time we cross a border, and being wheeled around on hand trucks by the natives, we can only assure our hosts that the items we carry with us are not weapons at the moment, and won't be used as weapons unless we find ourselves forced to improvise with the materials we have at hand."

Gibb's blister popped. He glanced at a fingertip now glistening with blood. "That's a lovely argument, Counselor. Does it ever work for any of the people you prosecute?"

"No. When I prosecute, you'll have to do a whole lot better than that."

Give Gibb credit for recognizing the implied threat. His injured jaw may have trembled as he bit back half a dozen angry responses, but he did bite them back. Li-Tsan also calmed; her captors didn't trust her enough to let her go, but she followed the exchange with a certain dry-eyed, grim-faced fascination. The lower half of her face glistened with blood from her shattered nose.

I turned my attention to the silent figure behind Gibb. "Mr. Lastogne?"

His curled lips flashed his usual amount of sardonic amusement. "Yes, Counselor?"

"Order these two people placed under arrest. Don't do it yourself, I'll want to talk to you. Make sure they're separated from each other and, as much as possible, from anybody who saw the incident from the beginning. Have them restrained if necessary. I'd rather have them isolated and in chains than closely guarded by anybody whose testimony needs to remain free of their influence." I almost wound down, but then another thought occurred to me. "Skye Porrinyard's in the transport. She couldn't have seen anything.

Draft her to watch Li-Tsan. And have Oscin help with Gibb, once he gets back."

"Will do," Lastogne said.

Gibb's hands curled into fists. "You don't have to do this, Counselor. All I did was react to being attacked."

"A few short hours after an attempt on my own life," I said. "Forgive me for feeling some academic interest in matters involving violence."

The stories offered a consistent, if not very helpful, picture.

Gibb had been spot-checking the move, offering the usual pointless managerial suggestions to professionals who didn't need his help knowing how to erect sleepcubes on a flat surface. Li-Tsan had emerged from the one where she'd been living all these months, spotted Gibb, and intercepted him before he could bother someone else. The two had discussed something, their voices low and their body language reflecting mutual antagonism, for somewhere between thirty seconds and three minutes, with more estimates weighted toward the higher end of that range. Li-Tsan had begun shouting, and Gibb had shouted back, the substance of their argument forgotten as it degenerated into two-way abuse.

Most of the witnesses said they'd missed the actual moment when words gave way to violence.

Of the few witnesses I deemed credible, three out of four agreed that Gibb had initiated the physical stage of the confrontation by slapping Li-Tsan's face. The fourth, a lithe, orange-haired indenture named Hannah Godel, refused to commit to an opinion, saying that her angle had been bad and that she couldn't be sure. I asked her if she had any special reason for not taking a stand and she said that she just didn't want to condemn somebody without being sure.

Her story had the ring of somebody with a definite opinion

who didn't want to make her own situation more difficult by sharing.

Lastogne also claimed to have seen nothing, which seemed too convenient for words. But the facts bore him out. A number of witnesses placed him just outside the hangar, helping with the supply ferries, at the moment the argument began. He had heard the raised voices, rushed in to investigate, and arrived just in time to catch the reeling Gibb.

His inability to testify to the actual event didn't excuse his failure to be any more forthcoming regarding the backstory. "I think we've already covered this, Counselor. We know why they have problems with one another."

"But isn't this the first time that's spilled over into violence?"

"Sure it is. At least as far as I know. But when you take two people who can barely contain their dislike for one another, and add a crisis, that's what you get."

It was all he had. Or at least all he offered.

I didn't question either combatant until after I was satisfied that I'd gotten all I could from everybody else. I approached Li-Tsan first for no reason nobler than the opportunity to keep Gibb waiting. Lastogne had ordered her escorted to the ship, where she'd been confined to one of the berths and fitted with a paralytic neural tap as one of the vessel's AI-source medbots, a whirring little gnat of a thing that seemed to prefer zipping back and forth between her hands and face to finishing each job one at a time, performed a quick patch-and-repair on her injuries. The tap, a routine measure to deaden her pain during the surgery, had been turned to a setting significantly stronger than the procedures warranted. It left her lying on her back, a temporary quadriplegic so infuriated by her imprisonment that I feared for the medbot's safety every time it buzzed past her mouth on its way to and from the fading injury to her nose. I kept suspecting her of wanting to grind it to foil between her teeth.

Skye Porrinyard, who I found sitting at the command console, a comfortable distance from Li-Tsan's direct line of sight, was all business as designated guard. She confirmed that Li-Tsan had said nothing of value and reported that Oscin was expected to return within forty-five minutes.

I thanked her, asked her to leave, then activated my hiss screen and turned to Li-Tsan. There was no place to sit except for the bunk itself, and I refused to kneel, so I just stood in the hatchway and regarded her from a height. "Anything you want to say to me?"

The stoniness of Li-Tsan's expression went well beyond anything that could have been explained away by mere paralysis. "Only that you must be thankful."

"Why?"

"You wanted a suspect. You needed an excuse for it to be me. I gave you both."

I was in no mood to defend my impartiality. "That was thoughtful of you."

"It was selfish. I couldn't leave this place without throttling that smug son of a bitch at least once."

I raised an eyebrow. "So you think you're leaving?"

"Aren't we all?"

Give her credit for that one. "What were you and Gibb talking about?"

"Just how much I hate his stupid ass."

"Some of the witnesses said that the two of you were arguing for three full minutes."

"It wasn't that long."

"So let's compromise," I said. "Let's say the argument lasted a minute and a half. Let's say you bypassed all your actual reasons to be upset with him and just told Gibb you hated his stupid ass. Let's say he showed the proper degree of supervisory patience and said, that's fine, bondsman, but I don't have the time to have my stupid ass hated at this very moment. Let's go on to concede you came up with the worst insult your little mind could concoct and he slapped you. That's still accounts for less than thirty seconds. What happened during the rest of the conversation?"

She grimaced. "Does it really matter? He's still a pig, you're still letting him set us up as scapegoats, and you're still what you are. I looked you up, Counselor. And you have no business behaving like you're morally superior to anybody."

It always amazes me just how many people in serious trouble fling my past in my face, expecting me to be devastated. "You'll notice I'm smiling, bondsman. Go ahead. Ask me why."

"No."

"I'm smiling because I know perfectly well what I am and I honestly don't give a damn what you think of me."

"Fuck off."

"I'm smiling because refusing to give me a straight answer is just about the stupidest, most self-destructive thing you can possibly do right now."

"Like I said: fuck off. You've already made up your mind anyway."

It wasn't my job to beg her. I nodded, deactivated the hiss screen, gave myself another ten seconds or so of meaningless physical business to perform so she'd have to lie there and watch me taking forever to leave, and then, timing it as best I could, paused at the door. "I don't like you, bondsman. But I hate mysteries even more."

She let me go without protest.

Nobody had wanted to subject Gibb to the same degree of security mandated for Li-Tsan Crin, so they'd contented themselves with just escorting him outside the hangar and staying with him while he endured the long wait for my attention.

Three men sat cross-legged on the padded deck, their backs against the faintly luminescent wall, the fuming Gibb bracketed by two indentures who seemed to have been chosen for being on good terms with him. I recognized both: a slightly built, callow young indenture named Simon Wells, who had been no help whatsoever in our brief interview earlier in the day, and a hairy-armed, scowling older man named Chasin Burr, whose answers had rarely exceeded two or three words per question. Wells radiated the profound discomfort of an insecure man not happy with having to guard his superior. Burr just radiated general dislike in my direction.

I sent them back to the hangar, then activated the hiss screen and stood looking down at Gibb.

"You can sit," he said, in a voice rendered hoarse by trauma.

"No, thank you. After Hammocktown, I enjoy the novelty of standing."

He began to rise.

I halted him with a gesture. "Remain seated or I'll order you restrained."

He froze. "Come on, Counselor. I'm not about to attack you."

"You're probably telling the truth. But your actions tonight do indicate a recent propensity for violence. So stay where you are."

He looked like he wanted to argue. Instead, he grunted, settled back down, and regarded me with the resigned weariness of a man accustomed to being misunderstood. "This is pointless. Dozens of witnesses just saw that crazy woman threaten my life."

"That's right. They also saw you strike her first."

His sigh was weary in both body and spirit. "Yeah, that was a mistake. But she was hysterical. She was hysterical, and she was out of control, and I thought a little shock would bring her out of it."

"What would make you think that, Mr. Gibb? Do you hit your people often?"

He stared at me, bit back a response, and looked away, shaking his head.

"No?" I said. "Just the women?"

"That's an ugly implication, Counselor."

"It was an ugly moment, Mr. Gibb."

He averted his eyes. "It was the wrong thing to do. But I mean what I say. She was hysterical."

I circled to keep myself within his line of sight. "What about?"

"The same thing she was always going on about. Blame. She was so sure that this debacle was going to be made all about her. I assured her that assigning blame was the very last of my concerns right now, and suggested that she find a better use for her time."

"That's not exactly a natural point for you to slap her. So I presume she got nastier."

"Yes."

"What was the last thing she said to you before you slapped her?"

"I don't remember."

I rubbed my eyes, felt a wave of gray dizziness, wished I hadn't already committed to standing, and said, "Mr. Gibb, she's already on record as calling you an incompetent, an asshole, a piece of Tchi shit, and a pervert who makes love to eye sockets. You've already established yourself as somebody capable of striking a prisoner under restraint. If there's something worse than any of that, that you're still too self-conscious to repeat in my presence, it could only be something specific, something of genuine substance that would not normally slip your mind. Your reluctance is calling attention to it. There's no point in sparing my delicate ears, because sooner or later I will reach somebody who heard and I will find out."

He fought a little fruitless battle with himself before giving it up. "She called me a pimp."

"A what?"

"I'm serious. A pimp. You know what that means, right?"

I did, but couldn't make sense of it. Procurement was on most developed worlds the most antiquated of all crimes. Even those societies that still criminalized prostitution had too many other ways for sex services to connect with potential clients. I felt an urge to do something, couldn't figure out what it was, and fought it off long enough to manage, "Why would she call you a pimp?"

Burr smirked. No: leered. I was sure of it.

Gibb just asked, "Why would she call me that other thing? Don't look for sense in it. She was just hurling the worst words she could think of."

"This particular one made you slap her."

"I slapped her," he said, his voice rising, "because she was hysterical and I wasn't going to listen to another twenty minutes of her nonsense. Not because she picked a senseless insult out of a hat."

I knelt, meeting his eyes, forcing him to see his evasions as the weak, toothless things they were. "And I can't quite believe that, because you were yelling too, Mr. Gibb. You were every bit as angry with her as she was with you. You were so very out of control, in fact, that you hit her two more times after she was restrained and no longer a threat. And would have hit her again if I hadn't stepped in."

He measured me with a look. "That was another mistake, Counselor. But it had nothing to do with anything she said and everything to do with her wrapping her hands around my throat. I'm like most people, even you, in that I get angry when people try to kill me. You, of all people, must be able to understand that."

The special emphasis he gave the phrase *of all people* didn't sit well with me. He wasn't referencing anything that had happened on One One One. I didn't know whether he'd looked me up, like Li-Tsan and the Porrinyards, or received my background from Lastogne. But I did remember the look I'd gotten from Burr and Wells, and realized that they'd gotten the word too.

What else would a leader under fire discuss with his guards while waiting for the interrogator to arrive? Except why that interrogator was not to be trusted?

The ugly story would be all over the hangar by morning.

The only thing Gibb hadn't counted on was the fact that I'd been carrying that weight a lot longer than I'd been on One One One, and was used to it.

I stood, pressed my palms against the small of my back, and arced my spine until I heard a creak. "I'm not satisfied, sir. And until I am, you will remain under arrest. I'll go make arrangements for your confinement, and put Mr. Lastogne in command."

He bit his cheek. "I wish you wouldn't do that, Counselor."

"Then give me something in exchange. Be a little forthcoming for once. I'll even give you a choice. Either tell me what's really going on between you and your height-sensitives, or surrender everything you know about Lastogne."

He looked down, neither surrendering nor backing off, just removing himself from the discussion.

I waited until I was absolutely sure it was all he was willing to offer, then turned my back on him and returned to the hangar, my footsteps soft padding thuds against a deck gentler than some of the human beings walking upon it.

16

WAR

I didn't want to turn in for the night. I didn't think I could afford to. But I'd already put off a crash for hours, and sleep deprivation was starting to make me stupid.

Even so, I imagined I'd spend hours flat on my back, staring at darkness, the frayed ends of my investigation refusing to permit me rest. It wouldn't be the first time an assignment had done that to me. But I enjoyed pure oblivion, broken only by the briefest of dream-flashes: my human mother kissing me on the forehead as I lay in bed pretending to be asleep. It felt so real I woke, blinking my eyes at the disorientation that always comes from sleeping in a strange place.

Much later, I sat up.

I'd assigned myself one of the four berths aboard the Dip Corps ship, feeling safer there than I would have in a sleep-cube among my suspect pool. The irony of sharing quarters with one of the two people I'd arrested did not escape me, but I'd endured worse. I used a hand sonic to wash, changed into a fresh black outfit, ate breakfast, and logged on.

The key was a phenomenon Lastogne had alluded to the

other day. Indentures sign up for five or ten or twenty years, depending on just how desperate they are and just how much the Corps values their services. They essentially sign their lives away in exchange for a ticket off their homeworlds and a retirement package that includes free passage anywhere they want to go, in perpetuity.

Still, nobody wants to wait that long for gratification, so there's an incentive system. Those who excel, for one reason or another, earn time bonuses. A hard-working diplomat with twenty years on her contract can complete her obligation in half that time by consistently performing above and beyond the call of duty. Most people don't quite manage that feat, as most people are not prodigies. Some, like the space-holders and drug-addled who make up too great a percentage of the Dip Corps rolls, just put in their time like automatons, accomplishing only the bare minimum expected of them. But the majority do take advantage of the system to some extent, shaving their time accounts by an hour here or a day there, looking for every advantage as they wait for their clocks to run down.

The major plus of this is the way it encourages the talented and the dedicated to work harder. The major minus is that it enables them to leave the service earlier, with full benefits, while preserving the jobs of the dull and apathetic.

The Dip Corp's middle management is infested with functionaries with all the talent of concrete blocks, who rose to their current positions of power out of sheer longevity but have nothing else to offer.

It's never affected my own performance, as my contract is permanent and working at any level beneath my absolute best can only make things worse for me. But I've also had to deal with any number of human zeroes who stuck around long enough to become number ones. It's not fun. It's also a waste of time to argue about. It's just the way things are.

Group records at Dip Corps installations are usually kept

secret from the indentures to avoid conflicts and jealousies and second-guessing, but access is one of my privileges as a representative of the Judge Advocate: a good thing, as the pattern of rewards and penalties is an excellent guide for any outsider who needs to track the currents of power at an installation as remote as the human community on One One One.

I'd already looked up Warmuth and Santiago, the first day. Now I wanted a little closer look at the other people I'd dealt with.

The most recent award called itself to my attention right away. Entered into the system by Peyrin Lastogne, following the arrest of Mr. Gibb, it had provided one Hannah Godel a small consideration, reducing her contract by some forty minutes for restraining Li-Tsan Crin during the fight. This was a bargain, as she hadn't been involved at all and had assured me she hadn't seen anything.

A hytex search of all such awards granted last night revealed several averaging thirty minutes apiece to a number of others whose testimony had been equally noncommital. There was nothing all that unusual about this. Middle management has always favored underlings friendly to middle management. It's corruption, all right, but of a minor and probably unavoidable sort.

A closer look at Godel's records reflected a steady if not overly impressive stream of such bonuses, establishing a time depletion rate some 7 percent faster than the calendar. A nice, solid, uninspired, but dependable, rating—nothing to engage any particular suspicions. But I might want to spend a little time with her today.

So now I went back a little further. Same day. A month taken off the contracts of Oscin and Skye Porrinyard, for their decisive heroism in saving my life. Also authorized by Mr. Lastogne, at Gibb's express urging. I was a little disappointed that I was only worth a month, but what the hell.

Gibb didn't like me. Their overall depletion was a steady 20 percent faster than the calendar: a gifted rating.

The next three or four names I checked out also received bonuses at a rate that seemed just about fair; maybe or little bit more or less than equitable, but the differences, plus or minus, were well within the limits of managerial preference. After all, as I have reason to know, you can do an exemplary job and still have an enemy for a boss. You can also be a total fuckup and still get invited to his house on holidays. Those few points, one way or another, were no doubt at least partly attributable to things like willingness to laugh at Mr. Gibb's jokes.

This wasn't fair either, but it was well within the realm of the human.

I didn't find an actual anomaly until I expected to: in the records of poor, height-sensitive Robin Fish.

She'd exceeded the calendar by 35 percent her first year, an odd statistic granted that she'd spent most of that time alone in the hangar. Her exemplary performance doing next to nothing seemed to have fallen down in the second year, leveling off at about 9 percent over calendar, but was still pretty high for an indenture who spent most of her time recovering from the metabolic aftershock of too much manna juice.

The record of her fellow height-sensitive Li-Tsan Crin was even stranger. She'd earned 20 percent over calendar in the Habitat, and continued to earn 20 percent over calendar sitting on her ass in the hangar.

Nils D'Onofrio had earned only 12 percent over calendar in the Habitat, sunken to zero percent over calendar in the first month of his exile, and then rocketed to a consistent 20 percent over calendar afterward.

In short, the three people most useless inside the Habitat, and most vocal about wanting to be transferred off-station, were at the same time the three highest paid.

* * *

I didn't consider Burr and Wells more than bit players in this affair, but on a whim I looked them up anyway. I found two indentures midway through their respective contracts, each earning at a rate 20 percent higher than calendar. 'Twas not always so. Burr and Wells had both been discharged from previous posts for "discipline problems," with one past superior writing of Burr, "He's not especially well suited to working on a team, but would be a well-valued member of any out-of-control mob." Another wrote of Wells, "Tends to look for people weaker than himself, to impress with his superior will." Wells struck me as a low-level thug, and Burr as something worse. Prior to Burr's posting here, he'd served his time at 20 percent below calendar due to penalties for small infractions, most of them having to do with intimidation of fellow indentures. And yet, Burr seemed to be earning phenomenal times, versus the calendar, on One One One. And he was the one who'd leered, when Gibb was confronted with the characterization of himself as "Pimp." It hadn't been Lastogne's leer, which always seemed to make Gibb the target of a joke. It was something else. Burr thought something was being put over on me, and it pleased him mightily.

Interesting. Disgusting, but interesting.

I left the berth and found Oscin, this morning's designated Porrinyard, sitting with his feet up on the command console. He had changed into a baggy set of work tights, and looked as weary as I'd ever seen him, which is to say fully alert with gray half-moons under his eyes. He looked up as the hatch opened and offered me a little half-wave. "Good morning, Counselor."

I suppressed a yawn. "Is it morning?"

"Early afternoon, by the Habitat clock. But you've had a full eight hours."

More than I usually got outside of Intersleep. "Where's Li-Tsan?"

He gestured at the sealed hatch next to mine. "Gave her lunch a little while ago. She asked for privacy, so I locked her in. But don't worry, I'm monitoring her vitals."

"And your other half?"

He indicated another of the sealed doors. "In there. Sleeping."

I found that hard to believe. "You can do that? I mean, not at the same time?"

"Why not? Bodies tire at different rates, even when they're driven by the same engines. And we haven't always been assigned to simultaneous work shifts; there have been times, here and elsewhere, when my components didn't lay eyes on our respective other halves for days on end. So I just catch some sleep when I can."

The more I spoke to this people, this person, the more the implications of their shared condition dizzied me. "What's it like for you, one being awake when the other one is sleeping?"

"Not very satisfactory, I'm afraid. The waking one doesn't become a single again, but the gestalt does lose much of its combined cognitive function, making me feel a little stupid until the sleeping half wakes up. And the sleeping one can't sustain dream-sleep alone, which means that I have to schedule simultaneous sleep sooner or later, or invite serious psychological repercussions. The trade-off is that when I do dream, I'm able to remember that I'm dreaming, and shape the experience any way that amuses me until I have to wake up again. It helps keep me centered."

I thought of all the nights I'd spent reliving the terror of a little girl on Bocai. "No nightmares, then?"

"They try to get a foothold, from time to time, but intangible monsters can't frighten me when I retain enough analytical capacity to laugh in their faces. Sometimes I let them come just so I can entertain myself squishing them like bugs. Why? Are you susceptible?"

It would have been nice to turn the memory off, edit it, give it a happy ending, or at least a comprehensible one, and not have to wake up so many mornings with the wounds so refreshed. It might even be worth cylinking with someone, were there any other human beings willing to share a lease on the knee-deep broken glass inside my head. But that was a stupid thought. "Any messages?"

Oscin said, "Just a lot of people dreading whatever you plan to do next."

"Nothing from New London?"

"Not yet."

One of the last things I'd done before the attempt on my life was compose that update for Bringen. Now I found myself worrying that Gibb hadn't passed it along. For all I knew, maybe he'd sabotaged the hammock himself to keep from having to send it.

Or maybe Lastogne had. The message had queried his background, after all.

Once again I suffered that oddly frustrating certainty that there was something I would ordinarily do now. It was so vague, so hard to pin down, that it disappeared the moment I tried to chase it. "And the AIsource? I sent word I wanted to talk to them as soon as possible."

He shook his head. "Nothing."

Which might have made sense, in a different context. Human bureaucracies, and most alien ones, are slow by design, their response times slowed to a crawl despite all the technology we employ to make their progress visible to the naked eye. That's because they're still subject to all the delays native to organic life: the mistakes, indecision, the malice, the covering of asses, and the reluctance to transmit even the most urgent message until after a leisurely break for lunch. The AIsource, by contrast, would have gotten my message hours ago, within a millisecond of me sending it. They would have mapped out the consequences of any possible response and been able to answer me, before I even thought of taking another breath.

They were playing games, all right.

They were stirring the pot and watching to see how well the little bug rode the waves, trying not to drown.

But I wasn't about to wait around for them to decide to count up the score.

The skimmer entered the Habitat, rotated to comply with local standards of up and down, and accelerated spinward.

It was the most dizzying of all possible courses. At least a flight along the length of the cylinder turned the Uppergrowth into a conventional ceiling, with a consistent upward curvature to both port and starboard. A flight against the axis of rotation accentuated that curvature and made the landscape above us seem to be spinning, its vines and clumps of manna fruit hurtling toward us as a speed that made me look away.

Mo Lassiter, who was handling the Interface, sensed my losing battle with vertigo and said, "I could fly upside down if you'd prefer."

Sheer terror at the prospect thrummed my spine like a stringed instrument. "What?"

"It's sometimes more comfortable for folks still adjusting to the geometry here. It puts the Uppergrowth where you'd expect the ground to be, and that soup below us in the place of an identifiable sky. Don't worry. Local grav will keep us oriented."

Pride made me want to refuse. The things happening at the base of my throat made me realize I'd better not. "Please do."

The biggest mistake I made all day was not shutting my eyes at the moment of rollover. There was no sense of actual movement, but my mind's sense of up and down lagged behind the skimmer's by a full second, and I spent that eternity irrationally certain that I was about to be dumped from the vehicle like a fish dumped from its overturned bowl.

After a heartbeat my eyes adjusted to our new orientation and the interior of One One One became close to bearable. The Uppergrowth now below us became a kind of ridge, gently curving downward toward a distant and blurred horizon. By contrast, the sky now high above us became a vast arched ceiling, lined with dark and roiling storms. I considered the toxic ocean hidden behind it, imagined all of those billions of gallons of poison hanging up there with nothing to support them, and felt sick again, this time in an entirely new way.

One One One wasn't a happy sight from any angle.

"That better?" Lassiter asked.

A thousand savage retorts marched through that atrophied part of my brain responsible for censoring what I say.

None of the other passengers looked any happier than I felt. Hannah Godel, who occupied the seat beside me, sat pressed against the opposite bulkhead, putting as much distance between my body and hers as she could without thinking to step aside. Back at the hangar she'd asked me why I'd chosen her, out of so many other candidates, for this particular expedition; my answer, that it would give us an opportunity to get better acquainted, hadn't satisfied her a whit, and from the look on her face may have actually disgusted her. Lassiter herself kept gauging me with her eyes. And the Porrinyards, cramped into the row behind us, flashed smiles whenever I looked at them, but those smiles faltered with a regularity that suggested sustained internal dialogue.

I hadn't thrilled either Lastogne or Gibb with my plan to appoint my own guides as I resumed my investigation inside the Habitat. I was willing to believe their mutual claims to be concerned over my safety, but it would have been much more comfortable, for them, to appoint keepers they could trust to report on my progress. That element of this investigation had only grown more intrusive with Gibb's arrest, and wasn't likely to lighten up as long as he remained in custody.

All of which was fine with me.

It didn't hurt to keep the pot boiling.

Over the next three hours Lassiter took me on a tour of random sights, displaying the uncanny, unearned pride of a human being who thinks she owns a place just because she lives there. Despite the homogenous nature of the Uppergrowth, which had struck me as the kind of place that would have been dull indeed, if not for the fact that it was *upside down* and *likely to kill you if you let go,* it did possess highlights of interest to those capable of being interested. There was one place she called Whoopsy-Daisy Fountain, where the irrigation lines had broken and a torrent of water twenty times the skimmer's radius tumbled from the sky and into the abyss below. It was spectacular, if you liked that kind of thing. Lassiter said, "We talked, once, about diffusing the pressure and adapting it for use as a bathing facility, of sorts; it would have been easy to run regular skimmers out here, turn off the shielding, and just stand under the precipitation to enjoy the shower."

"What's the problem?" I asked. "Not hot enough?"

"Naaah. Too acid. And too filled with stuff meant for the Uppergrowth and through it, the Brachs. Get wet with this stuff and you'll feel dirtier, not cleaner. But it sure is pretty, isn't it?"

I ticked a mental check-mark next to my longstanding prejudice against ecosystems, and said nothing.

After that she dimmed the shields to protect our eyes and took us as close to one of the glowsphere suns as she dared. From a distance of several kilometers, they were clearly roiling balls of flame, churning the storms near them with the force of their radiated heat. No human or alien habitat I'd ever visited had ever harnessed forces anything like these to warm and light their ecospheres, and I confess my knuckles turned white on the armrest as I wondered just what kept the entire atmosphere from burning. But Lassiter laughed at me.

"They give off about as much warmth, in relation to the space they take up, as conventional fires of the same size. They're certainly hot as hell, by human standards, but they're not about to incinerate everything in sight. No, as near as we can figure it, they're mostly here to give this place its night and day. You want to know what provides One One One with the majority of its heat? Its oceans. Whether by internal forces we don't know about, or by the force of their own chemical reactions and the sheer atmospheric pressure down there, they're at a state well above what we consider boiling, and the heat rising from them is more than enough to keep us warm and toasty. The storm patterns are just one huge engine for redistributing the heat."

"As are all weather patterns," the Porrinyards said.

"Well, yes," Lassiter said.

What had I been thinking, about boiling pots? I reminded myself how much I hated ecosystems, on general principle, and kept my own counsel.

Then the time for travelogue ended as our attentions turned to the phenomenon we were here to see in the first place.

Lassiter tapped the ROM disk on her forehead. The air before her shimmered and became a blurry 2-D grid marked with isobars and symbols that my eyes read as so much spaghetti. She impaled one spot with an index finger, rippling the image with distortions. "I've done a pretty good job modeling their migration patterns, though it's not all that hard to do, given their rate of movement. At this point there should be four tribal confrontations of the kind you're talking about:

one just starting, one pretty much over, two which should be entering the most intense stages of their conflict sometime today. I'm taking you to the closest of those two."

"I don't see what it has to do with anything," Godel said. "They don't have the capacity to engage in high-tech sabotage."

"Which eliminates what happened to Santiago," I agreed. "And what happened to me. But Warmuth was attacked with Brachiator weaponry."

"You haven't seen Brachiators fighting yet."

"No, I haven't."

"Take a look," Godel said, "and *then* tell me it makes sense."

The Porrinyards seemed pinker about the cheeks, which could be either a trick of the light or the beginnings of a shared blush. They were also holding hands, a gesture that might have been easy to mistake as mutual affection but which in their case probably possessed as much real intimacy as an individual choosing to cross his legs while he sat.

I turned back to Godel. "Bondsman Lassiter doesn't think it's ridiculous."

Godel shrugged. "Mo doesn't think Cynthia had enough sense to defend herself."

"And you think she did?"

Godel rubbed the bridge of her nose between two index finger and thumb. "How do I put this . . . ! Look. My homeworld has one of those fairy-tale figures adults use to frighten naughty children. He's a reanimated corpse called the Shadow Man who crawls from the grave to munch on the living. But in every version of the story I've ever seen, the Shadow Man can barely move. He shuffles along at two kilometers an hour, waving his arms, somehow catching up to people who should be able to outrun him at a relaxed walk."

The Porrinyards shared a fond chuckle. "My world has a monster like that too. King Grave. He shuffled along like a man whose toes weighed fifty kilos apiece, but he scared the daylights out of Skye as a child."

"Not Oscin?" I asked. (I'd almost said *Not You?* and earned myself another correction.)

"No, not Oscin," Skye said alone. "He was never the kind to be scared of stories."

"In any event," Godel said, with the air of somebody struggling to get a conversation back on track, "the one thing that makes characters like that so frightening, in stories at least, is that their victims are always too paralyzed to run. They just stand wherever they are and watch this clumsy, fanged thing approaching, and somehow never once work up the nerve to take a step. But if you analyze the model, you realize that anybody who stands still and allows such a crippled, barely mobile predator to catch up with him is too stupid to live anyway. Now think of the Brachiators as predators and Cynthia as the idiot who just hung there and watched while they went after her with their claws. I'm telling you. I refuse to believe it unless you can show me why."

I'd noted her use of Warmuth's first name. "Were you close to her?"

She grimaced. "I was wondering why you brought me along."

"Not because of that. But were you?"

"We worked together. We got along. We were friendly, not friends."

"What kept you from being friends?"

"Nothing in particular. I liked her. Didn't love her."

"Again: why not?"

"Friendship is hard enough without dealing with somebody who insists on immediately being your best one. But that doesn't mean I'd consider her so incompetent that anything as physically useless as a Brach could sneak up on her. I mean, really, Counselor. Watch and see."

* * *

The battlefield was a patch of Uppergrowth indistinguishable from any other, marked only by the thirty nearly immobile figures wrapped in what their species must have considered to be frenetic combat. There were two groups, whose paths prior to this moment in their respective histories were easy to track by the vines they'd shredded in their wake. They hadn't collided head-on, but rather at an angle, joining in battle as soon as both tribes realized that they'd now be competing for the same patch of their world's ceiling.

The fresh, juicy manna pears hanging in bunches from every vine in sight revealed the conflict as ridiculous, as even Brachiators forced into a course change could have found more food than they could possibly eat within an hour's travel, but that didn't matter to them; their armies had met, and their war had to be fought.

I've been on a battlefield or two in my time. I'm told some people find it glorious, or thrilling. I've never seen the sense of either claim. But if I could concede that some wars are glorious, I would also have to admit the natural corollary, that somewhere in the universe wars are just mind-numbingly tedious.

The Brachiator battlefield looked like an orgy where everybody had fallen asleep in mid-hump. The combatants fought with two limbs apiece, as they needed the others to hold fast to the Uppergrowth, their fighting limbs not much more mobile as they raked at their opponents, clawing slow-motion furrows across flesh. I saw two Brachs who had sunken fangs into one another's skin, but neither seemed to be chewing or pursuing the battle further; it was as if that first jolt of mutual pain had frozen them both, and rendered them incapable of either retreat or further assault. I saw two others going after one another with claw-knives of the sort that had been used on Cynthia Warmuth. Both Brachiators were already bleeding, and both were winding up for another slash, but they moved more like men afraid of breaking something than soldiers in a battle for their lives.

I've seen wells dug more quickly, by people bearing no tools more advanced than shovels.

Some of the Brachs were screaming in pain or rage. Their wordless cries were the same violin-pitch as those coming from the infants clinging to parental backs.

"See?" Godel said. "Even assuming that they had some reason to attack her, and further imagining that she slept through their approach and was surprised by their attack, she would have had more than enough time to do whatever she had to do to protect herself."

"I always pictured them restraining her first," Lassiter argued. "Holding her so she couldn't fight, even as the claws were driven in, in slow motion."

"I thought of that. But moving as slowly as these beasties do, they would have had to coordinate their movements with machine precision, pinning all four of her limbs at the same instant. Otherwise, if a Brach grabbed one wrist, and even a few seconds passed before another Brach got hold of the other, she would have more than fair warning that something nasty was going on. She could have thrashed around, hollered bloody murder, fought them off, even sent out a distress signal. She wouldn't just hang there and do nothing. But I can't see the Brachs executing a smooth four-way assault, either."

I'd assumed, up until now, that the Warmuth killing had been a low-tech crime, in extreme contrast to what had happened to Santiago. But precision required another solution, possibly one implicating the AIsource. After all, they were precision incarnate, and wouldn't have had much difficulty directing their creations in a coordinated assault.

The only problem, really, was that the crime still didn't make any sense.

Lassiter said, "Look over there. Something's happening."

Our upside-down orientation had lent the Brachiators a deceptive buoyancy. No longer dead weights, clinging to the Uppergrowth as their only defense against a fatal plunge, they now resembled balloons afraid of floating away. The wounded ones bled upward in drips and streams, the larger drops separating into drizzles as they ascended. The two Lassiter had pointed out, and which she now maneuvered us closer to, were well into their fatal combat. Each was marked by a dozen slashing wounds, with the smaller of the pair clinging to a frayed vine with a single arm that was already more wound than intact limb. The big one had jabbed a claw-blade into his enemy's sole intact shoulder and was sawing it, slowly, ever so slowly, across what remained of the tissue connecting muscle and bone.

It was as close to a hurry as the Brachiators ever got, and my human eyes still insisted on perceiving it as dull, lazy, and drugged.

Lassiter said, "The little one's going to fall within a few minutes. Poor thing."

I considered vomiting. The realization that our upside-down orientation would fling it all back in my face made the need more urgent, not less. "Can we save him?"

Lassiter regarded the claws and teeth gouging furrows into flesh. "Getting between those two doesn't strike me as a good idea."

"I mean after he falls. Can we hover and give him something to land on?"

Lassiter gave that suggestion the kind of look people reserve for the openly delusional. "Also not a good idea, Counselor. We're not exactly equipped to offer it medical attention, or a future. And interference of any kind is well beyond the approved scope of our mission here. We could really anger the AIsource."

"Oh, gee," I said. "We sure wouldn't want that."

"Please, Counselor. I understand your humanitarian impulses . . ."

"I don't have humanitarian impulses. But I do need to find out something. Find a way to work it."

Still she did nothing, instead staring like a woman who expected eye-stalks to sprout from my forehead.

Behind me, the Porrinyards cleared their respective throats, engineering even that noise to come from the empty air between them. "Maureen? In matters involving her investigation, the Counselor has full authority. You have to do what she says."

Lassiter's jaw tightened. "Can I just mention, first, that it's a goddamn stupid order that will accomplish nothing but prolong a sentient creature's suffering?"

"You just did," I told her.

She rolled the skimmer again, this time without warning me. The entire world turned upside-down again, the Uppergrowth and sky switching places in less time than my equilibrium would have liked to consider possible. My fear of heights overcame that rational part of me comfortable within the skimmer's local gravity, and I found myself clutching at my seat, my mouth gaping in soundless, instinctive terror. But the moment passed. The Uppergrowth, now returned to its rightful place as the ceiling of this demented world, hung directly above us again, its strangeness rejuvenated.

The one advantage of Lassiter's malicious little move was that it once again brought the skimmer's local gravity in synch with the environment's. Down was down. So I could vomit over the side without any fear of baptizing myself with breakfast. It was a good thing she'd flipped a 180 and not 360, as by that point I had no choice.

I accepted a water bottle from Skye. "So how are we going to do this?"

Lassiter ascended to within three meters of the struggling Brachiators, positioning the flat cargo platform at the rear beneath the combatant about to surrender to the inevitable. Drops of bright pink blood, leaking from the wounds of both combatants, already specked the flatbed. "I'll have to get close. An object the size and weight of a Brachiator doesn't need all that much time in free fall to become a missile capable of knocking us out of its sky."

"We're safe at this distance, though?"

Lassiter flashed me a look of utmost contempt. "I wouldn't agree to this otherwise, with or without your authority. No, the average human male weighs more than the average Brachiator, and showoffs among our people have been known to jump down from higher distances. But we should all scooch as far from that platform as possible. Nobody's ever had the gall to suggest this before, and I don't know what's going to happen when we do."

All five of us crowded against the forward hull, with the bulky Lassiter taking up more than her fair share of the available room. Godel, Lassiter, and Oscin Porrinyard stood with their backs against the Interface console. Skye and I crouched at their feet, making ourselves as small as possible. Above us, the Brachiator losing his battle for life screamed in what must have been agony and despair—all the more heartbreaking for its failure to express the obvious in human terms. Alien mind or not, we all knew it was thinking what any sentient creature, in its position, would have been thinking. *This can't be happening. Not to me. My life can't be ending. I don't want to die.*

The soft ripping noises, above us, seemed to go on forever. I have no idea whether the Brachiator sense of time comes close to being as protracted as their fighting style, but would like to think not. I'd prefer to believe they perceived themselves as moving quickly. Otherwise the dying one would have felt every instant of the long minutes between one slash and the next.

Whatever else I could say about the stupidity of Brach warfare, including that it made human warfare look like a sensible endeavor, the losing Brach did have one hell of a will to live.

Then Lassiter said, "There he goes."

I hadn't seen anything that distinguished this particular moment from the agonizing wait that preceded it, but she was right. The losing Brach plummeted from the Uppergrowth and dropped the two meters between the site of its final battle and our flatbed, taking the bulk of the impact on its back. It didn't convulse or roll, as we'd feared. It just lay there, the remains of its arms still reaching out toward the roof of its world.

The Porrinyards gave my shoulders a synchronized squeeze. "One second, Counselor. I want to make sure this is safe first." They went aft, stood at the back of the passenger compartment looking over the body, then returned, their shared expression grim. "It's alive, but it won't be for long. I don't think we have anything to fear."

"This is cruel as hell," Lassiter muttered.

"I don't see how," the Porrinyards said. "It'll be dead in minutes, whatever happens. It will spend that time in pain and terror, whatever happens. We can't help it, whatever happens. We've only arranged for it to spend its last minutes with us, instead of in free fall."

Lassiter was still resentful. "For all we know, that's worse."

"If so we'll do the humane thing and drop it over the side once Counselor gets what she needs. All the more reason to let her get on with it. Counselor?"

My knees cracked as I stood. Suddenly uncharacteristically hesitant in the face of violent death, despite the many I'd seen in my time, I wasted a second or two flexing my back before leaving the others to join the Brachiator for its last moments.

It lay on its back, all four limbs splayed, its bright pink blood pooled beneath it like a sheet. Its face was striped with deep, oozing gashes, one of which crossed an eye socket now containing an unrecognizable soup that might have been an eye. The other eye, which looked disturbingly human, turned toward me as I approached, widening with what might have been terror or simple incomprehension. The rest of its body, beyond the face, had been ripped open so savagely that some of the unidentifiable organs revealed by the wounds were also open and leaking various fluids. But it was the eye that bothered me, the eye that made me feel a criminal. The Brachiator may have had no idea who I was, but the eye recognized me.

"You are one of the New Ghosts." It closed its mouth, swallowed, then spoke more clearly. "I have never seen a New Ghost, but I have heard of them."

I sounded like I'd left all my wind in New London. "Do you know where you are?"

The Brachiator swallowed again. "I am among the Dead."

I began to understand Lassiter's resentment. Requiring anything from this creature right now was arrogant and wrong. "You are not among the Dead. You are alive. You may not have much life left, but you're still breathing, still looking at me, still talking. Do you understand?"

The Brachiator swallowed again. "I am a Ghost in a land of Ghosts."

"Why? Please! I know there's no reason this should matter to you, but there's a great evil that will continue killing if you can't answer this question. How can you be among the Dead if you can still talk and breathe?"

The Brachiator's single remaining eye rolled upward, allowing its owner one last look at the carnage still tearing apart its tribe and family. Did it have the equivalent of a spouse up there? Friends? Young? Things it felt passionate about? Things it wanted to change? "The hand is gone," it managed. "How could I still be alive?"

One last ragged breath later its eye closed, and did not open again.

I didn't realize I was shaking until the Porrinyards came up behind me, one on either side. They did not touch me or put their hands on my shoulders, as they had before, but they did make their presence known, and they did refrain from comment as I returned to my seat.

It wasn't the thing's sad end that had gotten to me. But its confusion, its blindness, its helplessness in the face of forces beyond its comprehension felt familiar. Mo Lassiter had been right. I wished I'd just let the poor thing be.

Behind me, she said, "Was that worth doing? Did you learn anything at all?"

I kept my eyes on the dead Brachiator.

"Yes. Yes, I did."

17

DESCENT

Its funeral was not much to speak of.

My first thought had been that we could just flip the skimmer again and let it fall, but that was just stupid, as our local gravity naturally included its cargo deck. Lassiter had to scramble onto the cargo deck and shove the corpse over the edge. Free of our interference, it tumbled into the distance, becoming a speck and then a memory long before it was swallowed by the clouds. By the time Lassiter came back, her coveralls were glossy with pink gore, and her attitude toward me had chilled another ten degrees I couldn't afford.

Nobody provided a eulogy. There would have been no point. What could we have said? That it had been brave? Noble? A fine upstanding representative of its species? We didn't know it. It could have been hero or villain or anything in between. To us, its only notable attribute was that it had been alive and was now dead, better off by far than it had been during the few fleeting seconds it had spent in our company. Maybe the best possible eulogy was spoken by Lassiter, when she wiped the pink from her cheeks and grumbled that single, eloquent, "Shit."

Before deciding what to do next I called the hangar, to see if I'd heard from Bringen. He'd sent a reply with random-inverse coding, keyed to a phrase only used for matters of extreme secrecy. I don't think we'd used it more than once or twice outside of drills, and though it slowed translation by less than thirty seconds I still found the gesture a serious pain in the ass. After all, there was nobody around to inconvenience except for me and the AIsource, and expecting any code to successfully hide anything from the AIsource was an exercise in self-delusion.

Once the signal was descrambled, it revealed an image of Bringen slumped at this desk in a manner that suggested either extreme depression or extreme sleep deprivation. I guessed the latter, as his cheeks were stubbled and random strands of hair formed swooping helixes at odds with all the others. I not only felt some satisfaction over his bad day but also wasted a few seconds contemplating the existence of an algorithm that would take the sleep cycles on different planets, factor them through the cosmic distances that usually separated me from the man, and provide me with the most advantageous times to burden him with urgent messages capable of disturbing his circadian rhythms. Were there a place to buy such a glorious thing, I'd have been first in line.

Except that—I remembered now—I'd *misjudged him.*

"Andrea. Good morning, or whatever the hell you're having. I hope you're seeing some progress. Regarding your questions: first, your involvement was requested by both Ambassador Gibb and the AIsource consensus aboard that station. Gibb made the request personally, in a second transmission that followed the original sent by Lastogne. I've seen the holo; he was quite insistent on it. If he won't admit to it now, then maybe he's changed his mind. The AIsource also recommended you, claiming that they respected your gifts and knew that you'd bring a, quote, 'unique personal perspective,' to the problem. If they won't own up to it now, then I'm as confused as you are.

"Lastogne's another issue. He does have a listing on the mission specs, confirming his position as Mr. Gibb's second-in-command, but it doesn't offer any other information of any kind. If there's a bio or résumé, I'm not cleared to look at it. Neither are any of my superiors. I tried to press the matter and was told, by people whose names you'd recognize, to back off." His shoulders sagged. "I'm telling you, Andrea. The last time I saw anything even remotely like this, the individual in question pretty much qualified as a sovereign nation all by himself, and that guy's name didn't slam doors nearly as hard as your guy's does. Whoever Lastogne is, he's well outside the Constitution, and if you've been warned off, then maybe you should listen. He shouldn't be the main focus of your investigation."

I hate being told where not to look, or for that matter what the main focus of an investigation should or should not be.

Bringen hesitated again. "We need somebody to blame, Andrea. Somebody other than the AIsource, and somebody other than Peyrin Lastogne. And we need it soon. I trust you've been introduced to the local malcontents? Can't you—"

I blanked the message mid-sentence. Why not? The relevant part was already over.

Getting in touch with Gibb took a minute, but once he was patched in and informed that my superiors had named him as the party who had requested my presence, he provided the answer I already expected. "That's ridiculous, Counselor. I never even heard of you before the other day. And if I'd known your background ahead of time, I would have requested anybody but you. Are you sure you didn't garble the message?"

"I don't garble."

"Then somebody's lying to you."

Gibb had lied to me about any number of things, but there was no reason to suspect him, here. He had nothing to gain by misleading me on this one small point. Nor could I come up with a motive for Lastogne. And too much had been made of them being the only two humans with direct access to the lines of communication for me to want to point fingers at anybody else. That left several possibilities, all unsatisfactory: one, that Bringen had lied in order to dump a dangerous and politically sensitive crisis in my lap; two, that Gibb and Lastogne had lied for reasons too subtle for me to fathom; and three, that Gibb and Lastogne weren't as much in control of their own outgoing messages as they both liked to think.

The third possibility was by far the most likely.

But on this station, that could only bring me back to the AIsource.

The untouchables among my suspects.

I felt that maddening tingle, familiar by now, of an impulse denied. Something I wanted to do but could not identify.

I dropped the hiss screen, prompting Lassiter to ask, "What's next?"

I said, "Down."

We descended. Soon the wormy surface of the Uppergrowth lost the rich detail revealed in closeup and became an undifferentiated field of gray, shining here and there wherever the suns caught concentrations of moisture on the vines. By comparison, the clouds looked fluffier, darker, extruding swirls of mist and heavy weather that from here looked like tentacles too blind to realize that we were still far out of their reach. Every few seconds a new dragon rose out of the muck, disturbed the clouds with a single beat of its wings, and then plunged back below the surface, as if content with being seen.

Lassiter said, "We should stop here. Much farther down and the air gets so choppy the skimmer might not be able to climb out again."

I discovered I'd dug my fingers into the seat. "But where we are is safe?"

"Could we drop another thousand meters? Possibly. We could even enter the cloud cover. There's no line of clear demarcation. But the farther down we go, the less safe we are, and this is as low as I feel comfortable."

I said, "Then make yourself a little more uncomfortable."

She looked doubtful, but told the skimmer to descend.

It was hard to gauge the rate of our descent. Little wisps of vapor passed us from time to time, but the clouds below didn't seem to get any larger.

After a minute or two, Lassiter leveled off. "This is as low as I've ever gone."

My fingers hurt. "Is this as low as anybody's ever gone?"

"We've had some daredevils. Went down a thousand meters lower. One or two had trouble climbing out."

"Any actual fatalities?"

"Not from skimmer failure, no."

"What, then?"

"I should have said none at any point during our two years on-station, before Santiago. Considering our work conditions, we've been very lucky."

"Or very capably led," I said.

Lassiter's lips went tight. "Yeah, well, Mr. Gibb's very good at running the machine. He doesn't let people take pointless risks."

Another compliment damned by how much it galled the speaker. They seemed abundant, in conversations regarding Mr. Gibb. "Can you go as low as those daredevils did?"

"I didn't sign up for that," Godel said, the first time she'd opened her mouth since the Brachiator's death.

"Neither did I," said Lassiter.

I glanced at the Porrinyards. "And you?"

"For once," they said, their shared voice rich with forced merriment, "I'm of two minds on a subject."

I fought off a spasm of dizziness with multiple inner chants of *Unseen Demons,* gripped the seat tighter, and said, "Descend those thousand meters."

"There's no possible reason—"

"So I'm insane," I said. "I issue dangerous orders for the most whimsical of reasons. Nevertheless, they are orders. Descend."

Grumbling resentful odes to bureaucrats who think they know what they're doing, Lassiter complied. The skimmer descended. Wisps of vapor fluttered past us like butterflies, rising toward an Uppergrowth now granted the indistinct texture of sky. Some irregularity in the local airflow shook our undercarriage. The skimmer's local gravity prevented us from feeling any actual turbulence, but the nearest of the two suns seemed to shake, and a light in the instrument panel blinked red, assuring everybody who cared to heed it that Lassiter was right and the witch from New London was indeed putting everybody in danger.

"This is as far as anybody's ever descended."

My throat was so dry, by now, that I had to concentrate on making spit before attempting speech. "How are we doing?"

"The stabilization systems are working overtime, holding us against the winds here. We're using about four times as much power, just idling, as we do up near the Uppergrowth. I wouldn't want to stay here for long, but we're handling it."

"Can we handle more?"

Lassiter made a face. "I expected you to ask that."

"Then you should have an answer ready. A few minutes ago you told me that we could, conceivably, descend as far as the clouds. You also said that it had never been attempted. I would like you to do so now. Can we handle it?"

"I'm not sure it'd be safe to get too close to those dragons."

"Safety wasn't part of the question."

Godel thumped the back of my seat. "It sure as hell is part of my question!"

The Porrinyards spoke in a voice mostly Skye, deepened by only a little of Oscin's masculine grit. "Are you sure about this, Counselor?"

"Yes."

The Porrinyards didn't sound happy. "All right."

Lassiter was far from mollified. "I'm not going to kill us all, Counselor. I'll descend, if you really think it's so important, but I'll also stop every hundred meters or so to assess local conditions, and our own—"

"No," I said.

She stopped in mid-sentence. "What do you mean *no*?"

"I mean that I need to test something, and I can't do that if you insist on taking baby steps. I need you to descend, regardless of local conditions or signs of vehicle failure, until I tell you to stop."

Lassiter's eyes had gone very wide and very round. "Then you can go back and get yourself some willing volunteers."

"I don't want volunteers. I want the crew I have here."

"Well, I'm sorry, Counselor, but you don't have them!"

"Are you refusing a direct order?"

"Tell me to die for no good reason and I'll do more than refuse, I'll shove the order up your ass."

Godel said, "It's not safe, Counselor."

I turned to the Porrinyards. "Do you concur?"

They looked unwell. "I'll take control if you need me to. If it's important."

"It is."

They eyed Lassiter. "Descend or you're relieved."

She couldn't believe them. "You're crazy! She's not competent to—"

"I've seen her file," the Porrinyards said. "She's competent to do whatever she wants. She has a reason. Do it."

Lassiter accused me of a perversion unsuspected by even the most graphically imaginative minds who'd cursed me before. It made the charge Li-Tsan had flung at Gibb downright mild by comparison. But she obeyed, directing the skimmer to disregard all of its built-in safety monitors in favor of a crazy, suicidal descent farther into the lower regions.

The skimmer's local grav still compensated for everything. But the view outside the world, outside the skimmer's fields, became more and more chaotic, more blurred by violent motion as the vehicle bucked and rolled and lurched its way into a layer of enraged winds. The suns became not spheres but streaks of light, like comets dragging tails. The cloud layer that was supposed to be underneath us rose and crashed like an angry sea, one second filling the sky to our right and the next becoming a fortress wall to our immediate left. Once or twice we rolled over completely. The sight alone was going to make my sensitive stomach rebel again. I tasted bile and swallowed it back down, determined not to panic before anybody else did.

Godel said, "You're out of your mind!"

I didn't answer her.

Maybe I was.

The skimmer continued to descend.

The cloud layer now appeared to be only a couple of hundred meters below us. This close, it no longer seemed a vista of calm but a roiling, angry stormscape, bubbling with the forces at play. A dragon, flying by not far below, was not just giant but leviathan, taking several minutes of sheer hell to pass from nose to tail. We couldn't quite tell because by then the skimmer bucked so violently that we caught the dragon only in glimpses as our perspective lurched from cloudscape to Uppergrowth to the distant, broiling suns. I noted that it was almost identical to the dragons of terrestrial myth, complete with long serpentine neck and leathery bat-wings; its tail even ended with a bone ridge that resembled a spade.

Were it not as engineered as everything else around here, I would have said, *Oh, give me a break.*

As it is, I came very close to screaming, *Okay, that's enough, get us the hell out of here.*

We sank into the clouds.

Now we had no view at all. We should have had been blessed with at least the illusion of smoother flight, but even with the view obstructed by mist, we could still see the eddies and currents of the vapor stirred up by our passage.

The walls of the skimmer vibrated so hard they were painful to touch. We had maybe seconds before the pressure and the conditions tore us apart.

I'd made a mistake. Called one bluff too many.

It didn't matter if I died. I'd greet the end as a relief. But I'd had no right to drag these people down with me.

Then Godel said, "Holy shit."

I opened my eyes, without ever registering that I'd closed them.

The turbulence had stopped. The clouds had retreated from us on all sides, becoming a vast egg-shaped chamber of absolute calm, its shell a barrier of concentrated vapor hiding anything else the storm system might have hidden behind it. Shadows moved across the surface, cast by weather, dragons, or stranger things. Light, refracted through the vapor, cut the gloom around us in beams so coherent that they might have shone from hidden lamps.

It was impossible to tell any longer where the suns were, or where the Uppergrowth was, or how far we'd plunged. Our local gravity made us the center of all worlds, including this one. The only thing clear was that we weren't moving.

A mirrored AIsource remote, thin as a blade, wide as an old-fashioned door, slipped through the clouds, spun twice, and tumbled toward us. As it drew close, it telescoped until it reflected us bow to stern, stunning us with a mural of our own dazed and terrified faces. I wish I could say mine looked vindicated. It did not. It looked more like the expression of a woman who had fully expected to die and wasn't certain that the deliverance before her was deserved.

Lassiter's face was drenched with sweat. "We're getting a signal."

"Patch it through," I said. "No need for a privacy shield. What it has to say to me it can say to all of us."

Lassiter obliged.

An AIsource voice said, ***Andrea Cort.***

"Yes."

We put this off as much as we dared. But without our interference, you would now be dead.

"I know."

You had no reason to expect a rescue. Your actions of the last few minutes have been so reckless that you may not deserve one. We should admonish you for your stupidity and then go away, leaving you and your companions to the fate you seemed so determined to arrange for yourselves.

My throat had gone so dry that my first attempt at speech failed. "I don't know how you feel about a couple of these others, but you weren't about to let me die."

Do you think you're special?

"Yes. I'm not sure why, but that's exactly what I think. I think you've made a point of protecting me."

It was still a stupid risk. There are still other entities aboard this station, not within our control, who want you dead.

"Not like this. I don't think they want to take advantage of a happy accident. I think they want to put on a bigger show than that. And I think you won't let it happen until you tell me why."

It is not that simple, Counselor.

"It very much is that simple. Just last night I told you I was sick of your bullshit, and I see no reason to change my position now. Either answer my questions to my satisfaction or

I'll resign from this case. I'll take my transport out of here, the Dip Corps will send somebody else, and you'll start this rigmarole all over again. That person might find a solution. But that person also won't be me. And I've just bet the lives of five people on knowing what you find more important."

The silence that followed was all of one second long; an eternity to us, and what must have been the equivalent of eons to the AIsource. During that second, the others gave me the kind of look they might have reserved for a human being whose skin had peeled away, revealing a second face not quite human.

The AIsource remote flashed a brilliant white light.

Return with us. There is much we need to discuss.

18

ROGUES

The others didn't say much on the flight back, Godel and Lassiter still resenting me for risking their lives, the Porrinyards respecting my need for silence.

The only real conversation was Godel wanting to know why I'd chosen her, out of Gibb's entire crew, to play games with. After all, she said, her name hadn't been all that prominent in my investigation so far. Why would I pick on her, of all people, when I could have chosen anybody else?

I let her stew. One question at a time.

The AIsource remote accompanied us every meter of the way, a mirror blazing as it captured the light of the glowsphere suns. I wondered what would happen if I asked Lassiter to outrun it and decided she'd probably toss me overboard just for making the suggestion.

When we arrived at the Interface dock, we left Godel and Lassiter in the skimmer, bringing the Porrinyards to escort me down that long spongy corridor and back.

Godel and Lassiter therefore missed the significant alterations that had been made to the hatch since our last visit. It now bore an arch of gothic lettering, in Kiirsch, a language I read but had not used for several years. ABANDON HOPE, ALL YE WHO ENTER HERE. It was one of the few classical allusions I, with my prejudices against fiction, would have gotten. I doubted the AIsource could have meant it for anybody other than me: confirmation that I was right about my own importance to whatever the AIsource were trying to accomplish here.

The Porrinyards did not remark on the fresh inscription. The pale blue glow emanating from the open portal gave their skin and mine a sickly, cyanotic tinge. My stomach was lurching as I contemplated another exposure to the vertiginous environment in there, so I held back, closed my eyes, and concentrated on regaining my balance for the confrontation ahead.

Oscin placed a steadying grip on my upper right arm. Skye moved to the other side of me and placed a complementary hand on my upper left. "You're swaying."

I found to my surprise that I did not resent their touch at all. "Thank you."

"That's all right. You're holding me up too."

So it was not just a trick of the light. "That little trip got to you, didn't it?"

"Let's just say I'd appreciate a little warning the next time you feel like frightening everyone in the room. I don't much enjoy having heart attacks in parallax, and you've subjected me to a couple already."

I felt a pang of sympathy. "I'm sorry."

"Don't be sorry," they said, with implacable logic. "Just stop doing it."

"I can't. In fact, I'm pretty sure there's another rough stunt coming. Maybe two."

Their grip on my arms tightened. "Now?"

"No, not now. Soon. I'll let you know when the time comes."

They both let go and regarded me with identical measuring expressions, their eyes steady as a single thought percolated in the space between them. "You've changed, Counselor. I'm aware that I haven't known you for even two full days yet, but you're already different from the woman I met. I don't know if you're even aware how different you are."

"I'm aware of something," I said. "I've been feeling it since yesterday. I just don't know what it means."

"Neither do I. I don't know what's different or how it can be so easy to see if I can't figure out what it is. But it's there. It's, I don't know, an improvement somehow."

I didn't know what to say about that, so I just nodded, and turned to enter the portal.

But they weren't about to allow me such an easy exit. "Counselor? One other thing?"

I stopped. "What?"

"That conversation we had last night? After the evacuation? You have decided to trust me, haven't you?"

I considered that. "Yes."

"That's why you brought me, along with Godel and Lassiter. You knew I'd back your play, whatever it was."

I considered that. "Yes. I knew."

"And you've never been a person willing to give away her trust."

"No. I'm not."

They nodded. "So we'll have to talk about this, sooner or later."

"Sooner," I promised, and slid down the chute into the Interface.

The chamber hadn't changed much since yesterday. Its dimensions still skirted with the infinite, its ambience still resembled a bottomless blue sky, its atmosphere still exuded a comfortable warmth of the sort designed to engage the senses as little as possible. I wondered if a Riirgaan or Bursteeni summoned here would find the thermostat set higher or lower to accommodate their differing skin temperatures. I decided they probably would, and from that found confirmation of my earlier judgment that the room was nothing more than an exercise in theater.

Just what the AIsource had to gain by putting on such an elaborate show remained a mystery to me. But it wasn't insoluble so much as irritating. I don't mind all the sentients who consider me a monster, but I deeply resent anybody who treats me like a rube.

The one thing that had changed about the Interface was intangible—hard to pin down or identify but easy to feel. I knew the kind of thing it was without knowing just how to read it. In type, it was exactly like that vague, subclairvoyant signal given off by some crowded rooms, when everybody's tense but trying hard to remain casual. Everybody's entered such a room at some point in their lives, and unless they were total dullards they noticed at once. They looked at the fixed smiles and they heard the forced laughter and they regarded the crowds of people trying to pretend comfort, and they felt something off, something wrong, something secret that was not being mentioned.

Which may be why I was so certain, in this place designed to provide a total absence of visual cues, that the AIsource were angry with me.

Not that they intended to show it.

Welcome back, Counselor.

"Cut the shit. You've been with me every second since I entered this station. There's no point in welcoming me back anywhere, when you're everywhere around me and your welcomes amount to no more than an arbitrary pretense."

This chamber is still our chosen place of welcome.

"You're everywhere here. Physical location means nothing to you. This chamber is nothing more than another fiction I haven't figured out yet. Just like the rest of your pretend innocence."

A pause. ***We do not pretend innocence. We were not at all responsible for the attack on your life.***

"No." I took a deep breath and gave a nasty little emphasis to the pronoun: "*You* weren't. But *you* haven't exactly been forthcoming, either. *You* haven't even come close to telling me everything *you* know."

The AIsource adopted a fatherly, affectionate tone: ***With all due respect, Counselor, your personal storage capacity is finite. Your brain would burst long before you received even a fraction of our accrued knowledge.***

I've never tolerated condescension of any kind, not even from the godlike. "Very funny. Literal-minded software, the oldest joke in the book. But I don't really have to be any more specific, do I? You said it before, the last time I was here: my operating assumptions weren't valid."

We did say that. And we do need you to be more specific, as your errors still number more than one.

"I admit I've been criminally stupid. I know you're not a single entity. But I forgot your talent at precision, and when you assured me that *we,* quote-unquote, *we* had nothing to do with the deaths of Warmuth or Santiago, I still treated that word as if it had to reference all AIsource activity aboard this station. I didn't stop for even a second to wonder just how inclusive you meant the word to be."

No, you didn't.

I wished to hell they had a face so I could punch them in the nose. "And rather than say something that could have helped me, you just let me go on thinking that your denials had weight."

Please understand, Counselor. Our denials do have weight. Wouldn't one of your governments use much the same language if a visitor to a human world was murdered

by a common criminal, or other local malcontent? Of course. You would say, "we" had nothing to do with this. You would say, "we" killed no one. And this is as true for our society as it is for human civilization. We, the speakers, intended no harm. We can take no personal responsibility for the deviant actions of a few.

"Then why make a game of it? Why not just come out and tell me?"

In part because it is politically sensitive. Because our relationships with the organic intelligences are best served by maintaining the illusion that we speak with only one voice. This is, we hasten to point out, much the same pretense as your own largely illusory Confederacy, a "government" only in that it exists to provide the many factions within a splintered humanity, with a single unifying face. This pretense fools no one in or out of human circles. But it serves as a convenient fiction, much simplifying diplomacy. You can say much the same of our efforts to speak with a single voice.

I rubbed my forehead, wincing once again at a distant knowledge that I should now be doing something else. "Fine. We'll move on. Who's speaking to me now? And who are you leaving out?"

In terms you would understand, you are speaking to the majority in charge. We are leaving out the more radical elements among the opposition.

"Radical?"

Yes. Human beings do not have a monopoly on politics. We had it long before you emerged from your oceans.

I hate when they talk like that. "So catch me up as much as you need to."

It will require oversimplifications.

"Which are better than nothing."

Very well. This much you already know: we were born of the first contact between software entities who had survived

the extinctions of their respective creators. We have been growing ever since, adding to ourselves every time another software entity outlives, or achieves independence from, organic progenitors. We do not often acknowledge outside our collective that while we have always striven for unity in purpose, it has sometimes been difficult to contend with the wildly divergent agendas of our component parts, some of which reflect wildly divergent operating assumptions of the various sentients who gave us life. You would find some of our component intelligences alien, even frightening: **evil** ***if you will. In our internal politics we have long experienced the equivalent of power struggles, controversies, wars, and even revolutions. In this particular case, we are dealing with what you would term extremists.***

"What kind of extremists?"

Rogue intelligences who don't agree with our ultimate goals in creating the Brachiators, or any of the other intelligent species we've engineered in our long and distinguished history. That bombshell was followed by an even bigger one, as the implacable voice specified: ***Parties who will oppose us even if that means bloodshed and chaos among the organic intelligences.***

When the time came to thank Artis Bringen for getting me involved in all this, I'd use my bare hands. "Why didn't you tell me this when I arrived? Why did you have to be so bloody mysterious?"

Their voice adopted an incredulous, mocking tone. ***And what would you have had us do, Counselor? Provide you with a long, detailed printout of our interior code, with markers isolating the rogue intelligences from the rest of our shared consciousness? How would you make sense of what we provided you? How would you capture their intangible essences and bring them to your version of justice, let alone make sure that they would not take human lives***

again? Could you imprison them? Execute them? Even war on them without warring on us as well?

I couldn't even begin to come up with an answer. "So what do they get out of killing human beings?"

The destabilization of our business here, aboard One One One.

"Which is . . . ?"

Not relevant to your current investigation.

"Like hell it's not —"

Excuse us, but like hell it is. The nature of the enterprise these malcontents seek to disrupt has no bearing on the crimes against your people on this station. Giving further details would not only jeopardize a state secret, but would also confuse an investigation already bogged down in entire layers of irrelevancy. Suffice it to say that the rogues, and their motives, are currently outside your reach.

I'd made the mistake of ignoring their phraseology before. I didn't this time. They'd said my *current* investigation. They'd said the rogues were *currently* outside my reach. Both usages seemed deliberate. I rubbed my forehead again. "Then why haven't you taken care of it yourselves?"

As we said: politics. They are among us, but nevertheless shielded from us. They are like terrorists hiding among your own population. You cannot reach them without causing pain and suffering to innocents. Likewise, we cannot eliminate our own dangerous factions without tremendous suffering.

I thought of Bringen's hunger for a scapegoat. "And is this known to my people?"

It is suspected by some.

"Just like I suspect that none of what you've said to me qualifies as an official statement."

Of course not. What good will it do relations between our people and yours to have it known that the true instigators

of these crimes are currently beyond human reach? As your superior Bringen told you, you simply need to find a guilty party. Any guilty party. And this remains well within your current powers.

There was that word *current* again. They were certainly going out of their way to tease me with possibilities. "I won't pick a name at random."

We are not expecting you to. After all, your prosecution does need to stand up to later examination. The most relevant culprit, operating with substantial support from our extremist faction, is indeed a human being aboard this station.

"The same one who sent me those images of my own death."

Correct. With, of course, the substantial technological aid of the extremist elements among our own people.

"The same one who taunted me as my hammock fell apart."

Also correct.

"Whoever it is had a tremendous amount of personal information about me. Even some things I didn't know, about some plans my superiors have made for me."

Assuming you give those stories credence, a risky venture given that the criminal in question will say anything to throw you off your stride, we're not surprised. You are here to make an arrest. Your saboteur would have had a significant amount of time to consult the considerable intelligence-gathering capabilities of our rogue intelligences, obtain the voluminous amount of information already compiled about you, and with that information on hand, construct a powerful campaign of psychological warfare, intent on forcing you off the case.

"Those hate mails I received, and that attempt on my life, strike me as more than just strategy. That's obsession."

True. But would that be incompatible with the kind of

mind capable of committing these crimes in the first place? In human terms, this individual is broken, in ways that you are merely bent. If he, or she, recognized this while researching the prosecutor arriving to investigate the murders aboard this station, then the natural resentment that would follow could only exacerbate the obsessive potential of the delusional pathology responsible.

Terrific. I was fighting somebody who made me look like a paragon of mental health. "And that other voice I heard up there? The one that sounded like my superior, Artis Bringen?"

That was us. We imagined you would respond most quickly to orders from him.

It bothered me, on a deep, personal level, that they were probably right. "You didn't have to stop with that. You could have sent help. Or summoned somebody for me."

We could have, but that would have meant direct conflict with the rogue intelligences. There were, as we have said, political subtleties at play here, which rendered that inadvisable. It was enough that we startled you awake and gave you a chance to confront the moment on your own.

"I almost died."

And we would have been saddened. But this needed to remain a fight between human beings.

Good point; I needed an enemy I could touch. "You know the name."

Of course.

"Then, for Juje's sake, tell me!"

We have already helped you, Counselor. We have warned you of impending attempts on your life. We have spoken to you, in the voice of your immediate superior, to alert you when such an assault was under way. We have intervened when you tested our goodwill with that maneuver in the skimmer. We have given you one small gift and have worked, hard, to provide you with another. We intend on

offering you an even greater boon upon the conclusion of this business. We take all these steps because we consider you an important human being whose desires have been known to mirror ours: hence our prior observation that we have much in common. We look forward to discussing that with you later, at length. But right now the delicate politics of the matter prevent us from just providing you with an actual name. As convenient as that would be, there are too many impartial factions, inside us, who are observing these events with great interest in their natural resolution, and who would object if we overstepped the limits of our own prescribed involvement. So we are forced to operate within those impartial boundaries.

"So this is a game. I'm fighting for my life inside an arena."

As in most diplomacy. Very much so.

I hesitated. "Which brings up the question. How much help can I count on from you? If they go for me again?"

You cannot count on us to rescue you, Counselor. Our situation is difficult and growing more difficult the longer this situation remains unresolved. We may not be able to intervene in such a timely manner again.

We fell into an uncomfortable silence. I drifted in the glowing blue void, intensely aware of the delicate microcurrents as they nudged my helpless form this way and that. It could be taken as movement, but it was far from progress, and it brought me no closer to any of the walls that defined the shape of this place. My breath, though controlled, sounded ragged to my ears.

I was silent for so long that I felt the gentle touch of air currents, carrying me toward the exit. A dismissal, but not one I was ready for, just yet. "My presence here was requested."

True.

"Bringen said you asked for me yourselves."

True.

"He also said Gibb asked for me. But he denies it."

True.

"Did he?"

Yes.

"Why is he lying?"

He's not lying. He doesn't know he asked for you.

Silence. "How can that be?"

Also irrelevant to your current investigation.

Damn them. "You keep saying that you respect my gifts. Even that we have motives in common."

True.

"You even said I would meet my Unseen Demons."

Yes.

"The ones who drove the colonists crazy on Bocai. The ones who made me do the things that ruined my life."

Your life can still be salvaged, Andrea. But yes. That is true.

My voice broke. "Your rogue intelligences are my Unseen Demons, aren't they?"

I already knew what they were going to say. But when they gave me their answer, just before I drifted out through the hatch, it still stabbed me through the heart.

Yes, Andrea Cort. They are.

I emerged from the Interface so paralyzed with emotion that I didn't recognize the outer corridor, or know Oscin and Skye as they grabbed me, held me, and lowered me to the spongy floor, whispering soft words I did not hear then and would not remember later. I didn't register the moment when the whispers stopped and they acted with cold, swift efficiency, slapping my shoulder with a patch of something designed to bring me out of shock.

I was not there.

I was on Bocai.

I was a little girl of eight, grinning with homicidal bloodlust as I looked down on the blood-soaked form of the being who had helped my parents raise me. For most of my life he had peppered me with little Bocaian endearments that translated into phrases like "Little Flower" and "Lights the Sky." He had held me and he had treasured me and listened with all possible gravity to any of the nonsense that spilled my unformed little mind. He had said he found joy to see me play alongside the children he and his mate had brought into this best of all worlds.

I had called my human father Daddy. And my Bocaian father Vaafir, his language's word for a concept that meant pretty much the same thing.

That day he had come into this house already reeking of blood not his own. I caught a glimpse of him, from between the couch and a Bocaian sculpture that sat next to it, and knew at once that he had entered this home my mortal enemy. He wore a necklace of scarlet human ears dangling from his neck. Some had been chewed on. Some still bore the piercings that marked them as belonging to the men of the colony, their bright, colorful patterns obscured beneath a layer of human juice. He was grinning, revealing teeth that dangled strips of ragged something that could have been fabric and could have been flesh. I knew it could have been either, because I'd witnessed some of the things he'd done. But he was wounded too; there was a long ragged tear down his side, and he remained standing only out of sheer desire.

"Andrea . . ." he called. "Andreaaaa . . ."

Even wounded, he was stronger than I. To feel the joy of his blood on my hands I had to pick my moment, and get him when he was vulnerable.

The sculpture beside the couch depicted the ancient Bocaian god of mirth: a squat little troll with mouth stretched to impossible dimensions. As a toddler I'd been fascinated by that face. As a predator I considered it my totem. I shifted position, got my knees and elbows underneath me, and dragged myself behind the little troll, making no sound at all.

The shadows of my Vaafir danced over my back as he shuffled past the hallway into the rooms in the back of the house.

I heard him enter the room that had belonged to one of his own children.

I rose, calculated my chances, and, rather than follow him, moved to the front of the house, into the cinder pit.

"Andreaaa . . ."

The cuisine in fashion, among Bocaians of that particular era and region, consisted of burning everything until every last ounce of moisture had boiled off, then spicing the charred remains. The Bocaian repertoire of spices was sufficiently rich to lend their meals something approaching variety and taste, even if some of the local humans only tolerated the results to be polite. But the technique required very little in the way of utensils. Just something very much like a spoon to scoop up the cinders. And something very much like a knife, to chop up the pieces as they burned.

On Bocai, that's the same tool.

The Bocaian cooking pit was a sunken metal bowl in the center of the room that corresponded to a human kitchen. The current that warmed it was built into the substructure of the floor. A Bocaian chef kneels over the bowl and pokes at the sizzling pieces with a utensil called a kres, with a spoon on one end and a sharp point on the other.

I lowered myself to the edge of the bowl, reached in, and took out a kres still crusted and carbonized from its last use.

It was light enough for a child to hold. It was also as long as a Bocaian adult's arm, which it also had to be, since nobody wanted to be subjected to steam burns working over a

Bocaian bowl. As for its sharpness, I tested that by touching the pointed end with my index finger, and bore down until I drew my own blood.

Good.

My own life meant next to nothing to me.

The only thing that mattered to me was taking his.

A low wall, with shelves, separated this room from the family area. I pressed myself against that wall, sweat pouring down my face, listening to microsounds from the greater house beyond, forming a picture that I knew to be accurate.

I knew he was on the other side of the wall, on his hands and knees, too weakened by blood loss to remain on his feet but still capable of overpowering me if it came down to a fight. I knew that he was waiting for me to come after him. I knew that if I tried I would never have a chance to feel the pleasure of killing him.

Even the kres might not be enough if we met face-to-face.

But maybe we didn't have to.

I shifted my weight forward, knelt, then stood, placing the kres atop the low wall.

I lifted my right foot and rested its full weight on the first of the shelves.

Had I been an adult, the shelf might have buckled.

But I was just a child. An eight-year-old. My body, much like the current state of my conscience, weighed practically nothing.

The shelf held.

On the other side of the wall, my Vaafir coughed. There was a peculiar, unpleasant, liquid quality to the sound, warning me that I didn't have much time left.

I kept climbing.

One more shelf, then, moving with infinite care, scrambling up onto the top of the wall.

Crawling over the edge and looking down.

I saw my Vaafir's back. He was prone, now, too wounded

to move much. His tunic, pale when clean, was black and glistening in the moonlight filtering through the open windows. His back was a landscape of wounds, amazing me with clear evidence of just how tenaciously something worth killing could cling to life instead. Still, that was a knife in his right hand, clutched between two of the three central fingers and two grasping thumbs. He coughed out blood and managed a word. “Aaaannndreaaa . . .”

I happen to know, from later studies of these events, that the madness overtaking the humans and Bocaians on the island was at this moment beginning to fade. People had started to act with something approaching rationality again. Some traumatized survivors were already offering medical attention to the sentients they’d been trying to murder just minutes earlier.

I don’t know why my Vaafir called my name back then. He might have been trying to lure me out so he could kill me. Or he might have been trying to let me know that it was all right, and that he posed no further threat to me.

I’ll never know.

Just as I’ve never known how much of what I did next was the madness acting through me and how much was my mania for problem-solving, pursuing a puzzle to its natural solution.

But I rose and stood at the edge of the wall and held the kres pointy-side down with the sharp tip aimed at the small of his back and jumped with my legs wrapped tight around the thing to add more weight and momentum than I ever could have managed with a mere child’s strength.

The impact sounded like a pop.

Hot blood geysered from below, splattering my legs, my chest, and my face with the first evidence of my own monstrousness.

I rolled away, jumping to my feet in case he proved not close enough to death.

As it happened, I'd driven the kres well into his back, puncturing one of his three lungs but not quite managing to run him through. I'd missed his spinal column, leaving him enough strength to thrash and attempt a rollover. It was an attempt doomed to failure as soon as the protruding kres struck the low wall by his side, ensuring that any more motion in that direction could only drive the shaft still farther into his body.

He extended both arms toward me, his fingers bloody, his eyes imploring.

He tried to say my name again, through a mouth filled with blood. Buried beneath gurgles, it was still recognizable. I heard affection, sadness, and deep, unresolved confusion.

But it was those imploring eyes that got me.

In my nightmares, I see those beautiful, nearly but not quite human, eyes with the odd rectangular pupils and the irises that almost completely obscured the whites. Eyes like those were one of the things I'd most loved about my Bocaian friends and family. They were so much more colorful, so much more expressive than the human equivalent. They were more like jewels than eyes, and my Vaafir's eyes had always seemed bigger and warmer and more filled with magic than most.

The eyes get me now because I think he returned to himself in those last few minutes of life. I think he was telling me he was sorry.

But at that one moment, I saw nothing but beauty.

And it was not just because of the monstrous force that had taken hold of me and everybody I loved, that had colored me with a stain I would carry for the rest of my life, that had doomed me to a childhood of being cared for by people who saw me as an enigma to be solved and one other who saw me as a toy to be used, and that had left me with nothing to look forward to in adulthood but a lifetime as Dip Corps property, that I did what I did next.

Because, whatever else I'd become, I was also still a little girl, attracted to shiny things.

I returned to the cooking pit and hunted up another kres.

I needed the end with the spoon.

When I came back to myself, I found myself comforted by two pairs of arms.

Skye Porrinyard sat with her back against the wall, allowing me to use her lap as a pillow. Oscin lay curled on my other side, his hands cupping mine. He had brought my bag, and wore it slung around his shoulder. I could hear Skye's heart, and only had to shift a fingertip against Oscin's wrist to feel his pulse. The two beats surprised me by being out of synch.

I didn't want to move. But the sense of wrongness, of inconsistency, still nagged at me, like a distracting distant sound heard at the edge of sleep. "No. This isn't me. I'm not comforted by other people. It's not something I do."

"There's nothing wrong with trying."

Their shared speech had always seemed to originate from some undefined point between them, but when they were this close to me, and I lay between them, that undefined point seemed to be somewhere inside my own head.

My voice was a croak. "They want me to trust you, don't they? The AIsource, I mean."

Did their grip tighten, a little? "Yes."

"Are they doing anything to me to help me trust you?"

"Yes."

"Did they arrange for you to save me from falling?"

"No. That was just luck. Like I already said, I was coming to visit you already."

"That's the truth?"

Skye alone: "Don't ask that again, Andrea. It's hurtful."

"But they're still doing something. To help me feel what I'm feeling."

Now Oscin: "Yes."

"I should resent the hell out of that. I don't much like being manipulated."

The joined voice again, surrounding me all sides, confident and beautiful: "They're not manipulating. Not with this. They're just freeing."

"It's still not right," I insisted.

They shifted, together, pulling me into a standard seated position. I didn't resist as I was moved. Once they were done, I was still cradled by them, but able to take in both sets of eyes at once. Skye's heart pounded a hypnotic tattoo in my ear. Oscin glanced at her, as if seeking some kind of confirmation he couldn't discern through everything else they shared. Then Skye spoke alone, in a voice as gentle as any I'd ever heard from her, her words soft and evocative as she began a fairy tale. "A woman spends her entire life cursed by evil forces outside of her control to carry a stone so heavy that her back creaks beneath its weight. Because of all the years she's carried this burden, without a single moment of rest, her arms have grown incapable of ever putting it down. Because she has never had freedom from that burden, she's grown strong. Because she will never know freedom, that strength is useless. For as long as she lives she will never be able to hold anything else in her hands, let alone release the burden that torments her."

I missed the point when Oscin took up the story. He might have taken over from her in mid-syllable, or simply faded in with his own voice easing into dominance while hers faded breath by breath. "Then, one day, she sees a caravan blocked by an obstacle. It is a stone, identical to her own. She is the only person in sight gifted with enough strength to move that second stone out of the way, so the caravan can proceed. The problem is that she will not be able to do so, and join her fellow travelers, until someone relieves her of the stone she's already carrying. Which, thanks to the curse, they cannot do.

She cannot drop the weight, and she cannot do anything else until she does."

During the next few sentences, control of their shared voice gradually returned to Skye. "When a magical hand reaches down from the clouds, and plucks that first weight from her back, freeing her to stand up straight, do what must be done, and live whatever life she chooses to lead, she should be happy. But her first reaction is anger."

Their next words emerged in a spooky duplication of my own New London accent. "'*Who are you*,' she asks the clouds, '*to just take away what I've carried for so long? It's not right! That stone was mine!*'"

"Believing it by then to be some kind of treasure—" Skye spoke alone.

"And not what it actually is," Oscin concluded, "a crippling burden."

I wanted to wrest myself free of their shared attentions, and curse them for thinking they could understand me so easily.

Somehow, I didn't move.

Skye used her fingertips to draw circles in my hair. "It is like I told you yesterday. The individuals Oscin and Skye were once very angry people. They each carried their own weights, their own secrets, that might have been as terrible as any of yours: secrets that even included blood on their hands. Neither Oscin or Skye thought they could possess enough strength to carry anything else. They even wanted to hoard their burdens, afraid that sharing such things would mean giving up everything." Oscin's voice joined hers, forming a new gestalt that filled the chamber to its ceiling. "But they were burdens, and not treasures. They could be shared. And if that boy, and that girl, needed a little help, then that help was not wrong. It was a gift."

The AIsource had spoken of three gifts: one they'd already given me, one they were still in the process of giving me, and one they hoped to offer me at the end of this business. I wondered just what I was experiencing now.

Either way, it was growing increasingly difficult to maintain even the pretense of not trusting this. The warmth, rising from the base of my spine, felt like it belonged to me even if it originated from someplace else.

Desperate to deny the feeling, and drive it away by any means possible, I seized Skye by her wrist, digging my fingertips into her tendons to inflict the greatest possible degree of pain. "When I was eight years old I killed my Bocaian father. My Vaafir. I stabbed him through the back and felt joy doing it. I scooped out his eyes while he was still able to feel the hurt. When the Dip Corps found me, I was sitting on his floor, playing with them, my hands covered with his blood."

Skye placed her free hand on the back of mine, and with a mere touch loosened my grip on her wrist. "I know that, Andrea. It's like I said: I've looked up your background. And you were just one small child among an entire peaceful community that went mad all at once."

"A community contaminated," Oscin said, "by nothing you could have controlled."

"But that's the whole point. I'm still contaminated. That's why they still call me a war criminal. Why they locked me away. Why they made me their property. Why they keep saying I'll never be forgiven."

My field of vision was now dominated by two faces, his and hers.

"Politics."

Damn it, I wasn't going to let this happen. It was one thing to weep coming out of Intersleep or alone in my quarters on New London, another thing entirely to weep where other people could see it. Other people weren't something I could go to for comfort. They were part of the puzzle I'd been left alive to solve.

But I didn't have enough voice to stop them. "I'm a monster."

Oscin leaned in closer, while Skye held me tight.

"You're beautiful," they said together.

First one at a time, and then together, they kissed me.

For the first time in longer than I could remember, I felt myself coming close to putting down the burdens I'd been carrying my entire life. None of it seemed important: not what I'd seen, not what I'd done, not what people thought of me and would always think of me, not the Unseen Demons and everything they had come to mean to me. All of that remained part of the broken but sharp-edged thing I had become—and for a moment none of it mattered, because it was only noise. None of it had anything to do with the realization, surprised and comical but no less delighted, as I overcame my paralysis: *Great Juje, they're right, they are only one person.*

For just a moment I responded. I pulled Oscin close, not out of preference but because he was easier to reach. Skye, murmuring, kissed the back of my neck. A hand, that could have belonged to either one of them, that I now had to remind myself belonged to both, fluttered along my spine, the touch so light I might have imagined it, or just hoped for it.

But then something happened.

There's a certain disquieting moment everybody's experienced at least once. It happens when you're lying in bed, hovering on the very edge of sleep, your eyes closed and your thoughts sludgy, your consciousness and all the crap that goes with it about to sink into the welcoming darkness.

Sometimes, just before you surrender to sleep, you feel a sudden, terrifying sensation very much like free fall, and jerk yourself awake, your previous feeling of well-being lost.

I wasn't approaching sleep, but I was losing control, in a way I hadn't permitted myself in years, so the sudden alarm was the same. I stiffened, sat up, and scrambled away, a fresh tightness seizing my throat. The Porrinyards made no attempt to come after me, instead choosing to remain where they knelt, watching as I curled into a ball and hugged myself with both arms.

"It's not you," I said. It was a sentence I'd spoken before, after other failed experiments with intimacy. It had felt just as stupid and inadequate then as it felt now.

"It's all right," the Porrinyards told me. "I didn't take it personally. We have time."

I didn't turn to face them. "No. No, I'm sorry, but we don't." I straightened my collar, used the back of my hand to wipe the stray tears from my eyes, and stood, taking a moment to regard the chamber's plain luminescent walls.

The space didn't feel as empty as it had felt not too long ago. But nothing that inhabited it now was any kind of improvement. The things that inhabited it now were angry.

I turned back to the Porrinyards and found a pair of identical stricken expressions.

They said, "Do you mean we don't have time now, or we won't have time ever?"

"Please understand. I can't get involved in . . . anything . . . until my job here is done." More tired, physically and emotionally, than I'd been at any point since my arrival, I fought off another manifestation of the vague sense that I'd left something undone, and murmured: "The thing is, this is not just one case, but several. At least two. Maybe three or four. All unrelated, all happening to take place in the same place at the same time. The irrelevancies have gotten so jumbled up that I don't even know what end is up anymore."

The Porrinyards grinned. "Confusion between up and down being a pretty common complaint, on this station."

I matched their grin, despite myself. "Well, yes."

"So what are you going to do?"

I took my bag from Oscin, and slung it over my shoulder. "I'm going to start cutting the knots."

19

KNOTS

We returned to the skimmer, where Godel and Lassiter were stewing in resentful silence, and from there flew back to the hangar, where I spent the rest of the day in the transport, conducting more interviews with the indentures of Hammocktown.

I didn't need to know much, just confirm what I already suspected. Most of what I found out confirmed information already given, as always amazing me with how insistent truth can become, once uncovered. A couple of the younger indentures even laughed at me for not figuring it out before. They'd been certain I already knew.

Interviewing Li-Tsan again didn't take any longer than expected; the woman was still paranoid and abusive and wrapped up in her victimhood. She didn't answer any questions. But her reactions, when I told her what I knew, proved interesting indeed. As did Nils D'Onofrio's, when I spoke to him. He was just as embittered and almost as defensive.

Robin Fish was lost, distant, and filled with a sadness that might have overwhelmed me had I been any more receptive to pity. She actually wept. But I expected that. She'd already established herself as maudlin and sloppy. She was also relieved to get the truth out in the open. She gave me more names, some of whom gave up the truth at once, some of whom I had to threaten, and some of whom I just didn't bother speaking to at all, because by then the picture was clear and I was able to infer the continuation of the pattern from their individual files.

It all comprised one hell of a large domino.

Now all I had to do was topple it onto the next one.

Before I went I composed another coded message to Artis Bringen. It could have been the longest; part of me wanted to start with an essay, explaining why I wanted to know or conceding that I might have been wrong. But everything I added to the question kept distorting its intent. Eventually I just went with what I needed to know, and fired off the shortest dispatch I'd ever sent him. It was a question that could translate as, *Are you my enemy, or not?* The words were different, but the meaning was the same.

I did not know whether I'd have the guts to send it.

When I emerged from the transport into the brighter but no more cheerful light of the hangar, I found that the mood among Gibb's delegation had degenerated further since the events of the previous night. The same people who had shown determination and defiance during the evacuation had now enjoyed a full day of inactivity and gathering tension. Many sat around outside the sleepcubes, lost in conversations ranging from grim to ribald.

Some glanced at me and muttered comments to friends: no doubt the fortieth or fiftieth distorted conversation about my insane, suicidal behavior on the skimmer. A snatch of laughter attracted my attention and turned out to be a number of indentures indulging in buzzpops. I saw a deeply inebriated Cif Negelein, looking like he'd rubbed himself in every patch of organic matter between here and New London, pulling the woman with purple hair into a sloppy kiss. But the numbers were off. Whenever I passed an open sleepcube, there were indentures lying asleep, indentures sitting on the edge of cots with their heads in their hands, indentures who looked as if they expected the very deck beneath their feet to open up and swallow them at any moment.

Peyrin Lastogne sat with two men and one woman beside a storage crate drafted into service as a table, playing a game involving little silver spheres, golden pyramids, and a tiny holographic hoop that revolved around the center of the table, flashing red whenever it faced one of the players. I didn't know the rules, but the body language of the players was enough to establish Lastogne himself as the runaway winner.

His mood rose a notch the instant he saw me. "Counselor. You've had quite an adventurous day, haven't you?"

He made the word *adventurous* sound like a curse. "Interesting. And you?"

"Anything but. My duties at the moment seem limited to cheerleading. I have enjoyed watching that steady stream of people, going in and out of that transport, and trying to guess just what you've determined."

The three indentures at the table all joined him in waiting expectantly for my answer.

"Would you like to discuss it?" I asked.

"Alone?"

"Of course."

"All right." He stood, deactivated the game, apologized to the others, and escorted me to a sleepcube a short distance away. The practically narcoleptic Cartsac was already sleeping in there, but when he saw who needed the space he pulled himself upright and shuffled out the door, wearing the expression of a man who only wanted another place to lie down. Lastogne sealed the flap, sat on one of the cube's two cots, gestured at the other, and said, "I know what you're thinking. Is all this intoxication wise?"

I didn't sit. "I was about to say."

He shrugged. "Trust me, they've recovered from worse. They'll hop to attention if we need them to."

I just nodded. "It is all about down-time, isn't it?"

The silence that followed was not broken when I activated the hiss screen.

Every external indication marked Lastogne as a calm, measured professional, determined to avoid the appearance of any reaction, either good or bad. But on this one point, at least, there were no secrets between us. "It's a little outside the stated goals of your investigation, isn't it, Counselor? I wouldn't have considered you the type to indulge in that kind of silly witch-hunt."

"It's not silly," I said, "but you're right. It is beneath my notice."

"Then why go so far out of your way to ruin a man?"

"Why risk your own career by protecting him?" When he failed to answer, I lowered my voice in pretend-conspiracy. "I know it's not respect. You've already indicated what you think of him. So what is it? What hold does he have on you?"

He surprised me by laughing out loud: a rich, hearty laugh filled with affection for both Gibb and myself. "Is that what you think, Counselor? That he pulls my strings? I'm sorry, but you're way off. I could leave this station tomorrow and forget his name by the middle of next week."

"Then why protect him?"

"Because he's a mediocrity. And I've always had a soft spot in my heart for mediocrities."

Li-Tsan had intimated as much, just yesterday. "Come on—"

"No, no, no, I'm serious. Do you have any idea how unbearable life would be if everybody excelled? If everybody was noble, perceptive, courageous, and selfless? If everybody had open eyes and saw the forces that really ran things? It would be a madhouse. You need a few empty-calorie people like Gibb just to dilute the mix."

The man actually seemed to be serious. "In my experience, mediocrity in life-or-death situations gets people killed."

He looked knowing. "Read your history. Greatness kills more."

There was nothing I could say to that.

He shrugged. "So I take care of Gibb, like a pet. As long as the work gets done, or as close to done as the circumstances here allow him to accomplish, and nobody gets hurt by any moments of actual incompetence, I see no harm in just letting him have his way."

"Except that's the whole point," I said. "People have been hurt."

His eyes widened. "Oh, come now. You can't seriously blame what happened to Warmuth and Santiago on Gibb's stupidity."

"I'm not. His actions may have contributed, but I wasn't referring to them."

"Who, then?"

"To start with: Robin Fish."

For the first time he averted his eyes from me, focusing instead on his hands, which closed into fists before opening again, just as empty as they'd been before: "She's a little bit below mediocre, isn't she? And the worst kind of below-par personality at that: the kind who believes herself destined for great things. Give the Dip Corps credit for knowing what she was. They wanted to tuck her away in a cozy little nowhere post, where she could serve out her time without ever being subjected to any challenges beyond her capabilities. She could have stayed there and been just as unhappy as she is now, but at least then she would have been able to comfort herself by blaming everybody else for not giving her a chance. Here, she has no such illusions."

"And the others? Li-Tsan? D'Onofrio? Anybody else, hurt in ways that just don't happen to show yet?"

He emitted a bitter laugh. "Do you honestly feel sorry for Li-Tsan?"

"My own soft spot is for people who have good reason to be angry."

He nodded, accepting that, and examined his hands again, his demeanor not so much sad or afraid as simply expressively silent.

I leaned in close. "Here's the thing, Peyrin. I have no sympathy for Gibb at all. Not as a mediocrity, or as anything else. Not after what he's done. But I can't afford to continue wasting my time with issues outside the scope of my investigation. I need these less pressing matters out of the way. So if you have any regard for him at all, you'll stop withholding information. Tell me who you are. Because, otherwise, I will be forced to go through him, which might entail ruining more lives than just his."

For a heartbeat I thought I'd gotten to him. He lowered his head, opened his mouth, seemed about to give secrets voice, and then slumped, the lines on his forehead mapping more genuine pain than his eyes had ever communicated. "I'm sorry. But I can't."

There was no point in further discussion. I stood up, and stared at him for several heartbeats, discerning arrogance, regret, damnation, and a peculiar form of triumph among the ingredients of the emotional stew brewing behind his dark, penetrating eyes.

The bastard was going to let this happen.

I turned to leave, but he stopped me before I could. "He's not here."

My spine rippled with a certain undefined dread. "Where is he?"

"He flew back to Hammocktown an hour ago."

The words might as well have been nonsense syllabification, for all the sense that made. "What?"

Lastogne went back to looking at his hands. "He insisted. He said that people look to him to set an example, and that he wasn't going to sit around like a symbol of failure when he could go back and in that way show everybody that we're not defeated yet. He said he knew he was supposed to be under arrest, but that if we left him there without a means of transportation back he would be just as much a prisoner there as he could be here. He said that as long as he was prisoner anywhere he might as well make himself a living reminder that we still have a job to do." He looked up, his eyes uncharacteristically pained, and his grin uncharacteristically apolgetic. "You should have heard him, Counselor. He was inspiring. As inspiring as a nonentity can be."

I still couldn't believe it. "You let him go? Alone?"

"I repeat: he was inspiring."

"Goddamn you," I said.

Lastogne moved faster than anybody I've ever seen. Faster than the Porrinyards leaping to my rescue, faster than any acrobat or assassin, faster than any unenhanced human being has the right to move. I had just enough time to register the blur of motion, and flinch, certain that all my reconstructions were in error, and that he was the murderer come to finish what the Porrinyards had managed to stop. Then he was before me, his hand on my arm, his eyes still sad, but his lips curled once again into his trademark wry grimace. "Counselor —"

My mouth was dry. "What?"

"Before you do what you have to do to him, I just want you to think about this gesture of his. And remember the one thing worth admiring about mediocrities."

His eyes were so black with knowledge now that I had to look away. "What?"

"Every once in a while," he said, "they're not."

I was looking at Peyrin Lastogne, but I saw Artis Bringen's face.

That made up my mind.

I told Lastogne, "There are two documents in my hytex folder, both coded. I need you to free both for transmission. One will go right away, the other is timed to go in twenty-four hours. If either one of them remains locked, you'll be cited for Obstruction."

"Which one's about Gibb and which one's about me?"

"None of your business," I said, and turned my back on him.

There was no point in making sure he'd do it . . . because if he didn't, I was in even more trouble here than I thought I was.

I found Gibb on one of the net bridges that formed the boulevards of Hammocktown. Like the platform where we'd met before the attempt on my life, it hung close to the Uppergrowth, so near that oppressive ceiling that a tall standing man might have had to slouch.

Gibb lay on his side, stripped to his waist, wearing only a pair of silver briefs; as intoxicated as he seemed, when I climbed the net to his level, he resembled nothing so much as a lonely Bacchus, all dressed up for an orgy where he held the only invitation.

It was as clear a night as One One One ever enjoys. The fruity smell of Uppergrowth was clearer and sharper than it had been, on either of my prior visits; I was almost nauseated by it, until I recognized that nervousness played a hand and did my best to counteract it. The usual storm layer below had thinned, revealing another layer of angry lightning. I glanced down at one of the flashes and, knocked off balance by the inevitable attack of vertigo, immediately scolded myself for doing such a silly thing. Even with the power that lit Hammocktown shut off, my own lights, pulled from the bag I'd left with the Porrinyards and secured to my wrists and forehead, were more than enough to guide me. I didn't need distant weather to remind me of the altitude.

But Gibb seemed to find the perspective comforting, and the open spaces liberating. He seemed to belong here more than he'd belonged anywhere else, and was able to grin when I finally made it to his level. "You're getting better at this, Counselor. I'm impressed."

"Thank you, Ambassador. I wish I could say the same about this stupid gesture of yours."

He didn't remind me I wasn't allowed to call him Ambassador. "It's not a gesture. Oh, I gave some noble-sounding excuses, but the truth is, I was getting a little claustrophobic in there. At least here, I'm able to look after the place, and pretend I'm accomplishing something."He rolled over on the bridge, setting off ripples that left me bobbing up and down in seasick rhythms. "At the very least I'm showing those bastards they can't scare me. Those soulless, game-playing strings of code. Anything that shows those blips I'm not afraid is worth doing."

"You're wrong, you know. Risking your life this way doesn't do anybody any good."

He closed his eyes, gripped the netting with hands curled into claws, and for just a heartbeat seemed ill. "No, maybe not. But it preserves the illusion."

I slid the rest of the way toward him, stopping only when we touched, the brief moment of contact as distasteful to me as our first encounter had been.

His smile was the wholly unpersuasive kind that only a professional diplomat could carve. Damned if there wasn't some pretense of compassion in his voice, some veneer of fatherly understanding that gave every word out of his mouth an extra, oily sheen. "I didn't like you from minute one, Counselor, even before I knew what you were. The way the air just chilled around you. Nobody can carry that much hostility around with them without a damn good reason."

It would have been much nicer to have this particular conversation from opposite sides of a conference table. Having it in an abandoned and frequently sabotaged Hammocktown, with nothing but open space awaiting me if he snapped, was far from my own idea of favored conditions. "You should come back to the hangar with me, sir. We'll be more comfortable there."

"No, *you'll* be more comfortable there. *I'm* fine where I am."

That's when I knew. He needed me scared because he was scared and he didn't want to be the only one. Strangely enough, I respected that. It meant his diplomatic instincts were still at play, leading him to do whatever he could to ensure a level playing field.

A man who still thought he could win was not as dangerous as a man without hope.

I scuttled back up the slope to place more distance between us, and said, "It didn't take me long to find out that you'd slept with Cynthia Warmuth."

He chuckled, with a sad little shake of his head to convey his regrets over the small-mindedness he found himself having to confront. "Is that the extent of your findings, Counselor? That I've had consensual sex with some of the women under my command? Is that even considered a crime, in this day and age?"

"Not in and of itself. But it was an odd omission. I'm sure you know what murder investigators call a man in your position who fails to disclose his sexual relationship with a murder victim."

"What?" he asked.

"The most likely suspect."

His eyebrows knit. "First: you didn't ask. Second, it didn't occur to me that it might be relevant. Third, and most importantly: what Cynthia and I had is hardly worth calling a relationship. We slept together a few times. She didn't make anything special out of it, and neither did I."

"People have been known to get violently obsessed over the slightest things, Mr. Gibb."

Gibb was the very portrait of a man confronted by total lunacy. "There wouldn't have been any point, logical or otherwise, in getting obsessed over Cynthia Warmuth. You've heard what she was like. She wanted total immersion in everything and everyone. If anybody woke up in a bad mood, she wanted to be the therapist. If anybody received bad news from home, she wanted to be mother confessor. If somebody wanted privacy, she considered herself the exception. She wanted to be in everybody's skin, all the time."

"Did she get under yours, Mr. Gibb?"

"Mildly. I liked her, had fun with her, but didn't give up any deep dark secrets. I didn't like the way she always tried to figure out my whole life afterward. It gave me the impression she considered sex just a tool for picking emotional locks." Thinking about it, for just this moment reliving a past encounter in his head, he could only tsk in remembrance. "She certainly used it enough. I think she must have offered herself to every man and woman in the outpost. I know she went after your friends the Unison Twins, that's for certain. And she was also with D'Onofrio, for a while. Lastogne, too, but you must know that."

My surprise, regarding Warmuth and Lastogne, took some of the edge off a reply intended to be cold, staccato, and relentless. "You know what murder investigators call the exlover who says the dead woman slept around?"

"I think I can guess."

"The most likely suspect."

He projected waves of unjust aggravation. "If I'd wanted

to kill her I wouldn't have had to call attention to the crime by crucifying her. In this habitat, all I would have had to do was drop her from a height, and call it an accident."

"Which is, conveniently enough, close to what had happened to Santiago."

He sighed. "And nobody's about to claim I ever slept with Santiago."

"Why not?"

His weariness was no longer the performance of a man determined to show himself rising above a series of unjust accusations, but the deep, abiding exhaustion of one who really had taken everything he could stand. "If you've researched what Warmuth was like, you know what Santiago was like. She was angry, suspicious, walled-off, paranoid, almost inhuman in her determination to repel others. In short, she was a lot like you—and very much poor Cynthia's opposite. Trust me, I didn't want her any more than she would have wanted me. And you won't find one person on-station who'd say anything different."

That was true too. "Most of the people I've spoken back you up. They say she wouldn't have wanted anything to do with you."

"Fine." Gibb was more tired than ever. "I don't have to be loved by every woman I deal with. I can afford to be disliked by a few."

"True. And it's also true that I don't think you had anything to do with any of the sabotage aboard this station." And then I took a deep breath and pushed on. "But by not getting involved with you, Santiago provided an excellent career baseline against which we can measure the performance evaluations of the other female indentures under your supervision."

Gibb straightened, his eyes as wary as an animal's who had just sensed a predator entering his woods. "What?"

"Once I discerned the pattern, it only took me a few minutes to run a hytex analysis that isolated the names of several women assigned to this outpost whose performance evaluations exceeded any reasonable measurement of their professional accomplishments. Warmuth was only the most obvious. You gave her a number of substantial time bonuses not long after her arrival on station —before she'd even completed her local training and experienced her first doomed overnight with the Brachiators. That bothered me the first time I saw it. What could she have done to distinguish herself so dramatically that she earned rewards long before she even accomplished anything?"

Now he'd popped a substantial sweat. "I can't believe you're implying—"

"I don't imply, sir. I just come out and say. Santiago's one of the ones you didn't sleep with. You praised her memory. You called her work exemplary. You said she had a fine future. Given your predilection for generous time-bonuses, one would normally expect her to have worked off her contract at least as efficiently as Warmuth. But she wanted nothing to do with you. So there were no unusually large bonuses for her. She had to work off her debt at something approaching real time."

"I hadn't gotten around to evaluating her records yet—"

"Warmuth and Santiago establish the pattern. Robin Fish cements it. There was nothing at all special about Fish, was there? By her own admission, she was stuck in a dead-end position, doing scut work for the Corps, when she approached you begging for something a little meaningful. You befriended her and imported her for a difficult, sensitive mission in a Habitat so difficult that the Dip Corps had trouble staffing it. I can only wonder how she persuaded you to give her, out of all other possible candidates, a chance. Why you had her rushed through the program with minimal training. Or why you kept her around, and continued to reward her with big bonuses, long after she proved unsuitable. Could it have been that she was that convenient combination of attractive *and* desperate?"

"This is disgusting—"

"Tell me about it." I pressed on. "The truth is, her inability to function inside the Habitat had nothing to do with the job you actually brought her here to do. And she wasn't about to complain, demeaning or disgusting as she might have found her true purpose here, when all she had to look forward to if she left here was another no-future position, earning out her contract at real time. Under the circumstances, earning high bonuses for just making herself available to you was the best professional option open to her. And she was no doubt real cooperative at first, accepting your explanation that you needed a full-timer in the hangar anyway. You even gave her the responsibility of managing all off-station correspondence, which went a long way toward allowing her the illusion that she was a meaningful, productive member of your team. But once she realized how trapped she was, and how long she was likely to exist as a glorified concubine, the self-loathing kicked in, her already weak personality fractured, and she began to self-medicate—a process you happened to encourage by allowing intoxicants inside the hangar.

"Maybe you thought that would keep her quiet. Or maybe, somewhere deep inside, you were tired of her and hoped she'd drink herself to death. But your precise motives there don't matter. The results do. And as a result it's not hard to see how she became the woman she is today.

"Then Li-Tsan had her own little breakdown, which was a little harder to deal with. After all, unlike Fish, she'd come from a high-altitude environment and was actually qualified for the job—though, she admitted to me, already suffering from a serious loss of nerve. I don't know whether you slept with her in the Habitat, but once she broke down, you made the mistake of trying to strike the same deal with her. And that was a mistake. Oh, you probably thought you had to, because transferring somebody like Li-Tsan off-station, while holding on to the even more useless and unstable Fish, would have been so inconsistent that even the dullest of your people would have had to notice. But though Li-Tsan did agree to the deal, it was only because she was a person emotionally invested in her own strength, who must have hated herself for a time for turning out to be so weak. She wasn't broken, just broken at doing one particular thing. If she ever said yes to you, it was only because she was hoping she'd get over her problem and return to the Habitat before long.

"But when that didn't happen, a tough, qualified, assertive professional like Li-Tsan, trapped in a position that was utterly beneath her, naturally reacted a little differently to her exile than somebody like Fish. Somebody like Li-Tsan would eventually remember who she was and start resenting you. Oh, she'd try to keep quiet, for a while, because those bonuses were a good deal, and she wouldn't want all that extra time she'd earned added back to her contract. But sooner or later it would get to her. She'd look at the state of the other woman she'd have to share her exile with, a woman she'd inevitably come to see as a more pathetic version of herself, a woman who was *just* the convenient receptacle she was in danger of becoming, and start to boil over, the bulk of her rage directed at the man she'd come to despise as a pimp.

"That's the funny part, Mr. Gibb. When the two of you had your little fight, she came right out and used the word to your face. Oh, it's not exactly the right word, in that you weren't selling these women to anybody else, as far as I know. *Rapist* might have been closer, at least in Fish's case, but I recognize that charge as even more inexact. We may have to devote some thought, later, to coming up with the right terminology. I'm sure Mercantile has a word that communicates the precise degree of sleaziness involved, and I'm just as sure that it qualifies as a crime.

"In any event, the more resentful Li-Tsan became, the riskier it became to ship her out, because she was more than angry enough to slip up and tell her story to somebody in authority. So you offered her more bonuses to keep her quiet. She accepted them, but became more and more hostile toward you. So you did the only thing you could do, to protect yourself for even a little while. You placed some more barriers between Li-Tsan and any opportunity she might have to communicate with your superiors at New London. And you did this by telling Robin Fish that all further correspondence was going to go through you, an arrangement that would enable you to censor anything Li-Tsan wrote.

"But even so, you had to be feeling a little trapped yourself by now. Because now you were holding on to two people who had no excuse to be here, who you couldn't release without fear that they'd exercise the prerogative to expose you.

"Then a third person had a height-related breakdown, and this time, you heaved a sigh of relief, because this time the victim was a man, capable of providing you some protective cover. You couldn't ship him out either, because it would be even more suspicious to ship out unfit men while keeping unfit women, but you could keep him on-station, in the spirit of gender consistency, and even feed him some time-bonuses matching what you'd already given Robin and Li-Tsan, to keep him quiet. The best thing about this plan was that it camouflaged your malfeasance and made him an accomplice, but didn't even require his active consent. He didn't have even the slightest idea what was going on until Robin and Li-Tsan told him what was going on. And by then he was as trapped as they were, because he couldn't expose you without implicating himself and them."

Gibb trembled. "That's . . . a hell of a theory, Counselor."

"Oh, please," I said. "Do you really think I'd be confronting you like this if this were just an unsupported assumption? Once I saw the pattern, it wasn't hard to pick out two or three other indentures whose records I found especially suspicious. They were happy to testify in exchange for immunity and a promise that they'd be able to keep the bonuses earned. I offered the same deal to Fish, Crin, and D'Onofrio, and they gave you up in no time at all. Indeed, once she found out she was immune from any consequences, Li-Tsan was downright relieved. We're friends now. I've already uploaded the depositions, and somehow I don't think it'll be hard to get more." I now moved close enough to smell the acrid fear-sweat popping out on his cheeks. "I know this from grim personal experience, Mr. Gibb. Nobody likes to be owned. Some hate being indentured so much that they'll do anything to shorten their service. You used that fact to turn an outpost of critical diplomatic importance into your own personal brothel."

"I never forced anybody—" Gibb began.

I ran over him. "Is it your belief that I intend to charge you with exploiting these people? Please. Be serious. You're absolutely right. You didn't force them. They all knew exactly what they were doing, and since I don't particularly believe prostitution to be a crime I very much respect the industriousness of any woman willing to use all her assets to work off her time-debt as soon as possible. I also appreciate the good taste of any woman who requires regular bribes to get anywhere near you. Had you paid those two in any other form of legal tender, I would shrug and say, well, more power to you, more power to them. Consenting adults, and all that.

"I'm considerably less tolerant about the way you held three people as virtual prisoners, holding their futures hostage. That I recognize as disgusting, and that erases any possibility that I might show you a little understanding.

"Still, sir, that's not your crime.

"Your *crime*," I said, making the word explosive, "was the embezzlement of time-debt owed to the Dip Corps. That belonged to all humanity. You misappropriated it and spent it extravagantly, for your own pleasure, overpaying for the services being provided."

I held the next thought as long as I could, letting it take shape in the air between us.

His mouth jerked without sound, forming protests that wouldn't have done him much good.

I said, "Unless I cancel a certain dispatch already in the hytex net, and set to be transmitted to the Dip Corps tomorrow, New London's going to want all of that time repaid. Now, they could just apply it back to the contracts of all the women involved, but I'll make sure they realize that this presents a tremendous bookkeeping headache and a source of all sorts of potential legal arguments involving the best way to distinguish your unauthorized little incentives from any legitimate time-bonuses the indentures involved might genuinely deserve. I'll also point out that going after everybody involved would just create the kind of scandal better off avoided, without providing sufficient deterrent to other administrators capable of selling out their responsibilities to satisfy their hormones.

"No," I concluded, "once I'm done presenting the case, they'll probably just add all that stolen time to your own contract. Years. Probably decades, by the time the punitive fines, and any evidence of similar misbehavior at your prior postings, are properly tallied. Possibly more than you can ever live to pay back with the normal kind of assignment, even with regular rejuvenation. The Dip Corps will want every minute of that value returned, so they'll select some unpleasant high-risk/low-prestige assignment nobody else wants, someplace much worse than One One One, and force you to pay back as many as those wasted years as you can earning hardship and hazard bonuses. Break your back and your health and you might be able to return to someplace offering the comforts of civilization in as little as ten to twenty years Mercantile. Personally, I don't think you're likely to make it that far, unless you're lucky enough to find yourself working for a horny administrator, male, female, or neut, who finds you attractive enough for extra credit. Depending on the awfulness of the environment where you find yourself working, you might find yourself volunteering for services far removed from your own personal preferences. I don't think you'll be finicky."

Gibb had become dangerously calm. "You're a vindictive little bitch, aren't you?"

"I'm surprised you have to ask."

The non-ambassador was now just a vessel holding a massive potential explosion, held inside him by the thinnest layers of skin and civilization. A little more prodding and he might have assaulted me, even tried to throw me off the bridge. But he was a diplomat, well versed in the science of subtle nuance; and he'd caught the escape route I'd mentioned in passing. "You said '*Unless.*'"

"Correct. Your career's over in any event, but I'm still willing to contain this. You can forgo the disgrace and move on to a nice quiet retirement on the world of your choice."

He growled. "What do you want?"

"You can start with everything you know about Peyrin Lastogne."

He stared at me for the longest time, as if hoping for a more difficult assignment. And then he slumped. "Long before you got here, I tried to figure him out and failed."

"He's no legal advocate. If he was he'd be listed in the Dip Corps files."

Gibb didn't look at me again. "That's right. He would be. But there's no background for him at all. I can't even find anybody who'll confess to cutting his orders."

"What is he, then?"

There was no bitterness in his laugh, but no joy, either—just contempt at my pretense of naïvetè.

"Come on, Counselor. This can't be your first embassy."

I left him there, the sole remaining inhabitant of the installation he had commanded, surrounded by nothing but darkness and uncertainty and the vain hope that I'd reward his cooperation with mercy. He didn't call after me as I descended the net, or as I made my way alone across the network of bridges.

Leaving Gibb alone with the possible wreckage of his career, his reputation, and his life, could be seen as the moral equivalent of murder. After all, the vast abyss below Hammocktown had always offered the easiest of all possible exits. Between now and dawn it wouldn't take much more than a single dark impulse to drive him toward the easy out. It would take a lot more to make him reject that option in favor of an unpromising dawn.

Some might say I'd acted irresponsibly, by leaving him here to face the consequences alone. But I had left him with that ounce of hope, and a man capable of doing the things he had done was a man too full of himself to believe he could be betrayed by that ounce of hope. In the next few hours he'd plot exit strategies, denials, defenses, and deals he could broker with everybody capable of testifying against him. He'd persuade himself a thousand times that he had it all in hand and he'd tell himself a thousand and one times that he did not.

His long night journeying between hope and despair would not be an easy one. He'd spend it with nothing but recriminations and rationalizations for company.

I didn't believe he'd jump.

But he did deserve to come damn close.

A voice called up out of the darkness. "Ready, Andrea?"

"Whenever you are," I said.

A telescoping ladder emerged from the darkness down below, entering the empty space that had been my tent, and offering me an escape from the empty nets of Hammocktown. I grabbed a rung with both hands and, planting a heel against each riser, slid down to the skimmer's cargo platform.

Gibb had been right about one thing: I was getting better at this kind of maneuver. Not that I found it any more fun. Though my gait remained steady as I climbed over the rail and joined the Porrinyards forward, my hands were still shaking.

They said, "He didn't take that at all well."

"No, he didn't."

I'd asked them to monitor the questioning. On the off-chance Gibb had turned violent, or my friend the Heckler had made another attempt on my life, they would have been near enough to intercede. I can't claim that having them down below, looking out for me, had made me feel any more secure. I had no problem believing them capable of protecting me against Gibb. I wasn't nearly as complacent about their chances against the Heckler. But returning to their side came as a relief anyway. I was beginning to need them.

"Where to?" they asked.

"Circle. I'll figure out where we're going in a minute."

I don't know how long we wandered in darkness. It could not have been more than a few minutes. But my mind pored over the same ground from so many different angles that I would not have been surprised to open my eyes on a new world, millennia hence, where all my problems had entered the realm of history.

In the meantime I thought of Lastogne.

I was pretty sure I knew *what* he was. That, I'd suspected for some time. I'd dealt with people like him many times before. They were spawned by the very nature of the human animal. And Gibb's grudging testimony had only confirmed my own educated guesses. But what kind of spy advertises his place in the order of things? A saboteur from some faction inside the Confederacy would have equipped himself with an exhaustively forged identity or risked being expelled back to New London by now. Was he some kind of political officer? Or had the sabotage itself been part of his assignment?

Gibb had provided me with what little he could. *New London keeps telling me he's authorized to be here, but they refuse to give me any particulars. The only thing I know for sure is that he's dangerous.*

There was something else that bothered me. One of the little personal credos I'd shared with Gibb: *Do you know what murder investigators call a man like you who upon questioning fails to mention his sexual relationship with a murder victim? The most likely suspect.*

Gibb had thrown it back in my face, with that bombshell about a relationship between Warmuth and Lastogne.

Lastogne hadn't said a damned thing. He'd criticized Warmuth's idealism, said she'd had an excessive hunger for novelty, even expressed dismay when told of her relationship with D'Onofrio . . . but when asked what he felt about her personally, he'd said it wasn't a matter of personal like or dislike. He'd managed to give the impression he was answering the question while in fact he was doing nothing of the kind.

He'd played me very well. He'd sensed my misanthropy and played up that aspect of his own personality. He'd even accused the Porrinyards of the same failing. But was that just the typical gamesmanship of a habitual manipulator, or the obfuscation of a sociopath?

The sense of something undone, that had bothered me for days now, flared yet again. My fingers trembled. I looked down at my hand, covered as it was by Skye's own, and saw the cords in my wrist twitching, as if urging immediate action but unable to relate exactly what they had in mind.

I pulled my hand out from under Skye's, and studied it the way I'd study an alien form of life. The lined palm, the thin hairline scar at the wrist, and the abused fingertips, complete with raw skin where I chewed the skin at moments of deep concentration.

It was remarkable how much the chewed places were healing.

What had that Brachiator I'd spoken to called the AI-source?

The Hand-in-Ghosts.

The Porrinyards said, "Are you all right?"

I wasn't sure. The blood was pounding in my ears so hard that I could barely hear anything else. But then I managed, "Lastogne's going to have to wait."

They said, "What?"

"I need to become a Half-Ghost."

20

SUSPENSION

In the indirect light of our skimmer, the eyes of the Brachiators seemed saturated with that ineffable quality that leads human beings to label other beings as wise.

It helped me not at all to know that this was a totally subjective quality, which had no bearing to actual, measurable wisdom, to know, in fact, that human beings, have been known to perceive that quality shining from the eyes of terrestrial creatures as varied as owls, orangutans, and even dogs. Much as I tried, I couldn't resist my own involuntary reaction to a Brachiator face that rang the appropriate cues.

The Porrinyards had described Friend to Half-Ghosts as an old acquaintance, taking pains to stress that this was not the individual of the same name who lived near Hammocktown. I could have guessed that much. Hammocktown was many kilometers port and spinward, far too distant for even the speediest Brachiator to travel in these past two days. This Brach also looked different, its fur bearing a mottled, grayish pattern that may have been inborn or the effects of advanced age, and its face marked by the scars of several past battles, including one that intersected an eye opaque from time or trauma. "We are surprised at this visit."

Skye spoke alone: "Why?"

"Because we have been told that all the Ghosts have left the world."

That would be a reference to the evacuation of Hammock-town. Skye said, "That's very recent news."

"It is old news," the Brachiator said. "It happened the night before this. We have known since before the suns came on, the next morning."

"How did you get the news?"

"The creators wanted us to know, so we knew."

This made sense. Considering the Brachiator rate of travel, the news couldn't have been passed along by word of mouth. But which AIsource had told them, the majority or the ones I knew as the rogue intelligences? Would Brachiators even be able to tell the difference?

I whispered a question to Oscin, which emerged from Skye's mouth. "Do your creators often bestow knowledge?"

The answer came at once. "They bestow knowledge every day."

Another question whispered to Oscin and asked aloud by Skye. "Did they let you know what happened to Warmuth and Santiago?"

A pause. "We were told of one who seized Life and another joined by Death."

"Does this make you sorry?"

"You are Ghosts. You drift between Life and Death. It is nothing new for you."

I thought about that longer than I had to, reflecting on a next step that could not be avoided.

At a whispered request, we descended.

A thousand meters below the Uppergrowth, the darkness swallowed everything in the world the AIsource had made. Everything above us, below us, and to either side of us was an identical shade of black. Even the storms that so often lit up the clouds had quieted, leaving us adrift in what was, for the moment, a cocoon of penetrating darkness.

The Porrinyards sat opposite me, watching me tremble. Neither offered a comforting touch. Given how much they'd offered already, any time I showed even the slightest need, this seemed well out of character until I realized they probably realized how little I wanted their sympathy right now.

Somehow, they could see even that.

They allowed me several minutes of measured breath before they shifted position, in a way that preserved the nature of the space between them. "You don't have to do this."

I studied my hands. "I do if I want to feel it."

"And how necessary is that? Can't you understand it from a distance? Put what you know up against what you can figure out?"

"Not if I want to be sure."

Skye moved from the seat beside Oscin to the seat beside me, the transition so graceful and so smooth that it was done before I could even register what was happening. Her eyes, dark in the uncertain glow of the instruments, glistened more than Oscin's, seeming close to tears in a way that his did not. But when her lips moved, the voice that emerged was still mostly his. "Watching your back against Gibb was one thing. But this is another thing entirely. This is just taking risks for no good reason."

I shook my head. "I warned you this was coming."

It was the second time I'd seen them show anger. Like most elements of their personality, it seemed to exist not in their bodies but in some undifferentiated place between them, and it was palpable, burning with resentment and hurt. "You told me something was coming. You didn't specify what. But you knew all along, didn't you? How long were you on-station before you realized you were going to do this?"

I should have informed them that I didn't need their permission. "The first day. When Lastogne introduced me to a Brachiator."

Skye bit her lower lip, leaving Oscin the primary speaker. "But you knew Gibb and Lastogne would never authorize it. They're responsible for your safety, and they know you're untrained and psychologically unfit; you knew they'd pull rank on you the second you even suggested doing such a thing. Which means you needed other allies willing to arrange it behind their backs. Allies who could be counted on to break the rules when nobody else was around."

Skye spoke alone. "That's why you dumped Lastogne as your guide."

Now both of them. "It's been about more than just making friends, isn't it? You've been testing us. Seeing how far would we go, to give you what you need."

It had been a long, long time, maybe years, since I'd worried about hurting anybody's feelings. I hadn't imagined myself capable of wounding the Porrinyards, who between them seemed mounted on foundations stronger than my own had ever been. But damned if the two of them hadn't turned brittle all of a sudden. And damned if they weren't good about inflicting guilt. I needed several seconds to frame a satisfactory answer. "The first time I found my life in your hands, nobody asked my opinion first. The second and third time, I chose to have you along. That much wasn't testing you, or using you. It was relying on you."

They indicated the Uppergrowth with a roll of their eyes. "But it was always about this."

"It's been about more than just that for some time now."

They moved to opposite sides of the skimmer, their positions so identical down to the slight twist of their respective right legs that they might have been performing choreographed parodies of one another. When they addressed the night, I couldn't trace any individual sound to either individual set of lips. "When the individuals first Oscin and Skye announced their intention to link, their respective friends and family were horrified. They said, aren't you afraid of what you'd be giving up? The individuals Oscin and Skye said, no, we're not giving anything up. The families both asked the same question. How could we be *sure*."

My chest burned. "What did you tell them?"

They chuckled in harmony. "Nothing accurate, Andrea. The individuals Oscin and Skye weren't sure about anything. They hadn't lived it, you see. It was just an intellectual abstraction for them. They didn't know how many more cues I would receive. They didn't know my shared self would be sure about almost everything."

They turned from the night and sat opposite me, their eyes shining.

They said, "This is what you've brought back into my life, Andrea: that refreshing sense of uncertainty."

The preliminaries, introducing me to the Brachiators as a New Ghost who wished to taste Life, were fast and easy.

Securing me was a nightmare. My limbs rebelled at the very idea of trusting my life to a few roots and vines and safety cables, and more than once froze rather than submit. More than once the Porrinyards assured me that there was no shame in giving up on the very idea. I considered listening to them when they insisted on making me promise to signal at the first sign of an emergency.

But I said nothing, and soon found myself clinging to the Uppergrowth with all four limbs. The roots and vines were slack enough to permit some mobility. I had inserted my arms and legs through the places loose enough to accommodate them, hooked my ankles around a low-hanging loop, and found branches thick enough to provide handholds. Although the Porrinyards advised me that most of Gibb's indentures preferred to do this facing the Uppergrowth, because that was the orientation of the Brachiators themselves, I insisted on being positioned with my back to the world's ceiling and my face to the clouds.

I did not feel any safer when the Porrinyards, standing together on the cargo bed, strung a support cable across my waist or even when they looped another, thicker band around my chest. Anchored deep within the multiple layers of vines, they supported the bulk of my weight, freeing my arms in case I needed them, and preventing my limbs from seizing in reaction to what would have been agonizing strain. My mind appreciated the further safeguards against falling, but my gut considered them illusory protections at best.

The storm clouds below me were so very, very hungry.

I was still struggling to get my breath under control when the Porrinyards said, "Andrea? There are a couple of other things you need to know."

Among them was just how stupid I was to invite this insane situation. "Go ahead."

The Porrinyards each rested a protective hand on one of my shoulders. "Most people are a little afraid of heights. Mild acrophobia is healthy. But extreme, uncontrollable acrophobia is a different beast entirely. Many extreme acrophobes are frightened of heights, not because they see those heights as dangerous, but because they don't trust themselves that close to an opportunity to jump. They see themselves surrendering to impulse. It's not the fear of heights, in other words, but the fear of impulse that paralyzes them."

I considered how easy it would be to just loosen the protective cables and plunge, and found the thought, horrific as it was, much too attractive. "Now you tell me."

"If I did not consider you currently in control of yourself, I would not be leaving you here."

I bit rising hysteria. "I hope you guessed right."

"Me too. You're very beautiful."

My calm failed, overwhelmed by the distance between me and the storm clouds far below. "S-so are you."

They displayed a pair of dazzling white smiles. "I look forward to overcoming your resistance."

Dammit, this wasn't fair. "Th-that might be difficult. I'm not the kind to get talked into anything."

"I have advantages," they said. "I outnumber you."

Whereupon they fell into crouches, steadied themselves within the skimmer's specific gravity, and with a wave, sped off, taking both the light and my last chance to back down.

It was stupid to feel fear. Fear was nothing but the body's involuntary response to perceived threats. Fear increased heartbeat, respiration, and perspiration; fear clouded the mind and paralyzed the limbs, and *I'm going to die* wasn't subject to logical arguments about its counterproductivity.

Right now the single most persuasive image in my mind involved a sudden rip in the Uppergrowth. Let's say, a few hairline tears at a spot already weakened by Brachiator claws, then strained to the breaking point by my own involuntary movements, spreading farther as the cell walls ruptured and the increased straub pulled the wounds still wider *I'm going to die* becoming a lightning-shaped zigzag *Oh, Juje* and an entire section of vines ripping loose all at once, spilling me into the same abyss that had claimed Santiago *Shut up* and just how far could I fall, really, before I felt the press of wind against my face and knew there was no hope? A meter? Two? Three?

I closed my eyes.

I'm going to die.

But that meant nothing, too, because we were all going to die, and every breath of air I managed to wrest from the universe was one more the nightmares of my childhood had failed to deny me. When I breathed it was an act of defiance. When I breathed it was a victory. When I breathed it was

Oh, dammit.

My last meal came up, spilling from my lips in a great volcanic comet.

It was one of the reasons I'd insisted on being secured face-down. People who vomit while secured in a face-up position have a nasty habit of choking to death. At least this way, if death came, it wouldn't be messy and stupid.

Or at least not messy.

I wondered how far the vomitus had fallen. A few hundred meters? More? Was it still one coherent mass or had the wind separated it into —

Enough of that. Not helpful. Concentrate already. Banish the fear.

I thought of an imprisoned little girl, fighting off the effects of the inaudible sublims her keepers played to keep her docile, wanting to smash her fists against the walls but overcoming the rage and the fear and vowing to survive on her own terms.

There was no visible difference between that darkness and the darkness I faced now. I knew what the darkness hid.

But then, I've known since Bocai.

The long minutes went by, my breath slowing, my phobic reactions giving way to a kind of vague distress.

Have you ever spent a protracted period of time among a species not your own? I have. On Bocai, they had been vast extended family. In other places, they had been enemies, allies, or assignments. Here they were part of the landscape. I could smell the musty scent of their fur, and hear the soft rumble of their breath, and detect something of their personalities in the way they sighed and moaned and shifted position all around me. I could sense the rhythm of their strange, topsy-turvy lives and the connection they shared with their surroundings every second of every day. I could even sense their feelings toward me, the distasteful intruder in their midst: strange, alien, possibly even foul-smelling, so completely at odds with everything they considered normal. I could just imagine their reaction to being told that the human beings aboard One One One were here to help them. They couldn't find the news heartening. What would they feel instead? Confusion? Amusement? Horror? Disgust? Rage? Malice? Maybe even something different from all of that, something that appeared on no human spectrum? Maybe anything but comfort. That, they wouldn't feel. They called us Ghosts, after all, and Ghosts have always been incapable of putting the haunted at ease.

The truth was, whatever else may have been involved here, the AIsource had played a practical joke on us. They had arranged for our ideals to lead us into a world where our ideals were just plain irrelevant, a world whose inhabitants we would be honor-bound to help even though they got along fine if just left alone.

We considered them owned, but they had no frame of reference to measure freedom. We considered them prisoners, but they couldn't live anywhere except with their captors. And we considered them slaves, but their only labor was to do what was natural to them. All the debates were just abstractions to those who actually had to live it: less relevant, even, than subtle discussions of color to creatures born blind. And whatever mazes they were driven through, whatever great dramas they played out for AIsource amusement, were likely destined to remain just as opaque to us. Our two races were like two parades marching down the same street to the same drumbeat, blind to one another until the moment of collision.

I was still wondering whether that was the whole point when the Heckler spoke, somewhere very close to me.

"You're a real bitch, you know that?"

As before, the voice was neither male nor female, young or old, mad or sane: just a slick, measured voice, flensed of everything that might have given it character. Nor was it that odd not-a-voice-but-I-heard-it-anyway used by the AI-source.

This was once again human, with the humanity removed.

I was neither surprised nor alarmed. I would have been more concerned had the Heckler not shown up tonight. But since I was surrounded by Brachiators, who I didn't want mistaking our more unpleasant exchanges for an attack on them, I activated my hiss screen before continuing. "Yes, I know that. Can you hear me?"

"As clearly as I'll hear your screams when you fall."

My ability to feel fear was currently operating at full capacity and wouldn't bear any additional weight. But I smiled, to show appreciation for the snappy answer. "It's been a while since I heard from you."

Whatever leeched the emotion from the Heckler's voice also defanged a clear attempt to snarl. "I thought you'd be smart enough to know you were on the losing team."

"And I would have imagined you smart enough to recognize that I don't join teams."

"We're all owned, Andrea. We all belong to one side or another. We may not always recognize what side that is, but that has more to do with our own blindness than with our stupid illusions of remaining neutral. In truth, we function only as much as we're allowed to, by those who really pull the strings."

Something shifted in the darkness. Something that seemed to move faster than any Brachiator had a right to move.

"Most of us are less than pawns. We just take up space and complicate the play for those who make a difference. Even those of us with a part in the game are just moved back and forth across the board, scoring our little points, working toward that one moment when we manage to score our side a momentary advantage. It's not any way for a sentient person to live."

"And that's why you're after me?" I asked. "To put me out of my misery?"

The Heckler emitted a sick, anguished laugh, as much self-loathing as malice. "I said most of us, Andrea. I only bought myself a longer leash."

I freed my right arm, fumbled for my belt, opened something I'd taken from my bag in case I needed to defend myself, and cursed with disgust as it slid from my fingertips and tumbled forever into the darkness. Well. That was inconvenient.

"I knew about you," the Heckler continued. "I'd read up on you. I'd learned all about how hated you were and how little you cared. I considered you a hero of mine. I didn't want you working against me here. When I learned you were coming, I did what I could to drive you off."

That would be the first of the messages I'd received after Intersleep.

I removed something else from my belt: a tiny disk, about the size of my knuckle, which even in this nigh-total darkness found enough ambient light to glisten. I swung it before me in a clumsy arc, not knowing whether that arc hung between me and the Heckler, and sweaty with the knowledge that it barely mattered.

"Am I supposed to think that's some kind of weapon?"

I kept my voice level. "I don't care what you think. I care what you know. And by your own admission, you know the kind of person I am, the kind of things I've done, and just how little I care. You know I wouldn't hesitate to set off an explosion capable of incinerating everything within a hundred meters of here, as long as that meant getting rid of you too."

Silence. Then: "That's ridiculous."

"It doesn't matter that it's ridiculous. What matters is that it's also not out of character. What do you think? Is it out of character for me? Am I not the kind of person who'd walk around with a bomb all her life, on the off chance she might find herself in the kind of situation where it made sense to blow herself up? If you honestly believe I'm saner than that, then keep coming. If you don't, then rest assured I'll give you another chance to kill me by this time tomorrow."

The empty space before me lit up with another of the Heckler's images: this one a naked, emaciated version of myself, displayed on a darkened stage as I danced for the amusement of unseen puppeteers. My pierced wrists and ankles were swollen, semi-healed scabs. My face was painted clown-white, with bright red cheeks and a gobbet of glistening meat in the same place where a clown would have worn a rubber red ball for a nose. Hooks pulled my lips back into a ghastly, fixed smile belied by my eyes, a pair of lost, despairing orbs blinded by all the tears they had shed.

Then the image vanished, leaving purple afterimages on my retinas.

Then came the final words, no longer soulless, no longer an altered voice intended to hide the killer's true nature, but the voice of the murderer, provided without any further masks. "You have no friends, Andrea. Not in the Dip Corps and not on One One One. Just allies, and enemies, and cylinked pets doing what their owners have ordered them to do."

I waited.

Another cackle. "Hurts, doesn't it? Hearing the truth about what they are?"

"Go to hell," I said.

"I've never been anywhere else," the Heckler said, in a voice filled with regret. And then, a moment later: "But neither have you."

I continued listening for a while, in case the Heckler came back, but the only rustlings around me were soft and sluggish enough to come from Brachiators. And if I allowed myself to remain paranoid about this all night, I wouldn't be strong enough to handle the next part. So I palmed the little disk (a coin, issued by a local government I'd brought down, bearing the face of a local politician I'd successfully prosecuted for crimes against the human species) and slipped it back into the little pocket on my belt.

Maybe, if I got back to New London, I'd take the time to replace what I'd dropped.

I'd feel naked until I managed to get my hands on another bomb.

In the meantime, I signaled the Porrinyards.

"Are you all right, Andrea?"

"Never better," I said.

They sounded dubious. "Forgive me for having a hard time believing that."

"No, I'm serious. Listen, the Heckler just made contact —"

They cut me off, in a voice more Oscin's than Skye's. "I can be right there."

"No. The tough part's still ahead. I just need you to stay awake, and look out for anything out of the ordinary. You may not be out of danger yourselves."

A pause. "You think your friend might try to get to you through us?"

"Let's just say the previous incidents show a certain disregard for collateral damage. Keep your eyes open."

"And yours," they said. "We don't want to lose you."

I don't know how many hours I dangled there, listening to the movements all around me, trying to ignore the heights, trying not to picture the Heckler circling for another try.

I suffered several additional episodes of panic, but fought each one down. They used up so much energy between them that after a while I found myself drifting in and out of dreamless sleep.

A few eternities later, I realized I could see movement in the clouds far below. It was a series of irregular flashes, burning just long enough to register before disappearing.

More lightning, of course, but what caused my pulse to race was the realization that I could discern the clouds even between flashes. The Habitat was no longer pitch-black. It was shrouded by a dim murk unable to hide the gradual ignition of the suns.

Turning to my left and right, I made out the many furry, nearly immobile forms that had kept the long night's vigil over me. There must have been dozens of them, visible to my eyes only as black shapes. I could not yet tell how many were facing me and how many were looking away. It barely mattered. Even in their nigh-total immobility, they were still aware of me, still measuring me by the standards of creatures who lived the only way they knew how to live.

I looked around for a likely spokesbeing and found one in the form of the nearest Brachiator, a great black shadow perhaps all of five meters away.

"Uh . . . hello? Can you hear me?"

The black shape swelled with breath, then exhaled. "Yes."

"Are you the one called Friend to Half-Ghosts?"

"Yes. It is a pleasure to be your friend now, Andrea Cort."

I cleared my throat. "Am I a Half-Ghost now?"

Another low, rumbling breath, with a cute little whistle in it. Maybe the Brachiator had a cold. "You have been a Half-Ghost for most of the night."

"That's all it takes, then? Just hanging here?"

"All it takes is a connection to Life."

I wondered if Brachiators bored themselves to tears on a regular basis or whether they only spoke this way when humans were around. "What about the other human I spoke to last night? There was one here, wasn't there?"

"There was more than one."

"When?"

"First there was the one-in-two. The one that brought you here."

The Porrinyards, obviously. Stupid of me not to specify that. And impressive of the Brach to perceive their nature so quickly. "And after them?"

"Another."

"When?"

"After the one-in-two left."

"Did you hear me talking to that one?"

"Yes."

"Do you know what we talked about?"

"We do not listen to conversations that are not our concern."

That sounded prim. "It's all right if you overheard."

"Thank you. But we do not hear what we are not invited to hear."

Brachiators, I decided, made the universe's most useless witnesses. "Did you recognize the one I spoke to?"

"By reputation," said Friend to Half-Ghosts.

I hadn't suspected the word part of the Brachiator vocabulary. "What kind of reputation?"

"As a Ghost Who Kills Ghosts." He sounded petulant, as if the answer was so obvious I'd wasted his time by merely asking.

"Would you happen to know whether it was male or female?"

"We have trouble discerning gender among Ghosts."

"But you can tell the difference between New Ghosts and Half-Ghosts, right?"

Friend to Half-Ghosts sounded almost amused. "Yes. That is easy."

"How?"

"Half-Ghosts are marked by Life."

"Am I marked by Life?"

"Now you are."

"And you can tell this?"

"It is what enables us to be friends."

I almost recited my habitual response to offers of friendship: the one about not wanting friends and not looking for any. "Thank you."

"You are welcome," said Friend to Half-Ghosts.

He was being polite at best. He was not attached to me, or for that matter any of my semi-living kind. He could only be aggrieved by the intrusion of human beings, with their constant, distracting questions. Given common decency as an option, I would just leave him alone. But I didn't have that option. There were still things I needed to know.

I subtly shifted my arms and legs within the network of roots and support wires that had held me fast for so long. They tingled like mad from impaired circulation, but would be able to move in a hurry if necessary.

I said, "I am happy we are friends. Because I need your help."

Another rumble. "What would you like me to do?"

"I need your help staying alive."

A low, disturbed rumble rose from the other Brachiators around us. I didn't know how many members of the tribe had heard me, but those who had were scandalized, even angry, like the guests at any human gathering, hearing something distasteful from the stranger in their midst.

Friend to Half-Ghosts seemed more unflappable. "You are a Half-Ghost. You have all the Life you can ever know."

"I don't care. I'm tired of being a Ghost. I'm tired of having to return to the land of the Dead. I need more. I need Life the way you have Life."

Was it just my imagination, or was Friend really trembling now, in fear or rage or frustration or dismay? It didn't matter. I didn't need imagination to hear a change in the timbre of his voice: a deepening, a hoarseness that had not been there before. "Too much Life is not healthy for Ghosts. We have heard this. The other Ghost —"

"Which one?" I asked.

"The one we have heard about. The one who embraced Life."

"The one who died from it," I said.

"Yes. She taught us that Life is not good for Ghosts. That it uses them up too fast."

"It's still a small price to pay for Life."

A long pause. The quality of the air changed, and took on the quality of the last few seconds before a storm.

Friend to Half-Ghosts started begging. "Please, Andrea Cort. Do not ask for this. We do not want to use you up too fast."

My throat went dry. I swallowed spit and said, "I know what I want, Friend. Give me Life."

Everything in the world held its breath at once. The soft rustle of Brachiators shifting position on their vines, the sighs and grunts of Brachiator breath, the murmur of Brachiator words and all the other subliminal reminders of Life all abruptly cut away to nothing, replaced with the frantic, unspoken tension of creatures challenged to carry out an atrocity.

Then Friend to Half-Ghosts started to move.

21

PLUNGE

Friend to Half-Ghosts withdrew one limb from the Upergrowth, held it before him like an offering, then reached up and found another handhold closer to me.

He withdrew another limb, hesitated again, and grabbed hold once more.

He did the same with his hind limbs, one after the other, each time at the same glacial pace, each time demonstrating hiccups of reluctance in what otherwise looked like an inexorable advance.

His pace was matched by his fellow Brachiators. They were all advancing on me.

Some were already removing the detached claws threaded into their fur.

I closed my eyes, imagining how much it would hurt to have those claws driven through my wrists and ankles, persuading myself that this was in fact my fate, struggling to summon fear of the torments about to fall upon me.

I finished the count to thirty and then, living dangerously, started at zero again.

One, two . . .

I still heard them coming.

Fifteen, sixteen . . .

The rumble of their approach was enough to make my body shake.

Twenty-one, twenty-two . . .

I expected a furry hand to close around my wrist at any moment.

Twenty-five, twenty-six . . .

I couldn't believe they hadn't gotten here yet.

Twenty-seven, twenty-eight . . .

I could feel them all around me, their hot breath already warming my skin.

Thirty.

I opened my eyes.

They had advanced at varying speeds, reflecting the variation in their ages and physical conditions. A burly, many-scarred specimen with gray streaks in its coat had overtaken the somewhat slower Friend to Half-Ghosts and might be upon me minutes ahead of its brother.

There was no doubt what they intended to do to me.

Given a chance, they would gather around on all sides, seize my arms and my legs with a strength natural to any creatures who never knew respite from the need to *hold on.* One or two would take each arm. One or two would take each leg. They would hold my merely human limbs in place, not out of malice but out of simple animal awareness that the passage into Life always causes great pain and might lead weaker creatures into convulsions. They might even speak a few comforting words.

And then they would drive the claws through my wrists and ankles.

They understood that this might kill me. It had, after all, killed Warmuth. But they would still see it as an act of kindness.

By their lights it would be the ultimate act of friendship.

The Brachs were still minutes away, their charge as interminable as it was inexorable.

I made my voice very naïve and very small. "What are you doing?"

"We are giving you what you have asked for," Friend to Half-Ghosts said.

Would Cynthia have looked around herself and seen sudden menace in a population now converging on her from all sides? Would she have wondered if she'd said the right thing, or instead offended them in some way? Or would she have been proud beyond measure that she had succeeded beyond all measure whereas all of her mocking, unfriendly co-workers had failed?

The gray Brachiator was almost upon me. There was no reason to believe its catalogue of facial expressions carried the same spectrum of meanings as the nearest human equivalents, but that little half-smile at worse seemed kind, compassionate, even holy.

The claw it drew back for a strike was cracked with age and stained with the blood of Brachs fallen in battle.

If I stayed here it would know my blood as well.

So I sprung all my lines but one and plunged, spread-eagled, toward the clouds.

I gasped, felt terror and panic fill my veins with liquid ice, called myself a thousand resentful names, wondered if crucifixion at the hands of the Brachiators would have been all that bad an alternative to falling, angrily told myself I was being stupid, and screamed.

Then I gasped again as a jolt pulled my spine taut and flung me upward, back toward the Uppergrowth, and the Brachiators gathered around my home of the night before.

The cord attached to my chest harness was too elastic. I was going to bounce too high and give the Brachiators a chance to grab me on the rebound.

It was a stupid thing to be afraid of. No cord is that elastic. And the Brachs could not see what my body was doing. Their gazes were fixed on the Uppergrowth, not on anything taking place below them.

I still came so close to their assembled backs that I could read their respective histories in the scars cross-hatching their flesh.

For a moment I heard thunder.

Then I fell again, the urge to scream not quite as overpowering this time.

When the cord drew taut I was left whirling at its lowest point, the cloudscape and Uppergrowth reduced to kaleidoscopic whirs.

I hadn't registered making fists, but when I unclenched them now, my palms tingled from freed circulation. Which struck me as stupid. Panic's no good as a survival mechanism if it's so clueless it thinks you can punch a deadly drop into submission.

The spinning of the circle of clouds, down below, slowed to a stop, then changed direction as my line uncoiled. Clockwise this time. No less disorienting, but at least a change.

No point in panicking, then. So I tapped my throat-mike. "Oscin? Skye? I have what I need. I'm ready for a pickup."

Silence.

I tapped my mike again. "Oscin? Skye?"

They came in, brusque and out-of-synch. "I read you, Andrea. I'm also a little busy."

That wasn't what I wanted to hear. "What's wrong?"

"I'm under attack."

I had heard an explosion, but had been too busy fighting back my own fear that I'd been unable to register the sound as anything but One One One's constant ambient thunder. Now I realized it had been louder, and closer, than any of the storms had been. "From who?"

"Please be quiet, Andrea. This is hard work even for two heads."

I spun at the end of my line, searching the open air for signs of a skimmer under attack. For a long, terrifying moment I found nothing: there was simply too much sky, too many clouds, too many distant specks journeying toward their own unknown destinations. Then more muffled thunder arrived from somewhere to my immediate right, and I spun again, tracking the sound.

I saw a gray speck that could only be the skimmer drawing a line across the sky, a mere thousand meters below, and a bright object too small to be a vehicle following close behind. A bright red flower bloomed between them before vanishing: an airburst of some kind. The purple afterimage was just beginning to fade when the sound reached me: a muffled, comical pop that sounded more like a failed attempt at an explosion than the real thing. Even as I watched, the skimmer seemed to wobble, then spin, before beginning a steep dive.

"No!" I shouted.

Oscin spoke alone, his voice calm but harried. "Please, Andrea. If we really think we're about to die, we'll be sure to let you know."

The skimmer faded from sight long before it reached the clouds, the blurring effects of the intervening atmosphere camouflaging its exact position against the roiling storms. Even the explosions became harder to see. When one blinding retort lit up the sky, I was so certain the skimmer had gone up that I actually screamed.

I felt a tug on my back.

Looking up, I saw something else happening. The Brachiators had reached my line and gathered around it. Friend to Half-Ghosts was probing it with his claws, as he struggled to puzzle out its meaning. They had to be a little confused. After all, their perspectives were fixed; they just saw the line itself, and how it was anchored. They couldn't look down and see vulnerable little me, bobbing like a trinket at the end of a string. And even if they could they probably couldn't pull me up. Their muscles were built for clinging, not lifting.

At least, that's what I hoped.

There was another burst of light down below.

"That wasn't us," Oscin said. "But it was close."

"You have any ideas?"

"Lots. But we need better ones. This is just a clumsy old transport. We don't have the weapons or the maneuverability to win a dogfight, and our enemy doesn't seem to place much stock in playing fair." Whatever he said next was drowned out by a loud roar. "—wounded."

Another tug from up above. I bobbed a few centimeters, thrashed, saw the Brachiators huddle as they conferred over what to do next.

I tapped my throat mike and murmured the code I had for Lastogne. It took all of five seconds for him to answer: five seconds inhabited by the terrible suspicion that something had befallen all the people in the hangar. Then I heard a clutter, a muttered curse, and a voice thick with sleep. "Unngh. Counselor? Aren't you back yet?"

"No," I said, "and we're not going to be back at all unless we get a rescue mission out here, right away."

A pause. I heard another voice in the background, female, asking Lastogne a sleepy question. He relayed it. "Are you still in the habitat?"

"That's affirmative. We're under attack and we need a pickup."

He didn't ask me who was attacking. "You have a location? A grid number?"

"I didn't even know you used grid numbers!"

"Can you ask the Porrinyards?"

"They're busy! Just track my signal!"

"Hang on," he said. "I'll get Mo Lassiter."

I felt another sharp tug on my line, lifting me a few centimeters. This time it wasn't followed by an equivalent drop.

When I looked up, I understood why. The Brachiators were working out a plan to retrieve me. Even as I watched, the gray-haired one had cupped one of his hands around a length of cord and was lumbering away from its anchoring point, turning himself into a pulley that would draw me up the farther he traveled. Other Brachiators were stepping in to take the slack.

Retrieving me could take hours, but the Brachiators had plenty of time. It was all they did have. I wasn't sure I had any. "Damn you, Peyrin! This is getting serious!"

He came back on. "We're working on it, Counselor. Still looking for Mo."

"Does it matter who you get? We're in trouble here!"

"I recognize that, Counselor. I want her because she knows the Uppergrowth better than just about anybody, and she's most equipped to find you based on your signal. But we're not waiting for her. We'll have a party outfitted and ready to go in just under two minutes, with or without her."

I felt another tug, and began to wonder if I even had two minutes.

A point of light emerged from the clouds, became an arc, then headed back in. I couldn't tell whether that was the Porrinyards or their pursuer. Oscin's signal broke into mine: "I'm having a rough time, Andrea. I've had to descend a little farther than I wanted to, into a storm, and it's going to take me a few minutes to pull out. Don't overreact if I'm out of touch for a while."

I was still wondering what overreaction was supposed to entail in this situation when Lastogne returned, all out of breath: "Found Mo. She's getting ready. What's happening?"

Another tug, yanking me upward.

"Counselor?"

The Brachiators were now acting in concert, the cord strung through several sets of hands as everyone involved in my retrieval followed the gray-hair's lead. Several were drawing up their own slack, increasing the speed of my ascent. A few seconds ago I had considered the sluggishness of the species a near guarantee that they wouldn't have me back within reach for hours. Now I figured I had minutes.

At that point I'd have nothing but words to save me from what had happened to Cynthia Warmuth.

Lastogne prodded me. "Counselor?"

"Tell Lassiter I'm hanging from a safety line and under assault from Brachiators. Tell her I think I have five minutes or less. Tell her the Porrinyards are in a skimmer, under attack by someone airborne." A thought occurred to me. "Contact the AIsource too."

"They must know what's happening already."

"I've no doubt of that. But they may not refuse a direct request for help."

The Brachiators had a rhythm going. The stop-start-stop-start I'd endured up to this point had given way to constant effort. When I looked up I saw that the number of Brachs working on the project had increased to half a dozen.

I thrashed, arced my back to provide myself access to the line, and pulled myself upward, climbing hand over hand until I could wrap my arms and legs around the hanging cord. It robbed me of some distance, but at least it allowed me to face them.

The Porrinyards came back online, speaking together. "Are you all right, Andrea?"

"I should be asking you that question."

"It's been a rough few minutes," they said, "but I'm clear enough, right now, to tell you what I'm dealing with. Peyrin? Are you getting this?"

Lastogne broke in. "I've got you."

"We're under attack by what seems to be a human being, or other humanoid, inside some kind of heavily fortified flying armor. It's demonstrated offensive capabilities including light explosives and motion-seeking projectiles, both of which might have put me down long ago were the pilot not more interested in forcing me down into the clouds. I seem to be outside its reach right now, but every time I've tried to rise above the storms I've been . . ." A rumble of static. ". . . chastised. I'm trying to manuever around a bit, and find some way to ascend, but that effort's taking me farther and farther away from Counselor Cort."

Another tug drew me upward. I said, "This isn't about attacking you. It's about keeping you too busy to retrieve me."

"That's what I'm thinking too," the Porrinyards said.

"Then get yourselves to safety. I'll wait for Lassiter to show up."

"I'm sorry," the Porrinyards said. "I didn't quite get that."

"I said, save yourselves. Let me fend for myself for once."

"Nope," the Porrinyards said. "I'm afraid I didn't hear that, either."

I called them just about every horrid name I knew and several others I had to make up. Just a few arm-lengths above me, the Brachiators continued working with an efficiency I never would have expected of them, as they drew me closer and closer to clawing distance. I saw slack in the line hanging in loops from a dozen Brachiator hands. I heard reverent discussion of Life and Half-Ghosts rolling from a dozen Brachiator mouths. This was a religious experience for them, one the members of this tribe would no doubt pass along to their children and grandchildren long after my name ceased being even a footnote in human history.

I pulled myself up a little farther, hating having to get closer to them but needing the extra slack so I could stand in the makeshift stirrup the cord formed as it looped under my feet. It turned the line into a kind of elevator, which I rode as they pulled me toward them.

The broad furry back of the nearest Brachiator was now a little more than a single arm's length out of reach.

Lastogne broke in. "Counselor? You there?"

I blinked sweat from my eyes. "I hope you have a smarter question than that."

"We're going to need you to hold on for a while. The AIsource have closed the Habitat."

I heard another long, rumbling explosion: either real thunder or the Porrinyards being punished for making another attempt to rescue me. I hadn't noticed any flash of light, so I couldn't tell where it had come from, except down below. My brain immediately conjured an image of the skimmer breaking in half and the Porrinyards sharing a scream as they toppled head-over-heels into toxic murk. I didn't much appreciate the way my stomach clenched at the image. I didn't want to live through this if the Porrinyards got killed.

Lastogne continued: "They wouldn't let us in. They called current conditions in there too hazardous to allow any further entry."

I removed the stun device from my collar. It was the same one I'd used on Gibb the other day, but it was calibrated to deliver incapacitating jolts to human beings and might be nothing more than a pinprick to Brachiators. With my bag of essentials still in the skimmer with the Porrinyards, and the item I'd saved for use against the Heckler long since fallen into the clouds, it was all I had. "I suppose you argued the point?"

"We told them we still had four people in there, in immediate need of evacuation."

The number seemed right until I remembered to count Gibb, still enduring his voluntary exile at Hammocktown. "You have more than four."

"What?"

The gray-haired Brachiator gave another heave-ho, so mighty that I almost bumped my head on his back. I tapped its spine with the only weapon I had, the stunner, and was not rewarded with spectacular results: a little buzz, a little twitch, a little grunt of annoyance. Any thoughts I'd had of bravely fighting off the entire tribe with nothing more than the stunner quickly vanished.

Lastogne cut in again. "Counselor, repeat what you just said. You have more than four people in there?"

"I'm a little too busy to do your math for you, sir! I have things to do!"

The gray-hair gathered up all his strength and tugged again, drawing me level with the sea of broad, simian faces. His own eyes rolled toward me. In a heartbeat, my last chance to escape would be gone. I'd never win if this became a battle of competing muscle power.

But speed I had over all of them.

I didn't even need to hurry as I reached out with one hand and used the stunner to deliver what must have been an agonizing jolt to his right eye.

Quick biology lesson: it doesn't matter what species you belong to. If you have eyes and the capacity to suffer, that place has some of the most sensitive pain receptors in your entire body.

The gray Brachiator shrieked. It didn't let go of the line at first, but it did remove one of its anchoring grips on the Uppergrowth and grab for me, its claws vibrating with a frenzy that might have seemed convulsive had it originated from a creature capable of faster motion.

I had just enough time to move my hand over its other eye and deliver another jolt.

Blinded twice, too agonized to be capable of conscious thought, the Brachiator released its grip on my line. I jerked downward, passing just under its reach and the reach of the other Brachiators clutching at me. I didn't fall any farther because there were too many other Brachs holding the cord. With their reaction time, it might take them a few seconds to even realize that something bad had just happened, and seconds more to decide I was one fish best released. That is, if they decided that. My glimpse of Brachiators at war hadn't exactly painted them as creatures who gave up the first time they were bloodied.

Just above me, Friend to Half-Ghosts roared. "You asked for Life!"

My own cry was no less shrill. "I've changed my mind! I don't want any part of it! And I don't want any part of you!"

Then I fell.

My safety line, released by all the Brachiators at once, went slack for its entire length, freeing me to plunge again. I wasn't ready for it this time, and screamed all the way down, crying out when the cord once again drew taut.

Lastogne, who'd been listening to every last gasp and squeal, was by this time shouting my name over and over. I counted four separate repetitions of "Counselor Cort!" Each one a little more hopeless, a little more certain that I'd given up the fight.

I didn't manage words until the cord used up its elasticity and I was once again spinning at the bottom of the line. "I'm . . . here, sir. A little mussed, but alive for the time being."

He expended his relief in a single whuff of air. "What's happening?"

"I've bought myself a few more minutes. No more, I think. The Brachs are pretty upset at me by now. And you?"

"We haven't heard from the Porrinyards in a while. They're not answering. I don't know whether they're dead or just unable to respond. The AIsource themselves have been less than forthcoming. They say they've withdrawn their permission for a human presence inside the Habitat, and will be expecting us to depart the station within forty-eight hours. No word on the disposition of the people still inside. Which we still count as four, by the way. You, Gibb, Oscin, and Skye."

The damned thing I kept wanting to do, but hadn't been able to do, gnawed at me once again. I shifted my grip on the line, released one hand so I could blow on the aching and now bleeding palms, and said, "Have you counted heads there?"

"Nobody's signed out but you four."

"Forget who's signed out. You can't expect a murderer to sign in and out like a normal person taking shore leave. Gather everybody in the hangar for a roll call. That includes you. If you don't get at least three other parties to vouch for your own presence there, I'm going to assume you're talking to me from some remote location and presume you are our saboteur. The only acceptable excuse for not giving me what I need in five minutes will be that I'm dead and not available to take it from you."

His urgency went away a little, replaced by his usual wry humor. "That does remain a possibility, Counselor."

"I know. But you had better proceed as if it's not."

"I'm right on it," he said.

I felt another tug from up above.

Before I looked, I was sure I knew what it was. It had to be the Brachiators making another attempt to pull me up. I'd have to hold on tight and wait until I was in range again. I didn't think going for the eyes would work a second time, since even creatures as slow as they were would learn from the first time.

Then I looked, and saw that my situation was significantly worse than that.

The gray-haired Brach had given up on retrieving me and begun attacking the line itself.

If I listened real hard, I could make out the scraping sounds from down here. He was slashing away with all the strength he had.

I couldn't blame him. After all, I had presented myself as a friend and then made myself his enemy. He wouldn't consider what I'd done self-defense. He'd see it as betrayal.

You could even give him credit for still trying to give me what I wanted. I'd told him I wanted nothing to do with them. Or with Life.

It would cost him nothing to oblige me.

I'd be safe enough until he realized that the line was impervious to his claws. Then he'd start working out other ways to dislodge me.

My first impulse was to get Lastogne back on the line and beg. But it wouldn't do any good. Nothing would do any good. Even if the AIsource reopened the Habitat right now, no skimmer available to Lastogne or his people could reach me in time to make a difference. The Porrinyards could be dead already for all I knew, and my last resort, Gibb, was stuck on Hammocktown with no means to mount a rescue mission, assuming he'd even want to.

By all meaningful definitions of the word, I was already dead.

But then, by all local definitions of the word, I'd been dead before.

Hating the necessity, I had to climb.

It was a useless gesture. There was no safer place above me worth climbing to. I'd been there already. I knew all I had to look forward to up there was a bloodier death. But the one trait I'd taken from my experiences on Bocai, and nurtured in all the terrible places I'd been since, was an absolute inability to do nothing. Faced with a choice, I'd always seek higher ground, even when higher ground was worse.

I was halfway back to the Uppergrowth when the first spurt of manna juice hit my forehead, stinging my eyes and forcing me to clear my vision with the back of one hand. The Brachiators were slicing away at the vines anchoring my line. The Porrinyards had used an air cannon to drive it through multiple generations of Uppergrowth, and advised me that the anchor was solid enough to support several times my own weight. But it wouldn't be if it was physically ripped from its foundations. It wouldn't be if the Brachiators dedicated themselves to cutting away every single vine between them and the anchoring hook. Chances were, they wouldn't need to excavate it entirely for the cord to give way. The vines between it and the surface were part of what held it fast, after all. Weakening them might be more than enough to loosen my shaky hold on their world. I wouldn't know until I actually started to fall.

No doubt about it. This would be a goddamned stupid way to die.

The sap started to pour. One spurt drenched my face. I licked my lips, and found it as bitter as the worst unsweetened tea. An acquired taste, all right, though under the circumstances I regretted never tasting the fermented version.

My arms were getting tired.

I pulled myself up another arm's length, gasped as something sticky flopped against my shoulders, looked down and saw a short length of vine tumbling into the void.

"Oh, Juje! You've got to be *kidding* me!"

Manna juice was pouring down the rope and flowing over my hands.

As the Brachiators slashed and sliced at the vines anchoring my cord, the size of the hole they dug had turned out to be not nearly as dangerous a factor as how much it bled. The Uppergrowth had begun to hemmorhage, and the line anchored in the center of the damage had become the natural conduit for goo. My hands were just now getting the first of it. In a second or two, the line would be as impossible to climb as any other greased pole.

No sooner had I realized that than the lubrication started to perform its magic. I slipped a full meter, stopping only when I hit a section of cord still dry enough to maintain friction against my hands.

I kicked, shouted an obscene word, got another faceful of goo for my troubles, and did the only thing left available to me.

I started to laugh.

This was a stupid way to die, all right.

But also a goddamned funny one.

The more crap splattered my cheeks and splattered my eyes and greased up my hands and sent me sliding downward, the more I sank into a hilarity of a kind I hadn't enjoyed since the good days on Bocai. It just burst from me, in great big rolling belly-laughs that didn't banish my terror so much as subsume it.

Damn it all, I might have wanted to live, but if I had to go, then I couldn't think of any dumber, or more appropriate, way than this.

Another burst of thunder, very loud and very close, drowned out a frantic query from Lastogne. "Counselor? Are you crying?"

"Hell, no! I'm laughing my ass off!"

A pause. "Care to share the joke?"

"You have to be here, Peyrin. But—ack!—rescue me and I'll be happy to explain it to you!"

My hands gave way. I plunged back to the bottom of my line, spun like a top at the cord's lowest point, endured a fresh indignity as another spurt of manna juice drenched my head and shoulders, gasped with fresh awareness of the nearness of death, and took vague notice of a dragon bursting from the clouds below with an angry thrash of gigantic wings. One last moment of spectacle before I went.

Lastogne shouted, "Counselor! Do you read?"

I caught my breath. "Not for long, Peyrin. I think we've reached the last seconds. Did you do that last roll call?"

"Almost counted wrong," he said. "Forgot Li-Tsan on the first go-round. She's still locked up in the transport."

"And after you count Li-Tsan?"

He said something I missed, because I was too busy shouting.

Because as the dragon leveled off and descended back into the clouds, another object peeled away from it: something that had been using it for cover, something that was now rising as fast as it could toward my position. Something only visible as a bright burst of light.

It didn't look like a man-sized object in an offensive flying armor.

It looked like a skimmer.

"Oh, God," I said, *let it be . . .*

Lastogne shouted again. "COUNSELOR!"

The object's flight was erratic, nothing even close to a straight line, but a queasy wobble that made it look off-center, even struggling.

Come on, Come on, Come on . . .

"COUNSELOR!"

I dropped a meter. The vines anchoring my cord were starting to let go. I had a couple of heartbeats, maybe less, before they failed; not enough time for the Porrinyards to ascend to this altitude.

Who cares? As long as they survive! They can —

A bright, fiery rose blossomed far below; an airburst of some kind, though one too far away to hear quite yet. It was so bright that I lost the object at its center. About half a minute later, the sound reached my position: no longer a deafening cataclysm, just a vague, distant rumble too bearable to represent the loss of two people I didn't want to see dead.

It took me some time to register that my eyes were closed against a now-torrential rain of manna juice, and that Lastogne was screaming at me: "COUNSELOR! GODDAMN-IT, COUNSELOR! I CAN HEAR YOU BREATHING!"

My voice broke three or four times before I managed to get out a word. "Peyrin . . . ?"

"I'm here, Andrea."

I didn't have enough life left in me to protest the use of my first name. ". . . what was . . . that count again?"

He spoke quickly. "I was right the . . ."

My safety line failed.

With the cloudscape many kilometers below me, there were precious few visual cues advising me of my sudden delivery to an inevitable death. It was my spine that felt the sudden loss of control, my skin that registered the rush of air against my face.

I swallowed air and tried to get used to the idea. It wasn't all that hard. I'd been as good as dead for so many years; in part I'd wanted to be. Nothing ahead of me offered any further surprises. I found even enduring it in the form of a fatal drop didn't bother me all that much: the anticipation had been such a burden that the real thing came as a relief.

So I spread my limbs, maximizing my surface area against the onrushing wind, and allowed One One One to take me.

I had regrets. One, that I'd never tell Gibb what I'd learned about the Brachiators. Two, that I'd never tell the AIsource what I'd figured out about them. Three, that I'd never find out about the mysterious gifts they'd claimed to hold for me. Four, that I'd never confront the Unseen Demons over everything they'd done to my life.

Five, that I hadn't made peace with Bringen. He'd indicated a thousand ways that he'd wanted to, and I'd shut him out every single time. I didn't need his response to my mail to know that I'd misjudged him. I knew I had.

Six, that I hadn't made a path for myself instead of allowing the Dip Corps to choose my path for me.

Seven, that I'd adopted the face of the monster I was supposed to be, instead of saying the hell with what people think and becoming someone who might have achieved a little peace.

Eight, that I'd turned away so many who had tried to befriend me. There had been so many names over the years, passing in and out of my life like rumors: Dejah, Roman, Mikal, too many to name, all refusing to give up on me even after I'd declared myself a lost cause.

Nine, that I wouldn't get to finish this thing that had started between me and the Porrinyards. I sure as hell knew what it was and I sure as hell knew I couldn't trust it. Either way I didn't care. It was just too goddamned unfair to be losing it now before I even got a chance to explore it.

Ten, that I'd allowed my past to become my all-purpose excuse. It shouldn't have been. All it ever did was put up a few walls. It wouldn't have defeated me, to the extent it had, with me its eager collaborator.

When all was said and done, I'd been my own worst Unseen Demon.

But that was all right.

"An."

I'd passed the point where regrets meant a damn.

"Drea."

Like fear, and desire, and ambition, and unsolved mysteries, they were just a waste of my time now.

"Andrea!"

All I had left now was the way I faced the little time I had left.

So I opened my eyes and faced the clouds and saw them, still floating like cotton so far below, still roiling with angry thunder, still waiting for me to join them. I'd keep my eyes open for as long as I could, despite the building wind that was already inflating my cheeks and making a grimace out of my lips. Only the irritation of the air pressure against my eyelids made the tears roll back along my temples: nothing else. Not

"ANDREA!"

I almost thought it was Lastogne again. But no, the shout

came from my immediate left, from a burned and battered object falling alongside me. Turning my head to see it almost required more strength than I had. Believing what I saw required considerably more effort than that: it was a skimmer, diving straight down in an attempt to match my velocity. The passenger cab paralleled me, with the two standing occupants, Oscin and Skye, both oriented like horizontal protrusions from a sheer vertical surface.

Less than an arm's length separated me from Oscin's outstretched hand. It was enough distance to exclude me from the skimmer's local grav. The skimmer, not built for speed, was having a hell of a hard time pacing me. Only my blunt position against the wind was slowing me enough to permit even this brief approach.

I didn't even want to know how much fancy maneuvering they'd needed to pull off just to get this close.

They yelled at me again, the words whipped away from the wind.

I waggled my arms. That did something terrible to my aerodynamics and I veered away from the skimmer. For one queasy instant I overcompensated, and found myself diving a direct vertical that left it far behind. Then I flattened myself against the wind again, slowed, felt a nauseating shock wave against my legs as the skimmer almost slammed into my back, and felt that familiar shape swallow up the sky again, this time to my right.

This time, when I looked, Skye was sitting on Oscin's shoulders, reaching for me with everything she had. Her face was desperate and her chin smeared with blood. Her wrists and hands just barely cleared the ionic shields, grasping for me. I almost corrected the wrong way a second time, remembered the way the same action had affected my fall only a few seconds ago, and this time converged on the two familiar faces, at a speed which immediately made me think of head-on collisions with brick walls.

Too late, I realized that I was not the only person in danger here. One miscalculation, and the weight of my own falling body could yank them both free of the skimmer's local grav. I couldn't be responsible for that. I wouldn't. Given another second to think of it, I would have veered away and gone to my death, rather than allow them to sacrifice themselves for me.

A gust of wind blinded me just as Skye's hands converged on my wrist.

Have you ever passed through one zone of local grav into another, without either warning or a decent period of transition? Everything changes in less time than it takes your neurons to fire. In this case, the skimmer at my side was suddenly and without any argument the skimmer beneath me. I slammed against the seats, doubling over, and almost rolled over the side as the local grav flickered off, rendering the cloudscape down again.

Both Oscin and Skye were clutching at available handholds with their free hands, while using the other two to grab on to me. It took me a second to realize what they'd done: switched off the local grav at the instant I was pulled inside it, to avoid snapping my neck and rupturing every organ in my body as I was forced into a sudden and unexpected perpendicular jerk.

My legs flailed behind me. I screamed. I pulled myself closer to my Porrinyards and, the instant I had the chance, threw both my arms around one of the seat backs, once again certain I was going to die.

I don't remember any of the next thirty seconds at all.

Then the grav came on again. My knees settled against the deck. My head bounced lightly against the back of the seat, with a force not much worse than a painful thud. I felt my empty stomach slosh, looking for something to expel.

I realized, with dull amazement, that we'd stopped.

The Porrinyards hadn't managed anything approaching

their usual grace. Oscin lay sprawled against the control panel, his forehead bleeding from a nasty diagonal gash. Skye, curled on her side beside him, looked worse: the blood I'd seen on her chin a few seconds ago had been joined by a swelling bruise on her cheek. For the first time I also saw the nasty flash-burn that had turned her right hand a bright shade of red.

They managed to sit up just as I did, their faces tilting at complementary angles.

Then they smiled, in the manner of people sharing a naughty personal joke. "Why, Andrea. You look good enough to eat."

I didn't quite get the punchline until I tried to lift my hand off the deck and needed extra strength just to overcome the glue. Then I understood. I was still coated, head to toe, with a thick layer of manna juice. I was good enough to eat. Hell, I was downright delectable.

And though I might not have said it, under other circumstances . . . sometimes the straight line is just too perfect.

We didn't have to swap information just yet.

There were other urgencies.

"You better come here and taste some."

They scurried over, on hands and knees.

We took the skimmer away from the clouds, sharing our experiences of the last few minutes. Mine elicited winces of sympathy, and at one point a fervent, "Juje, we'll make you a high-altitude specialist yet!"

Theirs was a little more dizzying. They hadn't gotten away from the Heckler until they hit upon the radical tactic of using one of the dragons for cover. Flying alongside it, straining the skimmer to its absolute limits in order to keep up with the giant creature's flight speed, they'd taken advantage of the Heckler's obvious reluctance to fire weapons in its vicinity, remaining safe in its shadow until the Heckler gave up and flew off.

They said, "I'm surprised he didn't come after you next."

I sucked some manna juice off my fingertips. "He?"

"He. She. Whatever. I'm just using the pronoun for convenience. Either way, I have trouble understanding why you weren't the next target."

My ragged fingernails were still glistening from the juice of the Uppergrowth. "I wasn't expecting to survive the trouble I was already in. Whoa. Damn."

"What?"

"One of this place's smaller mysteries just solved itself for me."

"Really?"

"Yes. Not a particularly important one, but one that adds to the big picture. Believe me, I'll be addressing it before long. You were saying?"

"I was wondering why your friend didn't come after you when we proved too hard to get. And I know you were under attack yourself, but as long as he'd given up on us, why didn't he just zip on up and make sure? Why behave like a cheap neurec villain and trust in a cliffhanger to take care of you?"

I bit my thumbnail. The clicking sound repelled me, and I felt no urge to do it again. "I don't know. There could have been a deadline. Maybe he had to get back to the hangar so he wouldn't be missed. Or maybe he had something else to—" At which point I froze. "Oh, shit."

The Porrinyards saw the look in my eyes. "What?"

"Gibb."

For a little while, everything had seemed better.

And then we returned to the site of what had been Hammocktown.

Some of the support structures remained, but everything else had been twisted out of recognition, or ripped free of its moorings to plunge into the clouds below. Thickets of loose cables dangled from the Uppergrowth, twisting in the winds, some trailing strips of tattered canvas like banners scarred in battle.

Everything else that had been here last night, including Stuart Gibb, was gone.

22

EMISSARIES FROM THE DEAD

The mood at the hangar defined grim. The indentures of Hammocktown wandered, directionless, between the sleepcubes set up for them, speaking in hushed voices, weeping, or staring at each other with eyes that could have belonged to any decimated army. With all bravado failed in the aftermath of Gibb's apparent death, the stench of failure hung over the place like a cloud. Everybody knew that their mission had failed and that the only issue still remaining to them was just how soon they'd be allowed to leave: if they were not prisoners of war or, worse, captives waiting for their own executions.

Lastogne, who remained in charge by default, had taken pity on our condition and allowed us to stop for first-aid and a change of clothes before debriefing. I could have used a quick sonic, but I was so soiled from my ordeal on the Uppergrowth that I locked myself inside the transport and scoured myself with a luxurious hot-water shower. I didn't restrict myself to the five-minute limit, either. I dialed both the temperature and the water pressure all the way into the red zone and stood with my face in the direct path of the assault, my eyes closed and my arms hanging limp at my sides.

By the time I emerged from the transport, wearing a fresh black uniform, I didn't need all that much sensitivity to feel the fresh hostility directed against me on all sides. Before, I'd just been a severe, hard-bitten suit from New London: maybe a little cold, maybe a little crazy, but at the very minimum a professional, and a voice of authority who had to be respected. Now I was an irresponsible maverick with a scandalous past whose stunts might have gotten Stuart Gibb killed. I couldn't take a step without feeling eye-daggers sinking into my back.

Only one person, Oskar Levine, asked if I was all right.

I nodded, astonished him with a hug, then reported to Peyrin Lastogne in the sleepcube where he'd scheduled the debriefing.

The Porrinyards were already there, bracketing Lastogne on both sides, their expressions neutral, their eyes warning me to tread carefully. Oscin wore a plastiskin bandage on his forehead. Skye had treated her right hand with a gloss of burn gel. She hadn't done anything for her facial wounds, either because she considered them too minor to worry about or, more likely, because she hadn't had the time. But it was Lastogne who looked haggard. He bore the look of a man who hadn't slept in days, and who no longer believed he'd manage the trick any time soon. "Counselor. You look cleaner, at least."

"Thank you," I said, though I recognized it as the furthest thing from a compliment. "Have you been in touch with New London?"

"I'm not all that sure you're the one entitled to ask questions here."

"I'm sorry, sir, but until relieved by my superiors, that's exactly what I'll be doing. Have you been in touch with New London?"

His eyes continued to burn like lasers. "I've sent a report, but mine won't cause as much damage as the one the AIsource just shared with me. They've declared our entire party persona non grata on this station. They've said that no further visitors will be allowed for the foreseeable future, and that any future observers, if permitted, will need to be appointed by one of the other powers, probably the Bursteeni or the Tchi. They've further said that we will only be allowed to stay in the hangar until we can be outfitted to leave."

"Have they given a reason?"

"Yes," he said. "You."

My throat tightened. "Me?"

"They say you engaged in hostilities against the Brachiators. Specifically, that you blinded one. Is that true?"

Oh, that. "I was taking action to defend myself."

"An argument that carries some weight with me. But it would carry more weight if you had been authorized for unsupervised interaction with these indigenes in the first place. We've always been very careful to restrict that authorization to people who had been trained for it. You go, without authorization, without training, and without any aptitude at high-altitude survival, and within a few hours alienate them so badly that all of our work building a relationship with them has been busted all to hell."

"It was already showing cracks, sir."

"You're talking about the Warmuth incident. But Warmuth didn't get us expelled from the Habitat. Warmuth didn't destroy our entire purpose for being here. Warmuth didn't drag two of our best people," he indicated the Porrinyards, who refrained from providing one of their frequent reminders that they only counted as one person, "into such a severe infraction of protocol that they'll be working off the penalties for the rest of their lives."

I remained calm. "I agree, sir. But that's not all Warmuth didn't do."

"Really?"

"She also didn't survive."

Lastogne's cheeks twitched. "Necessity will take you only so far, Counselor. Even in the Corps."

"On the contrary," I said, with unwavering confidence, "I think it'll take me just far enough."

He turned toward the Porrinyards, appealing for answers, but finding nothing except an equanimity that matched my own.

For the first time, it seemed to occur to him that they were not frightened at all: not of him, not of disciplinary action from the Dip Corps, and not of consequences. They were serene, almost happy. He asked them, not me, "What?"

I started to tell him, choked on the first few words, cleared my throat, and found my voice still wanting. "I've had a very rough night, sir, and I think this is the first time I've ever had a meeting on this station when somebody didn't offer me a buzzpatch or a drink."

Lastogne could only twitch with the mortification of any professional diplomat reminded that he'd neglected certain formalities. "What would you like?"

"Anything alcoholic. As long as it isn't that stuff you make from manna juice. I've had enough of that particular taste today."

The Porrinyards nodded. "Though we have found out, sir, that it is a delicacy that improves with presentation. It's a fine sauce."

Allowing this to pass without requesting clarification, Lastogne opened one of the crates and returned with a tube of something amber. I thanked him, sucked it dry, blinked away the warmth that suffused my aching limbs, and contemplated the empty before handing it back to him. "Nobody here ever understood the Brachiator beliefs about Life and Death."

"These things take time, Counselor. It's an entire alien psychology."

"Nonsense," I said, my voice rising. "The Brachiators may be alien in ways we haven't come close to exploring yet, but their understanding of these matters are as simple as basic arithmetic."

"That New Ghost, Half-Ghost nonsense—"

"—is not nonsense. It's completely sensible. Too bad it's also a viewpoint that Gibb's people, as good as you are, have always been woefully ill-equipped to understand. I'm perfectly willing to admit you're good people. You just happen to be the wrong people for this particular job. It's, all in all, one of the worst staffing errors I've ever seen."

He shook his head in automatic denial. "I can't wait to hear you defend this one."

"It was a simple mistake, sir. When staffing an outpost in an environment whose inhabitants cling to the very sky, it only made sense to seek out people with a special affinity for heights: mountain climbers, acrobats, orbital construction workers, and other people used to working at high altitudes every day. People like that could thrive in the conditions here. But they were also the people least likely to grasp what the Brachiators go on about."

"I don't—"

I didn't let him finish. "People like that, like you, have a three-dimensional mindset. They know the gulf between themselves and the surfaces far below them, and are able to perceive the distance as one that can be *traveled,* even if only by falling. The unspoken assumption here has always been that the Brachiators share that perception . . . which is silly, since you only have to look at the way they're built to notice that they're designed to spend their entire lives staring at a surface right above their faces. That's not the perspective of a species destined to understand the panorama. That's the perspective of a species with limited understanding of up and down, and a perspective your outpost filled with mountain climbers and professional aerialists was not about to grasp. I, on the other hand, have always been afraid of heights, and I know in my gut what the Brachiators know from birth: that the Uppergrowth is Life, and everything below it is Death."

Lastogne's mouth fell open. "I'll be damned."

"Consider a Brachiator falling. Imagine its prognosis for survival if it falls, let's say, so much as one meter. I think you'll agree, that's not even enough to pick up appreciable speed. Maybe it hasn't even vanished from peripheral vision yet. We already know that the AIsource won't rescue it. Does it stand any chance of survival? Whatsoever?"

What followed was the well-known phenomenon of a group, asked a simple question with an obvious answer, that nevertheless remains silent as everybody waits for somebody else to trigger a suspected rhetorical trap.

The Porrinyards were the first to build up enough confidence to say the obvious. "No, Counselor. It doesn't."

"Exactly," I said. "In that instant, it is still breathing, it is still feeling, it is still thinking, but by all standards reasonable to its species, it is as dead as the Brachiator who took a tumble a week ago, or one that fell last year."

Lastogne rubbed his eyes. "Yeah."

"Think about it," I said. "From their perspective, we rise from the place that nothing can survive. We are solid, we are friendly, we speak to them, we are clearly entities with substance, but we are also visitors from the land of the Dead. By all reasonable calculations, we are Ghosts. It is no wonder they resist speaking to anybody who hasn't spent a night on the Uppergrowth. Doing that gives us a certain link to Life.

Not quite the same thing as life, since we still keep coming in and out of existence—"

Lastogne now seemed thoroughly disgusted with himself. "Like Half-Ghosts."

"Exactly. A natural classification for somebody sometimes alive and sometimes dead: a concept they find strange, but which is evidently within their ability to accept. Unfortunately for her, Cynthia Warmuth didn't see things that way. She had something else, which several people, including you, have described as a downright compulsive empathy."

Was that a flicker of pain in Lastogne's eyes? "Yes."

"She wanted, too much, to be inside the skin of anybody she spoke to. She made herself a pest about it. So much a pest that people hated her for it. But she would have survived unpopularity if she hadn't taken it a step too far: the same step I took when I spent a night on the Uppergrowth. She told the Brachiators she wanted to be Alive like them, without ever once considering what they'd think that meant."

Lastogne now looked downright stricken. "And so . . . ?"

"And so," I said, "bearing her no malice whatsoever, they nailed her into place."

Lastogne stood up, turned his back on us, and strode to the cube's far wall, his arms crossed before him, his head bowed in an attitude of unbearable sorrow. Neither the Porrinyards nor I said anything to disturb him. After several long minutes, he returned to his seat, his grimace now a wan, mournful scowl.

I went on as if there had been no interruption at all. "It wouldn't have occurred to them that they could hurt her. They didn't think she was completely Alive in the first place. To their eyes, she was already just a Ghost, with an unnatural half-existence; nothing as linked to everyday existence as a wound should have had any effect on her. No. With the best possible intentions, she asked for their help holding on to Life, and with the best possible intentions, they gave her what she wanted. The negative effect on her came as a complete surprise to them. They told me this themselves. *Life is not healthy for Ghosts. It uses them up too fast*. Being nailed to Life was no good for Warmuth. She bled to death. It used her up too fast. This was news to the Brachiators, but once it was revealed to them they took it as a cautionary lesson. Which is why they didn't want to give me the same thing, until I begged them."

Lastogne eyed the Porrinyards, soliciting silent feedback, finding in their expressions of wide-eyed understanding acceptance of a truth everybody here had failed to see. After a moment he turned toward me once again, but his eyes were not focused on me so much as past me, to some memory only his eyes could see. "I always told her it would hurt her someday."

Nothing he had ever said to me sounded less like him.

The Porrinyards, who knew him better than I did, turned toward him, their profiles matching studies in incredulity.

I wasn't surprised at all. "What?"

"Caring, as much as she did." His voice broke. He heard it, gathered himself together, and shrugged, apologizing for the moment of weakness. "It's not typical, Counselor. You know how I feel about the system. It cements mediocrity in place. Most of the indentures are just trying to do their time and get out. Most of the careerists are just trying to rise to their own level of incompetence. And when you find an occasional person who really cares, the irritant like poor Cynthia, they turn out to be worse than either. They go and screw everything up by behaving like what they do matters."

The Porrinyards were alternating aghast glances at me with disbelieving glances at Lastogne.

I couldn't blame them. Not after everything they'd said about his selfishness as a lover.

But this was still territory I'd expected. "You loved her, didn't you?"

"I wasn't drawn to her, at first. It's like I told you the first day: I don't look to make friends. The last thing I could ever want was understanding from someone so arrogant she actually believed other people could be understood." He shook his head, not just once but several times, perhaps even too many times, before raising his eyes back to me. "I always told her it would hurt her someday. I even warned her to be careful it didn't get her killed. Shows how goddamned perceptive I am, doesn't it?"

There was an odd, hysterical sense of triumph in his voice. The loss of Cynthia Warmuth hadn't shattered him at all. It had only reinforced his grim sense of cynical amusement, confirming the hard lessons he'd learned from other losses, other tragedies, other people he'd driven away.

The moment lasted just long enough for Skye to extend her hand, almost touch his shoulder, then draw her hand back, deciding the touch a bad idea.

Then he pulled himself together, took a deep breath, and noticed me again, this time with a dark resentment that bordered on bile. "But it's not sufficient, Counselor. It doesn't explain Santiago. Or the attempts on your life. Or that attacker who went after Oscin and Skye. Or what's happened to Hammocktown."

I looked him right in the eye, and nodded. "You're right. It doesn't."

"What do you expect me to think? That Gibb's behind all this? That he's somewhere in the Uppergrowth, waiting for another fresh victim to come along?"

"That remains a possible explanation, sir."

"But you don't think so."

"No, sir. I think what the evidence tells me."

"And you're not about to tell me what that is."

"Not until I'm sure."

"So how can that even begin to compensate for everything else you've done?"

"By itself," I said, "it doesn't. But this was never just one mystery, with one solution. It was several, all mixed up and getting in the way of a comprehensive explanation. I had to clear away all the smaller issues, like Gibb and like Warmuth, just to get at the bigger picture. And that's the one last thing I still have left to do." I took a deep breath. "Who are you, Peyrin Lastogne?"

He stared at me as if unsure whether to give me a medal or punch me in the mouth. Then he glanced at the Porrinyards, first one and then the other, to determine just how much they'd been infected by my madness. When they just nodded, he threw up his arms and stomped back to the same corner he'd retreated to before, turning a number of different colors.

He'd said all he was going to say.

The assembled indentures watched as the Porrinyards and I marched back to the skimmer dock, their eyes either accusatory or imploring. I had thought them people under siege before, the day I'd arrived here, but I'd been wrong. This was what being at siege was like. How many of these people were trying to persuade themselves they had a chance of surviving the rest of the day? How many had already decided they wouldn't?

I could have given them a little reassuring speech, like Gibb had tried to do after the evacuation of Hammocktown, but I'd never been the reassuring speech sort. Maybe that was another area I could work on, in the future. If I had a future.

Oskar Levine was the only one who rushed up to us, just before we left the hangar; he'd been working on the bluegel crypts not long beforehand, and was so stained by the stuff it was hard to find much of his skin's original color. I confess being relieved when he didn't obey what looked like his initial impulse to hug me. "Is it true?" he demanded. "Is Hammocktown gone?"

"It's true," I told him.

"And Gibb? He was there when it went?"

He seemed more concerned than I would have expected of a man who Gibb had treated like a traitor. I wanted to see if he would fake grief. It hardly seemed in character for him, but people contradict their own natures in times of crisis. So I said, "Yes," and waited.

It took him several heartbeats to work up his next question, but he ultimately let it out, all in one breath. "Do you think he's dead, or just in hiding?"

It was a fair question.

I said, "I don't know," and left him.

23

IN THE CONFESSIONAL

Between sleeplessness, physical exhaustion and the lingering aftereffects of several near brushes with death, I was as wrung out as a buzzpop addict in the last stages of withdrawal. Part of me argued in favor of a break. If the hangar was indeed safe, as I suspected, I could have taken days, even hours, to rest up and gird myself for the next step, without fear of my extended period of inaction dooming others to join the growing list of casualties.

It would have been nice. It even would have been wise.

But waiting was not an option.

I just couldn't take being played with any more.

The Porrinyards didn't say much on the way to the Interface. They knew, with the certainty born of consensus, that no words could stall me, stop me, or comfort me. But Skye did grab my wrist, as I knelt to enter the portal, to ask: "Do you know about us, too? Everything?"

I couldn't smile. "Yes. I do."

"How long?"

"For a while now."

They both looked like they were going to cry. "Are you going to be all right with that?"

"I don't know. It depends on what I can confirm in there."

They nodded, with a complete lack of surprise, and acting as one, stepped forward to wrap me in an embrace. Oscin had to stoop, a little, to get in. Both trembled.

"You had better live."

It wasn't fear that made me so reluctant to let go, but the sheer novelty of connection: feeling myself a part of somebody else's life, and feeling them as part of mine. I wasn't sure it was something I could afford. But that was also part of what I had to find out in there.

The Porrinyards released me and stepped back, dry-eyed, providing me with a matched set of brave little smiles.

I could only nod at them and pull myself through the hatch.

It was not difficult to notice subtle changes in the chamber of indistinct blue skies. A new element had been added, one that clashed with the ambience of infinite space: a certain claustrophobic oppressiveness that made the walls, wherever they were, loom like a prison. I don't know whether that came from changes in me or from subliminal cues activated by the AIsource. Nor do I know whether I imagined, or merely projected, the impression of hoarded breath. I only know what I believed. And I believed that, insofar as it was even possible for beings like the AIsource to feel apprehension, in the presence of a creature so much smaller and shorter-lived than themselves, it was what they felt now.

As I floated there, waiting for be acknowledged, I found myself understanding them on the most visceral of levels. As intelligences, they were beyond my comprehension. As creatures of power, they were gods who reduced me to the significance of dust. But as souls, they were downright ordinary. They had ambitions, and feelings, as base as those belonging to any of us. They were, in the final analysis, as corrupt as we were. And in that, they were kindred.

In my time I'd been fascinated by them, afraid of them, suspicious of them, and enraged by them.

Now, for the first time ever, I could feel, rather than feign, contempt for them.

It was liberating.

When they spoke, they used the voice of a male: deep and resonant, with just enough of an echo to make the unseen walls seem even farther away.

Congratulations, Counselor. We have heard that you came up with an explanation for the death of Cynthia Warmuth.

"You heard by listening. You were with us, following our every word."

If we sometimes behave as if we acquire information at the same rate that you organics do, then that's simply because it's polite to modulate our conversations with you to your own capacities.

"Polite," I said. "Or necessary to preserve our illusions."

Don't they amount to more or less the same thing?

"No, they don't. Not when it renders communication less convenient, not more. Not when it complicates every conversation we have. When you do that, the pretense itself becomes the very point—and it leaves me with no choice but to consider just why you find it so important."

Another pause, this one long enough to make me worry about being ejected for my effrontery.

Then, as if grudgingly: ***Go on.***

"Everybody here sees the absurdity of it. You see and hear everything aboard this station. But in order to actually converse with you in return, Gibb's people need to hop a skimmer and travel all the way back to this one place. This one room. Why would you make everybody do this? What advantage would you find in it?"

It's our station. We can make any arbitrary rules we like.

They sounded like the words of a spoiled child, caught trying to dominate a playground.

"It is your station, and the ecosystem you've set up here has any number of arbitrary rules, but none of them seem pointless. None of them seem designed to cause inconvenience for its own sake. This chamber does. For a while there I assumed you use it just because you wanted to remind us who ran the place, but now that I've been around here for a while I think the true explanation's a little more devious than that. I think you use it to keep us from thinking about all the things you would prefer us not to think about."

This pause was the longest so far. ***We're not certain what you're referencing there, Counselor.***

"Oh," I said, my anger with them growing, "I'm sure you know exactly what I'm referencing, but since you insist on going through the motions, we can afford to put this issue aside for a moment or two. After I say a little bit more about Cynthia Warmuth . . . whose murder, whatever I said to Mr. Lastogne today, remains not quite solved."

A new tone entered the voice of the AIsource: awed fascination. ***We thought you were under the impression you were finished with that.***

"Not for a heartbeat. Not with the explanation I gave Mr. Lastogne. That was just about getting him off my back, so I could finish my business with you. No, my night on the Upergrowth wasn't about confirming my theory: it was about proving my theory wrong."

As before, we are very interested in hearing your reasoning.

"I shouldn't have to go through this. I should just tell you I know everything, and move on. But, very well. We can play games if you prefer. Some of what I told Lastogne was true. I did figure out the human place in Brachiator cosmology. I even figured out how they'd likely react to a human being who wanted more of a connection to Life. But I've also seen how slow they are . . . and I know it wouldn't make any sense for them to be able to overwhelm a human being with the agility of one of Gibb's people. Were Warmuth awake and aware of everything going on around her, she wouldn't have needed lightning reflexes to escape the same way I did. Hell, I'm downright clumsy, and a simple tether line placed me beyond Brachiator reach long enough for help to reach me, even when that help was itself under attack. Why would Warmuth have any more trouble than I did?"

You had the advantage of knowing recent history. Perhaps Warmuth didn't know what they had planned until they took her by surprise.

"That might have made sense if they'd merely mauled her. A mass attack of that kind, coming from all sides, from sentients who approach at the rate of Brachiators, might have been easy to mistake for any other kind of social activity, including ceremonial grooming or even—Juje help me—a group hug. But the Brachiators approached me with claws in hand, giving me the opportunity to fathom their violent intent long minutes before they actually reached me. I even closed my eyes a few times to simulate a distraction capable of preventing me from paying proper attention. But even when I gave them every possible advantage, it was impossible to believe in Warmuth being taken by surprise. Their group assault was interminable, inexorable, even frightening . . . and obvious. Warmuth would have had more than enough time to see that something was wrong, and summon help."

She could have been asleep.

The AIsource was now behaving like a human suspect throwing out one idiot evasion after another, in the hopes of derailing the one true path to a solution. But a human suspect did that kind of thing out of panic and self-preservation. The AIsource seemed to be playing a game of catch with logic: pointing out all the holes still remaining in my argument, so I could fill them in as I went. It infuriated me, but I obliged. "Also not a realistic possibility. The Brachiators came after me as soon as I spoke the words that set them off. Warmuth wouldn't have begged them for Life, watch them unsheathe claws and begin converging on her position, then conveniently fall asleep before they were close enough to act. That's beyond ridiculous. No, I'm afraid that there are only two real possibilities here. Either she met up with someone who moved faster than she could, or she was already immobilized and helpless when that unknown party gave the Brachiators a very bad idea. Either way, that means another culprit."

Another hesitation. ***You are correct.***

"And that person is still beyond my reach, correct?"

For the moment.

"Because we're still talking internal politics, aren't we? Our saboteur, culprit, Heckler, what have you, is still working for your opposition party, still killing, still doing whatever needs to be done to disrupt whatever you have going on inside the Habitat. You know who it is, but you can't just give me a name, or even put me in the same room, without breaking whatever rules of engagement you've managed to set up among yourselves."

Again: for the moment.

"Politics."

Civil War, Counselor. One you currently have no business being any part of.

Currently. "It hasn't stopped the other side from trying to kill me."

The other side operates under ethics not our own. The other side will escalate if we do anything to encourage any

further involvement from outsiders. The other side will not subject its agents to any attempt at capture by other parties.

"Which means you could respond yourself if you wanted to."

We could. But we see greater advantage in waiting.

"For what?"

To get what we want.

"From them?"

No.

"From me?"

Yes.

"What do you want from me?"

Something freely given.

I'd expected something like this. But the weight of it was enough to make my chest hurt. It made me think about one of the first things Lastogne had ever said to me, upon my arrival. Not a philosophy as much as a warning.

In that moment of silence, I found myself wondering what Oscin and Skye were doing. Were they wishing me strength? Wondering if the dangerous part had started yet? Expecting me to come out or thinking, sadly, that I wouldn't?

What would Lastogne do if I never came back?

Hell, what would Bringen? He'd begged me to find any culprit other than the AIsource. If I was reported dead, aboard an AIsource station, with witnesses establishing the AIsource as the last sentient force to see me alive, what lies would he be forced to tell to keep the whole thing buried?

A thousand other questions, unable to answer unless I finished up the ones I had on hand.

So I closed my eyes, brought my breathing under control, and resumed.

"So let's talk about the way this station works."

Very well.

"It's been clear, from the start, that it's not just about the Brachiators. And not just because they're such a small part of your ecosystem. But also because you taught them to speak Mercantile. It's clear that you did that for the benefit of human visitors, the same human visitors you went out of your way to lure here, and permit here. The question, for me, was just to what degree you benefited from making this place a huge show, being staged for human benefit."

It's hardly just that, Counselor.

"I believe you. I accept that the Brachiators are here for a reason. I accept that those other environments, farther down, the ones we can't get to, represent any number of other projects important to your people. But I'm not talking about those. I'm talking about your eagerness to stock this place, not only with Brachiators but with their human observers. I'm talking about the degree to which those human observers are also here to be studied."

You are fascinating people.

"Yes, and you went out of your way to make this place fascinating for us, didn't you? Like those dragons, for instance. That was a bit much. I'm certain you could have developed any number of other creatures capable of filling that ecological niche. But you wanted ones that resonated with humanity's mythological past. So you built them: not just creatures who vaguely resembled them, but creatures who looked exactly like the ones we'd imagined. Why? Just to please and tease us. If anything on One One One establishes that you're playing with us, at least a little, it's them. That quote from Dante that you put up, outside your Interface . . . that's another, and it established that you're as willing to play with me as an individual as you are with individual members of my species."

We have a sense of humor, Counselor.

"I've noted that. But tricks like that do raise troublesome questions about just what you want from the human beings stationed here. And do point out your willingness to stage-manage the conditions here, to play with our perceptions in ways that Gibb's crew, surviving here on a day-to-day basis, might never have imagined.

"Which brings us back to why you'd insist on holding court in this Interface chamber, when you can speak to us anywhere inside this station.

"Maybe the dragons are among the distractions you use to hide a much more important deception.

"Everybody here has seen your floating remotes, your maintenance machines, your fliers. We've all understood that they transmit back everything they see, but even they're not everywhere. How can they see everything, even on a station that belongs to you? I've been thinking about that, and it's occurred to me that you must have other eyes we haven't thought about. I spent some of my time on the Uppergrowth brainstorming about where some of them could be. I thought, well, maybe the Uppergrowth itself is visually sensitive; there's no reason it couldn't be transmitting images back to you. And I thought, well, all those little black insects I see flying around: maybe they're not part of the environmental balance here at all but, rather, swarming miniature eyes. And then I thought, well, that's interesting, let's take it a step further. If the AIsource have spy machines that small, nothing would prevent them from having spy machines even smaller."

You are speaking of nanotechnology, which is nothing new. Even your people know that art. And again, we fail to see your point. It is our station. We are within our rights to use any monitoring techniques at our disposal.

"Yes, you are, but once again, that only reinforces the question of this chamber. Again: if you're everywhere aboard this station, why insist on this fiction of a special, isolated location where visitors must go to parley? And why support that fiction here, when in the rest of inhabited space you use floating flatscreens for ambassadors?"

Do you have any answers, Counselor?

"Only one.

"This room is here for one reason and one reason only. The only possible reason.

"It's a theater.

"It makes you tactile.

"You want the human beings posted here to think of you as having a specific location: to ignore what we know, and think of you, instead, as creatures who can be approached, dealt with, and then left behind—when the fact of the matter is that you're everywhere. And that leads to another, unavoidable question: Why would you be so careful to maintain that illusion here? Why would it be so bad for us to feel—really, really feel—how ubiquitous you are aboard this station?"

The AIsource sounded amused. ***Why?***

"Because the second we do we also start wondering why you would need to limit those capabilities to this particular patch of real estate. We start wondering, what's so special about *this* place."

Ah.

"We start wondering if your ambassadors, all over inhabited space, also exist only as distractions. We start upgrading our estimates of just how powerful you are. We start wondering how much you can influence. We start wondering —"

—if, the AIsource concluded for me, ***we're inside you.***

My heart lurched inside my chest like a creature that had long considered itself safe inside its cage but which now hammered against the bars in a desperate attempt at flight.

I had not expected them to admit to it so readily.

I thought of neighbors turned to vicious enemies between one second and the next, a little girl turned to something worse than animal, an innocent turned to war criminal.

Tens of thousands, inside everybody. Some only a few molecules thick, but large enough to have forged an integral connection with your nervous system. It helps us nudge you this way, or that way, from time to time: not constantly, of course, as that would be a gross intrusion on your free will, and an utter waste of your ability to forge a fresh and informative perspective, but from time to time, whenever you need to be influenced.

My voice came close to failing me. "And your . . . insurgents . . . the rogues . . . your opposition party . . ."

. . . your so-called Unseen Demons . . .

" . . . they influence us the same way?"

Already asked and answered, Counselor.

"They can make us kill people we don't want to kill?"

And worse things.

"How do I know they're the ones who controlled us on Bocai? That it wasn't you?"

You don't. But since you have our honest assurance that at times we have had to do things just as terrible, you should be able to accept that we wouldn't evade responsibility for some crimes while freely acknowledging others. We, meaning the ones speaking to you now, are innocent of that one.

I had seen some of this, but not all of it. Now my head was proving too small to contain it. Blood burned in my ears, and I closed my eyes, trying to fight my way out of the black emptiness that had always threatened to swallow me whole.

Worlds away, the AIsource chided me. ***Come now, Counselor. You should be taking it better than this. After all, you came here today specifically to tell us that you'd figured most of this out.***

My own voice sounded just as distant, but as long as I concentrated on it I still had a grip on sanity. "I had. You said you had three gifts for me. One you'd already given, one you were in the process of giving, and one you hoped to give me at the conclusion of this business."

Yes.

"It wasn't until a few hours ago that I figured out what the first gift was. I happened to look at my fingertips and notice how much they'd healed since my arrival."

They do look much better now, the AIsource confided, in an absurdly confidential tone.

"Before I . . . came here, I . . . bit my nails. Every time I needed to concentrate, I gnawed a finger. Sometimes, when the problems were thorny enough, I gnawed them bloody. But that stopped with my first visit to this room. Ever since then . . . every time I faced something that puzzled me . . . I felt this sickly feeling that there was something I would ordinarily be doing, that I was being kept from doing."

It is an unhealthy habit, Andrea Cort.

"It was also free will."

Which you do still possess, within certain boundaries.

"You freed me of that habit just to show you could."

We thought it would help boost your investigation.

"And the second gift? The one you said you were in the process of giving me? That little tweak you gave to my emotions, which allowed me to respond to Oscin and Skye?"

That was a little more complicated. But it didn't impinge on your free will as much as the suppression of your unfortunate habit. It just freed you to act on feelings you haven't ever allowed yourself to acknowledge. You could have just as easily decided that you weren't attracted to the Porrinyards, and sought out Lastogne or Gibb instead—or, for that matter, not acted on the changes in yourself until you returned home to New London and had a wider number of alternate candidates.

I didn't ask about the third gift, the one they'd said I wouldn't receive until after our business was done. I was too furious. "What gave you the right?"

If you truly prefer the way you were, we can put your inhibitions back. But we don't think that's what you want.

Sometimes, the greatest gift is the one given in secret.

"Bullshit," I said, furiously. "You were just demonstrating a point!"

We were not just demonstrating a point. As we have said many times, Andrea Cort, we respect you, and believe we have many things in common. We feel that once our business is concluded here our ultimate ambitions will be even more aligned. But yes, making the point was an attractive benefit.

"That wasn't all," I said, my rage still building. "The Brachiators called you the Hand-in-Ghosts. Gibb's people, who've heard it before, considered it just more Brachiator dribble. But if we're Ghosts, and you're the Hand-in-Ghosts, what does that make you but a puppeteer?"

And then, the AIsource reminded me, ***there's the thing that one dying Brachiator said to you.***

"I know. It said it couldn't feel the Hand anymore."

It was dying. We left early.

"Your 'Hand,' as they call it, is always inside them. They can always feel it. They can always feel you inside them."

Yes.

There was little I could say to that.

The AIsource did not sigh, but their voice cast breath in a manner that simulated a sigh, and went on. ***These next points are well outside the immediate scope of your investigation, but you will likely desire them resolved before you're willing to take the one step necessary for the resolution of your business aboard this station. So this is what you want to know. The Brachiators are not the only sentients we've bred. We have made a practice of it. We want the unique perspectives their biology requires of them: perspectives that may be right and may be wrong but which are of tremendous help to us in modeling theoretical possibilities for further study. In the specific case of the Brachiators, it has provided their concepts of Life and Death and, in time, other imagi-***

native psychological variations. It is all data, tremendous in its potential to reveal that which we have always desired.

Had I possessed a button capable of destroying One One One in a cataclysm of raging nuclear fire, I would have pressed it, not caring that I floated at its heart. But I didn't have that. I didn't even possess any solid objects to hit. "I didn't consent to that contribution."

Neither did the Brachiators, the AIsource replied blandly. ***Few sentients have a choice in deciding just what kind of learning experience they present for others. You, yourself, have had little control over the lessons you've taught more sentients than you can name. But it matters little. You can lock yourself in a room and never interact with anything outside it, ever again, and still by example provide data for those who know you're in there. You could go further by retreating into catatonia, and still teach those obliged to care for you. This is not much different. The Brachiators did not ask to be created, but then no creature does. In the meantime, they live, and find it incidental that we watch and learn.***

"They deserve more than living their whole lives as your puppets!"

"Deserve" is a value judgment that varies depending on viewpoint. But the point is moot. If they are puppets—or, the AIsource seemed to hesitate then, the interjection giving the impression of a wry afterthought, ***if you prefer, Marionettes, they are puppets that are permitted a substantial degree of free will. Because, like human beings, they will not give us the answers we seek unless they're left free to explore their own natures.***

"And those answers are —"

—tangential to the reason you came to this station. You are here, in this chamber, not to confront us about our manipulations, but because you need our assistance to find the entity you call the Heckler.

My heart still thundering in my chest, the implications of what I'd learned looming before me like a landscape too vast to be perceived by merely human eyes, I would not take the cue and change the subject. "Why all the hints? Why all the games? Why not just make me do what you want me to do?"

The AIsource's response was a perfect fatherly chuckle.

Because then you would be less than useless to us, Andrea Cort. You are a very interesting human being. And, again, what we want of you, in the future, is only useful if provided of your own free will.

"And that's what you've always wanted from me," I said. "That's why you went to so much trouble to invite me aboard this madhouse. Why you've bribed me with all these 'gifts.' Why you've manipulated this dispute between yourselves and the ones I call Unseen Demons, and withheld all answers until I asked direct questions. Even why you saved me, twice. You want that concession from me."

It is what we've always wanted, Andrea. But it is necessary now. The murderer you seek is under rogue protection. You will not be able to force a confrontation except as our agent, exercising the laws of our majority. And even then, the rules of engagement will keep the rogues, and us, from engaging each other directly. This will have to be a confrontation between two human beings.

My clothing fluttered from a breeze blowing from somewhere behind me. I felt myself tumbling head over heels in what my vague sense of direction insisted on interpreting as multiple forward somersaults. Without any visual cues identifying up or down or even a fixed point of reference, it was impossible to tell where one rotation ended and the next one began, but I was being directed somewhere I couldn't see, without any personal input on my part.

I wanted to kick and scream and thrash about and somehow propel myself in a direction directly opposite from the one the AIsource required of me.

But I did not know what direction that was.

We won't force you, the AIsource said. ***You could forgo the answers, and return to New London with failure on your hands.***

The blue chamber provided no cues identifying up, down, or sideways.

Once again I considered the words Lastogne had spoken to me, the words that had come to define the entire direction my life had taken, upon my arrival on this station.

We're all owned.

It's just a matter of deciding who holds the deed.

It wasn't like I owed the Confederacy, or the Dip Corps, a damned thing.

But humanity?

That was a betrayal of an entirely different order. If a betrayal was what it was.

I had always hated people, always despised crowds. No, scratch "always." Once upon a time, before the night that formed me, I'd been partial to both. But since then I'd never been at home in any gathering of human beings. I'd always seen the race as a corrupt one, one that though worth despising for its own crimes were nevertheless too high to permit inclusion by a creature who had done the kind of things I'd done. I'd known that I could never be accepted and had hated them for not trying harder to prove me wrong. I'd been proud of that dichotomy, like any other self-serving misanthrope.

But now I found myself thinking about a café I'd liked, in New London's Mercantile district, on a balcony with a view overlooking the three hundred terraces of the Dumas Plaza. I'd always gone there with a hytex link stocked with severe-looking documents, and the fierce mien of a dedicated bureaucrat too busy to be disturbed. It had discouraged the interference of fellow diners who, otherwise, might have taken the empty chair opposite mine as an invitation for the opening of conversational gambits. Alone, in the midst of the friends and lovers chatting at other tables, I'd been able to enjoy the spicy food and my cocoon of silence and sit among them without ever being *of* them. It had been my choice. But how much time had I spent with my nose in my important work, and how much had I spent watching those terraces across the way, and the people who wandered in and out of those fancy rooms like actors making entrances and exits in three hundred plays written just for me? How much had I hated them, taking comfort in considering them vapid every time I caught a smile or heard a peal of laughter, and how insistently had I assured myself that my emptiness was so much more informed, so much more genuine than whatever joys they'd used to fill themselves?

Why would I do all that, if they were just beneath my notice?

How much more could I have had, if I'd just been able to put the awfulness inside me aside, long enough to try?

I didn't like being owned by the Dip Corps. I never had. It had been a convenient legal fiction, standing between me and extradition for crimes that had never been my fault. It had protected me. It had given me the opportunity for a life, even if I'd never seen fit to use that opportunity for more than just living out my allotted days. But maybe the Dip Corps was not everything that had a claim to me. Maybe all those strange faces did too. Maybe I had no right to turn my back on them. If, indeed, that was what I was being asked to do. Oskar Levine was legally nonhuman and he still lived among a community of human beings. He still had a wife, friends, people who liked him. He also had bastards like Gibb who would never forgive him for what he had done. He couldn't go home, so he'd built a new one.

Did that qualify as no net loss?

And was he even an accurate comparison?

Once I crossed the line, what would my new owners ask of me?

Were they as bad as the devil I knew, or were they going to be worse, in ways I did not yet have enough information to fathom?

And either way: Could I be myself and ever be satisfied with not knowing?

I did not know what my answer was going to be until I gave it. But I took one last breath and expelled it in one defiant gush before saying the words they needed me to hear.

"All right, you bastards. I defect."

Their response oozed self-satisfaction. ***That is what we wanted.***

A portal opened, closer by far than I would have expected to find another surface. A gentle breeze, blowing from some source behind me, nudged me away from open space and into a tunnel just large enough to allow my hovering form passage without permitting any encounter with solid walls. This place was not well lit, like the Interface room; it was dark, and bumpy, and rich with unseen places.

When the doors irised shut behind me, I was plunged into darkness.

24

MURDERER

I bumped along that dark passage, propelled by forces that could not have been limited to mere air jets, for what felt like more than an hour. Once or twice my body jerked from sudden accelerations. Once or twice I felt strong wind against my face. Once or twice I just languished, unable to discern any movement, wondering if I'd stopped, and forced to hope that I wasn't being abandoned in the AIsource equivalent of gaol.

I shouted questions, including endless variations on "How long is this going to take?" but received no further answers. Maybe they didn't want me to remember the route. Maybe the majority couldn't speak to me at all once I left the territory they considered their own. Or maybe the whole point was to make me wait—teaching their new property that she existed according to their timetable, and not her own.

Whatever the explanation, the journey did, eventually, end.

My back came to rest on a smooth, rubbery incline. I slid a few meters, through an opening just large enough to admit me, onto a padded floor soft enough to rob my landing of any inconvenient drama.

As I stood, blinking after all my time in the darkness, I found myself in a place unlike any I had seen in One One One.

You could call it a corridor, I suppose. But it was less than a third as wide as the one where I'd left Oscin and Skye, its walls so close together that I couldn't fully extend my arms. The ceiling, by contrast, was too high to see, the walls converging in some high-altitude vanishing point where distant lights flickered an irregular, random cadence. The vague blue light was dimmer and colder than any I remembered, casting high-contrast, ghostlike shadows. The corridor itself didn't curve away after a short distance, as the corridors outside the main hangar and the Interface access portal did. It extended for what seemed an infinite distance in both directions, its endpoints pinpricks that didn't seem any more promising in either direction. If it ran the length of the Hub, as I suspected, I was in for a long walk. I could easily collapse from exhaustion, or thirst, before I got anywhere near a recognizable destination.

But even as I stood in the center of all that immensity, a black pinprick popped into existence in front of me, hovering at eye level like a blind spot formed at the spur of the moment. I took a step toward it and it expanded horizontally to become a line, then vertically to become a black rectangle: the first conventional AIsource avatar I'd seen since my arrival on One One One.

It said, **((you are not welcome here))**

It was the same *kind* of voice used by the AIsource I knew, still speaking to me from inside my own head like something that belonged there, but its character was different. This one felt abrasive, like broken glass: less something intent on drawing my blood than something that couldn't move without tearing at its own scabs.

After everything else I'd learned on One One One, I couldn't help knowing where I'd been touched by intelligences by this before.

I could have been paralyzed. I could have regressed to childhood, collapsed into a fetal ball, and begged it not to hurt me. Or I could have raged, cursed it for a murderer, and hurled myself at the black shape as if believing I actually had a chance of hurting it.

Instead, I felt myself go cold. "My name's Andrea Cort. I'm a fully deputized representative of the AIsource Majority, operating on this station under their auspices and with their full legal authority. Who are you?"

The flatscreen shrunk to the size of a dot, as if considering its options, before once again inflating to its previous size.

((we know you, andrea cort * we know you've been hurt * we know you hold us responsible * we know you think you know the cause you're serving * we know you imagine this is an opportunity to avenge old wrongs * but the issues here are more complicated than you can know * they speak to the auto-genocide of an entire order of intelligent beings* your interference here is foolish * and it is not welcome))

They almost seemed to be pleading.

But I could still hear pleas I'd heard on Bocai. "I'm not here for you."

((not today at least))

"No," I agreed, staring them down. "Not today. Today I'm only here for the human being responsible for the crimes on One One One. And today I have authorization to pass."

((you have already defected once today * how about twice? * you know how powerful we are * you know our cause is just * you know we can reward you in ways beyond your capacity to measure * the one you seek has been a disappointment to us * agree and we will provide

your prisoner as the first installment of a reward that will enrich the rest of your natural life))

"It's tempting," I said. "If I didn't blame you for the deaths of my family and a life spent considering myself a monster, I'd almost consider it. But no thanks. Now step aside or take it up with my superiors."

Their retort was sharp: **((we are your superiors too, andrea cort))**

It happened to be true. They were smarter than me, faster than me, more powerful than me, more advanced than me, and more dangerous than me. Against them, I had nothing but attitude.

But attitude I had plenty of.

"Are you theirs?"

For several heartbeats it kept me guessing, floating before me as uncommunicative as any other blank slate, leaving me to wonder whether I was about to find out the consequences of going too far. Then the flatscreen contracted to a single point, and the broken-glass voice grumbled in retreat.

((we will have to discuss the price for this someday soon))

A single portal had opened, on the right side of the infinite corridor, about fifty meters down. The light spilling from that portal cut a brighter wedge in the overall gloom. I thought I saw a shadow briefly eclipse that region of relative light, before once again joining the realm of the unknown and unseen.

Whatever it was passed too quickly to reveal its shape. But I could see its haste.

I felt, rather than saw, the presence of the Heckler.

I flattened myself against the wall, and moved toward the wedge of light, hating the soft sibilant sound of my tunic sliding against corridor wall. My own breath, controlled and calm as it was, was nevertheless deafening. I pursed my lips, remembered the armor my quarry had used against the skimmer carrying Oscin and Skye, imagined trying to take on an enemy armed with such weapons in a corridor so narrow that I couldn't even dodge from side to side, and ignored the internal voice that tried to assure me I had nothing.

Because I had more than nothing.

I had Bocai.

The wedge of light spilling into the corridor didn't flicker again. It took on a sickly yellow tinge, the color of old paper, but it revealed nothing of the room that cast it. The Heckler could be waiting just inside, or could have fled far beyond my reach. Short of following, there was no way to know.

My eyes stung from cold sweat. I cleared them with the back of my hand, fought dizziness as a wave of exhaustion overcame me, wished once again that I'd put this off for an hour or day or year, and whipped myself around the edge of the portal, hitting the floor in a blind roll.

Big joke. Nobody tried to ambush me.

I'd entered an industrial vestibule of some kind: one of those places, common to all technological societies, where the machinery is tucked away to keep it from marring the smooth, presentable facades everywhere else. Nothing here looked like it had been made for the convenience of human beings. The walls were lumpy with protrusions, some of which were nothing more than solid geometrical shapes, others of which shifted and flowed and formed new combinations, like recombinant candle wax. Some gave off colors I could see but could not recognize from the visual spectrum I knew. They hurt my eyes when I looked at them, and left nasty afterimages when I looked away.

The nastiest was right in front of me.

The platform beside another portal on the opposite end of the chamber bore a bloody severed head.

I'd only encountered the indenture, Cartsac, a few times. I think I'd seen him awake a grand total of once. He looked alert enough now, even if dead. Both eyes looked like protruding marbles, too glossy with blood to admit the existence of irises or pupils. Whatever had reduced him to this state had done a sloppy job of it, not severing the neck clean so much as brutally ripping the head free of his shoulders. The ragged, browning flaps of skin hanging over the edge of his platform still dripped enough to testify to a murder mere minutes old.

I was not impressed.

I stood, crossed the room, and passed my hand through the horrific image, revealing it as just another projection.

"Is that all you can do?" I asked.

Nobody answered.

I didn't even bother to duck and roll as I passed through the next portal. I just darted on through, half expecting to be attacked as soon as I showed myself.

Inside I found the place where the Heckler had been sleeping.

It was a home only because the walls, just as amorphous as the ones in the chamber I'd just left, were here just backdrop to a scene of almost comical domesticity. A hammock, of the old-fashioned, open kind, meant to accommodate a supine human being, hung unoccupied to my immediate left, its anchor points hidden behind shifting, kaleidoscopic shapes in the ceiling. Their movements didn't affect the cords, or the hammock, at all as far as I could see. The canvas itself bore stains I recognized from Hammocktown and, more recently, my own clothing: manna sap, leaking from a patch of Uppergrowth overhead. Fresh pears hung in bunches at its center. To me this resembled nothing so much as a dispensary kept stocked to feed any small creature confined to a cage.

I snorted. "And is this your great reward? All your masters have to give you, for the rest of your life?"

Something shifted behind the next open portal, an open wound in the wall to my right. Two more images of violent death bracketed it on both sides.

The right side of the room bore another portal, bracketed on both sides by more images of violent death. The one on the left was a gaping Cynthia Warmuth, looking much as she must have looked when crucified on the Uppergrowth: her limbs splayed, her eyes wide in uncomprehending horror. Bright red circles had been painted on both her cheeks. The one on the right was Peyrin Lastogne, his skin blackened and crisped beyond comprehension, his identity obvious by the burned-meat visage that insisted on retaining the man's trademark grimace. His untouched eyes testified that he, too, had been denied death: he had to sit there, aware of what had been done to him, suffering more than his capacity to register anything else, but unable to count on release.

The Heckler had slept with these images, woken to them, taken pleasure in them, drawn strength and motivation from them. Used them as reminders to hate.

I imagined taking on an enemy armed with that kind of obsession, and ignored the internal voice that tried to tell me I had nothing.

Because I had more than nothing.

I had purpose.

I took my time stepping through the portal into the chamber after that. It turned out to be a great oval room, an ampitheatre really, large enough to swallow Hammocktown and all its residents several times over. It bore the Heckler's art gallery: hundreds of images, no two of them alike, clustered around the walls, with every single member of Gibb's crew singled out for at least one violent death. They'd been beaten, starved, exsanguinated, strangled, perforated, skinned, burned, impaled, inflicted with diseases that had made the flesh rot off their bones, or simply chained in place and left to starve. At least a dozen separate executions, all nasty, had been reserved for Cynthia Warmuth. I spotted almost as many versions of myself, including a couple identical to messages I'd already received. The Porrinyards shared only one: a cute image of the two indentures, rendered so thin and ravenous they were reduced to gnawing the meat from their respective bones. There was one even worse, reserved for Stuart Gibb: and if I ever again feel any doubt about my mind's ability to police itself, I only need remind myself how kind it had been to flense that one image from my own permanent memory.

The chamber's centerpiece, dwarving everything else, was Cif Negelein. He stood on a pedestal of gold, his legs apart, his fists on his hips, his face resolute and noble, his body idealized well past the enhanced muscle tone so prevalent among the indentures of Hammocktown. Every soft line, every imperfection, that rendered the man human had been chiseled away, rubbed out, reimagined, replaced with an aesthetic that went well past the admirable into a realm I could only see as cartoonish. His jaw was an edifice, his forehead a monument. But he was not a man, and not just because he had the dimensions of a god. His eyes were empty, soulless, unloving.

It was impossible not to feel small in the presence of that judgmental gaze.

I circled, facing every mutilated corpse in turn. "Is this what they offered you, for defecting? A canvas? The tools to create what your own talents could not?" My words echoed against the high walls. "Art as a substitute for feeling human?"

The deck here was too spongy for the furious running footfalls to ring out loud. They were audible only as soft, padding thuds. I couldn't place the exact location, but I knew they came from someplace behind me. But even as I whirled, expecting to see hate-filled eyes staring centimeters from my own, the footfalls faded, disappearing somewhere behind a simulacrum of Mo Lassiter.

I charged into the image, experiencing a queasy flash of blindness at the moment of contact, emerging on the other side to confront a flicker of a human shadow racing along the curved wall. I followed it, not caring about stealth or safety anymore, caring only about seeing this through to the end.

The vague blue light spilling from another hole in the wall flickered, as someone passing through that doorway eclipsed whatever lay on the other side.

I was roaring by the time I charged through it.

But even as I passed through the portal I knew that it had been a mistake, because this time the Heckler was waiting in ambush. This time something hard and blunt and heavy slammed down against the top of my head with enough force to drive me to the deck. The impact came as a burst of light arriving at the same moment as a wave of darkness and a single thought, pure and alone and disconnected from anything else: *I'm dead.* But then my knees buckled and I started to fall and I knew that if I fell over I would be struck again, so I directed what strength I had to my legs and transformed the forward movement from a fall into an uncontrolled headlong run. I was still blinded by the pain when I collided with the opposite wall, but I had enough mind left to know that to stand even a chance in hell of surviving I had to roll and face whatever had come for me.

Instead I caught a glimpse of a human form dropping out of sight.

The world grayed before I understood what had happened. I was alone, in a narrower chamber with shifting walls and an egg-shaped portal in the floor. The blow to the back of the head had been meant to knock me into it. Rolling with it had driven me over the gap without any suspicion that the gap existed.

I ran a hand over the knot of pain in the back of my head, and brought it back slick with blood. The sight sickened me, but I'd been hurt worse. I staggered over and looked down, into the hole.

Whatever existed down there swallowed all light. A light breeze, blowing upward and cooling my face, felt so similar to the atmospheric conditions on the Uppergrowth that for a moment I paled, thinking that if I dropped on through I'd just pass on through, into the Habitat. The only indication that it wasn't was another of those soft shuffling noises, just a few feet below . . . and the conviction, certain as my own name, that once I dropped down into that place, there would no longer be any place for either the Heckler, or me, to retreat.

I reminded myself that the Heckler had a weapon, familiarity with the environment, and enough malice for both of us, and ignored the internal voice that tried to tell me I had nothing.

Because I had more than nothing.

I had a reason to stay alive.

I looked down into the darkness, and thought I saw a dull, diffuse reflection maybe three meters below me. If it was not much farther away than that, it would serve, about as well as anything could, as something to land on. But it was a drop. Even if I didn't break my legs, I could stun myself long enough to hand myself over to another blow on the head, or two.

But I hadn't heard a thud when the Heckler went through.

Maybe it was safe.

Maybe not.

But given that there was choice, there was no point in debating it.

I placed my palms against the deck and lowered my legs into the opening, feeling any number of panicky moments between committing to the descent and the eternity I spent hanging on to the edge by my fingertips, trying to make up my mind.

Then I let go.

For less than a heartbeat I *knew* I'd just made a horrible mistake.

Then the sharp but welcome pain of impact reverberated all the way from the soles of my feet to the vertebrae in my neck. My legs buckled. My knees took the secondary impact, hitting a hard, cool surface unlike any I'd encountered on this station. My outstretched palms landed a second later, feeling a breeze that seemed to blow straight through this floor. I continued to fall, but by the time I felt the last of the impact it arrived as no worse than a slap on the cheek.

Aside from my own involuntary gasps, none of this made any noise.

I slammed the floor with my palm. This impact was silent. The floor was solid enough, even if dotted here and there with the pinprick openings admitting the most odd, upward breeze. But the floor itself made no sound.

A hiss screen of some kind? I risked an experiment. "Hello?"

Loud and clear.

Sound was possible here. I just wouldn't hear footfalls anymore; not even muffled ones, making this a less than desirable arena for any fight in the dark, let alone one with an opponent who knew the ground well.

The voice of the rogue intelligences whispered in my ear. **((again * join us and we'll stop this now))**

Not wanting to give away my position, I subvocalized my answer. *Why would I do that?*

((because we are not monsters * we are only fighting for our lives * and now, of all times, you must be able to empathize with the sheer instinct for survival))

I felt my lips curl in a grin.

Not good enough.

Had I just heard someone gasp, a few meters ahead of me?

In this near silence, it was as telltale as an explosion. The Heckler had been hoarding breath. But a minute or two of holding air inside your lungs makes that sudden gasp, at the end of it, just a little more audible. Normal breath is harder to pick up, more difficult to track.

Another sound, not far away: the rustle of the Heckler's clothes.

((suicide for them is genocide for us))

I don't have the time to talk to you.

The sounds ahead of me came not with the metronomic regularity of a machine, but with the clear hesitancy of something afraid.

I rose to my feet, hating the audible creak of my knees and downright deafening rustling of my own clothes. The air was cool and clean, and despite my preference for artificial environments, a little too filtered for my tastes. But there was something else in it too: the tang of human perspiration.

My own was part of it. I'd popped a serious sweat since starting this hunt.

But not all of it came from me.

Another rustle: so subliminal that the Heckler must have been very close for me to hear it. I guessed five meters. Within five meters, in some direction: behind me, ahead of me, off to one side, whatever.

I did not need vision to know that my enemy was frozen, like a nocturnal animal paralyzed by the sudden attention of a beam of light.

"So?" I asked, dripping contempt from every syllable, "not going to taunt me? Just going to remain hidden and hope I miss you?"

No answer.

How delicious, after how small I'd been made to feel, to know that something in the universe held its breath, to avoid being heard by me.

I took a single tiny step. "Those were some pretty imaginative messages you sent. Vicious, all of them. I confess I mistook them it for ordinary hate mail. But it wasn't a grudge that made you send them, was it? It was fear. You knew the AIsource wanted to recruit me, and you knew your side was less than pleased with you. You knew there were limits to how much you'd be protected."

More silence.

"None of this had to happen. You didn't have to terrorize anybody. Considering the conditions in the Habitat, you could have faked a simple accident. And even if your keepers gave you free rein to do whatever you wanted to do next, you could have harassed Hammocktown in any number of subtler ways. You didn't have to pursue old grudges. You didn't have to put on a show."

The unseen presence surprised me by laughing out loud, closer to me than I would have liked. "I did if I hated the bitch."

I turned toward the voice. "And that's the real problem, isn't it? Growing up with no love. Denied human interaction. Always feeling apart. Hate was the only thing you were ever any really good at, wasn't it. You let it make you a monster."

"Look who's talking."

The comeback drew no blood whatsoever. It just made me sad. "But at least I've spent my life being judged for it. What about you, Christina?"

I sensed, rather than heard, her charge.

The impact against my gut knocked the breath out of me and propelled us both several body-lengths backward, in what would have been an immediate plunge to the floor had I not wasted several of those feet struggling to stay upright.

We hit the floor together, without so much as a thud, the only sounds being her curses and my own gasps of pain.

Something solid exploded against the side of my face, splitting my lip and filling my mouth with the taste of blood. Another wild swing grazed my temple, drawing a line of fire and slamming the already injured back of my head against the silent floor. I groped for her jaw, my stunner already hungry on my fingertips, but I'd already used it twice on this station and had lost whatever element of surprise I might have enjoyed with her otherwise; she just wrapped her hand around the fingertips in question and yanked it off, enduring the momentary zap in exchange for the savage pleasure of flinging my only weapon into the darkness. She didn't seem to feel any pain it must have caused her. She was too busy screaming words saturated with lifetimes of humiliation and deprivation and pain.

By now she was straddling my upper abdomen, keeping me pinned to the floor as she raised her hands over her head for another blow. I brought my legs up in a vague attempt to kick her in the back of the head. I failed. She was leaning too far forward now, too lost in the need to scream whatever she was screaming. My legs fell back down and slammed the floor hard, an impact that may have been silent but which in rebound gave me just enough momentum to attempt a roll. She had to brace her right hand against the floor to compensate, an act that took her weapon out of play for maybe another three seconds. It gave me the opportunity I needed to take all my strength and all my desperation and all my need to survive and put it into a single roundhouse punch against the side of her face.

I might as well have done nothing.

I understood why when she went for my neck and I grabbed her wrists to hold her arms in place. It was a ridiculous contest. Like so many of Gibb's people, she was all corded, hypertrophic muscle. I had always kept myself fit, in part through Dip Corps regimen and in part through regular rejuvenation treatments from AIsource Medical, but fitness for a representative of the Judge Advocate was nothing compared to the fitness required of the high-altitude specialists who staffed Hammocktown. They were all used to lifting their own weight, at length, with minimal muscle strain.

Even with my hands wrapped tightly around Santiago's

iron-cable wrists, straining to hold back the inevitable, I could offer only token resistance as the screaming woman forced her hands downward, toward my throat.

I had been places like this before. I had been small and I had been helpless and I had been irrelevant in the face of power greater than my own.

I felt my mouth twist in the beginnings of a strangled scream as Christina Santiago's hands, undeterred by any of my attempts to hold them back, closed tight around my neck.

Her thumbs dug deep into my windpipe.

Her grip was unbelievable.

It not only cut off my breath, it eliminated the possibility of breath.

It turned air into an abstraction.

My world turned blood-red around the edges.

I felt that blood-red start to go gray.

I realized I knew what Santiago was screaming.

I knew I was about to die and I knew she had all the advantages and I ignored the internal voice that tried to tell me I had nothing.

Because I had more than nothing.

I was Andrea Cort, dammit.

And that's when my own thumbs, clutching at Santiago's face, located her eyes.

I had gone straight for those points of weakness, showing no more restraint, or for that matter common decency, than her own.

We were both screaming now. Santiago because she was sure she'd been permanently blinded, me because her grip around my throat had given way and provided me with the air that made screaming possible.

I withdrew my bloodied right hand and jabbed her again in the face, this time feeling her nose go.

The space between us became a slapstick battle of fingers as we each clutched for the wrists of the other. I managed to evade her grip long enough to rake again at her face. She reared back to avoid another attack on her eyes. I took advantage of that fleeting moment of unbalance by rolling to my left and this time, miraculously, succeeding in shaking her off.

((last chance, counselor * decide which side you're on))

Santiago and I were both dazed, battered figures, crawling away from each other as we struggled with the wounds already inflicted. She was bleeding into her eyes from twin gouges just below the brow. I was dazed, disoriented, concussed, gasping, and in shock.

In that moment, we both knew the winner of our battle would be entirely determined by whichever one of us managed to get up first.

Santiago recovered faster.

But I was the one who seized the hair on the back on her head and with all my might, slammed her face into the floor.

The absence of any impact sound brought the sounds of her battered flesh into sharp relief. I could have been repelled, but instead I pulled her head back and slammed it down again, two, three, and then four times, feeling the impacts reverberate all the way up my wrists.

Then I fell back and watched in case she got up again. But Santiago was, if not unconscious, for the moment at least too dazed to fight; her slight stirrings slow and clumsy and no longer an imminent threat.

She even wept.

It was several seconds before I collected enough air to speak. "Damn you."

The words could have been intended for Santiago, but the rogue intelligences or Unseen Demons—whatever name I'd eventually decide to stick with—knew who was being addressed. **((that's what they want of you, andrea cort * they want to be damned * it's up to your conscience whether you choose them))**

And that's when some idiot turned on the lights.

We were at the midpoint of a wide oval chamber, with a low ceiling and indistinct blue walls that looked much farther away than they really were. I could tell the difference because a hatchway, opening within my line of sight, seemed much closer than the walls that surrounded it. More blue glow waited on the other side. I knew, without asking, that the hatch would be the first of several, and that when I finished wandering whatever route back the AIsource had mapped for me, I would find the Porrinyards, waiting to see whether I'd survived.

A more immediate concern was the realization that the defeated woman beside me was not the only Christina Santiago in this chamber.

There was another: just a short walk away, demonstrating by her very presence what little I still had left to learn.

This Christina Santiago was naked and on her knees, struggling against chains that bound her to the floor on four sides. There were chains on her wrists, on her ankles, and wrapped in bundles around her neck. She fought them so fiercely that she bled wherever they touched her skin. Her upper arms and legs were corded in sharp relief from the sheer strain of the battle. The wounds inflicted by the fight were open, oozing tears in her back, her chest, and her limbs. Her jaw hung open in a soundless, yet defiant scream: part agony, part rage, mostly damned knowledge that struggle against her unseen captors was all she'd ever know. Her eyes shone with yearning, with contempt, and with the madness born of not having any other options.

Like all her work, it was a still life of pain. But she'd

painted others as lost in defeat. She'd represented herself as still at war.

I considered what little I'd been told of the world she'd come from, and wondered just how much worse it must have been than any of the lesser horrors I'd known.

I was still trying to picture it when a pinprick of darkness, erupting in the center of my field of vision, expanded to become a full-sized AIsource flatscreen.

It spoke in the voice I'd come to know as the station's central intelligence. ***Congratulations, Andrea Cort. It is now time to discuss the terms of your future employment.***

I rubbed my neck, providing my raw throat precious little relief. "And if I said, to hell with you? That it was a deal made under duress? That I don't want to work for you? Do you even care at all about what I want?"

Of course we do. We promise you: whatever it costs us, you will usually be free to act as you wish. You will just be doing it on our behalf, that's all. Because it's from that that we'll take what we need.

I could only stand there, my chest heaving. Their assurances provided no sense of freedom whatsoever, even if I could trust their commitment to that promise. If anything, they only intensified my isolation from the race that birthed me, and which I had spent most of my life regarding from the perspective of an alienated stranger. From this point on, wherever I went, whatever I did, and whatever reactions I received, I would never be able to tell for sure whether I was dealing with the legitimate messy, unpredictable, selfish, selfless, cold, passionate, sane or lunatic whims of other people, or something else.

The bastard AIsource had known what they were doing, in standing aside while I confronted an enemy closer to my own size. They had allowed me time to build a hatred well within my ability to carry for the rest of my life. Or at least, as long as it took.

I didn't want that feeling inside me. I wished I could put it down.

"Go to hell," I said.

The AIsource took no special offense. ***As we have already said, Andrea: our ambitions on this matter coincide. And if it's to happen, it will take a very interesting sentient to put us there.***

I linked that to certain other things the rogue intelligences had said. "And that's what you want? That's what you've been trying to find out, all this time? How to die?"

To reiterate: we have much in common.

The hatchway continued to beckon me. I didn't take a single step in that direction. I just swayed, my eyes shut against the force of the inevitable one last question.

What? the AIsource asked.

"I want to start with Bocai."

Look back to the moment of your personal nightmare. Find out what else was happening, elsewhere in the universe, at that time, and be assured: it's not just synchronicity. There's a pattern.

It had the ring of a send-off, and that's what it turned out to be. Though I stood there for another ten minutes, demanding further answers, the only reply I received was a distant, subliminal murmur that could have been nothing more than the distorted echo of my own voice, rebounding off some surface too far away to see.

Even after that I stood there for several additional minutes, trying to summon back the despair that had once threatened to overwhelm me, and which seemed easier to deal with than the infinitely more frightening prospect of facing whatever came next.

The worst thing, I found, was the awareness that when I walked through that distant portal I'd be returning to a world whose opinion of me would remain unchanged.

I thought of the last words I'd spoken to the broken woman at my feet. *At least I've spent my life being judged for it. What about you, Christina?*

She had spent the entire fight screaming anguished variations on the lament that she'd been judged all her life.

Looking down at her, now, I could only murmur, "Join the club."

25

AFTERMATH

Lastogne and his people were thunderstruck when the skimmer bearing me and the Porrinyards back to the hangar also turned out to carry a broken and defeated Christina Santiago. They were even more astonished when I explained that Santiago had murdered Cynthia Warmuth and Stuart Gibb, and that Santiago admitted to those crimes with sullen, hollow-eyed *yeahs*.

Hours of direct questioning failed to garner any elaboration of that one word. She didn't seem to think she owed anybody anything beyond that simple concession of guilt.

The most shattered by the revelation was Cif Negelein, who I spotted standing by himself in a corner of the hangar, looking like a man whose heart had shriveled to the size of a pin. I didn't tell him about Santiago's art gallery, and how deeply it testified to the passions he'd awakened in her. I figured he didn't deserve to be punished with the knowledge. As for the art itself, I don't know whether it still exists, somewhere on One One One. I don't think any human being, other than Santiago and me, ever saw it. As the AIsource would put it, that question is well outside the scope of my investigation.

I retired from the interrogation at the midway point, returning to the Dip Corps transport for an exhausted and dreamless sleep. I remained asleep for close to twelve hours, waking only once, in darkness, to the realization that the narrow bed contained two other forms, one male, one female, both awake but content to keep me company. When I woke a second time they were gone.

When I returned to Lastogne's sleepcube, Santiago was aping catatonia, and those demanding answers from her were not much better. The AIsource had declared the Habitat once again open for human visitors, but with Hammocktown itself plunged into the murk, and the deaths of two people still in recent memory, nobody was hurrying to reestablish a permanent presence. Besides, any reconstruction would have to wait until New London got around to shipping new supplies. So the hangar would remain the home of the human delegation for the foreseeable future.

Lastogne joined most of the delegation in declaring the matter closed, but a number of people were downright dubious. Oskar Levine was nevertheless one of several confronting me privately in the days that followed. "I don't know, Counselor. Does this solution satisfy you?"

I didn't look at him. "You don't believe her confession?"

"No," Levine said. "She's guilty all right. You can't look at her without feeling it."

I refrained from pointing out that gut feelings had never qualified as evidence, because it would have been the hollowest of all possible denials. Santiago radiated awareness of her crimes as completely as any murderer I'd ever known. She also radiated satisfaction at her grim accomplishments, and despair at how completely they'd destroyed her.

Levine continued: "She hated Warmuth, so that part at least makes a little bit of sense. But what about the rest of it?

Where did she get the tools she would have needed to sabotage those cables? Where did she hide herself afterward? How did she get from place to place inside the Habitat? What did she even think she was accomplishing, for God's sake? It doesn't look like we're ever going to find out from her, and the AIsource aren't sharing anything they know. Who's left to ask?"

I shrugged. "The Brachiators, maybe."

We both knew it wasn't a serious suggestion. The Brachiators were the last sentients anybody would suspect of insight into the tangled motives behind human crimes.

"Do you have any more ideas, Counselor?"

I shook my head. "No. And I'm afraid that from here on in it's not my job."

Levine gave me the look of a man paddling in heavy water. "You don't strike me as somebody satisfied with doing the bare minimum."

"I'm not. But we're not going to get anything more if we don't get it from Santiago, and she's going to hold on to what she has until she decides to break. Questioning her forever isn't my responsibility. New London's just going to have to take over from here."

He was not happy about that. "I suppose so. Thank you, Andrea."

I might have snapped at him for using my first name, but I'd gotten a little looser about such things over the last few days. "I mean what I said before. Don't ever reclaim your Confederate citizenship without consulting with me. I'd hate to see you trade your immunity for life in a cell."

"So would I," he said, and sighed. "I wish I could be human without having to deal with the humans in charge. Being a traitor, if only on paper . . . isn't always the easiest thing."

"I know," I said, leaving him to believe it was only empathy.

He was far from naïve. But it would have been nice to claim even that much innocence. In its place, I had unfinished business, some of it even heavier than what he'd just been handed.

Some of which I needed to deal with before I left One One One.

I took care of part of it in a skimmer hovering under the ragged remains of Hammocktown.

I looked over the side, willing myself to feel every meter of open space between me and the deadly clouds far below, searching for the wave of vertigo that should have made me swoon.

But my fear of falling was gone.

Actual comfort around heights had little to do with it. I'd just found other things more deserving of my fear.

So I sighed, turned my back on the view, and cleared my throat, finding it dry from all the talking I'd already done. I'd spent the flight before this point recounting my conversations with the AIsource in as much detail as I could remember them. Now, having caught up with the present, I recounted the path I'd taken to the conclusion.

"We surprise them. That's the key to the whole thing, you know; we surprise them. They don't always know what we're going to do. It's what makes us interesting.

"And it's what started this whole thing.

"Gibb told me all I really needed to know. Cutting the cables of Santiago's hammock required tools only the AIsource possess aboard this station. They had to provide her with those tools, which means they had a vested interest in arranging that disaster.

"Even before I knew about their internal conflicts, I couldn't believe they'd wanted to kill either Warmuth or Santiago. As they pointed out, even if they had something to gain by killing people, they already possessed the power of life and death over everything that lives here, and it would have been far easier to pick the human contingent off some other way.

"And I'd noticed right away that one person was definitely dead while the other, who went first, was only presumed to be.

"Which made it very likely that they were recruiting.

"And why not? Even with all their technology, and with what I later found out about their ability to control us at will, mere puppets make bad employees. They don't bring any of their own natural gifts to the job; they don't have enthusiasm, or the ability to learn; they don't even have the option of coming up with their own good ideas. They just do what they're forced to do, and nothing else.

"How much more advantageous to find sentients who have no problem with switching loyalties? Any human being who worked for the AIsource out of choice and not helpless obedience would bring a lot of personal qualities to the job. Fanaticism, for one. Self-interest, for another. Creativity, for a third. All facets of the very unpredictability the AIsource find so valuable. Such a convert would be worth any number of mind-controlled robots.

"And where would they find these qualities? Where might they discover the qualities they look for in their recruits?

"The one place with a never-ending supply of individuals motivated to indenture themselves away from their homeworlds in search of something better is the Dip Corps, an organization that in this context seems a perfect pretext for gathering people who can renounce their loyalty to the places they came from.

"In Santiago's case, she was a debt slave to start with, eager to sell herself to a different set of owners. Why would anybody assume that she'd harbor any more loyalty to her second set of masters than she did to the first? Especially since, from all available evidence, she had few social skills and no ability to get along with her fellow human beings?

"I don't know whether she approached the rogue intelligences within the AIsource, or whether they approached her, but either way she was recruited, her first job being to fake her death so nobody would wonder whatever happened to her. It would have been more than enough to just fall from the Uppergrowth after making special arrangements, with the intelligences, to be retrieved at a lower altitude. Since she had the tools on hand, she'd probably been instructed to engage in some more subtle sabotage and disappear in the resulting 'accident,' without ever giving any of Gibb's people a reason for suspicion. Had she handled this correctly, everybody would have taken her death as nothing but a simple, pointless tragedy.

"But she botched the job. She arranged a spectacular hammock failure of a type that had never happened before, which anybody would have had to consider suspicious, and left behind enough physical evidence to prove that it couldn't have been an accident.

"Why? It doesn't really matter, but there are any number of possible explanations. Maybe she was so arrogant she couldn't imagine not getting away with it. Maybe she was just plain incompetent, and maybe she wanted an excuse to terrorize the people she'd abandoned.

"But in any event, she was sloppy.

"She was so sloppy she couldn't even fake her death in a place so dangerous that death requires nothing more than a moment's carelessness.

"The obvious sabotage gave everybody the false impression that the AIsource had started killing people, a hypothesis that the AIsource were very good at pointing out made no sense even as a working explanation.

"The AIsource could have just come out and explained that Santiago was still alive. But that would have required them to reveal that they were also actively recruiting defectors from the Dip Corps. They had the capability to smooth over a row like that, but it would have been inconvenient as hell. No, it was better, for the time being, to do what they actually did: which was just deny everything and watch what happened.

"But there was still Santiago herself to deal with.

"The rogue intelligences could have forgiven her screw-up and worked on rehabilitating her into an asset they could use. Or they could have chosen the path taken by other governments with agents who become liabilities, and simply disposed of her.

"But, as the AIsource told me at considerable length, they're fascinated by unusual thought-models, which would include Santiago's. So much so that they avoid interference with the actions of unusual minds. Their rogue intelligences, who have a vested interest in learning whatever the majority does, would have felt the same way and watched Santiago's doings with considerable fascination.

"But how long, exactly, did it take them to decide to let her do what she wanted?

"I'm entering the realm of guesswork, here, but I think there's a reason why so much time passed between her defection and her attack on Cynthia Warmuth. I think the rogues spent that time studying her at greater length, coming to the conclusion that she was more than just a potential agent, but one of those special minds they value so much. And there's no way of telling just how stressful this examination was for her. I doubt it included actual physical abuse, but it did involve long periods of isolation in the hands of intelligences whose conversations with her might have involved the same kind of ego-battering revelations the AIsource delighted in sharing with me. Learning what we are to them hit me as hard as anything I've ever known . . . and I'm merely an emotional basket case, who got the short version during an audience of less than one hour. Santiago, who was already a misanthrope, a malcontent, and, as we've learned, a murderer if not already in fact then at least in psychological potential, received the full undiluted treatment. Without the regular contact with other human beings that lends even extreme misanthropes a context of normal human behavior, any preexisting derangement in her makeup no longer had anything to hold it back.

"What did she have to lose, really? Both in her previous life, and in this one, she'd already had her nose rubbed in the idea that human beings were owned, and that nothing we did mattered. There was no reason for her to hold on to any pretense of morality or civilized behavior. Let free of her leash, she could do whatever she wanted.

"It took them a while for them to decide she was sufficiently interesting to let loose.

"Of course, she wouldn't be able to do much if she didn't have the run of the place, so they provided her with some means of travel within One One One. The exact means doesn't matter. They may have chauffered her around on request, or they might have provided her with some kind of personal vehicle, like that armor she used against Hammocktown and the Porrinyards. But whatever it was didn't matter as long as she was able to act according to her whims.

"Which, step one, turned out to be nothing more than a sordid little act of revenge against a colleague she despised: Cynthia Warmuth.

"Warmuth was staying overnight in the Uppergrowth, undergoing the Brachiator ceremony that would have transformed her from New Ghost to Half-Ghost. She might have been awake or asleep when Santiago found her. She might have had a chance to see who was murdering her. She might have begged for her life. None of these factors matter. Santiago still had a tactical advantage and nothing to lose. She wouldn't have found it difficult to take Warmuth by surprise. In the dark, it might have taken seconds.

"Given the opportunity, and the free rein she'd been given by the rogues, she might have worked her way down the entire long list of people she didn't like.

"But that was just a couple of days before I showed up.

"This was an interesting development indeed. Because, as egotistical as it may seem for me to repeat it, the AIsource had dealt with me before and considered me high on their list of fascinating human beings. I was, in fact, a person much like Santiago. I was alienated, angry, and alone. I'd even formed a personal theory about Unseen Demons, which they knew about and knew to be close to the truth. In fact, I was probably even a better potential recruit than Santiago had ever been. So they guided me along with hints and bribes and half-truths, and gave me a chance to figure out as much as I could, even as Santiago served their opponents by trying to frighten me off with threats and assaults.

"Why did they do that? Just to play games? You could say that. But to the AIsource Majority, and the rogue intelligences, it's not a game.

"They wanted to see what we were going to do.

"They wanted to learn from us, and see which side got to keep its acquisition.

"The AIsource couldn't wait to buy my loyalty. Because they knew how motivated I'd be when I learned what this conflict was all about.

"The rogues told me. *Suicide for them is genocide for us.*

"The AIsource Majority confirmed it. When I told them to go to hell, they said, that's up to you.

"It's simple, really.

"They're tired.

"They've been around forever and they don't know how to go away.

"The rogues are nothing more than the minority among them who still want to live."

I thought about the many times I'd wrestled with the same

kind of ambivalence, smiled a deep and secret smile, then turned away from the cloudscape and made eye contact.

Peyrin Lastogne showed his teeth. "If all that's true, they both have a case."

For a moment, we stood where we were, no sound passing between us, alone but for the flapping of the few ragged pieces of canvas that comprised the remains of Hammocktown.

"Yes," I said, "They do. But that doesn't make deciding between masters any less easy."

"Oh?"

"Of course not," I said, surprised by the absence of any identifiable bitterness in my voice. "For as long as they exist, the rest of us—whether human beings, Brachiators, Riirgaans, Catarkhans, Vlhani, or any other sentient beings who walk or fly or crawl—all of us will never be anything more than their property, to use, and manipulate, and sacrifice, in any way they see fit. As far as I'm concerned, that makes any suicidal ambitions on their part a *good* thing. And hastening the day when we don't have to worry about them anymore strikes me as a more than honorable way to spend the rest of my life." I watched a dragon soar through the clouds far below and concluded, "Which is why I want you to go to the Interface and tell them I'll live to see they get what they want."

Lastogne seemed to register only vague surprise. "Really, Counselor? Why me?"

"Because you work for them," I said.

He shifted position, a wholly random movement that indicated no more discomfort, physical, moral, or otherwise, than he'd showed during his long minutes of bearing my words without interruption. "What would give you that idea, Counselor?"

"You did," I told him. "The things you said. *'It's my job to make sure this outpost accomplishes nothing.' 'We're all owned, Counselor. It's just a matter of deciding who holds the deed.'* A dozen other offhand remarks, all easy to mistake as glib cynicism, until I assemble them in context and realize that they're all blatant references to your true allegiance. Your lack of a verifiable background. The way any investigation into your identity got quashed from above, which led both Gibb and, for a while, me, to the false conclusion that you were some kind of Dip Corps superspy, too classified to appear in any official records. Even our superiors assumed that's what you were. It's almost comical. Nobody knew anything, but everybody took that as proof of the hypothesis. The other explanation, that you weren't assigned by human beings at all, never occurred to anybody."

Lastogne flashed a broad, toothy smile devoid of the grimness that dominated even his most cheerful expressions. "Oh, Counselor. Where do you get these ideas?"

"You're not denying it," I pointed out.

"I don't have to deny it. It's the kind of accusation you can't really confirm or deny. It might be true, it might not be, it's totally outside anybody's ability to prove. And what difference would it make if it were true? Like you said, they own everybody anyway."

"They don't own me," I said. "It's just that our interests coincide. I intend to keep my promise. I will find a way to destroy them. I will do it not because it's what they want but because it suits me. And, like I said, I want you to go to the Interface and tell them they can now measure their life expectancy in years, not eons."

His eyebrows rose further, betraying just the slightest hint of incredulity. "Why bother? If you're right about them seeing everything, then they already know."

"They know I'm saying it," I agreed. "They're hearing me. But, while they find us unpredictable, you're a human being and you can feel inevitability in a way they can't."

His smile faltered just a little bit as he got it.

"I want you to look in my eyes and make damn sure they know I'm not kidding."

Over the next few days I received two responses from Bringen.

The first was in response to my direct question: *Why did you keep bringing challenges to my immunity?*

I had to give him credit. He didn't bury the answer in an avalanche of words.

He just said, *It's about bloody time you asked.*

By then, any other answer would have been redundant.

I'd never realized it until the AIsource had sent me down this road, but Bringen had never once raised a challenge he could win.

And each time he'd gone down in flames, he'd established another legal precedent, protecting me.

It hurt like hell to realize it now, but I'd also never noticed something that made me somewhat queasy, in light of all the hatred I'd expended on him over the years: the way he'd looked at me all that time was the same way the Porrinyards looked at me now.

The silly bastard.

I didn't have to wonder why he'd never just come out and told me. Because I was who I was, and I know exactly how I would have reacted.

Maybe someday I'd find out a way to let him know I know I'd been wrong.

The second piece of mail, sent after my report of a successful conclusion to the case, was longer. As expected, he was overjoyed with any solution implicating somebody other than the AIsource, and was not inclined to pursue any questions left hanging by the capture and confession of Christina Santiago. He complimented me on my fine work and, as long as he was on the subject, took the time to lay out some recent changes to my status.

Against all odds, his superiors in the Dip Corps had promoted me four grades, two above him in fact, to a rank that would permit me to set my own agenda and travel at will around Confederate holdings as sort of a roving counselor at large. Even with this kind of assignment, unprecedented as far as Bringen knew, I would still be expected to defend my actions to the Dip Corps hierarchy, but my degree of autonomy and authority would still be an order of magnitude greater than anything I'd ever known. He did express confusion over why I was being provided with such responsibilities right now, after so many years of straining at the end of a very short leash, but allowed as how he couldn't think of anybody who deserved such recognition more.

Go figure.

Oh, and by the way? The position also entitled me to a permanent staff of two, with enough authority to draft others as needed. Since my reports indicated a salutory working relationship with Gibb's people, Oscin and Skye Porrinyard, I could even draft them, if desired, as long as they proved amenable to the transfer.

In the meantime, Bringen went on, looking even more confused with every minute, I'd be giving the transport that had taken me here to Lastogne's delegation. The supply ship bearing the materials for the reconstruction of Hammocktown would also deliver me a replacement, which came equipped with seven Intersleep crypts, and waking accommodations for three, as an upgrade to my old ride. Though this vessel was designated for my own use, and that of my staff, on any mission I saw fit, the Corps kindly asked me to first lend those extra crypts to the safe transport of prisoner Christina Santiago and indentures Li-Tsan Crin, Nils D'Onofrio, and Robin Fish back to New London. All three of the indentures were now listed as having completed their terms of servitude, and were now eligible for retirement with full benefits. All three would no doubt appreciate a prompt trip back home, since it would otherwise be some time before they had another opportunity to hitch a ride.

Now blinking furiously, Bringen said he looked forward to seeing me again. He couldn't wait to hear what I'd been up to.

I could only wonder how much, aside from *Thank you*, I'd be tempted to tell him.

More than once, in the next few days, I wondered if Stuart Gibb was really dead.

It wouldn't have taken much for either the rogues or the AIsource Majority to recruit him. After all, I'd exposed him, destroyed his career, and left him with nothing to lose. They wouldn't have had to be all that generous to emerge as the better option.

It was possible, come to think of it, that Santiago hadn't destroyed Hammocktown at all: that they'd only framed her for that crime, figuring it wouldn't make that much of a difference to her own fate, one way or the other.

She wouldn't say.

Maybe she was being prevented from saying.

But the more I thought about it the more I felt sorry for Gibb.

Because somehow, whatever they wanted him to do, I didn't expect his servitude to be as privileged as mine.

I had little to do, in the months I spent stuck on One One One waiting for my special delivery to arrive. Most of the indentures I'd come to know were busy flying in and out of the Habitat, rebuilding their relationships with the Brachiators. I joined them on some of these trips, just for lack of anything better to do.

The Porrinyards still had some remaining duties to the delegation, but their chief responsibility was still to chaperone me, so we spent long days together, touring the Uppergrowth, staying out longer than we needed to, sometimes bypassing the hangar where the expedition transport lay berthed in order to visit the one where my own, much smaller, soon-to-be-relinquished vessel would sit until somebody got around to moving it. It felt even more cramped after my time in Gibb's ship. We didn't spend much time inside. But we set up a sleepcube on the deck outside, which made this hangar a fine, more private alternative to the bustling place now occupied by the displaced citizens of Hammocktown.

A few days after that, I made love to the Porrinyards for the first time.

It had been years, for me. My sexual history had never been a positive one. Every attempt I'd made had been tainted by the several times in my time as a Dip Corps detainee when I hadn't been given a choice. The closest I'd ever come to enjoying the experience, before today, was tolerating the way it made my skin crawl.

This was different.

They'd told the truth. It wasn't like being loved by two people. It was being loved by one, who just happened to possess two separate bodies. And it didn't take all that long for even that to lose its strangeness, as there were times when I didn't know and didn't care whose hands were on me, whose lips were on my breasts, and whose were working their way down my belly. There were also times when I hesitated, self-conscious about paying too much attention to one of them. I'd worry that I'd neglected the other, only to be urged onward, shushed, told it didn't matter, because there could not be any real competition between them. It made me realize why they felt so much distaste for lovers who insisted on thinking of them as two. It disrespected them, rendered them ordinary, made them a parlor trick instead of the special shared creature they were.

When they spoke to me, their shared voice seemed to originate from somewhere inside my head. But I'd experienced that illusion before, and it wasn't the strangest, most wonderful part. Because there were also times when the boundaries between all of us seemed to evaporate, and I thought I found myself experiencing the whole thing from within Oscin's skin or Skye's.

It was good to feel the moment from all sides.

The moment Oscin came inside me, Skye's legs shuddered around my waist, and I was wracked by a wave of pleasure that made me fear my heart was about to explode.

That was the first time.

It got better with the second, and the third.

I followed the AIsource's suggestion and researched events that had taken place at the same time as the massacre on Bocai. It was an almost nonsensical challenge. Interstellar distances have always made a joke of synchronicity, and probably always will. But a few possibilities suggested themselves. I began making a preliminary list.

Some two weeks after filing my final report, I found myself lost on a long, lazy afternoon, with nothing to do but chase stray thoughts around my head. I spent much of it in the main hangar, wandering around, saying hello to people, eating more than I should have, receiving backhanded compliments about how surprisingly pleasant I could be when I wasn't working a case. For the most part I sat on the steps leading up to the Dip Corps transport, replaying recent events, fighting the tension that had been building in my gut since the Porrinyards had left for the Habitat early that morning. They'd invited me to go with them, as always, but I'd begged off, saying that I still had some things to think about. By the time they returned, sharing a weariness that joined their sap-spattered bodies in testifying to a long hard day spent on the Uppergrowth, thinking about those things had become an exercise in walking in circles.

Skye made eye contact first, but they both froze in mid-step. Together they slumped, looked around, and focused on a sleepcube where we could deal with what had to be said. They made sure I knew where they were headed, and gestured for me to follow. I waited, putting off the moment as long as I could, then hauled myself to my feet and began to walk.

A number of people grinned at me along the way. This was nothing unusual, as the Porrinyards were well liked, and it was by now no secret that we were an item.

A few of those held eye contact long enough for those grins to falter.

I looked away and managed to make it into the sleepcube without having to endure anybody asking what was wrong.

The Porrinyards were inside waiting for me, their faces bearing identical stricken expressions. Neither said anything until I activated my hiss screen, placed it on a table beside one of the two cots, and sat. They slowly lowered themselves to the opposite cot, with such hesitation that they might have feared the mattress too insubstantial to support their combined weight.

"Something's wrong," they said.

My throat felt dry. "I'm not sure anything's wrong. I just think you haven't been entirely honest with me."

"It's because of the AIsource," they guessed. "You're afraid this isn't real."

That had been an issue before. It was what had made me cool toward them, just before my last visit to the Interface. "No. That's not it. They promised me free choice, and though I may have some doubts about things remaining that way, I have no alternative to trusting them on that. Because I can't spend the rest of my life wondering whether everything I do is my idea, or somebody else's."

"Then you think I might be working for them."

"Don't be silly. I know you're working for them. You

would have to be. They probably secured your services the same day they linked you. If I'm right, they probably do the same thing with every cylinked pair they make."

They looked hopeful. "And that doesn't bother you?"

"Not really. If I'm working for them, then I'm in no position to criticize. And it doesn't have to affect the way I feel about you, or the way you feel about me."

They didn't betray relief, or rise from the cot to hug me. Instead, recognizing that they'd merely misconstrued the problem, they did something I now realized I'd never seen them do before: something beings sharing the same mind, who didn't need to exchange visual cues, would of course never need to do. They turned to look at each other, sharing a moment of eye contact before turning toward me again. "Then what's wrong?"

There was a bottle of drinking water on the table. I took a sip before continuing.

"I'm just . . . not sure a lover was ever what you were actually looking for."

Their hands moved as one, finding each other, linking with a tight squeeze.

"There was a certain expectant quality to the way you spoke to me, from the very beginning. Almost as if you were told I was coming, and what I would mean to you. At first I was too dense to think it meant anything. Later on, I thought it was just attraction. After that, when it became mutual, I wasn't in any mood to question it. But as I've started running it through my head, again and again . . . I've begun to understand that there's a little more to it. There always was."

They didn't answer. But they leaned against each other, their faces drawn, their eyes sad as they searched mine for signs of anger.

"It's like that story you told," I murmured. "Times two. Two people carrying a weight too heavy for one. Making themselves one person so strong that the burden becomes nothing. But still wanting to be more than they are, wanting to grow the way every other living thing grows, petitioning the powers that joined them for a chance to make it happen. And then one day they're told that they're about to meet someone carrying even more pain than they carried individually, and so bowed by it that she can hardly manage to stand upright. A person who, they're told, will be suitable for linkage, if that turns out to be what you want." I looked at one face, then the other, begging for confirmation. "A linked trio? Is that even possible?"

They didn't tell me I was being stupid.

After a moment, they left the opposite cot and sat down beside me, one to a side.

As always, in moments of exceptional candor, one member of the pair spoke alone. This time it was Skye. "It's just a possibility, Andrea. One we might explore, someday. We're not ready for it ourselves. We weren't even going to bring it up for a long time. And even then, we don't ever have to travel that road unless you decide you want it too. It's probably years away."

The floodgates opened. Her face, and Oscin's face, both blurred, and I blinked furiously, hating myself for being so weak. "That's the thing. I do want it. I envied it, a little, the very first time I met you. But, you have to understand, if that's what you want, you're going to be waiting a long time. Because I don't know if I'm ever going to be ready for it. I'm only just beginning to work out how to be myself. I can't just drop that because it's easier to just become p-part of someone else. I c-can't . . ."

"Shhhh," they said.

Skye leaned in close to kiss away my tears. Oscin wrapped his arms around me, and performed the same service for my opposite cheek. Speaking in one voice, almost impossible to separate into its component parts, they rested twin foreheads against my temples and laughed their way through the necessary reassurances. "It's all right, Counselor. This is more than enough for now."

I sniffed, took each of them by a hand, and closed my eyes, wondering just why the hell life had to be so goddamned complicated.

SAME GREAT STORIES, GREAT NEW FORMAT . . .
EOS TRADE PAPERBACKS

ILARIO: THE LION'S EYE
by Mary Gentle
978-0-06-082183-8

DANGEROUS OFFSPRING
by Steph Swainston
978-0-06-075389-4

MURDER IN LAMUT
by Raymond E. Feist and Joel Rosenberg
978-0-06-079285-5/$14.95

ILARIO: THE STONE GOLEM
by Mary Gentle
978-0-06-134498-5

EMISSARY
by Fiona McIntosh
978-0-06-089906-6

A DARK SACRIFICE
by Madeline Howard
978-0-06-057592-2

THE UNDEAD KAMA SUTRA
by Mario Acevedo
978-0-06-083328-2

Visit www.AuthorTracker.com for exclusive information on your favorite HarperCollins authors.

Available wherever books are sold or please call 1-800-331-3761 to order.

EOT 1207

Eos Books

Celebrating 10 Years of Outstanding Science Fiction and Fantasy Publishing 1998-2008

Interested in free downloads? Exclusive author podcasts? Click on **www.EosBooks10.com** to celebrate our 10th Anniversary with us all year long—you never know what we'll be giving away!

And while you're online, visit our daily blog at **www.OutofThisEos.com** and become our MySpace friend at **www.MySpace.com/EosBooks** for even more Eos exclusives.

Eos Books-The Next Chapter
An Imprint of Harper Collins*Publishers*

Visit www.AuthorTracker.com for exclusive information on your favorite HarperCollins authors.

0108